Daisy Buchanan is an award-winning journalist, author and broadcaster. She has written for every major newspaper and magazine in the UK, from the *Guardian* to *Grazia*. She is a TEDx speaker, and she hosts the chart-topping podcast You're Booked, where she interviews legendary writers from all over the world about how their reading habits shape their work. Her other books include the non-fiction titles *How To Be A Grown Up* and *The Sisterhood*, and the novels *Insatiable* and *Careering*.

Also by Daisy Buchanan

Insatiable
Careering

limelight

DAISY BUCHANAN

SPHERE

This book contains some scenes that
readers may find upsetting

SPHERE

First published in Great Britain in 2023 by Sphere

1 3 5 7 9 10 8 6 4 2

A CIP catalogue record for this book
is available from the British Library.

Hardback ISBN 978-1-4087-2559-7
Trade paperback ISBN 978-1-4087-2560-3

Typeset in Sabon by M Rules
Printed and bound in Great Britain by
Clays Ltd, Elcograf S.p.A.

Papers used by Sphere are from well-managed forests
and other responsible sources.

MIX
Supporting
responsible forestry
FSC® C104740

Sphere
An imprint of
Little, Brown Book Group
Carmelite House
50 Victoria Embankment
London EC4Y 0DZ

An Hachette UK Company
www.hachette.co.uk

www.littlebrown.co.uk

For Dale, my light and my home

Sometimes an image stands for
something that will only be understood
in due course. It is a mnemonic, a
cryptogram, very occasionally a token
of precognition.

Look At Me,
ANITA BROOKNER, 1983

Prologue

A photograph is a paradox. In pictures, we become still, and silent. Less than a second's worth of our feeling, breathing selves exists within the frame. A single image can flatten a full life.

Yet, in photographs we never stop moving. Our old ghosts come back to life, and we command them to animate our memories. These ghosts are cursed to exist within an eternal loop, reliving our hazy recollections for us with precision. We demand that the ghosts save us from our greatest fear: being forgotten.

I have another great fear, which is vanity. I *am* vain, I suppose. I take photographs of myself, and I look at photographs of myself. I am not comfortable with this compulsion – but it is a compulsion. It stopped feeling like a choice, long ago. I am desperate. I search the pictures, hoping the camera has captured proof of my value. When I blinked then, was I beautiful? Did I lose myself in a laugh, a sigh, a turn of my neck? Will I ever become real, vivid, alive?

I have been blessed and cursed with a litmus test. My big sister, Bean. She glows. On and off film, she is filled with life. Filled with light. It's a beauty that promises warmth. Yet, to stand beside it is to feel cold. It casts a shadow on me.

I cannot admit this to anyone.

There's a particular picture that haunts me. I begged my mother for her copy, claiming I 'loved' it, that I thought we looked 'adorable' together. The truth is that it fills me with such longing and envy that I want to stare it down. If I can only atomise my feelings, I can steal its secrets.

Bean looks beautiful, of course. Amber eyed, sweet and serene. Undeniable. There is something about her face that reads as a statement of fact. This is the way a cheek is supposed to curve. This is the exact place that a nose ought to begin and end. My face is a naughty, unruly classmate beside Bean's. She is the eternal example. Even when aesthetically on my best behaviour, I shall never be good enough.

Here, I am definitely on my best behaviour.

My tummy is pulled in tight, and I am clasping my hands over a chocolate ice cream stain. (I can still remember the stickiness and scratchiness where my palms touched the net of the tutu.) I'm beaming adoringly at my big sister, convinced that if I can only open my eyes wide enough, if I can make my smile big enough, a little bit of Bean might be projected inside me. Just enough to light me up. My right foot (chubby leg encased in neat white pointelle sock) is placed before my left, an imitation of ballet's third position, concealing the other white pointelle sock, which has unravelled itself again. I can hear my mother's muttered 'Beatrice never does this', feel the breeze of her breath against my calf as she bends, sighs, yanks me back into place.

I see my hair, yellow as marigold petals, a buoyant

balaclava tufting up from my scalp. I see my nose – or rather, I look at my nose and see Bean's all over again, and wonder what life might have been like if it were half a millimetre shorter, or narrower. If I could have been half a millimetre happier. I see my clown mouth, too big, too bright, too false.

The precise moment captured is clear to me, if not the occasion itself. The recitals, concerts, pageants and fund-raisers are blurred into one long opportunity to be good and help. Being pulled out of bed before it was light, being bundled into the back seat long before breakfast, being urged to 'think of the less fortunate'. I remember rationed sweets – rarely chocolate because, as evidenced, I could not be trusted not to spill. Bean whispering, Bean worry-ing, then Bean bored, something thrilling and unfamiliar pulsing from her headphones. Tugging on the rubber cord, begging to hear what she heard. Then listening anxiously, feeling confused and frightened.

I did not understand what I had asked for. Getting what I wanted never felt as good as the wanting itself.

I have probably looked at this photograph on nearly every day of my adult life. Sometimes I try to see the picture through a stranger's eyes, hoping to surprise these girls into switching places. I know what I crave and I'm ashamed of it. Just once, I want to be the pretty one.

Chapter One

Fit, fuckable, fake

For once, my body isn't the problem. It's my face that won't follow the rules.

If I turn and tilt my torso, lifting and twisting to the left, the roundness of my belly dissipates. The action creates the illusion of muscle tone. At least, according to my reflection. I stand on one leg. My body looks amazing.

Of course, I don't have my glasses on, and I've left the lights off. It's a dull, dark day. The room is only just illuminated by the (surprisingly flattering) blue light coming from Wingz'n'Thingz opposite. From the neck down, in my smudgy, grubby mirror, I look like the sort of girl who could give you a good time. Sharp angles and firm curves, a generic babe, reality TV bait. Not bad, considering that half an hour ago I caught sight of my own outline in a shop window and wondered why I'd gone out dressed as a lady vicar. I long to be sultry. In real life, my vibe is 'hearty', 'jolly', 'ruddy'. I've had more than one conversation where it has been assumed that I spent my school days playing a lot of hockey. I'm certain this never happened to Brigitte

Bardot. No one ever looked at Julie Christie and offered her a big bowl of apple crumble with extra custard.

In this position, my waist is narrow, my legs are longer, my thighs are slimmer. But I'm obviously suffering, and I do not look beautiful. As I try to keep my body in place, my eyes bulge, my eyebrows hit my hairline, my pout becomes a grimace. I remember a Groupon yoga class, a teacher telling me off during a terrible attempt at Crow Pose. 'You're carrying too much tension in your face,' she sang, serene in Lululemon, seeming to float off the ground. She had a point. When I looked at myself in the studio mirror, it seemed a wonder I hadn't shat the mat.

I'm making a face like Frankie Howerd, from the *Carry On* films. It's not a great look for anyone. And you really, really need to avoid it if your name is Frankie Howard. Frankie Howard from nowhere of note. Frankie Howard from a handful of awful castings, an advert for the Thriller Griller barbecue, last shown in 2017, and from the Bazowwwww! box. On the box, I am actually making a Frankie Howerd face, opening my mouth and pointing with delight at man named Ken, who is supposed to be impersonating a donkey. Perhaps that's why the game sold so badly.

Planting my bare feet on the floor, I breathe in, slowly. My body is beautiful. I hold the breath for five beats. My body is useful. I try to breathe out even more slowly, and my tits wobble. Jelly on a plate. Fuck you, William Morris.

I have set alarms in order to wake up fifteen minutes early to look into this mirror and tell my body that it is beautiful. I have written affirmations. I've bought too many crappy crystals from Etsy sellers. I own at least thirty sachets filled with fragments of murky Himalayan rose quartz.

Apparently, the secret to lasting self-compassion looks like something you'd put on your chips.

I have spent money that I do not have on sessions with faith healers in village halls on Saturday afternoons. I've drunk the Kool-Aid literally, as well as figuratively. Miriam, my boss, is best friends with a white witch, and she made me a self-love potion. I downed it and I was sick for seventy-two hours. I puked all over my duvet cover, washed it three times and eventually had to burn it.

For a while, there was no limit to the amount of expensive nonsense I would engage with in order to try to love my body better. After years of experimentation, I have discovered there's only one thing that works. The trouble is that for me, it really works.

I twist again, but I keep both feet on the floor. It's about manipulating the curve of my hip. It's simple physics.

If I fold and hold my left arm against my bare flesh, and let my breasts fall against it, the effect in the mirror is ... compelling. Coital. The heaviness of me is shaped and contained.

Licking my lips, I cast my gaze to my feet. No, too subservient. Too sad. I shake my head, so my lion's mane falls in my eyes. That's the only bit of my body I like, all the time. It's thick, and wild, just like the rest of me – but in hair alone, these qualities are permitted and encouraged. I train my eyes on the floor and look up, through the curtain of hair.

I set the timer on my phone, before propping it against a pile of battered paperbacks. Then I resume my position, recreating the pose as precisely as I can. *Focus!* I think. But *relax!*

When the brief barrage of clicks has ended, I pick up my phone and examine the images. It's the ultimate act of narcissism, staring at myself while thinking 'Would I want her?'

My own face is such a mystery to me. The smallest movement in my jaw, or of my eyelid, makes all the difference. There are twenty photographs here, and twenty different Frankies. I see Menacing Frankie. Knackered Frankie. 'No, thank you, I don't need any help, I'm just browsing,' Frankie. Finally, Fuckable Frankie makes an appearance. Thank goodness. Number seventeen.

That's the shot.

The full-length ones always do well. I'll take more – on the bed, augmented by pillows, carefully positioned to conceal and reveal – but this is the photo I was hoping to get. The fuckable one. The fit one. The fake one.

It needs careful editing – a process which requires just as much time and attention as striking the pose. It's funny, there is a sense that filtering photographs is evidence of a superficial nature; it's something to sneer at. But it's hard to get it right. It's difficult to create something that looks easy. Even though I've done scraps of modelling, I don't look or feel like a model. Yet, alone in my bedroom, teaching myself how to make the most of my phone camera, I tell myself I am almost a proper photographer. Or maybe an *im*proper one.

One day I would like to own a proper camera, though. I'm always half-heartedly 'saving up', scouring various auction sites to see if I can find a decent second-hand model, almost asking for one for Christmas. I scrape money together, I read reviews, blogs and magazines, I start to dream about what it might be like to be *behind* the lens, for a living – and then I picture myself in six months or a year, still here. Still stuck. People like my photos because people like tits. Not because I could be the next Corinne Day. A camera would be evidence of ambition, and audacity. And then, photography would just become another thing I failed at.

That said, in this context I know what I'm doing. Making infinitesimal adjustments to the light settings, I check my skin tone, clean up a little shadow and make sure I look as polished as possible. Smooth, pliable and pliant. Ready for the website. A safe space, where even a girl like me can pass for perfect. A place where I can be nearly naked, while hiding in plain sight; where I can stay invisible while secretly seeking to be seen. It's impossible for anyone here to find a context to frame me or fix me in place. No one knows my real name. I'm just @girl_going_alone.

A handful of users even start their messages with 'Girl' or 'Girlie'. It sounds offensive, but I love it. I don't want to be 'Frankie', here. Frankie has a hairy little toe. Frankie has been known to hide under a table if she thinks she has heard a wasp. But a 'girl' is a fairy-tale thing, an amorphous fantasy. Anything that anyone wants or needs her to be. Here, a 'girl' can never disappoint.

The lie I tell myself is that I need to alter the image enough to make sure no one I know could ever recognise me. But I don't believe anyone from my real life could ever find themselves here, looking for a cheap thrill.

The truth is that I love the sense of control that comes with photo editing. It's a contradiction that knots and loops. I couldn't explain it or justify it to anyone else because it doesn't even make sense to me. Fake Frankie gets to experience complete release. What I do in front of my phone is an uncontrolled explosion. And then Real Frankie, the nerd, the obsessive, steps in and carefully moulds the material. There is nothing false about filters; they allow me to reconcile my inner and outer selves.

The money will come. The messages will come. And today, I'll try not to think about the men who might be staring at me, touching themselves, maybe telling their partners they'll be ten minutes, that they've got to make a call or check something in the shed. I mean, it's Valentine's Day. It's depressing that I'm all alone, in Paddington, stuck in my damp attic room, turning myself on with my own vanity. But it would be much more depressing to be somewhere else, and someone else's girlfriend, wishing there could be one night when my partner put down his phone.

I like the attention. I like the validation. I like knowing I can create something that makes these men forget themselves for a moment. I especially like the knowledge that none of them would ever look twice at me on the street.

Usually, I am invisible, my spectacles misted with condensation, a woolly hat pulled over my ears. Once a week the odd one will shout, 'WHY ARE YOU SO TALL?' Last year, I found a beautiful jade-coloured coat in a charity shop. I had to donate it again after some teenage boys followed me down Edgware Road, shouting, 'Shrek! Shrek! Shrek!'

But online, the comments are kind. It's not just that these men think I'm hot – or rather, think that pretend, digitally manipulated me is hot – this is something I'm *good* at. I don't really have any skills or abilities. I'm not special, I'm not exceptional. I'm always coasting, drifting, stuck on the sidelines. It isn't that I've missed my chance;

I'm just not the sort of person that inspires the stars to align in any way.

Still, my relationship with the site is complicated. It's completely legal, and I tell myself that I have nothing to be ashamed of, but I *am* ashamed. I don't yearn to be loved as much as I long to be looked at. I'm an attention seeker. The worst kind of woman.

But I need it. When I'm posing and posting, I feel as though I'm in control of my life. It seems *safe*; it's a space where I will only encounter kindness. And yet, I cannot bear to think of what I'd have to do if anyone found out. It is not a happy secret.

I'm scrutinising the image, trying to work out whether I could make myself look slightly more attractive, when my phone screen flashes. My naked body is instantly replaced by an image of a truly beautiful woman grinning broadly, her face flanked by two beaming little boys. Bean.

'It's your secret admirer!' she says. I squash my phone against my ear and under my chin as I grab my dressing gown from the back of the door. I'm extremely close to my sister but not naked-phone-call close. As she once said, 'Taking baths together when we were kids doesn't mean there's a lifelong clothes amnesty happening. In fact, we should be less nude together – we've used up our allowance.'

'Happy Valentine's Day! Did Paul pony up with a fabulous gift? A champagne hot-air balloon ride? Fireworks in the back garden?' My brother-in-law isn't typically a man of grand gestures, but he might surprise us all.

Her laugh ends with a sigh. 'Hardly. He's working late and we're getting a takeaway. I got a very sweet card from

Jack, though. He made it at school. "I love you Mummy. You shout in the car."'

I like my nephew's style. 'He's not wrong, Bean. You do shout in the car.'

'He drew a picture. Stick Me, standing by my car, with a speech bubble that said, "I HATE YOU." When Social Services call, will you plead my case?'

I picture Bean's pristine kitchen, my nephews in their matching dinosaur T-shirts, and snort at the idea. Then I make the mistake of looking around my room. You could sell the contents and it wouldn't pay for Bean's fridge. I barely have furniture; just piles of books, and piles of dirty underwear. Sometimes I wish Social Services would come and remove me from myself. With a shake of my head, I push the thought away. Comparison is the thief of joy. Although, so are bras with loose wires – I really must sort out some of these piles.

'What was Mrs Beardley's brief, exactly?' I ask.

Bean sighs. 'I asked her, and apparently she told the kids to focus on what their parents' hobbies are.'

Given Bean has an actual Pilates instructor who comes twice a week, at 5 a.m., this seems unfair. But it jogs my memory. 'Did I send you that hilarious piece Maz Clarke wrote about hobbies? The one where she panicked about not having any, and lied about being able to juggle, and then became addicted to juggling ...'

'I'm not sure,' says Bean. 'I might have read it somewhere. Anyway—'

'Or it might have been Caitlin Moran? I can't remember. I wish I wasn't so clumsy, I'd love to try to juggle. I wonder whether juggling can cure clumsiness ...' I drift off, picturing myself throwing balls in the air, then breaking mirrors, windows.

Bean interrupts my reverie. 'Listen, Frankie, can you do me a favour?' She sounds tense, and a little breathless. 'I've got an appointment and I'm going to be running late. The boys are at Becky's, would you mind picking them up for me and bringing them over? You'd be a lifesaver!'

I look through my window, out at the blue gloom, and think *Yeah. I would mind.* I picture Bean at her appointment. My photo addiction is sordid and secret but the whole world is happy to indulge my sister and *her* addiction to gel manicures. That's 'normal'. Lifesaver, indeed. Bean would miss major surgery if it was scheduled when she was supposed to be getting her nails done.

I consider putting my coat on, and I can already feel the dank winter air seeping into my scarf. The sogginess. The scratchiness. '*Bean*, I just got in! And I'm in my dressing gown. Can't Becky bring them to the nail place?' Damn. I shouldn't have told her about the dressing gown; she's always on at me to be less slobby.

'Franks, I'm not at the nail place,' she says, sounding hesitant. 'I'm at the hospital.'

Panic seizes me. 'What? Shit! Oh my God, are you OK?' I hear a siren, which seems like an awful omen. 'Are you in an ambulance?' I add, picturing Bean prone, surrounded by paramedics, speeding past my door.

'Frankie, calm down. You're so suggestible! Was that a siren? You live near St Mary's, you're on the route. I always hear sirens when we're on the phone; I've seen you sleep through them. I'm fine. I'm not in an ambulance. It's just a boring old UTI,' says Bean.

13

She *sounds* fine. A little tired, a little grumpy, but not as though she might be bleeding from the head. 'Poor you, though,' I say. 'You'd only just had one, too!'

'Yeah, last month,' says Bean. 'It got sorted pretty quickly, but my GP followed up. There's some bullshit initiative, a clinic aimed very specifically at mothers under forty living in south-west London with Aries rising and bladders the size of geriatric hamsters …'

'Is that too big or too small?' I ask, gravely. 'I have a theory that my bladder is half the size it should be, but maybe *stretchier*? Because sometimes if I drink a lot of coffee—'

'Frankie, please.' Bean sounds exasperated. 'Just get the boys. I'll owe you one. I'll owe you one million. You remember where Becky lives? I'll text the address, she's just fifteen minutes' walk from us. Have you got keys?'

No, I threw them out of the window. It was a piece of performance art. I called it 'The Feckless sibling'.

'Yes, I've got keys,' I say, wearily. 'I'll be there within the hour.' And I am rewarded for sucking in my sarcasm, because Bean says, 'Thank you, Frankie. I don't know what I'd do without you,' and she sounds like she means it.

With great care, I save my photos into a hidden folder, which nests at the core of a series of Matryoshka-doll dummy folders: 'Boiler Instructions' hides the ambiguous 'People and Places!' Which hides the truly off-putting, appalling sounding 'BANTS HOLIDAY ADVENTURES'. I don't know who I'm trying to convince. It's obvious to anyone that I don't have the sort of wide social circle with which one has BANTS ADVENTURES. It is even more obvious that I don't know how my boiler works.

Then, with less care, I attempt to put on as many items of clothing as possible in under three minutes. Leggings, jeggings, sweatshirt, jumper, woolly hat, scarf and gloves are unrolled and layered with as much speed as I can muster.

There's an old-fashioned party game in which this burst of activity would be followed by an attempt to eat a bar of chocolate with a knife and fork. Instead, I pat my pockets, lock my door, and hurl my body down the stairs while wondering why the scientific community has made such strides in things like 3D printing, yet has not come up with a fast and painless way to get to Clapham.

Chapter Two

Valentines

Before I'm at Becky's door, I can smell vanilla, sweet and warm, beckoning me from the pavement. Shivering, I pull my scarf a little tighter. I'm still sweaty from the Tube, but the projection of warmth and the idea of future cosiness is making me especially aware of the current cold. As I press the doorbell, I remember what I'm wearing – more or less all the warm clothes I own – and feel a bit shabby and self-conscious. I've only met Becky a couple of times, but I know she is the very essence of Middle Class Womanhood. This door is the portal to Pure Clapham. She makes Bean look like ... well, me, I suppose.

'Sorry!' says Becky, by way of greeting. Her jumper is very pink, and very fluffy. It matches her very pink face and her very fluffy blonde hair. 'Oh! It's you.' She looks up at me fearfully, as though I have come to steal her eggs. 'We made cookies, which was terribly naughty of us. I hope Bean doesn't mind.'

Bean doesn't give a shit, mate. You haven't set her kids up in a commercial meth lab. It's just some chocolate chips.

'Your secret is safe with me. Anyway, Bean is just super grateful to you for looking after the boys,' I say. 'Are they ready?'

'I think so,' says Becky, indicating for me to follow her into the hall. 'You don't want a glass of wine, do you?' She peers up at me from over her shoulder, fearfully. I suspect she thinks she ought to be offering me the blood of a freshly slaughtered virgin, or a nice mug of petrol.

From what Bean has told me, I know I am Becky's ultimate nightmare come to life. Becky has a perfect home, a perfect child (Aloysius – I *know*) and a perfect marriage, apparently. But she believes, quite sincerely, that all her good fortune rests entirely on her ability to maintain a classic size-eight figure. She will not have eaten a single cookie. In her eyes – and it's my height as much as my weight – I am a monster from another realm.

To her credit, she has only ever spoken to me in a manner that is polite, kind and civil. But she looks at me as though my body might be catching. Bean is offended on my behalf. I choose to find it hilarious.

'You're sweet to offer,' I say, 'but we'd better get the chaps back.' See? I might look like the Iron Giant, but I speak fluent Clapham.

'Boys!' I call out. 'Are there BOYS here? Jack! Jon! Get your shoes on!'

And then, the magic rush, the swelling, soaring, ascending notes of my heartstrings as I hear my name, followed by footsteps tentative (Jon) and thundering (Jack). A pair of sweet, hot, sticky little dark brown heads hurl themselves at my knees.

'Careful, boys!' calls Becky. 'Don't get chocolate on your auntie!'

I drop to a crouch and wrap my arms around them both, squeezing hard.

'Fuh— Frankie, I mean, Auntie Eff ... anyway, please can Ally have a hug?' whispers Jon, entirely audibly.

I look. Aloysius is standing behind the boys, grinding his right heel against the floor, clasping his hands. His eyes are downcast.

'Of course!' I reply. 'Ally, would you like to join in with the hug?'

'I suppose so,' he says, solemnly. He walks towards us slowly, before stretching his arms around my back and burrowing under my armpit. I daren't look at Becky, but I try to send her a psychic message. *It's safe. I'm not going to snatch Aloysius up into my jaws and fly off with him.*

'Now, has everyone got everything?' I ask, preparing to carry school bags and book bags and dinky embroidered drawstring PE bags.

'It's alright, they dropped everything off at home before coming here,' says Becky. 'But please take the cookies. Please.' She proffers a giant Tupperware box.

'Mummy, they're not taking them *all*, are they?' says Aloysius, sounding bereft. 'Because you promised, after last time ...'

Shamefully, I don't think I have the energy to intervene on Aloysius' behalf. Becky is fierce – if I tried, I suspect I'd end up in a Tupperware box myself.

'Right, let's get going,' I say, quickly. 'Shall we sing a song on the way home? Thank you so much, Becky. Bean sends her love; you'll see her soon, I'm sure. Say thank you, boys!'

'Bye, Ally. Thank you, Mrs Becky!' calls Jack. 'Auntie

Frankie, I learned a song at school today, can we teach it to Jon?'

'Sure,' I say, as the door closes behind us. 'What's it about?'

'It's about being friends!' says Jack, excitedly. 'It's by the Spice Girls.'

'Right,' I say, taken aback.

'Auntie Frankie, what's a lover?' he asks. 'Mummy wouldn't tell me but I thought *you* might know.'

'Um . . . I'm not sure!' I say, brightly, not certain of what is about to come out of my mouth. 'Is it to do with not liking the sea? People who don't go to sea are called landlubbers – maybe it's another way of saying that?'

Jon puts his hands on his hips and stares up at me. 'I am the littlest, and I do not know things. And even *I* know that is stupid.'

'Maybe,' I shrug. 'But I am the biggest. Maybe *I* am the stupidest! Maybe being big has nothing to do with being clever.'

'Not nothing,' says Jack, meaningfully. 'I think *sometimes* being bigger must make you cleverer-er.' And that discussion takes us all the way to Bean's front door.

We have opened negotiations about teatime, bathtime and bedtime when I hear a key in the lock. Bean is back. 'It's Mummy!' I squeal, and we all assemble before my sister can step through her own threshold.

Bean looks like a Christmas card. Swaddled in her navy coat and red tartan scarf, she should be stressed and sweaty. It's the end of a long day, when most of us feel frayed and unstuck, a little blotchy, a little slumped. But Bean is predictably perfect. She looks like a fresh fall of snow at sunset, deep and crisp and even. Her dark hair swings and shines, perfect molten chocolate. It's a wonder she isn't followed by a chef brandishing a whisk.

(Once every six months, when work is especially stressful, she sends me a picture of Emma Stone or Maz Clarke and says, 'I'M DOING IT. I AM GOING GINGE.' My responses range from 'But u r already FOXXXX' to 'Don't you dare, I will stage an intervention, I will phone the salon and tell them not to let you in.')

After the office *and* the hospital, Bean still looks good enough to advertise bubble bath and life insurance and dating apps for when you're tired of swiping and you're ready to meet the Disney princess of your dreams. She even still *smells* good. (Jo Malone English Pear and Freesia – she claims it's the official fragrance of SW4. 'You're legally required to wear it; if you rebel, the council will put you on the most punishing bin schedule.')

She is holding a heart-shaped balloon.

'Hello, my lovelies! Have you been good for Auntie Frankie?' Bean steps inside, and with a tremendous effort of will, I stand back and allow her children to hug her first.

'Mummy, Auntie Frankie says that being big doesn't mean you're clever,' says Jack accusingly, beady as any 1960s Soviet informer.

'Does she, now?' says Bean, looking up at me, and then drawing herself to her full five feet four inches. 'I think she has a point. Now, boys, because it's Valentine's Day, I have a very special treat.' She produces two red, foil-wrapped, heart-shaped lollies from her coat pocket. 'These are for you. Because you have been so good for Auntie Frankie, you can eat these and watch *Hey Duggee* in the den.'

20

Jon graciously accepts a lolly and says, thoughtfully, 'Not *Hey Duggee*. I like *Bing*.'

'I suppose that's also acceptable. We'll be in the kitchen; come down if you need us. And remember, boys, it's a day of love! Be nice to each other. Or Saint Valentine will ... um ... tell Santa on you!'

The boys run off, and I say, half joking, 'Where's my lolly?'

'Frankie, you're twenty-nine,' says Bean, sighing. 'Here you go. Happy Valentine's Day.' She produces a third red heart. 'I knew you'd want the bloody chocolate.' Then she hands me the balloon. 'But I saw this and thought of you.'

As Bean peels off her layers, I make my own way into the kitchen, straight to the fridge, where the wine is. By the time she enters, I've filled two huge glasses, and I'm sitting, serene at Bean's kitchen island. My favourite place on Earth. Exactly where any lost soul would want to wash up.

It's fabulous – glossy, but not show-home glossy. Just scuffed and stained enough for a person to feel completely comfortable about undoing the top button of their jeans to make room for more potatoes. The faintest flush of a red wine ring gives a healthful glow to the granite countertop. Gleaming copper pans are piled up on the shelves. Giant feathery ferns line the windowsill, as well as a sad, spindly spider plant called Sid that Bean rescued from a student house share. ('I thought I'd give Sid a little dignity, so that he could see out his last days in peace,' she explained. 'But the bugger *will not die*.') A fridge that looks big enough to drive, covered with robot pictures, report cards, and grinning, gurning photos of Jack, Jon and Auntie Frankie. Bean's house is my home from home. In fact, it's more home than home.

'Sure you've got enough wine there?' she says, shaking her head slightly.

This isn't like her. She seems exasperated. Firstly, this is part of our ritual. I must have got wine out of her fridge a thousand times. Secondly, I just left a distant postcode and went out in the cold to pick up my nephews, without a moment's notice. What happened to 'lifesaver'?

'What's up with you?' I ask, grumpily. 'Did you want red instead? Or a gin and tonic?'

'I'm sorry, Frankie, I'm a bit all over the place ... Look. Listen, I don't know how to tell you this.' She reaches across and puts her right hand over mine. 'I lied to you. I don't have a UTI. I just got the results of a biopsy.'

My hand flips over and squeezes hers tightly, my body responding to the word more quickly than my brain can. 'Right.' A *biopsy*? That sounds scary. That sounds serious.

'So, the good news – and it *is* good news – is that they've caught it early. Really, really early. All things considered, everyone is optimistic.' Bean's hand squeezes back, but she's looking at my chin, avoiding eye contact. She's speaking at a quarter-pitch too high, a quarter of a second too quickly. She's doing an impression of herself, and it's almost convincing. But I *know* her. Something is very wrong.

'Bean, please, I'm sorry, I'm not following. Slow down. What have they caught early?' Just in time, I stop myself from saying *use your words*. I must not panic. I don't want her to protect me from her horror, to babysit me through it. If she catches me panicking, she'll go Full Big Sister. She won't tell me anything.

'OK, don't worry. Promise me.' She pauses, and now her speech becomes too slow. '*Promise me* you won't worry.'

22

Too late. Worry is gathering at the base of my belly, shooting through my arms and legs, spikes forming across my back.

'I promise,' I lie.

Bean pauses for about a hundred years.

She makes eye contact, at last. 'There are some cancerous cells in my right breast.'

'Right, right.' My mouth is busy, buying time. 'Cancerous cells. Cells of ... I see.' That can't be the same as cancer, can it? She would have just come out and said cancer, if it was something so dark, so frightening. 'Cancerous' is technically a different word. It sounds more like 'cruciferous'. Which is, I think, something to do with broccoli. Broccoli isn't serious. 'So, cancerous cells – but not actual cancer?'

After my last smear test, I got a letter telling me I had 'abnormal cells' and I *freaked out*. Then I got another letter telling me that they'd sent the sample off, had a closer look, and there was nothing to worry about. 'Cells' must be medical code for 'sounds scary but is actually fine'. Because Bean can't have cancer. Bean *cannot* have cancer. Bean is so healthy that she claims to actually like green tea. I don't think Bean has ever had a cold sore.

I'm taken aback when she starts laughing. She snorts, she barks, she clasps both my hands in hers, and tears of mirth start sliding down her face. At least I *think* they're tears of mirth. 'Fuck!' she says, snorting again, wiping her eyes on her sleeve. 'That will teach me to try talking like a doctor. Franks, cancerous cells are cancer. I'm sorry. It's shit. I'm so sorry that I'm telling you this shitty, shitty thing.' Now she's really crying, and I take her in my arms, trying to fold her into me. Comforting her the only way I know how. I need to play the big sister now, if only physically.

The funny thing is that I've been rehearsing for this moment. Not breast cancer necessarily, but some kind of tragedy.

I knew disaster would strike at some point. I had always believed I would automatically become Useful. This is supposed to be my cue. In this instant, I should be transformed from Shabby Half Person With Crap Job and Crap Flat to Mary Poppins. I'm meant to be coming down the chimney with a bottomless bag of nutritious home-cooked meals, exuding a perfect ratio of practical cheer to sympathy.

Instead, as I cradle Bean I'm searching for loopholes, pacing outside the emotional courtroom, determined to keep her out of jail. And hallelujah, I think I've found one!

'Hang on. You're much too young for breast cancer, aren't you? I saw it on TV, I think it was on *Real Housewives*. You don't even have to get screened before you're in your forties, and you're not even thirty-five yet!' I drop an imaginary mic. The defence rests, your honour.

Bean laughs, again. Why does she keep laughing? 'Oh my God, Frankie, for goodness' sake! I went to the hospital! They stuck needles in me! But by all means, offer me a second opinion. I mean, what's medical school and years of training compared with a half-remembered episode of *Real Housewives*?'

I'm flooded by a wave of shame. 'I'm so, so sorry, Bean. I'm being stupid. I think it's the shock.'

She sighs, again. 'I'm sorry, of course you're in shock. I was. I still am, a bit. You're right, too. It's really unusual for this to happen when you're thirty-four. But the doctors

24

have said that in a weird way, that could be good news. Generally, I'm strong and healthy. In fact, I noticed nice and early because I'm pretty vigilant about health stuff, and everyone I've spoken to says that's a huge plus.'

'What happened? What ...' *Why didn't you tell me before?* is the question I want to ask. I should have known, all the same. I should be intuitive enough to have sensed something, the very second anything started going wrong.

But then, this is Bean. I've never needed to comfort her. She's never been fired. She's never been dumped. She glides through the world. Everyone smiles at her, steps aside for her, as though they have been expecting her. I'm the fuck up. If Bean has bad news, the apocalypse can't be far away.

She shrugs, as though she's talking about getting her car fixed. 'My right one has been a bit weird ever since I was breastfeeding Jon. Do you remember when I had mastitis? I was keeping an eye on it, and I had a cyst about a year ago, but it turned out to be benign—'

'A cyst? You never told me that!' I'm hysterical. I'm gulping for air.

'Frankie, this is why I didn't tell you. For fuck's sake, you need to calm down, yeah? I'm scared, Franks. I need to believe that this is going to be OK and I can't have you bringing the drama. You're worse than Alison. And I'm not telling Alison – at least, not for the time being.' From Bean, this is a damning indictment of my behaviour. Our mother can be Difficult.

'Do you want me to tell her?' I ask, tentatively. I want to be generous, to save Bean from the horrible task – it's *not* going to be an easy conversation – but it's not an entirely selfless offer. I don't trust Alison not to drag it out of me,

25

somehow. Bean has built parental boundaries of reinforced steel; mine have the structural integrity of wet toilet paper.

'NO!' says Bean, grabbing me by my shoulders and giving me a small, brisk shake. 'Absolutely not! She'll make it all about her – and I need some more time to get my head around it before that happens. It will bring up all the Dad stuff for her. You know. She'll go full Tragic Widow. And it might trigger another crazed fundraising phase. She'll have you tap dancing in church halls and selling raffle tickets. I don't want to be her good cause.'

Dad died of lung cancer when Bean was seven and I was two. I don't know whether I have any real memories of him or if they're just photographs, reconstructions, Bean's efforts to make sure I knew we'd had some happy days.

I find it hard to imagine him as part of our family. I find it harder still to believe that his death did not mark the start of a curse. I try to tell myself that we've already had our share of bad luck, that the worst has already happened. Sometimes this eases my fear. And sometimes I wake up in the early hours of the morning and count down the minutes until I can message Bean or Alison – ostensibly to send a cheery greeting, but really to make sure that they are still alive.

Even though I barely remember Dad, I suspect he accounts for much of my genetic legacy. Alison and Bean are tiny brunettes. Dad was well over six foot tall, Celtic, freckly. I'm always searching for scraps, seeking out clues. Who was he, and who does that make us?

'I know I'm being silly,' I say, cautiously, 'but is this connected with Dad? Do your genes affect anything? I suppose it's a completely different kind of cancer.' I've forced my face into a smile. I'm trying to be optimistic, but I know I sound callous, ridiculous. As though I'm claiming that Dad crashed a red car, so Bean will be fine in her blue one.

'Obviously I asked about that,' says Bean, and I'm grateful. I'm not completely stupid if she's had the same questions. 'I don't think I fully understood what cancer actually was – is – before. I've been going deep with Dr Google. What I have is ultimately a different sort of illness. The good news, I think, is that medical science has made some truly phenomenal leaps. A diagnosis is not a death sentence. Treatments have changed completely since Dad had it.'

'He was a smoker too!' I say. 'You don't smoke.' Why am I telling Bean this fact about herself as though it might be news? I'm addressing the universe too. Someone needs to fix this administrative error. Growing up, Not Smoking was our religion. Smoking kills – we had evidence. Surely if you don't smoke, you're supposed to live forever?

Bean laughs. (How?) 'Now that I think about it, I probably drew him a card that said, "Daddy, I love you and you love Benson and Hedges".'

'I suppose it was a different time,' I say, dully. That catch-all excuse for all the pain and horror that happened in the past.

'And, most importantly, science is on my side!' says Bean, pragmatically. Anyway, I'm sorry to give you the world's biggest Valentine buzzkill. But we will be fine. Just promise me you'll never say, "You got this!"'

'Cross my heart. We absolutely, emphatically, do not got this. Seriously, though, what do you need? What would be the most helpful thing for me to do right now, and generally? Is it childcare, or coming to hospital, or cooking, or what? Daily check ins?'

'Honestly?' asks Bean. There's a tremor in her voice. 'Please, just be as normal as you can. I'm not in denial, but I figure this is going to be a lot of my life now. And I desperately need a place – a person to be with – where I can pretend to be fine, someone who is never going to say, "How are you?" with their head tilted. I don't want you to be sorry for me. I don't think I could bear it if I thought you were putting your life on hold, for this. I need you to make me laugh. That's what you're best at. That and Strategic Alison Management.'

'When are you going to tell her?' I ask, cautiously. 'You do need to tell her, at some point.'

'Mmm,' says Bean. This means, 'The course of action that you are suggesting is entirely correct – but I'm not going to do it.'

She looks at her hands and fidgets with her wedding ring. 'It will be easier when I have a team assigned and a treatment plan, which should be soon. I can tell her when I've worked out the best way to keep her calm – or, ide-ally, oblivious. Otherwise I'll have a house filled with fruit baskets and she'll be dragging me to mother-daughter mas-sages. No thank you.'

Making a face, I think about Alison's possible reactions. 'In old films, they have singing telegrams. I can imagine her hiring someone to come and sing on your doorstep.' I attempt an off-key, off-colour, improvised melody. '"Sorry, to hear the news! A shame, about your boobs! We hope you get well soon! Thanks to this healing tune!"'

'News and boobs don't rhyme!' gasps Bean, but she's

28

laughing again. 'That is exactly what I needed. That's what I want you to do. Don't ever stop being you, around me. Please be as dark and crude and funny as possible. That's what will help.'

'I might not "got this" but I've got dark, crude and funny,' I say, forcing a smile. I've never felt less funny in my life.

Chapter Three

The worst possible taste

Usually, the best thing about travelling in London is that you're guaranteed total privacy. You could get on the Tube with a dead body under your arm and pinch someone's *Metro* from under their nose to mop up the blood. They might tut, but they wouldn't look up.

I was relying on this to get through the journey home. I was hoping to be left in silence so I could wait for the sadness to hit. I want to feel completely and instantly heart-broken, filled with despair, screaming at the sky and renting my garments. It's going to happen, and the longer I wait the more frightening the feelings will be.

But there's an emotional airlock. I can't cry, I can't release anything. I feel too solid, stuck on the brink, unable to hurl myself into the canyon. This is Bean. *Bean.* I try to picture her in hospital, in a room decorated with Jack's pictures. Bean in a skimpy cotton gown. *Paul* taking charge. Oh, God. It's just not possible. None of this is possible.

It's also hard to focus on my feelings because I'm attract-ing some unexpected attention.

At first, I ignore the smiles from the man sitting opposite me. I reckon I've got his number – at least, metaphorically speaking. Ruddy face, stripy shirt, four pints after work, north of fifty, 'still got it', will try 'it' with any woman who seems young-ish and blonde-ish.

But when I look away, I see his neighbour smiling at me, too. It seems much friendlier from her – a woman who could be in her seventies, wearing a beautiful green brocade skirt suit. (Also a matching hat, which is *immaculate* – how? How has she escaped the relentless misty, soggy rain?)

Is this a very strange message from the universe? God, saying, 'I know you're ambivalent about me, but I'm here! Reminding you to depend on the kindness of strangers!'

At the other end of the carriage, a little girl in a unicorn hoodie beams at me and looks above my head. And that's when I remember it's still Valentine's Day, and I have a heart-shaped helium balloon tied to my wrist.

This is my tragedy balloon, but to everyone else it's a symbol of love and fun. It's *festive*. I look as though I'm just a few stops away from a glass of prosecco with a strawberry bobbing to the surface. I smile back at the little girl. Maybe I should give her the balloon.

No! It's *my* Valentine from Bean. It's precious.

There must be a Valentine I can send to Bean. Something to lift her up and make her laugh. It's probably too late to send flowers. And if Paul hasn't got her anything, he'll sulk, and that's no fun for her.

Not flowers, I think, as I get off the train and walk up the platform. *Not champagne,* I think, as I jog up the escalator. We'll have champagne the second she's better. I'll buy her magnums! Double magnums! What are those giant bottles called? The ones named after the Three Wise Men? But no, that's too celebratory. That doesn't feel appropriate right now.

Plodding through the drizzle, I consider and reject a box of posh truffles. My sister loves 'basic bitch chocolate' – her term – she doesn't want 95 per cent cacao anything. That nice blue jumper in the window of Whistles? No. She probably already owns it; she has every single 'nice blue jumper' Whistles ever made.

With minimal dexterity and a lot of luck, I get my body and my balloon through the front door and up the stairs. I see a red envelope on the mat, addressed to 'sexy Stella', which means my neighbour is out – probably having an exciting time with someone other than the card sender.

No one left a Valentine by my door. Everything in the room is exactly where I left it. The bed is unmade. The space is in a state of disarray. The balloon looks incongruous. My giant, distorted red face is reflected back at me in its curves.

You were supposed to be bringing me to a party! it seems to say, accusingly. *I belong somewhere exciting! I used to model for Jeff Koons, you know.*

I look back at the balloon. Maybe it wants to have its picture taken? Smile for the camera, baby!

I think about how I might lure the balloon to my casting couch, and I snort. *It would be classy. Discreet. You know I'm legit, I've got the 'e's in the right order.* Then I'd tie the red ribbon string around my ankle, spread my legs and snap. Or I'd take a picture while holding the balloon against myself, obscuring my body while 'accidentally' displaying it on the balloon's metallic surface.

32

It would be impossible to wrangle both phone and balloon. I would need to be more discrete than discreet – for my two separate selves to manifest and take corporeal forms. The slut, to pose and pout and straddle, and the nerd, to click and tweak and position, and prevent the balloon from floating away.

How can I think this, today of all days? I'm a monster. This balloon is the last thing Bean gave me before she told me the news. She presented me with a giant, inflated heart because she knew she had to break my real one. She is an angel, a tragic angel, thinking of me when her thoughts should be fully focused on herself and her body. And here I am, joking to myself about turning her generosity into a cheap prop.

But what if this is exactly what I need, right now? Maybe I should do something normal. Well, normal for me.

I haven't posted any photos today. I haven't finished editing them. If I finish what I started, I can travel back in time. I can pretend the last few hours did not happen. I can escape my feelings for a little bit longer.

Even as I'm trying to resist the urge, my thumb is itching. It's as though it has its own brain, which is much more powerful than the one in my head. *Just a little photo. Just a little play. This feels nice. This will make everything better. If you carry on as normal, you can pretend life isn't happening. Just for now. It's safe here.*

Compulsively, I pick up my phone and go straight to my hidden album.

In the olden days, after a big shock, you'd have a whisky, a Valium. This is my Valium.

I start to edit, completely absorbed in the task. I can push thoughts and facts aside for a moment. The *feeling* – the acid ache immobilising my body – has leaked out of me. I'm comfortably numb. Moments ago, I felt as though someone had wedged iron girders under my shoulder blades. Now they have dissolved.

I adjust the settings, playing with the colour saturation and enhancing the sense of chiaroscuro. I try making the room even darker, so the brightness falls on my body. This is the part of the process I love the most. I'm making something. I get to be creative. I am not flesh and blood, any more; I'm a stick woman, tits and teeth and big hair. Let me be your fantasy, creepy men of the internet. I want to render myself unreal. In this universe, nothing can touch me, and I cannot be hurt.

I can barely recognise myself. I post the photos to my profile before I can change my mind. Thank goodness for this. A tiny online corner, just for me, where life is all likes and approval and bad news can't reach you.

Then, I have an idea. Maybe there is a way to share this with Bean, to make it about her too. Well, not *this*, obviously; not my secret profile. But there might be a way to doctor this image, make her laugh with something crude and crass. A funny Valentine, an echo of Jack's homage to her hatred of other motorists.

Is this a bit *too* weird?

No, I can never be too weird for Bean.

I re-edit the photograph, cropping out most of my bare skin. Now, it just looks slightly suggestive. My namesake would have approved – it's more 'Matron!' than 'Think of the children!'

I add bright blue squiggles under my eyes. They're

34

supposed to look like tears. I draw a speech bubble and insert the text, 'I love you, Bean! Your tits are shit'. Then, the crucial detail. A pair of poo emojis where my breasts should be. My smirk to camera, my big hair and my slightly guileless expression all add to the effect. A joke in the worst possible taste.

Obviously, Bean does not know about the website. She's seen the odd photo on my phone, and has reacted with strong curiosity, and mild alarm. I claim it's for dating – that no one will consent to meet me for a bowl of noodles unless I send nudes first. (Sometimes she asks why I don't ever seem to go out on any actual dates. I shrug and look sad and it shuts her up.)

HAPPY VALENTINE'S DAY!!!!!! I write. Is this dark and funny enough for you? Cannot believe cancer is made out of cancerous cells. I've had an educational day. Sending love and light to you and your wabs. WE DO NOT GOT THIS XXX

I don't know if it will make Bean feel any better. I hope so. I feel a small jolt of optimism – as though being dark and rude and irreverent is a force that could hurt the thing that is hurting her. It's an invader, a body bully. Together, we shall shrink it by dismissing it.

My attention is tugged in two different directions. I want to see what Bean says, but I also want – no, I *need* – to see what the men of the internet think of me. I'm aware of notifications piling up, and I can't focus on anything else.

STUNNING, says @Rob_1963.

IMACULAT, says @Leon_thelover, which is more than I can say for his spelling. That's such a weird response to a picture of a naked woman, too. As though he has thoroughly checked me for smears and smudges before announcing that I meet with his approval, and he is prepared to drive me off the garage forecourt.

Surfing an endorphin rush, I check to see whether Bean has responded. I'm warm, anticipating praise, a lovely message from my big sister about how hilarious I am.

Fuck. Wrong group. How have I done this? *How?*

I have sent the picture to Bean and Alison.

I didn't think things could get any worse, but I have *made* them worse. Alison will be freaking out. She's all alone. What if I have to go out *again* and calm her down? Otherwise, she might turn up unannounced at Bean's, weeping on the doorstep and clutching a strange and inappropriate gift. Miniature tuxedo jackets or a giant packet of toilet roll. (She has previously shown up with both.)

I have many separate messages from Bean. The first one reads, SERIOUSLY????

I call her. She does not pick up.

Looking at the group messages, I begin to piece it together.

No, honestly not serious, stay calm.
Very early.

I didn't tell you because there isn't anything to worry about.

Really nothing to worry about.
Frankie's idea of a joke.

36

Oh no.

This gives me an idea!💡 I read. An Alison emoji is a bad sign. Every drop of blood in my body seems to turn a little colder.

Holding my breath, I read on.

Why don't we all do some fundraising together?

I don't know why she has bothered with a question mark. In the gap between messages, Alison has probably already booked the Rotary Club and phoned the local papers.

This is pure punishment for my fuck up. Before the week is out, I'll be in a threadbare boa and ancient leotard, trying to remember the words to 'Big Spender'.

Didn't people do selfies with no makeup for cancer awareness? SEXY SELFIES!!!

Ah. Three lightbulbs this time.

#breasts4breasts!!! #Checktitout! CHECK TIT OUT!

Is she joking? She *must* be joking.

ARE YOU JOKING???? types Bean.

Sex sells!

Not this again. Alison briefly temped at an ad agency in the eighties, and she's never quite recovered.

Dead serious. This would get loads of attention.
Important cause. We could raise £££.

A line of flying dollar bills, and inexplicably, two peaches and an aubergine.

This is an emergency. I press the call button.

'Mum? It's me,' I say, trying to regulate my breath, while fixing my gaze on a pile of dirty pants.

'Yes, I know, darling. My phone tells me! Isn't modern technology *clever*?' says Alison, breathily. It's a good job I'm not in a laughing mood.

'Listen, I don't think fundraising is a good idea just now. We need to focus on being there for Bean. At some point, we'll definitely get involved with a charity, but she'd want to do something more low key. Maybe we could all do a five k.'

'A five k ... television?' she asks, and I hold my phone away from my mouth so she does not hear my long sigh.

'A sponsored jog, Mum. But sexy selfies ... would be really inappropriate. People would hate it. Not just Bean; everyone who has, or has had, breast cancer. It's a sensitive issue, they don't want to see a load of sexy pictures. And you know what Bean's like. She hates attention. She's having a bad time. We don't want to make her feel worse.'

'But she says it's fine! Nothing to worry about! And it wouldn't *be* Bean in the picture, would it? It would be you!' says Alison, as though she's delivering a flawless piece of logic. 'Besides, it's sexism, pure and simple.'

'Pardon?' I can't wait to hear how she has worked this one out.

'People are always criticising women. If a man took a picture of his penis to raise money and awareness of prostate

38

cancer, people would applaud him!' My mother is, among other things, a twisted genius. She's completely ridiculous – but the next celebrity caught in a dick-pic scandal should really hire her to do his PR. And she's presenting her argument to me with the confidence of someone who has a warranty in one hand and a defective toaster in the other.

As I try to gather my thoughts, I bite the inside of my wrist. Otherwise, I'll start laughing until I cry, and I'm not sure I'll ever stop. It occurs to me that she's so obsessed with fundraising that she hasn't stopped to ask why I'm taking pictures of my tits in the first place. That's a worrying sign.

She keeps talking. 'The thing is, Frankie, you have to take risks in life. Do the bold thing, the brave thing! Sure, a few people might not like it, but what really matters is the *cause.*' She pauses dramatically, and I attempt to stick a spoke into her mental wheel.

'Exactly, Mum! *Bean* is the cause! We focus on her. No matter what we *think*, we do what she asks us to do. And if she doesn't want us to do anything, we don't do it.' As the words leave my mouth, I shudder. I've already failed at this.

'But . . . ' Alison sounds confused. 'This isn't a big deal, is it? She said it was a routine thing, early treatment. I mean, she would have told me if it was serious. She would have called me, straight away.' I detect the tremor in her voice and remember my brief.

'Yes! It's a good prognosis—'

She interrupts, sounding panicked. 'What do you mean exactly by "prognosis"?'

This is going to be really hard. I don't want to lie. 'This is something that is treatable. The main thing is that we don't create any extra stress. She doesn't want us to worry, and she doesn't want us to give her extra things to worry about. So let's think about fundraising in a few months, when she's better. A way to celebrate and say thank you!' And a problem for Future Frankie. Silently, I promise the universe that I will do anything if Bean gets better, up to and including a fully nude fun run.

'OK, I understand. Leave it with me,' says Alison, ominously. 'I'd better let you go. Oh, that reminds me, have you been using a retinol? Because it's never too early to start. I got you some cream I saw in Boots; the woman said it wasn't for young skin but I thought, well, you're certainly not getting any youn—'

'Oh, that's the door! BYE, MUM! Love you! Speak soon!' I don't have the energy for a bonus half hour of Alison skincare chat.

I'm an idiot. I'm such an idiot. But sometimes it seems so exhausting. Alison needs so much ... *management*. I don't even tell her when I go to the opticians. When it comes to her daughters' health and wellbeing, she has far too many opinions. No wonder Bean wanted to keep this from her for as long as possible.

Chapter Four

Foreboding

On Wednesday morning, my brain wakes me up with a tickertape instruction. *Don't think don't think don't think about the bad thing.*

Still sleepy and searching for context, I answer back. *What bad thing?* Did I have a nightmare? I wiggle my toes, and the rough skin on my heels catches and scratches against the bedsheet. I feel spooked, polluted, *haunted* by something that happened. Something I did? Is this a hangover? Was I drinking? No, I had one glass of wine, with Bean, and I didn't even finish it. Which is unusual for us. Why didn't I finish it? What happened with Bean? Oh. That's the bad thing. Bean has cancer.

I need to cry, or scream, or break something. I repeat the words in my head, over and over again, trying to make myself believe them. I can't do it. I can't *absorb* it. I try to picture Bean in hospital, being cured. I can almost imagine a consultant in a white coat, praising her for her bravery, telling her she's made a full recovery, as a roomful of doctors applaud.

Then, I picture the worst possible thing. Jack and Jon, sad and solemn, in tiny black suits, Paul and I helping them with their shoes, saying, 'Mummy wouldn't want you to be sad today. She can see you, she loves you so much,' and I roll over, push my face against my pillow and howl.

Every time I start to get my breath back, I see something else. I imagine Bean's precious, saved up for, special occasions only, size-five Bottega Veneta leather boots, sitting unworn forever in her hall. I imagine walking past Bean's favourite bars and restaurants and seeing her old, happy ghosts, thinking, 'She used to love it there'. I imagine a future in which I screenshot stupid memes, or try a new flavour of Starbucks, or walk past Cumming Street in Islington and start to message Bean about it before remembering . . .

Every single scrap of anything that's good in my life is stitched together by Bean. Embroidered with Bean.

When both sides of both pillows are soaked through, I sit up. Crying has made me feel infinitesimally better. No one has mentioned *anything* about dying yet. As Bean said, medical science is constantly evolving. Surely brand-new breakthroughs are being made every day?

Feeling optimistic, I google 'breast cancer survival rates', and read, 'Around ninety-five of every one hundred women survive their cancer for one year or more after diagnosis. Around eighty-five out of every one hundred women will survive their cancer for five years or more.'

Oh. Those numbers aren't quite what I was hoping for.

I can't find any website that says, 'Within the next three months, a total cure will become available that means one hundred out of one hundred women are totally fine.'

Sighing, I pat my puffy face and remember that Bean is

also really angry with me. But *maybe* that's a good sign? If she didn't think she was going to be OK, surely she would insist that I rush to her bedside to be with her for these precious final moments? She's pissed off with me, because of something Alison has done, which is the most normal thing in the world.

Normal is good. Normal is safe. Normal is what Bean said she wanted. And she might be cross with me, but I think she'd be even more cross if she found out that I spent the day in bed, weeping and googling, instead of going to work.

Standing in the shower, I manage about twenty seconds of 'up and at 'em!' positive thinking, before I shudder. There's Another Bad Thing coming today. What is it? Not *as* bad, a minor irritation but laced with major dread. It's nipping at my heels, pinching the knuckles of my toes.

In fairness, my bathroom does not generally inspire positivity and confidence. The water never really gets warm, and the curtain never really gets dry. I always try to cower in the corner, but my body is too big. The clammy plastic gets stuck to my legs, and my head looms over the top of the rail. In my more whimsical moments, I feel like Alice in Wonderland, stuck in the White Rabbit's house. Today I just feel awkward. As I unpeel the curtain from my body for the third time, I remember the other bad thing. Rupert. I'm supposed to be having coffee with Rupert.

It's not that it ended especially badly. Or that I still want him. Obviously no smart woman could possibly have any unresolved sexual tension with a man named Rupert. I just didn't particularly enjoy spending time with him when he was my boyfriend. And when you haven't heard from some-one for years, a text saying, Would love to catch up, I've got something important to tell you – well, *why?* I am 99 per cent sure he's getting married and is on some crazed 'laydees, look what you could have won!' tour. And 1 per cent sure that he has waited until now to tell me that one of us has given the other an incurable STI.

Still damp, I look at the sad pile of black and grey things in my 'wardrobe area' and spend half a second wondering whether Rupert is worth dressing up for. If anything does happen to Bean, it will be all my fault. I've tempted fate – every single outfit I own is in a sad, funereal palette. And she's always trying to get me to wear bold, bright colours, even though she's a navy addict herself. If Bean is OK, I will wear neon pink leopard print unitards every day, until the end of forever.

If only I owned a T-shirt that says, I'm sorry for your loss. I could wear that to meet Rupert.

I don't care about looking good for him; I just don't want him to pity me. The trouble is that I have even less going on in my life than I did when we were together. No new boyfriend. Terrible flat. The same job in the copy shop, with absolutely no prospects – well, the prospect of the admin-istrators remembering they still have a barely functioning branch of FinePrint in west London and shutting us down. Miriam tells me to relax and 'trust the universe', but then she occasionally forgets to pay me.

I decide to compromise with bad clothes and good under-wear. My favourite bra – a gift from Alison, who took me to Rigby and Peller last birthday while muttering passive aggressive things about my terrible posture – is a pointy, lacy instrument of torture. However, it makes me feel slightly more confident under my baggy beige jumper. I've layered up against the chilly air. If I'm very warmly dressed, I might be able to trick or spite spring into coming early. My torso is shapeless, broad and round, yet my nipples are visible through thick wool and thin cotton. I look like a bowl of porridge, with a couple of raisins lurking under the oats.

It's ten to ten. I *hate* being late, even though Miriam doesn't give a shit. She often turns up half an hour after I do. As I scan the room, I pat my pockets. How can I have lost my phone already? Oh, it's in my hand. I lock the door and hurtle down the stairs.

I've leaped down half a flight when I hear a familiar, husky voice. 'Frankie? Where's the fire?'

'Ah, hello, Mrs Antrobus! How are you?'

'For fuck's sake, child, it's Estelle. Never mind about me, how are you? I've not seen you for a week! Although that's on me, I guess. I vowed I was going to sit at home and stay out of trouble, but my willpower was no match for Gstaad.'

Estelle Antrobus is standing grandly outside her door at the top of the stairs. There are several steps between our feet, but our heads are level. With the light behind her, shining through her pale gold hair, she looks like God's favourite angel. The leopard-skin coat and the jewelled buckles on her fuchsia mules do not bely the impression.

'Oh, you know! Keeping busy! Mrs— Es— I'm so sorry, but I really do need to get going. Are you OK, for everything? I'm doing a shop tomorrow, and you know I'm always happy to pick up some extra bits.'

She tosses her hair and rolls her eyes. 'Frankie, honey, I don't need anything. I can go to a store. But I worry about

45

you. Always working, always rushing ... but how are you *living?*' She pauses meaningfully and waves a tiny, pink-tipped hand in my direction. She does not approve of my 'look'. 'I mean, what is it with you today? You're going on a polar expedition, but you're stopping at a wake on the way? Listen, come by soon, girls' night. I've got a bottle of pink champagne with your name on it. I want to fix you up! I want to see you in my Halston!'

I force a smile. Mrs Antrobus has tried to 'fix me up' before. She is wilfully blind to the fact that I'm twice her height and three times as wide as she is. I covet her collection of couture – but it really should be in a museum. There's no noise more frightening than the sound of chiffon ripping. Vintage chiffon. From Dior. That your septuagenarian neighbour got married in. She shrugged it off, saying, 'It was like, my third wedding. No big banana.' I nearly crapped myself, and not figuratively. My bowels still twist when I think about it.

'Let's hang out soon,' I say.

'Sure, sure. Just give me a knock. I'm busy this weekend, though. I have a date!' Her smile spreads across her face, slow and sure. The look of a woman who knows she's getting laid.

'Someone nice?' I ask, feeling terribly, awkwardly British.

'Nice!' she snorts. 'He's rich, that's the main thing. We're going to the country. This is the point where I usually get bored. I'll keep you posted.'

'Do! I want the gossip!' I smile, I wave, and then, inexplicably, I give Mrs Antrobus a Paul McCartney-style double thumbs up. I can hear her sighing as I thunder down the stairs.

It has come to this. My neighbour, who has nearly fifty years on me, is having a thrilling fling with a rich man. I know 'the country' could mean Marlowe or Monaco – and I'm going to be sitting in Caffè Nero with bloody Rupert.

The shop is in darkness when I arrive. It's a weird space. No matter what time of year it is, it always feels like a shock to leave and learn that it's still light outside. The shop consists of a long, narrow corridor with a tiny cash desk at the front. Most of the window is blocked by a coin-operated photocopier. It comes up to my waist, and I reckon I could climb up and lie across it if I wanted to. It's so cold today that I'm tempted to turn it on and straddle it for warmth.

Our tiny kitchen is freezing. I try turning on the radiator, which emits a series of alarming clanking sounds but no heat. So I make do with the kettle, filling it up and trailing my fingers in the steam. I make a sludgy cup of instant coffee – two sugars, but I use a soup spoon (while wondering, as I do, every morning, about how the soup spoon got here). I've clasped my hands around the mug when I hear rustling and scratching.

'Flossie? You in?'

'No, it's a burglar!' I stick my head around the corner of the doorframe and see a reassuring, soft shape, a perfectly balanced ratio of glitter and henna. 'Do you want a coffee, Miriam, or are you on the special sauce?'

'Eh, Nescafé will do me for now. I had some apple cider vinegar before I came out. Got it from my herbalist; it's supposed to do wonders for the gut, but it tastes like anus.' Miriam's head briefly disappears as she sits down while peeling off a black, woollen poncho. She emerges, in red stripes and yellow tassels, exposing a second layer of poncho.

'Did you get up to much last night? Any Valentines?' she asks, plucking a wisp of wool from the corner of her mouth.

I think for a minute. Miriam would be sympathy itself, if I told her about Bean. But she would also be full of unsolicited advice about homeopathy. And if I don't mention it, maybe it will go away on its own. Work will be an exclusion zone. 'Not really. No cards. No news. But I have my hot date with Rupert later.'

She frowns. 'Which one was Rupert again? Did he have the very chiselled jaw? Or was he the one whose mum had the famous dog?'

'No, that was Ryan, whose mum was the petfluencer.' I tried really, *really* hard to like Ryan. On the first date, I had major misgivings. On the second date, he dumped me for being too tall. 'No, Rupert ... had no distinguishing features, really. We went out for ages and I honestly don't remember why. But he wants to meet.'

'He wants to get back with you! Of course he does!' Miriam is smiling indulgently. She has often told me she'd be proud to have me as her *shiksa* daughter-in-law, that she'd stand up to any rabbi on my behalf. It means a lot. The fact that she has no children and never goes to Temple is immaterial.

'No, no, I don't think it can be that. He's not given to big, mad, passionate gestures. And even if he did – *no!* Urgh! Not now. Not for me.'

Miriam narrows her eyes, as though she knows a secret. Sometimes she's worse than bloody Alison. Alison *loved* Rupert. Not necessarily as a potential son-in-law, either.

There were a couple of occasions where I was worried that the flirting was about to get out of hand. I wince, remembering it. Then I remember that I really do need to speak to her. But I should probably try to fix things with Bean first.

'Is it OK if I call my sister? Mum's being a bit dramatic about something.'

'Go for it, good luck! You might as well use your desk phone, although' – she is definitely trying not to laugh – 'don't tie up the line for too long. Our many customers need to be able to reach us. Ha!' Miriam believes this joke becomes funnier every time she tells it.

I take a deep breath and dial. 'Bean? Hey! It's me. Calling from work. And I want to say it again. I'm so sorry. I know I fucked up badly, and I want to fix it. I'll do anything to fix it.'

'Oh, it's you,' she says. She sounds grumpy, but not actively hostile. And most importantly, normal. 'I've talked to Alison, I've played everything down, I think I've contained it. The main thing is that she's not hysterical, she doesn't think I'm dying.'

The 'd' word seems to slice straight into my gut. 'You're *not* dying, though, really, right?' I ask. I beg.

She sighs. 'Frankie, we are all dying, all the time. That's the direction we're heading in. *You're* dying, right now.' A note of levity creeps into her voice. 'You could get hit by a bus at lunchtime.'

I take the bait. 'Actually, I got hit by a bus on the way to work. I'm ringing to tell you I'm a ghost.' I pause, for dramatic impact. 'I just called to say "woo".'

'Well, "woo" to you toooo,' she replies. 'Actually, I'm glad you phoned. I've had a thought. And you're not going

49

to love it, but it might solve some of our problems . . . ' There is a faint wheedle her voice, and I feel a glimmer of hope. This may mean I have something she wants, and there's *nothing* I wouldn't give her. 'Go on.'

'So,' says Bean. I recognise her Project Manager voice. 'Our mother is desperate to do *something*. Some fundraising, "awareness raising", whatever that means. She loves to shake a collection tin, and she wants to feel like the hero of the hour. We need to give her a job. Get her off my back for a bit.'

'Right,' I sigh. 'And "we" means "me", doesn't it?' Bean has a point, but I'm not wild about where this is going. 'Please don't say tandem sky dive.' Although if the universe can *guarantee* Bean's swift and total recovery in exchange for my offering, I'll do it without the parachute.

'Frankie, don't worry,' she says, and she sounds like she's smiling. 'I was only thinking of a bring-and-buy. A charity bake sale, or something. Dead easy. Brownies and trestle tables. Completely in her wheelhouse. And you just need to ask stupid questions about rotas, burn some buns, keep her off my back. It's simple.'

Simple, but genius. Bean has been promoted four times in the last three years, and I can understand why. Alison might not understand her, but Bean has a doctorate in Alison manipulation.

Still, I realise Bean needs to feel as though I'm making a proper sacrifice. I know my role, I know my lines, and I know exactly what my sister expects to hear. 'Bean!' I wail. 'Alison? At a bake sale? Running around telling everyone how many calories are in their cupcakes?'

She cackles. 'I know! I'm *evil*, aren't I?' Hearing Bean's

laugh is medicinal. I begin to feel a little better. 'But you made the mess. You clean it up. Parenting 101.'

'Is this revenge?' I say, teasing.

'Yes! Distract Mommie Dearest, and we're Even Stevens. If you want some bonus points, you could supervise Jack and Jon with some cake decoration. Get everyone off my back for a bit, and we're golden.' Bean is happy, I can hear it. I smile too.

'Even Stevens,' I repeat. 'Operation Bake Sale is on. I deserve it,' I say, in sorrowful tones.

'Thanks, Frankie,' she says. 'You know – we have to believe I'm going to be OK. This isn't going to kill me. But ... ' she pauses, and my heart starts pounding. She speaks again, sounding grave. 'I strongly suspect this may kill you!' She snorts.

'You bitch!' I squeal, because you can call your sister that if she's robust, and healthy, and *not* dying. 'Can I ask – if she hadn't seen it, if I hadn't fucked up, would you have thought the photo was funny?'

'Hilarious. You're a regular LOL-a-saurus Rex. Sorry, Jack has just learned about sarcasm. No, really, it made me laugh a lot. Now go! Practise your Victoria sponge!'

Miriam is looking at me with a raised eyebrow. 'I wasn't eavesdropping,' she starts.

'You were *absolutely* eavesdropping,' I counter.

'Is Bean OK? Tell me if it's none of my business.' Miriam looks pale.

'You make everything your business. And I love you for it. She's fine,' I say, hurriedly.

Miriam says nothing. She waits for me to speak again.

'She's not fine. She's just been diagnosed with breast

cancer.' As I say the words, I feel numb. I look at my right hand and concentrate on the creases of flesh between my fingers and my palm.

Diagnosed with. Those words are doing a lot of heavy lifting. Heavy lying. I cannot quite bring myself to say 'she has'.

I think about the last week. All the time I've been living my nothing life – shop, bedsit, shop, internet, preoccupied by pointless things – while my Bean was waiting, worrying, making appointments, *having a biopsy.* What has been going through my sister's mind, in surgery corridors, on the phone, while the post arrives? Why didn't she tell me the moment she started worrying? I hate myself for not knowing. I hate myself for thinking about me, again, when I should be thinking about her.

I look at a dark, sticky patch on the floor, and wonder whether it's ink or coffee, and if Miriam made it or if it was the work of another woman who worked in this shop while she waited for her life to start. And I want to see a butterfly, or a balloon, or some Rorschach shape that means I'm creative and unique and filled with untapped, sparkling potential, but all I can see is a splodge, a nothing, an amorphous nothing, and I start to cry again.

'Sorry, sorry, sorry. It's early. It might not even ...' Miriam comes to me and pulls me against her. Her arms are warm, and she rocks me, and I breathe her in. She always smells incredible. She doesn't wear traditional perfume; she buys orange blossom essence from the Waitrose baking aisle and dabs it behind her ears.

I shake my head and murmur apologies into her right tit, and she shushes me and reaches up to stroke my hair.

She elbows me in the nose, but she means well. Now she's saying, 'Sorry, sorry, sorry,' and I'm sobbing with laughter.

'You know, and I know, what I could say. There are words of comfort I could use, and I'd mean them. But it's very sad, and it's scary. I think what you're feeling now is an early stage of grief. You're in shock, you're in denial.'

Sniffing, I nod. 'That's exactly it. It doesn't make any sense. I don't understand how everything is still normal. My walk to work was the same as usual. The pigeons were not respecting my privacy at this difficult time. It's as though there's a way I *should* feel, but I can't tap into it. I want to be strong and resilient for her. But I'm ninety-five per cent denial, five per cent pure dread.'

She looks thoughtful. 'You grew up with so much grief and loss, but that doesn't mean you have a manual or a mode for this. The truth is that it's just another drop of pain in the cup. Rationally, you realise it's not probably going to be like it was with your dad, but you don't know that emotionally.'

Bean teases me about my tendency to swallow Miriam's 'hippy bullshit', but in some ways she's the smartest person I know.

'Thank you. And thank you for not mentioning ground-up turmeric root or suggesting she tries transcendental meditation,' I say, sincerely.

Miriam looks thoughtful. 'Oh, we should all do that. Still, I think this is a sign of sorts. When we are reminded of death, we must all live harder! When I lost my friend Lily, I moved to Amsterdam. I ended up working in a peep show for six months. It was good fun, actually. Loved the locals, hated the tourists. And I got quite good at this clever trick with bunting ...' Miriam looks into the distance and smiles. 'Anyway, we're a long time dead. Now, let's pretend to do some work. I'm going to order some paper. You do some googling and see if you can find someone to fix the photocopier. Don't commit to anything, just ... research it.'

The morning does not go quickly. I google 'breast cancer early signs easy curable' and shut down every page before it loads. I sing along to the radio, which, like the rest of the office, is stuck in 1986. At lunchtime, I go for a walk and try listening to a podcast about anxiety. It makes me feel anxious, so I give up and count my blessings. *I'm grateful that it isn't raining. I'm grateful that Miriam is kind. I'm grateful that my little fingernail is starting to grow back after I caught it in the doorway.*

Back in the office, at quarter to three, I remember Rupert. Or rather, I remember that I might have forgotten him on purpose.

I start mentally composing the message that might get me out of it. *'Really sorry, my neighbour urgently needs ...'* No. It's karmically off to bring poor Mrs Antrobus into this. *'I've got an important work meeting ...'* That is so obviously a complete lie. *'Family emergency ...'* That's far too close to home right now.

I'm five minutes into typing, *'Think I might have food poisoning, I've got explosive ...'* when Miriam makes a gasping noise. 'Your young man! Three o'clock, wasn't it? Go, go, go!'

I shake my head. 'Sorry, I meant to wait and take a late lunch for it. But I've gone out already.'

'So? And stop saying "sorry", Frankie. We've talked about this.' She raises a warning finger.

'Sorr— yes. I was going to make an excuse.'

Miriam rolls her eyes. 'Face him! Find out what he wants. I need the gossip. And you need something to take your mind off . . . things. A distraction. Excitement. A change of scene,' she finishes, firmly.

'Hardly a change of scene, I'm only going a few doors down the road,' I say, sulkily.

Miriam ignores me. 'Normally I'd tell you to go straight home, but you're to come here and report back. Have you got your scarf? Do you want a little bit of brandy first?'

I pull my hat over my ears. 'No, I'm fine. It's only Rupert.'

Chapter Five

The usual

I'm six doors down from the office, in a dead zone of smooth jazz. It's not yet school-kicking-out time, so there's a palpable absence of voices, of excitement, of conversations about fingering. Just a lingering smell: cheesy, yeasty and stale. Trails of paper packets, straw sheaths, scattered sugar. Time has been killed here, thoroughly. It's dead. And at the back of the shop, facing the door, in a brown stripy scarf and a navy peacoat, my ex-boyfriend sips a Giant Foamed Something and sighs with satisfaction. He exhales so loudly that it drowns out the tinned saxophone on the stereo.

I find it hard to describe Rupert, even when I am looking at him. His hair isn't brown, especially not compared with his scarf, which is a definite chocolate colour. It's just browner than any other shade that hair comes in. I think of Rupert as being 'freckled', but he doesn't actually have any freckles. Or he's 'like a mouse', but I'm *fond* of mice – they are sweet and snuffly and big eyed. Rupert simply looks as though something is always irritating his imaginary whiskers.

Feeling guilty, I walk straight past the coffee counter. If I don't have a drink to finish, I can get this over quickly. I can always buy Miriam something on the way out – souvenir mints, or a dusty muffin. A passive aggressive present, so she's forced to acknowledge her part in ruining my afternoon. Rupert stands up, flinging his arms out in welcome. A montage, a highlight reel – or rather, a lowlight reel – flickers to life in my mind's eye. I remember Rupert flirting with waitresses, being rude to shop assistants, the drinking songs, the drinking games. The aggressive sense of entitlement he brought to every single room he walked into.

Do I really have to hug him?

'Frankie, Frankie!' My left cheek is kissed, then my right. I feel cold, clammy, self-conscious. 'Long time, no see! So good of you to meet with me!'

'It's nice to see you,' I lie, trying to straighten my spectacles, which he has almost knocked off my face. My vision wobbles; I grab the table and watch as a wave of latte crashes over the rim of his mug. 'Sit ye down!' he booms, seconds after I've started pulling a chair out. 'So, I've got some seriously big news. I'm getting married.'

Ha! *I knew it!* Most predictable man in the world.

'Congratulations! That's incredible!' I cry. And I mean, in *every* sense. Because this means some woman, somewhere, has looked at the man in front of me and thought, 'Yes please, I'm going all in with this one!' I'm hardly the best feminist in the world, but is there really a woman alive who is desperate enough adhere to patriarchal, heteronormative standards that she'd marry *Rupert*?

'Anna's the lucky laydee.' He actually says 'laydee'. I strongly suspect that's how he spells it. 'Did you ever meet her? One of the old gang – she was going out with Andrew, she has a PhD in modern theory.'

'Modern theory of what?' I ask, sweetly, laying him a trap. Idiot. I cannot *wait* to tell Bean all about this.

'Of ... modernity,' says Rupert, who barely scraped his third in Land Management, even though as far as I can tell, his only course requirement was 'learn how to wear a gilet without dying of self-conscious shame'.

He pulls out his phone. 'Anyway, let me show you a picture.' There's some corporate-looking lettering on the phone case, and I squint over my spectacles, trying to read the acronym. It can't be. In capitals, above the words 'Adams-Robert Investment Strategies,' it says ARIS. My ex-boyfriend, the desperate-to-impress, blowhard corporate climber, is going around with a phone emblazoned with the cockney rhyming slang for 'arse'.

Biting the side of my cheek, trying not to laugh, I focus on the photo Rupert is showing me. Anna is a brunette, with delicate features, smiling through the screen in a sensible black jumper. Our only superficial similarity is the specs. And unlike me, she looks as though she's modelling hers: clunky black frames that emphasise her femininity and fragility. This woman has never had an accident with a packet of mayonnaise and spent the rest of the day squinting through an oily patch on her lenses.

'Lovely!' I beam. 'Um, she's beautiful!' Surely this is the greatest possible compliment anyone can come up with, but Rupert is waiting for something else. 'Um, well done,' I add. That's the right answer.

'Isn't she something? So, the other big news is this – it's baby time!' Rupert punctuates the plosive by banging his fists on the table and splaying his fingers, as though he's announcing the dawn of a brand-new era. Confused, I look around the café, half expecting to see that it has been taken over by a flash mob of line-dancing babies. 'You're having a baby? Anna's pregnant? Well, that's double congratulations!' Just what the world does not need. More Rupert.

He looks slightly abashed. I did not know he had it in him. 'Yah, well, no, early days, early days. She's not preggo yet, but *we're trying*. We thought that it can take a little while, so if we get going now, by the time we've had the wedding ... Her idea, really. I suppose it doesn't matter if *she* gets up the spout beforehand, I can still get smashed at the bash!'

When I broke up with Rupert, there was a general sense of head-tilting disappointment. Poor, poor Frankie. She lost the game. She tanked it. She didn't work hard enough, she wasn't lucky enough, when she could have had the ultimate prize: a man who can't wait to get blind drunk at his own wedding.

'Frankie.' Rupert takes my hand in his, pulling my wrist into his latte puddle. His skin feels cold and clammy too. Ew. Bloody Miriam, making me come here.

She was not wrong, though. It has taken my mind off things. Now, I'm aware that I have managed not to worry about Bean for four whole minutes. Was this supposed to make me feel better? I don't want to stop worrying. I don't want to be distracted. Life is heartbreakingly short, and I have already wasted quite enough of it with Rupert.

I have spent the last twenty-four hours being reminded that I have one life to live, and every moment is precious, I'm here. Of all the places. *Holding hands* with this all-time aris. An engaged-to-be-married aris, at that! I'm desperate to snatch my hand away, but no matter how many frantic messages my brain sends, my body will not respond. *Sorry, we don't speak logic here.*

I have made no effort to project a pleasant expression onto my face, so it's entirely possible that I've been gurning my way through my horror soliloquy. But Rupert is oblivious. Rupert has always been oblivious.

'Listen, I've been thinking. I miss you. And all of this ... *grown-up stuff*, it's a bit of a shocker, yah? I'm ready, I'm looking forward to it, Anna is definitely the one. But I think about you ...' His thumb traces a line along mine. I should whip it away, but I'm frozen on the spot. My bones betray me. They have become too heavy to move.

'Right,' I say, weakly. Oh, I hope I don't know where this is going.

'I thought we could,' he raises both eyebrows, and looks expectantly at me.

I don't react.

'I mean, for old times' sake.' A wink this time. No. I don't want to respond with so much as the flicker of an eyelid. He keeps talking. 'I mean you were always so wild. Good old Frankie. And Anna, and all this stuff, and baby-making – it's a bit of a boner killer, you know?' says Rupert, as though he is in a meeting, making a reasonable point. There is not a scrap of self-awareness on his face or in his voice. I am half expecting him to pull out a graph – a jagged red diagonal line crashing – to represent the disappointing annual performance of his penis.

'Are you *serious*?' I must have misunderstood. He cannot be asking me what I think he is asking me. I laugh, awkwardly. 'Sorry, Rupert, I don't think I heard you properly. You don't want to ... I mean, you can't want to ...' I trail off, waiting for him to blush, get flustered and course correct.

'Call it a wedding present?' There is zero shame on his face.

Gasping, I pull my hand from the table, aiming it at his face. I miss, swiping at the air. Attempting to claw back a little dignity, I hiss, 'Fuck off! Rupert, how dare you? It's disrespectful to Anna *and* it's disrespectful to me.'

He chuckles, as though this was an expected part of negotiations. 'You're not seeing anyone else, are you?'

'Well, no, but I don't see how that possibly—'

He cuts me off. 'I thought not. And, ah, how's work? Are you still at the, whatchamacallit – is it a café?'

'Copy shop,' I say. 'I've been there for a while now, I got tired of temping. It's not the most stimulating job, and the money isn't great, but I really like my boss.' If I can keep talking nonsense, I might be able to distract him and make him forget about his ridiculous idea. Politely, I ask, 'And are you still at the, um ...' Oh, fuck, what was it? 'Company?' I smile, brightly.

I'm a genius. This will prompt Rupert to start blathering on about his monthly quarterlies or whatever it is, and I'll let him bang on for twenty minutes and then say, 'Oh, gosh, is that the time? I must fly!' *I must fly?* I don't understand how I can be such an awkward freak, even in my own mind.

Rupert nods sagely. 'Frankie, I know your work situation has always been a bit wobbly. I wouldn't expect you to do this purely for old times' sake. But I am looking for someone who might be interested in some kind of ... arrangement, you know?'

'An arrangement?' I say, dumbly. I think of flower arranging. When we met, I spent a lot of time arranging chairs, in conference rooms. Is he offering me a job at his company? I'd better try to remember what it does.

'Nothing ... sordid, you understand.' I *think* he's blushing, but it's hard to tell. He lowers his voice. 'Nice trips. Gifts. The ... usual.'

It's as though he's speaking in French. If I concentrate hard, I can translate it, but the words aren't landing. Out of the corner of my eye, I see a woman enter the café. She's festooned with bags. A small pink glittery rucksack on her chest. A matching one hanging from her shoulder. Tote bags, book bags, a carrier with a tiny sparkling trainer peeping out of the top. She stands in the doorway and exhales slowly, as two small blonde girls in matching pink hats run to the counter. *She could probably use a nice trip,* I think. And then Rupert's words start to sink in. I'm an idiot.

'The *usual*?' I'm screeching. That word in itself suggests that I'm probably not the first woman Rupert has sought an arrangement with. 'Look, I'm going to go.' Because if I don't get out of here soon, I'll try to hit him again. I'm not worried about hurting him. I'm worried I'll miss.

'How dare you come here – and show me a picture of your fiancée! – and suggest I might want to ... ' Panicking, I pull a fiver out of my pocket and let it fall to the table, even though you pay at the counter, and I haven't actually ordered anything. 'Shove this up your fucking aris! Don't contact me ever again.'

I yank my hat back on and pull it so hard it covers my eyes. I'm too angry and embarrassed to fix it. God, I *hope* I'm walking in the direction of the door.

'You change your mind, you know where I am,' booms Rupert at his natural volume, shouting over the engine of a Land Rover. 'Wait, let me walk you to the door.' It's so weird that he brought me here, to do this, and yet he plays the 'nice guy' to the bitter end. He takes my hand again and squeezes it, so that I can't snatch it away. 'Look, I didn't mean to offend you. I just thought . . . I found your pictures online. Your profile. I started subscribing. Hot stuff! I just assumed you might be in the market for something.'

Even though I can't see very well, I know the barista is looking at me and wondering what Rupert could possibly mean. How can this woman, in her seventeen jumpers, be hot stuff in any sense other than the literal one?

'How on Earth? Were you looking for me? How dare you! That's *private*,' I hiss. I can't deal with this. I can't cope. I'm sweating, burning up.

He laughs, the rat. 'It really isn't, Frankie, anyone can sign up . . .' He registers my distress, and his tone softens, slightly. 'Look, I stumbled across it, I recognised you. It's just one of those things, a coincidence.'

'Could you unsubscribe, please?' I mumble, looking at the floor.

'But surely . . . OK, fine. You could just block me.' He looks at me and shrugs. 'OK, sorry, I just assumed you wouldn't mind.'

'It's a secret project. It's a hobby, it's not for you, it's not for men like you, it's . . .' I howl with frustration. 'Oh, fuck this! I don't owe you an explanation. How dare you do this to Anna? How dare you present yourself to the world as this respectable fiancé person, when you're going around looking at women. Well, I forbid you! I forbid you to look!'

Ironically, I am aware that I am probably attracting quite a lot of attention to myself. My heart is pounding. Beads of sweat are gathering under my hat.

'Steady on!' says Rupert. He puts a hand on my shoulder, only to instantly remove it – possibly because I look as though I might bite it off. 'Look, it's just some food for thought. If it bothers you so much, I'll stop subscribing. But you know where I am if you want me.'

I can't look at him. I must say something dignified, cutting, perfect. Instead, I make a squeak – it's an exact imitation of Miss Piggy, in a bad mood – and stomp out of the café.

Food for thought.

I know, in my bones, that my subscribers are not all respectable, respectful single men. I'm sure some have fiancées, girlfriends, wives. There are whole lives being compromised by the people who look at my pictures. But when those lives are shadowy, vague or wholly unknown, it's easy to shrink the thought down and push it away.

How did Rupert find me, anyway? There are less than fifty people following me. Why must one of them be him? I don't know how to process this. Is it really a coincidence, or a warning? It has to be a fluke.

'You're back early! I thought you'd still be reminiscing about old times. What did your young man want, anyway?' asks Miriam, as soon as I open the shop door.

I can't quite begin to explain the last hellish half hour. 'He's getting married,' I say, wearily.

Miriam grins. 'Ain't love grand! How sweet. Good for him.'

Chapter Six

A surprise

The sun isn't up yet, and there seems to be a bee under my pillow. I think I was *dreaming* of bees, or perhaps I'm still in the dream, I'm not sure. But I'm reaching for the source of the buzzing. My muscle memory is kicking in before my eyes are fully open and I can calculate the risk of getting stung.

I hold the bee to my ear and I'm rewarded with a cry of 'Great news!'

Oh, lord. Have I been woken up by one of those automated 'You have won a competition, just call this premium rate number for a million pounds a minute to register' messages? Ah, no, hang on. It's Alison.

'Mum?' I say. 'Great news about Bean?' I rub at my eyes and manage to fully open them both. Hope has woken me up.

'About you and Bean! You've made *MailOnline*!' Alison is jubilant.

'What? Why?' My brain is working furiously. Maybe the doctors have found a miracle cure. Am I to be the world's

65

first ever boob donor? I'll do it! Although, I think, as consciousness starts to dawn, it would be *odd* for the doctors to tell a national newspaper before they told me.

Alison is saying something about responses, about positivity, about kindness, and the 'lovely surprise'.

'Mum, hold on, sorry, can you slow down a minute? I've just woken up!' I pull my laptop out from under my bed and google my name. Usually, the first result is 'Do you mean Frankie How*erd*,' with an invitation to watch a load of *Carry On* films on Amazon Prime. Not today.

Little sister's adorable list inspires
us all to #BeKind4Cancer

I gasp. I start to shiver. I recognise this, vividly. But why is it here? It shouldn't be here.

It's my seven-year-old handwriting. I remember the way those colouring pencils felt in my sweaty, pudgy hands. The red one, worn down to a stump. Trying to write in all of the colours of the rainbow and running out of rainbow. Pressing down extra hard on the yellow, because it was so difficult to see what I was writing, and breaking the lead.

Why Bean is the *best big sister*

1. She is the kindest human I know
2. She knows all of the wurds werds words to all of the songs
3. She lets me eat her jelly babies (exept green Is)
4. She thinks bullies are BAD!
5. She let me use her headphones when I was ill

6. She gets to wear a BRA
7. She can dance
8. She isn't scared of dogs en any more
9. She brought me a dinosaur magnet on the school trip
10. She can make a wish on an ey lash

Below, a wobbly drawing of two stick girls holding hands, with purple triangle skirts. Bean's hair is two straight, black lines. My hair is an orange coil. And below that, a photograph. The pair of us aged seven and twelve, in our matching tutus. Bean serene, while I beam like an idiot. I can feel the ghost of my sock falling down.

Breathing rapidly, I try to work out when I last spoke to Alison. About thirty-six hours ago. How has she done *this* in the last thirty-six hours?

'Frankie? Are you still there?'

I'd tuned Alison out, I hadn't noticed that she stopped speaking.

'Um, yes, I'm here, it's very ... goodness! How did you find this?' I blink, rapidly. This might be a night terror. This is Classic Alison – exactly the sort of thing my stressed, anxious, knackered brain would come up with, as a sort of torment. Any moment now, Rupert will burst in, bellowing 'HEY LAYDEEZ!' and then I'll sit up suddenly and wake up properly, gasping and grateful.

I refresh the page. This is real. This is happening.

Looking at my hand drawn picture makes me feel as though I'm seven years old again. Convinced that if I worked neatly enough, I could make Bean feel better. I still remember colouring carefully, while worrying and wondering what had made my strong sister so sad. Was it a boy? Something at school? All I can remember is Bean, alone in her room, silent. Standing outside, holding my breath, listening, wishing I could hear her. I wanted her to cry, to scream at me and tell me to leave. I remember the way my heavy, scribbled lines felt slightly waxy to the touch. I remember sliding the paper slowly through the slender gap between her doorframe and the carpet. Trying not to be impatient, trying to keep the paper flat and perfect.

But I still can't remember why I needed to write the list. Or how she felt about it, at the time. I do remember seeing it pinned on her noticeboard during her first year of university and laughing at my own naivety – but secretly feeling deeply touched, too.

'Where did you get this?' I ask, again.

'Well,' says Alison, who is clearly desperate to explain her process. 'When I spoke to Bean yesterday, she was very keen for us to do a bake sale at the community centre, but I was worried that it all felt a bit low key. Our girl deserves something bigger! So I was looking through some things from when you were little, trying to remember some of the charity stuff you did, and this fell out. And I thought, how adorable!'

'Right. It is,' I say. 'But – this is something I made for Bean. It was a private thing. A family thing. And it has nothing to do with what's happening to her now. I don't understand why it's in a newspaper. Or why a newspaper would be interested in it.'

'Well,' she says, again, 'it's just *lovely*, isn't it? Sisters being sweet. So warm, so relatable! I thought they could put it on tea towels or mugs or something ...'

Who are *they*? That can't be right. 'Sorry, Mum, I don't think I heard that last bit, the signal is awful in here.'

'Anyway, I rang up the local *Gazette*, spoke to this chap. I thought it might be a nice human-interest thing for them, and he told me to leave it with him. I think he popped it online and I guess the *Mail* picked it up! Apparently that's quite common; he did say that he sometimes passes stuff on to the Press Association. The news is so awful, and this is just the sort of thing that will cheer everyone up!'

I look again at our triangular skirts. This will cure the nation's ills. Ah, I see: Text KIND to 87707 to donate five pounds to Young Survivors UK. That's something. Still, 'Be Kind 4 Cancer'. I'm not sure Bean wants kindness, so much as the very best that medical science has to offer. What does 'be kind' even mean here, as an instruction? Who decided to bother with the 'e' of 'be' but then thought everyone would be in too much of a hurry to write out 'for'? And surely no one wants to do anything *for* cancer. It's not even proper alliteration. I want to compose alternative slogans. Be Itchy 4 IBS. Be Diplomatic 4 Deep Vein Thrombosis.

'Does, ah, does Bean know?' I ask, cautiously. Maybe, just *maybe* Alison ran this by her before contacting the press. And maybe Bean said, 'Brilliant idea! Let the fund-raising commence!' There's no way. Bean would eat a newspaper, page by page, before she would voluntarily consent to appearing in one.

'It's a surprise!' says Alison. 'Bean said that as long as I didn't use that *rude* photo you sent, I could do anything I liked. It made me so happy to find it, it brought back a lot of lovely memories. It could have been yesterday.'

'I . . . see.' If I'm going to manage this situation, I can't scream at Alison. I have to keep her calm. Even if the effort of doing so induces a small stroke in me.

Looking again at the list, I feel an intense cellular memory. My body is revisiting an old sensation that I can't quite decode. Being a kid. Being powerless. Being caught in the middle of Alison's relentless, oppressive optimism and Bean's rebellion.

'Frankie! Don't you like it?' The pitch of Alison's voice is becoming higher and higher, and I know that this signals a role reversal. I need to mother her, right now. I speak carefully. 'I love the list; like I said, I'd forgotten about it. It really is a surprise!'

Scanning the article, I feel confused.

When Bean Andersen, 34, was diagnosed with breast cancer, her little sister Frankie Howard, 29, wanted to give her a boost.

'I'm sharing this list because I believe kindness is more important than ever,' says Frankie. 'Bean means the world to me, and I'm hoping this will res-onate with anyone who loves someone and doesn't want to lose them.

'Frankie hopes that people will share her list with the people they love – and eventually she's plan-ning to raise money for anyone who is affected by cancer by selling merchandise decorated with her moving words. For now, here's how to donate to the campaign. Text this number . . .

But *I* didn't share this list! I'm not a spokesperson. *What* campaign?

'Mum,' I say. I take a deep breath. 'Mum,' again. The rage catches in my throat. The irony could choke me: I'm too scared of my anger about the words she has put in my mouth to find my own words to express it.

I can't do it. I don't know where to begin. This is the all-time fuck up. It doesn't matter *how* much money this might raise, this is Bean's biggest nightmare. She didn't even want Alison to know. Now Alison has told the world, and it's all my fault. Bean wants normal. Bean doesn't want anyone to treat her differently. Becky might be reading this on her phone right now, her little pink face puckering into a frown, as she works out what she'll say, how she'll clutch Bean's arm. The murmurs from the other mums. *So* sad. *Such* a shame. Everyone talking about my beautiful, brilliant sister as though she's a ghost.

There's no point screaming at Alison now that she's done it. She'll get upset, she'll get defensive, she'll accuse me of 'throwing it all in her face'. She honestly believes that the greatest gift a mother could give her child is a feature in the *Daily Mail*. Last year she tried to persuade me to persuade Bean to enter Mrs UK – a beauty pageant for married women. ('I know she *says* it's not her thing, but that bone structure is wasted in – what exactly is it that she does again? Insurance? She could get presenting work! Something nice at teatime.')

Alison and Bean could not look more like mother and daughter. But when I compare their personalities, I'm not convinced they're part of the same species.

'Mum,' I try one last time, attempting to find the words to explain the situation. I can't do it. 'I have to go because the ... washing machine man – person – has come.'

'Really? Before 8 a.m., goodness!' trills Alison. Then, conspiratorially, 'I know you're a feminist, darling, and that's all well and good, but it usually *is* a man ...'

'Got to go!' I hang up and throw my phone across my bed. As though the problem can't be *so* bad if there are enough pillows between me and it.

Thank Christ I don't have a proper job. I send Miriam a text that simply says, FAMILY EMERGENCY XXXXX and scramble into an ancient pair of leggings and a vest of unknown provenance. In two shakes of a deodorant can, I will be heading to Clapham. I have no idea what I'll do when I get there.

Chapter Seven

Mothers

Usually, I love going to Jack's school – even though I truly hated my own school days. It's nothing like the hell I remember, just lots of neat, sweet, solemn boys and girls skipping, running, whispering and laughing. Once Jack's friend Jeremiah walked towards my knees, looked up to the sky, and introduced himself by saying, quite formally, 'Hello. I am the frog monitor.' Jeremiah ought to run a course for socially anxious adults.

Today, however, everything feels off. There is a feeling of barely controlled chaos. The air seems thick and muggy, despite the wintry chill. I don't even know if Bean will *be* here, and I haven't told her I'm coming. As I approach the gates, I hear her voice.

'No, no, honestly, that's really kind, but I'm fine.' I know without looking that the bottom half of her face will be forced into a grin, but her eyes will not be taking part.

I stride towards the group. The attack of the six-foot woman, bearing down on Clapham's yummiest mummies. (I can't stop myself from thinking that none of the clustered women look robust enough to birth a child, and yet I'm so enormous you'd be forgiven for assuming that I eat them.)

'Bean!' I cry. 'I just thought . . . ' I panic. 'I couldn't remember if I said I'd pick up Jack later,' I finish, pathetically.

Bean does not respond with a fake smile, or a real one. I reach out to her, but someone, or something is tugging at my elbow.

'Oh my God, are you Frankie?' shrieks an elf in a pale grey skirt suit. Oh, no. I remember this woman. George's mum. She hates me. When I went to the nativity play she all but asked me to give her a blood sample, to prove I was a real auntie and not a child snatcher. George is a little shit, too.

I nod, weakly.

'*Such* a lovely thing to do! What a good, *kind* person you are! And of course, let us know if there's *anything* we can do to help. We'd *love* to organise a fundraiser with the PTA. Nice to get some media coverage for the school too.' She grabs my hand. 'Give me your number!'

Um, no.

'Lovely to see you, I'm in such a rush,' I gabble. 'I just need to grab Bean for a quick word, but I've got your email!' I lie.

With all my might, I fling out my arm, shaking George's mum away. I reach for Bean. She looks at me with pure hatred, but she holds on to me and lets me pull her out of the crowd.

We walk around the corner, and I don't know where to begin. 'Are you OK?' I ask, softly.

'Fuck! Don't you start,' she snarls, looking away from

74

me and wrapping her arms around her chest. 'I can't have this. Jesus, Frankie. What if I do die? What if I die, and my last months on Earth are spent listening to people saying "there, there" and talking to me as if I'm already dead? Now everyone knows! And it's going to be awful! What the fuck were you thinking?'

It's the loudest 'fuck' I have ever heard. Especially impressive given we're about ten yards from a school.

'I'm so, so sorry. I wasn't thinking. I mean, this wasn't my idea. This was all Alison.' As I say it, I know how weak it sounds.

'You. Were. Supposed. To. Make. Her. Do. A. BAKE SALE.' Bean looks up at me, and down at the ground, and up at me again. Then I'm aware of a twinkle of diamond, a flash of pale lilac polish, and a fist landing against my chest.

An ancient indignation unfurls in my gut, rushing to my heels, tingling in my arms, burning the back of my neck.

'Bean!' I cry, in a register several octaves above the voice I recognise. 'You can't beat me up! I'm your *little sister*!' I put my hands on my hips, my mouth agape. 'I'm—'

'Telling? You're going to *tell* on me?' She stares up at me, eyes shining. She's about to either laugh or hit me again.

'No!' Yes. That was exactly what I was going to say.

Sighing, I slide against the wall, into a crouch. She waits a moment and does the same.

'This is the last thing I wanted, believe me,' I tell her. 'Maybe second last, after Alison pitched "sexy breast selfies for awareness". I honestly thought we'd corralled her. She called me this morning and she was so happy. So pleased. She thinks she's helping. But I'm struggling to get my head around how this happened. I still don't understand how she got hold of the list.'

Bean sighs. 'You know, I really do love the list. I've been hanging onto it for years – well, I thought I had. I've been looking for it. I was hoping it was in a box in the loft.'

'I was going to get you some green Jelly Babies, but I could only see Haribo in the shop. And it looks like only one of us gets to wear a BRA today!' I say, gesturing to my wobbling chest.

Bean presses her forearm against her eyes. 'Sorry. Sorry. This is bad. The situation is bad. But also, I am thirty-four years old, and my mother doesn't have any idea of who I am. I know she didn't deliberately set out to hurt me, or stress me out, but I almost wish she had. How is she so clueless? We only have one parent, and she's a disaster. I think she'd have done a better job with a pair of Yorkshire terriers.'

'For what it's worth, I often wish I was a Yorkshire terrier,' I say.

She smiles and leans against me. 'I'm really late for work,' she says. 'Still, I have the best of all excuses.'

'Me too. Late, I mean. I have no excuses.' I tent my fingers, push my palms away from my body and count to five. I count again and take a deep breath. 'Bean?' I say, tentatively. 'I know this is probably the worst time to ask, but what's going on, exactly? What happens next? And how are you feeling?'

'It changes every day, Frankie. Earlier this morning, I was feeling sort of optimistic, if you can believe that. But then, I have periods of feeling unbelievably sorry for myself. My consultant is calling later, to discuss the treatment plan. She said, "I'm hopeful that we can save most of the breast." Which is great, right? But I *hate* that "most of". I *hate* myself for being so scared, when so many women go through so much worse. And I hate Paul for saying, "Lucky I'm a leg man!"'

'Bastard!' I say, with feeling. 'Surely that's worse than the national news coverage?'

She gives me a faint smile. 'I think he was trying to make me laugh. But I'm bone tired, and I'm honestly not sure whether it's really worse than normal, or whether it's because I am always quite tired. I'm worried about work and money and what the health insurance will cover, and yet I just spent almost three hundred quid on various vitamins and supplements. The boys are great. It turns out that an intense discussion about robots is a fairly effective way of taking my mind off things. But it looks like I'm going to get a surgery date for next week. Tuesday afternoon, unless anything comes up sooner.' She sounds far too casual about this. She could be talking about a manicure. Tuesday is scarily soon – and yet, somehow, not soon enough.

'Why didn't you tell me?' I windmill my arms towards the sky and let them fall, as though I'm conducting a particularly dramatic piece of music. As if I could control an orchestra. I can barely control my mother. I'm picturing Bean, pale and naked under a papery gown, surrounded by masked men wielding shiny tools. It's a horrible image.

'Well, I am telling you, Frankie. This is me telling you. And I know you're not *great* at following my instructions, but – please don't freak out. Tell me it's going to be fine. Because it is. It's just a little lumpectomy!'

I bark a laugh. 'A lumpectomy! Ha! That's adorable. A nice, safe, friendly de-lumping.'

Bean smirks. 'I know, right?! I can't believe that's what it's called. It's as though someone said, "That will do for now, we'll think of a proper name later," and never got round to it. Anyway, Granny Andersen is on standby; she's going to have the boys to stay.'

'Can I come? I'd really like to come,' I say, quickly.

'To Granny Andersen's?' Bean nods. 'Sure, she'd be delighted to have you. She'll make you line dance, though. She's bought the boys these miniature Stetsons, and Paul said something about boots—'

I shake my head vigorously. 'You know I am even more terrified of your mother-in-law than you are. I meant Tuesday. Can I come on Tuesday?'

Bean frowns. 'I don't know if that's a good idea. I might be there for a while, Frankie. And I'm not sure if patients are allowed to bring an entourage. Paul will be there. I'll be fine,' she says, firmly.

'Please,' I say, my voice cracking slightly. 'I really want to see you, before you go in. It's important to me. Miriam won't mind. In fact, I think she'd be surprised if I wasn't there.'

I clamber to my feet, and Bean motions for me to pull her up. 'OK. Fine. It would be lovely to have you there. But between now and then, *please* sort Alison out. No more news. No more fuss. Promise me that you won't tell her about Tuesday. We have no idea what's going to happen, or how long this is going to go on for. There may come a point where I really can't not tell her stuff, but ...'

'Promise,' I say. 'We can't trust her not to turn up with,

78

I don't know, a circus, or a merch stand, or a camera crew. I'll keep mum, as it were. And I'll get her to rein this in.'

The trouble with Alison is that she's like a naval destroyer. Once she's set in motion, it's hard to turn her around.

Chapter Eight

Good person

By the time Bean and I have hugged it out, and I've boarded the bus, I feel a little better. She offers me a lift – the ultimate act of love, driving into Central London, when her office is in the opposite direction – and I tell her I'll be fine on the 39. She looks relieved.

Staring out of the window, gazing at the grey, I go back to feeling worse. We're not fighting, but she still has ... might ... If I start crying on the bus, I won't stop. I could count blue cars, or silently recite the alphabet backwards. Tuesday. Treatment. Treatment makes people better. She is going to get better. And if – *when* – she gets better, I will be kind and good and patient and stop staring furiously at the other passengers as I try to work out who isn't picking up their phone. Some of the passengers are giving me equally dirty looks. The bus is very vibrate-y, as we wait at this red light ... ah, shit. My phone. Withheld number.

'Hello?' Somehow I drag a third beat out of the word, trying to place some syllabic sandbags between me and the bearer of bad news at the other end.

'Is that Frankie Howard?' She sounds friendly enough, but that's how they get you.

'May I ask who is calling?' I say, crisply, impersonating my own imaginary secretary.

'My name is Emma, I'm calling from *South London Today*—'

The name sounds vaguely familiar. Do they do electricity or water? 'Listen, I'm not sure where you got this number but my landlord looks after the bills. I don't have his number to hand ...' In fact, I'm not entirely sure who he is, where he is, or whether he's still alive. To be a successful city subletter, you need the original landlord to forget that they own your flat.

Then, I have a dark thought. 'Is it – you're not going to cut off the electricity, are you?'

'No, Frankie, *South London Today*,' says the voice, patiently.

'Right!' Nope, doesn't help.

'Are you free later this afternoon? We love your campaign, and the adorable list. We think what you're doing for your sister is so sweet. We were wondering whether you and Bean could come on this evening's programme. It would be brilliant to do it live, but if the timings don't work, we could prerecord ...'

'Yes, I think I'm free,' I say, without thinking. 'And Bean ... actually, no. Sorry, that won't work.' She's from the telly! Bean can't go on TV. I can't go on TV and talk about Bean. She'd *hate* that.

'Tomorrow, then? Or next week?' asks Emma, brightly.

'Not next week, Bean is going to—' Just in time, some instinct stops me from saying the word 'hospital'. 'I'm really sorry but this is a difficult time for the family. My sister wants some privacy.'

'But your mum gave me your number,' says Emma, sounding puzzled. 'She thinks it's a great idea.'

Of course. Of bloody course.

'I think there's been a mix-up. Emma, I'm really sorry for wasting your time. Thanks for calling.' I hang up. I need to call Alison. I don't want to call Alison.

Staring at her number on my phone screen, I think that if I speak to her now I might scream at her. I need to come up with a cease-and-desist strategy, but one that she can own. If she's going to stop, she needs to believe that it was her idea to stop. Could I come up with a new slogan? Be Silent 4 Cancer? Leave Your Poor Daughter Alone, 4 Cancer?

'Mum,' I rehearse in my head. 'Mum, listen, I think we need to talk.'

I'm about to hit the green button when my phone starts ringing again. I'm too slow to stop my thumb's trajectory. Another withheld number.

'Hi, is that Frankie? My name is Ria, I'm calling from the nightly news desk of *Aspect West*—'

'Sorry,' I say weakly. 'Wrong number.'

By the time I get into work, I feel as though I've been awake for about a year. I stagger through the door and Miriam arches an eyebrow.

'Sorry I'm late,' I say. After all, a girl's got to have a catchphrase.

'You're not, really,' she replies. 'You messaged. And it doesn't matter anyway. But Flossie! *Be Kind 4 Cancer*?'

Staggering towards my chair, I sigh. 'None of this was my idea. Or Bean's.'

'Alison,' says Miriam, knowingly.

'Got it in one.' I turn on my monitor and it makes a rumbling, grunting noise of protest. 'I know how you feel,' I mutter at it. 'I'll go and make us hot drinks in a minute. Right now, I haven't the strength.'

'That photo of you both is adorable,' Miriam says, evenly. 'This is horrendous for you – well, mostly for Bean, obviously – but I think you're going to raise pots of money. Greatest good for the greatest number, and all that.'

I frown. 'How do you even *know* about it? I only found out this morning when Alison rang. This is a nonsense story. It's nothing. She called the *local* paper with it. I don't understand.'

Miriam shrugs. 'It came up on my phone, not long after I got your text. Actually, it *keeps* coming up. The *Independent* did something, it's in *Metro Online*.' She taps her keyboard. 'Oooh, you're in *Panache*! "Why Frankie Howard is inspiring us to celebrate sisterhood".'

'Is it hot in here? It's hot! I think I need to get some water,' I say, standing up and then sitting again. I take a deep breath. 'I feel a bit sick, maybe it's because I haven't eaten yet ... '

'Oh, Floss, sit. Take a minute. I'll get you some water.' Miriam gets to her feet, and I put my head between my legs. Breathe. My forehead is slick with sweat, and my head feels weird. Ah, because I haven't taken my hat off. That's better. I remove my coat, and I'm about to peel off my jumper, when I remember that I dressed in a hurry, and I'm not wearing anything underneath.

'How are you feeling?' asks Miriam, peering down at me, concerned. (She's only just taller than me when I'm sitting and she's standing up.) 'Here's some water, and here's a weird tisane thing I found in my handbag – it's mugwort and something. I think it's for cramps, but worth a try, eh?'

I gulp at the water and force a smile. 'Thank you. I'm fine, I think. I will be.'

'Do you want to go home?' She pats my shoulders. 'I think you should go back to bed.'

'Can't I stay here?' I say, desperately. 'I just want everything to be normal. I think I'll feel even less normal if I'm at home, worrying and googling. Thinking about Bean. This is awful for her. It's all my fault, really. I've let her down.' I rub at my temples and try to imagine the sort of day she's having. Whether everyone in her office will have read the news and be whispering about it. The messages she'll get. The notifications on her phone, telling her about her own body, her own news. Sighing, I slump forward, letting my forehead hit my desk. 'I'm a terrible sister.'

'It's blindingly, bleedingly obvious that you're Team Bean,' says Miriam. 'You're always on her side.'

I sigh. 'I set this whole mess in motion. All I had to do was not tell Alison. And I told Alison. Bean does not like any kind of attention. She gets embarrassed when you sing *Happy Birthday* to her. She doesn't want to be in *Panache*.'

Miriam squeezes my shoulder and returns to her desk. She taps at her computer. 'Frankie, these are some of the things people are saying about you: "Kind Frankie Howard", "Generous Frankie Howard", "Cancer campaigner Frankie Howard's fundraising gesture is a sister act – and a class act!" "A cheerleader at the forefront of the cancer battle!"'

The nausea starts to engulf me again. 'Cheerleader? Bloody hell. I'm *not* a cancer campaigner, am I? I'm a shop assistant.

I don't even assist anyone – we never have customers.' *Model, Frankie Howard,* whispers my subconscious. *Pornographer, Frankie Howard. That's not true!* I think, angrily. But I guess it's much more truthful than 'cancer campaigner'.

If any of these people knew about @girl_going_alone, they wouldn't say any of these things.

But then, no one who knows about @girl_going_alone knows about any of this. I still have a secret space. I still have an escape hatch.

I feel a treacherous twitch between my legs. Throbbing, longing.

It would be so nice to hide, online, for a while. To get a little respite from being Frankie the list-making little sister, just for half an hour or so. To get the kind of attention I'm used to, the kind I understand. The kind I can control.

But that wouldn't be responsible. This is my mess. I can't run away from it. I have to face up to reality. Reflexively, I glance at my phone. The missed calls and messages are piling up. The screen is screaming at me, and I'm aware of my lungs pushing against my ribs. It's as though my own walls are closing in.

I close my eyes. I dig my fingernails into my palms. I can ride this out.

I want to go home. I want to take pictures. I want to pose and pout and pretend this isn't happening, I want to be my shadow self, the beautiful monster. Even though I know it won't help.

It might help.

Think of a single good reason why you should go home, right now, I challenge myself. *Explain yourself. You can't, can you?*

I can't. I just know that I'll sit there, in misery, thinking about it, until I do it. And that everything else will feel just about bearable once I have done it.

'You know what, Miriam,' I say, weakly, 'maybe I should go home for a bit. Is that OK?'

She smiles. 'I think that's a really good idea. Text me later, let me know how you're feeling. I know how worried you are, but I know you and Bean are going to be fine.'

I force a smile, and nod. Maybe Bean will be OK. I'm not so sure about me. After all, you're as sick as your secrets.

Chapter Nine

Dressing up

As soon as I have closed my door behind me, my breath becomes a little steadier. There's so much peace in this moment, after I have stopped fighting with myself and resisting myself. Lately, and perhaps worryingly, I keep thinking of the famous Twelve Steps: 'We admitted we were powerless'. The urge makes me feel completely powerless, yet submitting to the urge is empowering. It doesn't make any sense.

I'm not an addict. I just want to be wanted on my own terms. I am allowed to have secrets. I must be able to deal with this grief and shock in any way that works.

I have been sent home sick. All I am doing is prescribing myself some specific, highly effective medicine.

Justified, I can lose my clothes to the floor. I step out of my leggings, shedding my coat. Now, I'm naked, apart from a pair of grubby pants covered in pugs (a gift from Bean). These won't do at all.

I go to The Drawer.

Some of the money I make from the website covers rent,

food and any shortfalls left by my paltry print-shop pay. If anything is ever left over, I spend it on something for The Drawer.

Some of the messages that men send me suggest that certain clothes, certain looks, would make me more money than others. From their phones and laptops, they shout out their favourites, as though they're screaming for songs at a festival.

STOCKINGS!!!!!!!!!!
  Bra no panties please

and memorably, once,

Nood + feathers?

There are lots of blogs and newsletters about 'maximising earnings'. One of the website's superstars, @lola_bomb, claims that her earnings go up by over 20 per cent when she wears a blonde wig and black lingerie. I bought a black baby-doll nightie, and sure enough, it almost paid for itself. And then I felt weird about it. I didn't like myself in it, and I wasn't turning myself on. It felt too much like a chore, an obligation, and I haven't worn it since. Apparently @lola_bomb makes a six-figure income from her photos. That sounds a lot like hard work to me.

So I don't do requests.

I like to wear sheer things, silky things. Hold-ups that reach the very top of my thigh. I did a special set, once. My face was not in the frame, just one of my outstretched legs, and then ... me – bare, and shaved, completely exposed

88

against the black band of the stocking. I slid one, two, three fingers inside myself, my nails painted the palest and most ladylike pink. But I think the most shocking, erotic photograph was the one where I also slid my thumb under the band of the stocking, against the mesh.

My pussy, my cunt, my whatever – I change my mind about names every day – it *is* my 'whatever', really. Anyone can buy those pictures and fantasise about penetration. I'm sure they're engaging in the ultimate straight male fantasy. They think I *want* them inside me, that their magic penis will make me gasp and climax. And I want them to want that. I'd never want them to *do* that.

Most importantly, they will never, ever know how good and smooth it feels at the very top of my thigh. They can have the cunt; I'm not even giving it away – I don't feel as though it's ever really belonged to me. But I get to keep the context. Perversely, I feel that's the private part.

My real clothes are crumpled into chaotic piles, mostly on the floor. Anything that has made it into one of the other drawers is wedged, screwed up, and making a bid for freedom. But The Drawer is as neat and orderly as an ice cream counter, organised into candy stripes and shades of sorbet. Every time I see it, I feel the same thrill, and I have to push the same thought away. It makes me think of the chapter of *Lolita* in which the unspeakable Humbert goes clothes shopping for Lo. That is the relationship I have with myself. I'm the predator and the victim. And it's the most satisfying sexual connection I've ever had.

Tensing myself against odd thoughts of *Lolita*, I pull out a peaches-and-cream layer of dull, matte silk. It should look weird – it probably does look weird, it's only slightly pinker than my own skin. But as I drop it over my head, I shudder with pleasure. It feels like supple suede against my body, against my *cunt*, which it does not completely conceal.

For a long time, I have fantasised about form-fitting vinyl, rubber catsuits, 1980s sex-shop nightmares. But as well as being expensive, they seem quite admin heavy. If I was going to go in for that, I'd need an unlimited supply of talcum powder.

But this is easy. I *feel* easy. I look to the girl in the mirror, and she smoulders back.

She's *all* breast, fierce and unfettered; her tits are fighting the scooped neckline and winning. She turns and looks over her shoulder, admiring her smooth back, her body almost entirely exposed, but for an enormous bow, which prevents the outfit from being completely obscene. The bow should be ridiculous, frivolous, a total turn-off. But it makes her look younger, sort of sculpted. Coy ... but *dangerous*. She tests this with a finger, pulling at her lower lip, a little-girl gesture.

She knows what she must do next. She'll blacken her lashes, and paint on a pair of pale, glossy lips. She'll twist and lean, and find the angles that conceal, while promising to expose. She'll perform a series of contradictions. She'll balance on the highest heels, clicking and capturing and cycling her way from baby doll to homewrecker. Here, now, she believes she can be everything. She has sexual omnipotence, with no responsibilities. In the wrong hands, on the wrong phone, these pictures could ruin *lives* – but she's just a kid. She's playing dress up. She's anonymous.

I pick up my phone – my studio, I suppose. I look at the list of notifications, and I throw it across the room. Then, staring at the girl in the mirror, I push my index finger against my lips before forcing it into my mouth, sliding it backwards across my tongue, making myself gag.

When I remove it from my mouth and push it between my legs, I do not break eye contact. I touch, and stroke, and rub, and gasp my way into oblivion.

Afterwards, when I have finished the pictures, the posing, the posting, I wonder whether I should feel ashamed, or angry with myself. I have been fiddling while the real world burns. But I don't think I'm hurting anyone. And I feel better.

Chapter Ten

The centre of attention

My new pictures generate a small, warm response. A handful of 'beautiful', 'gorgeous' and 'more please!' messages. I have four new subscribers, which means I have made sixty pounds – a little more than I get for a shift in the shop. It's a nice boost, and I reply with my usual 'Thank you!' 'So glad you like them!'

I'm reminded of the more avuncular men who used to gather around Bean and me, after we'd spent an afternoon singing songs in a church hall. It's surprisingly cosy, this community. My 'subscribers' are almost friendly, almost respectful. I recognise their user names. It's strangely comforting. For a moment, I panic – what if one of them is Rupert? But then – he *promised* he'd unsubscribe. My ex is not a subtle man, either. If he was still here, I'm sure he'd be making his presence felt.

Right now, it's quite easy to be @girl_going_alone. All I have to do is be nearly naked, stay close to my laptop and respond to the occasional site user. Being Frankie Howard requires a great deal of effort. I can't do it. I'm deleting all my messages. I've hidden my phone in a shoe.

I've stopped googling myself, but people keep sending me things they've found online. People I haven't spoken to for years are messaging with clips and pictures. I'm wondering whether someone has scrawled my phone number on the wall of the world's biggest public toilet. I had no idea that I had so many friends and well-wishers. Capital Radio had a 'fabulous Frankie fundraising phone in'. Bean and I, and our tutus, have been in the *Toronto Star* and the *Sydney Morning Herald*.

It would be hilarious, in any other circumstances.

I'd hoped that if I hid from the world for twenty-four hours, I'd feel rested, and ready to re-enter it. I'd come up with a plan. Instead, I feel exhausted, hollowed out by half dreams and night terrors. Haunted.

I would like to spend today in bed, too. Ideally with the covers over my head, hiding. With a great effort of will, I throw off the duvet and plant my (cold) feet on the (freezing) floor. I inhale and breathe in compassion for myself. I breathe out compassion for Bean (easy), Alison (challenging) and everyone who works at a global media company that has been tasked with finding a vaguely cheerful news story (almost impossible.)

I thrust my right hand into my left Air Force 1 and brace myself. It is just a phone. It is not a Molotov cocktail. It's not poisonous. It will not bite me. It is not on fire.

I am always slightly stunned by the size of my own feet. This trainer is *capacious*. I could use it as hand luggage.

Shutting my eyes as I close the notifications, I find my Favourites and press the Bean button.

It doesn't have a chance to ring. 'FRANKIE!'

'Hello?' Oh, fuck, it's Paul.

He does not sound very friendly.

'Why don't you pick up your phone?' he hisses. 'I spent all day yesterday trying to get hold of you.'

'I was sleeping,' I say, defensively.

'Good for you!' he snaps. 'I'm so glad that you got your rest. Here in Clapham, we weren't so lucky! We haven't had such a relaxed night of it, which is a shame. What with all the reporters ringing us up and trying to think of things to say to Jack and Jon to explain the situation.'

'I'm sorry!' I say. 'I'm really sorry, but you have to ...'

He isn't listening. 'Fortunately, the family managed to get to sleep at oh, what was it, three o'clock in the morning? Yes! Because guess who woke up again at four? Guess who had to leap out of their warm bed, on a frosty February day, to investigate a *tremendous banging* coming from outside our front door?'

'Oh, no!' I gasp. 'Reporters came *to your house*? Paul, I don't know what to say.' This is awful.

'Not exactly,' he says, sourly. 'A cat got into a fight with a big bin lid, and I had to rescue it. But the *point*, Frankie, is that it might have been reporters. I didn't know. I thought that a stranger might be breaching the threshold, where my wife – my *sick* wife – and my kids were sleeping! Because of your family's ridiculous antics!'

I wish I'd just had a relaxing read of my notifications.

'Paul, please, listen. I'm so, so sorry. I do not have the words to *tell* you how sorry I am. None of this is OK, of course it isn't. I will do anything I can to fix this. But this is something Alison has done. I don't think she believed it would get beyond *her* local paper. It's not even a paper,

94

more of a pamphlet. It usually comes with a sheaf of leaflets about something called Wayne's Drains.'

'It's typical, though, isn't it?' he says, sounding more sad than mad. 'Bean is so worried – we're all worried – and you make it all about Frankie, again. You're the centre of attention, again. This is serious, Frankie. She's looked after you, for all your life. Isn't it your turn to do that for her? She doesn't need some silly stunt.'

I bite my lip. Because he's right, and I hate him for being right.

I hate him for thinking that he knows his wife better than I know my sister, and I hate myself for thinking such a ridiculous thought. I *should* apologise, again, and never stop. I *should* ask him what Bean needs, specifically. Because I can't claim to know Bean best unless I acknowledge what Paul is saying: That she's never going to ask me for anything. She's never going to lean on me. She needs me to need her.

However, if I open my mouth I'm pretty sure that what comes out will go along the lines of 'OH FUCK OFF, YOU CONDESCENDING CUNT!'

I breathe in more compassion for myself. I breathe out compassion for Bean – not because she has cancer, or because she is being hounded by the press, but because she has to be married to Paul. Ha! That's a good, sneaky loophole that Buddha would absolutely not sign off.

'Listen,' I say, trying to sound calm and steady. 'I appreciate your points. I am going to see Alison today and sort it out. This is the eye of the storm. In a couple of days, everything will be forgotten about, and things will be back to normal. Not normal, but ... you know.'

'Frankie, I'm sorry too,' says Paul. 'Obviously this is

hard for all of us. The last few days have been so—Well, I'm trying to be normal, for the boys. I'm trying to be positive around Bean. I'm shi—shimmying it. Sorry, I think Jon is hovering in the doorway. But I haven't slept, I'm not thinking straight, I realise this isn't anything that anyone wanted. Any of it.'

'Yeah,' I say, softly. 'Thanks, I really do appreciate that. It's weird – I'm not sure I'd mind being in the papers, if it was for some other dumb thing. But the "lovely little sister" angle – it feels wrong, generally, to be praised for something I did with crayons when I was seven. And especially wrong, now. For this.'

Paul clears his throat. 'I did see something, on some website – I have no idea where the numbers came from, or whether this is true – but apparently that "text to donate" number has already raised close to a hundred thousand. So that's one positive thing. Do you know if Bean still has that leotard?'

'Paul! What's *wrong* with you?!' I have the upper hand, now. 'Shall I come over and look after the boys, later? You can both catch up on some sleep.'

'Thanks, Franks, but you're alright. We wanted to spend the weekend with them; my mum is coming to pick them up on Monday. They're staying with her for a few days, for when Bean goes into ... you know.' I don't know if he doesn't want to be overheard saying 'hospital', or if he just doesn't want to contemplate it.

'Bean tried to put me off, but I want to come on Tuesday, if I'm allowed.' I'm trying not to sound grudging. Under normal circumstances, I'd be due at theirs for Sunday lunch tomorrow, but I daren't mention it.

96

'That would be really nice,' he says. 'She's having a general anaesthetic. I'm not sure if you can hang around, but you should be able to see her before she goes in.'

'Thank you. Please keep me up to date, let me know if you change your mind about babysitting. And I hope today is a bit more peaceful.' I hang up. Weirdly, that may have been one of the nicest conversations that Paul and I have ever had. Maybe this will bring us together. Maybe Bean will be fine. I'm willing to do whatever it takes for the happy ending.

With that in mind, I shuffle towards the shower, trying to generate some optimism. Positive thinking is petrol, and I need all the petrol I can get if I'm going to survive the journey to see Alison.

Chapter Eleven

Taking turns

The train ride to Alison's is short, but fraught. There is a game I like to play, to survive it. Gazing out of the window, my cheek grazing the glass, I stare at suburban back gardens and think, *What is it like to live here? What is it like to be you?*

There are so many trampolines. Webs of black netting, stretching endlessly west. If you weren't familiar with the route, you might assume we were passing an Outward Bound centre, or a military training area. But I think these are straightforward, suburban homes. Normal kids get to have trampolines. These are families who weighed up the expense, the space, the aesthetics of having a giant, grubby octagon in front of the French windows, and thought, 'You know what? This will be fun!'

These families, I imagine, sit outside together on long summer evenings. Days and weeks pass where no one uses the trampoline at all, and no one notices or minds.

Maybe one kid in twenty or fifty is an aspiring gymnast. Maybe they find joy in their dreams, the blood rushing, the imaginary crowd cheering, as they bounce higher and higher and higher. Hope brings them joy, a sense of weightlessness. They experience gravity, but they do not feel its pressure, in the physical or emotional sense.

I have convinced myself this is what it would have been like to grow up in a normal family.

That's what Bean has been desperate to create, though, and her children aren't entirely free from anxiety. They have started learning about space, and now Jack is struggling to understand the nature of reality itself. 'How do we know we're here?' he asks, furious for an answer. 'How do we know we're not all ... running around on the tip of a giant's finger?' Jon, as always, is more scared and solemn. 'Sometimes,' he told me, trying to make a case for not going to bed, 'I worry that it's all a lie. That people only get up and run around because I'm there, and if I'm not in the room with them, they sort of stop. Like robots. I don't want you and Mummy and Daddy to stop until morning.'

As I racked my brains for something that would make scientific sense and reassure a small child, I realised that this is what Alison did to us. When other people were there, we moved, we shone, we existed. As soon as there wasn't an audience, a camera, a person to show off to, we all slumped over.

'Charity begins at home!' Alison would say, filling our little house with posters, flyers and fabric swatches. It took me a while to realise she was scared. She wanted to plug all the gaps and make sure there wasn't space for anything else to seep in. What else do you do when you're all alone in a haunted house? You wear the sequins, you sing the show tunes, you never stop moving.

Bean taught me to be kind to our mother. My first conscious memories are framed by Bean's slogan: 'Let's make Mummy happy!' Mummy was queen, and it was up to us to distract her from the fact that she didn't have a king any more. If Mummy asked us to be quiet or to tidy up our toys, we did it. And when Mummy started asking us to dress up, and sing and dance, and help the people who were even less fortunate than we were, we did it. It was easy, and it was exhausting.

Bean taught me too well. She couldn't show me how to ascend to the next level and break free, to lift the curse of that kindness. When Bean started to say no, it was as if she'd stumbled upon a superpower.

Even now, I can't say no to Alison. In fact, I'm still saying yes for the two of us.

Everything changed when Bean stopped being cute. At first, I feared for her. I believed that we would always be rewarded for following the rules. When she started to break them, I felt bewildered. Clumsily, greedily, I tried to gobble up her prizes. I didn't realise that she could win the game for herself, forever, by deciding not to play.

The train has stopped. We're in a tunnel, and the window has turned into a dark mirror, filtering my face into something blurred, almost flawless. Almost beautiful. If I really looked like this, I'd look more like Bean. If I really looked like this, I think I'd be happy. If I really looked like this, I wouldn't be so vain. I wouldn't need to keep staring at my reflection, wishing and hoping.

After a few seconds, the train starts to move again. My perfect reflection is left behind.

I learned about the world by looking at people looking at

my big sister. They stared at her with reverence, sometimes fear, and even I knew that her beauty made us separate. Bean startled people into stillness. She let me tease her and touch her as much as I needed to, but even with paint on her shirt and spaghetti in her hair, I knew there was something arresting about her. She flashed, and glowed. It was in the very lines of her being, the curve of her jaw, the feather and ink of her lashes. As she grew into her beauty, she seemed less touchable. Less reachable. She was still mine, but not just anyone's.

Then, Bean got breasts. We laughed about it later. 'I swear, I went to bed one night, woke up in the morning and found these *things* on my chest, pushing up the covers,' she said. 'It took me years to get over the shock. It's ironic, it's not even as if they've become particularly vast. Literally, a storm in a B cup. You got the Community Chest.'

Right around that time, I started getting terrible headaches. Alison, an alarmist, rushed me to the GP, making noises about specialists and MRIs and how terrible it would be if anything happened to her daughter – her darling, perfect, precious daughter – after the awful loss of her husband, and who would curse a widow so, and Dr Sanders gave her a sharp look and said, 'She just needs glasses. Take her to the optician.'

Bean's breasts were bad enough. Alison is not a patient woman, and she was a resentful seamstress. She did her best to let out the tulle, but suddenly our matching dresses looked obscene on Bean. We embarked upon the period of the Sash Wars, and my sister's dresses would be tied as tightly around her waist as possible. Bean would rebel – if simply wanting to breathe can be called a rebellion – and

101

undo the bow, even though Alison would be hissing from the front row, 'Tie it up! Tie it up! You look like Demis Roussos.' She also banned me from wearing my glasses during performances. That did not go well.

We were in Market Harborough, booked to sing 'The Trolley Song' for the Let's Cancel Cancer! regional fundraiser. Bean and I were barely speaking to each other at the time. I hated Bean for causing so many arguments, for making our mum so angry. I didn't understand why she wouldn't shut up, smile, get on with it. Alison made enough scary scenes; she was responsible for constant tears, shouting and drama. Bean was supposed to be on *my* side, not making everything worse.

I was determined to deliver the performance of a lifetime. I spun, bounced and pouted. I was Shirley Temple. I mimed the actions perfectly, while Bean shuffled and mumbled. In front of an audience, with a song to sing, and steps to follow, I could relax. I had to excel, to make up for Bean. My brilliance would compensate for her reluctance.

After the performance, when the photographer from the local newspaper turned up, it made sense to me that he would push Bean aside. She was grimacing, downcast, staring at her shoes. If you didn't get close enough or look hard enough, her mime was completely convincing. She was purposefully playing ugly, so I didn't protest when the photographer implied it. 'No, not you, love, just the pretty one.' He turned to me. I stood on my tiptoes and smiled. I'd been waiting for so long. Maybe it was my turn, at last.

Chapter Twelve

Too big, too small

Alison refers to her maisonette as 'the townhouse'. She has a predilection for brass knockers shaped like bees and pineapples. When she sold the house we grew up in (handy for the airport, and not much else), Bean and I both assumed she would keep heading west and end up in the Cotswolds. 'It's Alison-idyllic,' said Bean. 'Nothing scary like actual mud, and plenty of opportunities to pay sixteen pounds for a handmade jar of artisanal carrot jam.'

We were stunned when she settled in Southfields, especially because she doesn't seem to like it much. 'I just can't be too far from my babies,' she explained. 'I'm already eaten up with guilt about leaving The Laurels and all of your precious memories.' Bean and I knew our lines. We hugged her, we nodded, we bit our lips and did not say, 'Nothing good ever happened to any of us in that house. And *you* were the only one who called it The Laurels; it was number ninety-two. You don't name a 1930s semi.'

Maybe one day our mother will come to her senses and find herself a picturesque cottage with roses round the door and underfloor heating. For now, she spends shocking sums of money on decorative tat, convinced she's only ever one hanging basket away from transforming the rest of her street into Chipping-Wimbledon-on-the-Wold. We know we should probably stop enabling her, but it makes her easy to buy for at Christmas.

As I approach, I gather a McDonald's carton, an empty beer can and a silver gas canister from her doorstep and shove them in my coat pocket. These litter land mines have the power to make my mother explode. Later I will detonate them in the relative privacy of the train station car park municipal bin.

Alison's newest knocker is shaped like a dragonfly. She opens the door before I have a chance to grab its tail. I was vague about my arrival time, and I hope she hasn't been watching and waiting. I don't want to think that she might not have anything better to do.

Alison defies all known laws of physics and looks down at me. I am a full ten inches taller than her, including her beehive. The top three inches of her is made of backcombed hair, swept into a bright, lacquer-shiny bun.

'Darling, are you ... have you ... you look ... a little bit *bigger* than usual,' she says, gesturing to my parka pockets, where the bloody litter is. I've put gross, revolting things in my coat to stop her from doing her nut, and the nicest thing she can say is, 'You look bigger'. Then, 'Is everything alright? Or have you been living on toast, again?' She squeezes my forearm, her face a tragic mask. 'It's our true family tragedy, darling. You're at the end of a long line of women who simply could not digest bread.'

There's a number of things I want to say about what our

true tragedies have been, but I mumble, 'I think it's just my pockets.' Then, pointlessly, pathetically, 'Sorry.'

As I follow her hair up the stairs, I renew an old suspicion. I believe that Alison's house is designed to make people feel fat, or ungainly. The stairs are so narrow that there's only room for the toe of my size 43s. In the hall, there's a chandelier – an *actual fucking chandelier* – that's too broad to walk around. You can't go over it, you can't go under it, you must go through it. The crystals skim the top of Alison's bun. They tinkle merrily, grazing her daintily before smacking me full in the face.

'Coffee?' she asks, oblivious to the fact that I have a mouth full of crystals.

Her sofa is a hell of a thing. Pale pink velvet, brass legs, entirely occupied by fat, silver satin cushions that cost £195 from Selfridges – each. You find this out fast if you have the audacity to move one in an attempt to sit on the sofa. Which is less comfy than a gym bench. Bean is convinced that all of Alison's furniture comes from a place that makes Borrower-sized stuff for show homes, in order to make the room seem larger. When I am here, I always feel far too big – and yet, very small.

Alison emerges with a tray bearing two steaming mugs and a plate of biscuits. Hers is covered in tiny hand-painted hearts, with the word 'Mummy' stencilled in rainbow cursive script. Where did she get this from? Maybe it was a present from Bean, a manifestation of panicked, hysterical guilt. I hope she didn't buy it for herself.

Mine is graffitied with little pink lowercase letters – l, o, v, e – over and over and over. The biscuits are layered: a tier of long brown Bourbons, golden custard creams, a

Jammie Dodger heart crowning her efforts. She places the plate on the coffee table (pink and white, fake marble, too narrow) and I reach for a custard cream. 'Darling, are you absolutely sure that's wise?' she asks, shaking her head. 'I put Splenda in your coffee.'

The plate is purely decorative. I don't think Alison has allowed herself to eat a biscuit since 2008. I wouldn't be surprised if that is the best-before date on the packet.

Fixing my gaze at a point above her bun, I try to prepare myself for an awkward conversation. Right now, I wish I was anywhere but here. About to sit a maths exam. Or at the car-hire kiosk at the airport, trying to explain that there was already a scratch on the wing mirror. What does it say, in *How to Win in the Workplace?* Good posture commands respect. Speak low and slow. Be compassionate, but not emotional. Be firm about your boundaries.

'Mum,' I imagine myself saying. That's the trouble, right there. It's easy to promise Bean that I'll sort things out with 'Alison', but I've never been able to stick to any sort of boundary with Mum.

I breathe in, and splutter slightly as a sip of coffee bubbles in my throat. 'Mum, I—'

'I've got some really exciting news!' she says brightly, ignoring me. 'It was the funniest thing, I was just about to call you when you said you were coming over, so I thought I'd *save* it, and it would be a *lovely* surprise!'

Given Alison used to wake us up at 5 a.m. on Christmas morning to open our stockings, the greatest surprise might be the fact that there *is* a surprise. Still, I feel a wave of anxiety breaking and sloshing in my gut, though it might just be the effects of drinking coffee on an empty stomach.

If only I could distract her for just long enough to palm a custard cream.

'A lovely surprise?' I say, cheerfully. 'How, ah, lovely!'

'This terrific young woman from the *Post* has been in touch, she's called Leticia. She's been following your story over the last few days, and she wants you to be in a photo shoot!'

Oh, no.

'Mum, that *is* a surprise, but I don't think Bean—'

She cuts me off. 'Oh, don't worry, I did tell her that it probably wasn't really Bean's thing. She was very keen to have both of you, and recreate that *adorable* picture, but I wasn't sure if Bean was available. You know, with the boys, and her job keeping her so very busy . . .'

And the fact that she's about to be spending most of her time in hospital for treatment, I think.

'Mum, Bean wants all of this to die down. She's finding the attention difficult to deal with. It isn't nice for Paul, or the boys. It's been stressful for everyone, and I don't think this is what she had in mind. She thought we'd be doing something simple, she wanted us to do a bake sale for Cancer Research. So maybe we should say—'

Alison hasn't heard me. 'It's been crazy. And so exciting! Frankie, I had no idea that this would happen. I thought this would be a little local-interest story. It's gone beyond anything I could have dreamed of. I've never been so proud of my girls! And we're raising so much money!'

Here comes another great big wave of anxiety. 'How exactly is that working? People are texting that number – who set it up?' I ask.

It is not outside the realms of possibility that Alison has

linked it to her own PayPal account without realising the scale of the operation. That she does not understand that this is not the same as writing a cheque for £32.96 to the local Dogs Trust after relieving me of the small hatful of coins I have amassed by spending the afternoon outside Marks & Spencer strumming a ukulele.

She grins. 'The chap from the local rag was *so* helpful. Really charming, actually,' she says, flushing sightly. 'It turns out they have everything set up, it's one of those big media companies that owns everything, just like in *Succession*!' She laughs.

I bite down on my thumbnail, picturing the giant yacht that some faceless billionaire has probably already bought with everyone's donations. 'Frankie, darling, don't! With hands like yours, you can't afford stubby fingernails. Think of Bean, now – her nails are *beautiful*.' Alison splays out her own hands for inspection. 'She takes after me. Selenium every morning, cuticle oil every night. You know, it was awful when your father died, but it did mean that I could start sleeping in gloves.'

Right. Regroup. Focus. Shelve that for another time. For my future therapist.

'So, can we be absolutely sure that the money is definitely going to a cancer charity?' I say, slowly. Pre-emptively, I shove both hands under my thighs because Alison's reply could drive me to an insatiable fingernail binge.

'Darling, do pay attention. Get with the programme.' I'm certain that wherever Bean is, she can sense the shift in atmospheric pressure as I roll my eyes at Alison. 'Of *course* it's going to charity. So, this company – Heritage, I think they're called – I didn't realise that they own most of the local newspapers too. They also publish the *Post*. They do loads and loads for charity, Heritage. They pick a cause every so often and push it and they get loads of donations from their readers. It's wonderful! Actually, the timing couldn't be better.'

'How so?' I ask, cautiously. Because I want to scream, 'What do you mean? The timing is *appalling*! What about Bean? Aren't you worried?' But then she'll cry, and I'll cry, and we'll get nowhere.

'Well, the *Post* was about to do something with this anti-bullying charity. They were going to run a big interview with the founder. But they've had to drop it because of this massive scandal. It hasn't come out yet, but she's been bullying her own interns.' Alison drops her voice. 'Apparently one woman has come forward to say she was repeatedly pelted with Maltesers.'

'What?'

'I know! You'd think they'd be light little things, only eleven calories a pop. But it sounds as though they hurt if you throw them hard enough. Anyway, the *Post* was about to do this big push. All of their branding was around kindness, so "hashtag be kind for cancer" is a win for them. And you make the perfect spokesperson. You could be the face of the Heritage charity arm! As long as you haven't been hurling Maltesers at anyone.'

I am starting to think that the only way to get out of this is to start committing random acts of violence with confectionary. 'How can I be the face of an arm?'

Alison tents her fingers. The vein in her forehead throbs visibly, and I know she is forcing herself to remember that I am twenty-nine, not nine, and that this would be a bad time to give me a telling off.

I use this pause to my advantage and try to state my case. 'Mum, I don't think Bean would want me to do this. We've raised some money, which is wonderful, but we've taken it as far as it can go. I'm sure the *Post* can find someone else to be a spokesperson. I'm not going to do this.' Despite my best efforts, I fail to speak 'low and slow'. I sound like a pressure washer. The last part squeaks out of me, with a rising inflection. I'm leaning forward, adopting the brace position, waiting for Alison to scream, weep or shout. I'll probably get all three.

'Darling,' she says, huskily. It simply isn't fair that *she* can manage 'low and slow'. 'I understand. I did wonder whether you might not be keen initially. But all of this has taken me back to the lovely times we had when you were little. I know the fundraising was rather more low key. The odd fifty quid, here and there. But you did so much good work. You were such a trooper. I remember thinking of your dad, and how very proud he must be, looking down at you.'

She is completely transparent, I think. I look at her, hoping to shock and shame her into self-awareness. But she blinks and beams, childlike. Alison is an arch manipulator. It's her world; we're just living in it. But she's impossible to argue with. She's completely committed to doing the 'right thing', no matter what it takes. It has never occurred to her that the 'right thing' looks a lot like getting her own way.

I open my mouth and close it again.

'The thing is, Frankie, I have been a tiny bit naughty.' She smiles, and I try not to sigh audibly. Alison is almost sixty, and she still sometimes speaks as though she's wearing a frilly party dress and holding a lollipop. I half expect her to put on a lisp. 'The *Post* really needs a feature for this slot – the Maltesers lady has left them in a bit of a jam. They're desperate to do this on Tuesday morning, otherwise poor Leticia is in a real pickle.'

So, a lot of condiment-based drama, over at the *Post*. Poor *Leticia*? What about poor Bean?

'How is that our problem?' I say, stiffly. 'I'm sorry, but I promised Bean I'd try to calm things down. This is the opposite. She needs to be as relaxed as possible, and this isn't relaxing for her at all.'

'But Frankie, that's the whole point,' says Alison, patiently. 'Bean won't be involved. This is such a lovely thing to do for her, really. A tribute. At the moment everyone is focusing on both of you. This is an opportunity for you to step in and take the pressure off. She'd *want* you to do this.'

I shake my head and feel my brow puckering. Alison wags a finger. 'Darling, careful. Think of your complexion. I just read that frowning is worse than smoking. Anyway' – she lowers her voice – 'Leticia thinks the *Post* could raise *vast* amounts of money. Their last charity drive generated *ten million*. Money for research, treatment, counselling, provision for families. All sorts of stuff for kiddies who need their mummies, like Jack and Jon. Of course Bean would want you to help.'

Anyone who uses the word kiddies should automatically be placed on some sort of community safety register.

She keeps speaking. 'So you wouldn't have to do very much, really. It's just like the bits of modelling you used to do. You were always so good at it. Turn up, get your picture taken, maybe talk a tiny bit about the stuff that you and Bean used to do when you were little. That's the end. They'll take care of the rest.'

111

'Anyway, I don't think I'm free on Tuesday,' I say. 'There's ... something I need to do in the afternoon.' I'm longing to tell her about Bean's appointment, but I bite my lip. She'll have Paul. She'll have me. And if our mother knows, it may well turn into *Alison's* appointment.

'Well, that's perfect, then.' My mother claps her hands. 'Wonderful! Shoot in the morning, and then the day is yours. It won't take long.' I wait for her to ask me what I'm doing on Tuesday afternoon, but she is wholly incurious. 'I'll get Leticia to give you a ring. They'll sort out hair and makeup and everything – it's *terribly* professional. So, lots of water, but not too much, because you do retain it. I've got you some nice Clinique toner, hopefully that will sort out that little dry patch on your chin. Do you still have that wrap dress? The blue one, like Kate Middleton wore in the photo?'

The wrap dress still has its tags on. 'Flattering for *every* figure,' Alison had trilled when she presented it to me. It makes me look as though I have four arses.

I grimace. 'Lovely to have a bit of colour, don't you think?' she carries on. 'Obviously I think they'll put you in all sorts of fabulous designer clothes, but do turn up looking smart and neat. Darling, I know it's the fashion but you do look as though you're always wearing pyjamas.' She taps her nose and frowns. 'No, not pyjamas. What is it they always wear in prison? That sort of thing. If I saw you, and I didn't know you, I'd worry that your house had just burned down.'

I can hear Bean, screaming at me from somewhere in the universe. 'Why do you let her say this stuff to you? Why do you sit there and take it?' 'Because she means well,' I reply in my head. 'It's just her way.' So I don't challenge Alison.

I look down at my thighs and smooth out the puckered fabric of my leggings. The wrinkles immediately pop back into place.

'Frankie, I know this is a difficult time for you too,' says Alison. 'It breaks my heart to see you stuck. You've got so much to offer, and so much going for you. I wonder whether this might be the making of you. An opportunity for me to give you the life I dreamed of. For you, I mean. I feel so guilty, watching you, the days slipping by. You and your sister are so different. Bean is so sorted, so together, and you're so vulnerable. You haven't had that chance—'

I panic. 'No, Mum, it's OK!' I feel guilty enough for both of us. 'I'm happy enough. I like my life, really.'

Alison takes my hands in hers. They're chilly, I realise. Her hands are impervious to the warmth of her coffee cup, and that worries me. Is she healthy? Does she eat enough? She seems frail; much older than the woman who exists in my imagination.

She tilts her head, and her bottom lip protrudes. I know this expression well. Bean says she is always auditioning for the role of 'Alison' in *Alison! One Woman's Courage.* She lowers her voice. 'I wonder whether things would have been different if you'd had more security. If only I'd been able to give you some stability, growing up. We could have sent you to a proper stage school, maybe. You'd have been able to make something of your life.'

I snort. 'Mum, really, I'm fine. I promise.' And because she seems so fragile, so desperate, my words tumble out in a rush. 'I'll do the shoot. I'll wear the wrap dress.' Which is a pointless thing to say, because it isn't my decision at all. Or Bean's. It's always Alison's.

Maybe this will do more good than harm. Maybe we'll raise money and change a lot of lives for the better, and maybe this will take the heat off Bean. I can't say no. I tried, I failed. This is simply the latest in a series of events that is just going to happen to me, no matter what I do.

As I walk back to the station, my subconscious is whispering viciously. *How can you say that? All of this is your fault. Take some responsibility, for once.*

And then, *Grow up. Grow up now. Because Bean might not always be there to fight your battles for you.*

Chapter Thirteen

A natural

While Alison will never completely understand Bean, Bean is the only one who understands about Alison. And Bean is braver than me. She's built her own life, but as the younger sister I'm stuck at age seven. Bean tries to intervene but Alison and I will always be parent and project. And Bean and I keep saving each other. She tries to remind me that I am an autonomous human being, and I tap dance on tables, figuratively and literally, to soak up the excesses of Alison's attention and give Bean the peace she craves. I'm not sure that it still makes sense. I don't know how to do anything else.

I started to wonder about our strange family dynamics around my thirteenth birthday, when Alison took me to my first photo shoot. It was a present, supposedly.

By that point, Alison had offered us both up to every reputable agency in town. And every slightly sketchy one, too. She didn't tell us what she was doing – not straight away – but there was one morning where she opened a plain, white envelope and sighed so heavily that her crumbs scattered, rising from her plate and falling again, a tiny toast tornado.

Looking back, the fact that she was eating carbs was a clear indication that she was in a bad way.

'"Not suitable for any of our current projects."' She looked at me, at Bean, and then back to me again. 'Lord knows who they're taking on. Perhaps it's the fashion to look plain. There are enough of them about. That kid who gets the ice cream on her nose, she's nothing to look at. You could both do that.' She sighed again, announced that she was getting a migraine, and went to bed with the Yellow Pages.

There were more white envelopes. I grew to loathe the girl with ice cream on her nose – not because she had what I wanted, but because she made my mother so unhappy. Her existence seemed to be evidence of my failure, although I wasn't sure what I had failed at.

Then Alison discovered that you can buy success, temporarily. I was given the Star Search Makeover and Portfolio Package as a birthday gift.

'The brochure says you get up to three outfit changes, but I think we might as well bring some extras,' said Alison the night before. 'Have a look under my bed.' Bean and I were watching *Home and Away*. Bean told me it was OK to like it 'ironically' but I really, really liked it. One day, I'd move to Australia, a land where everyone was so gorgeous that nothing could really hurt them – not divorce, not car crashes, not discovering their sister had been swapped at birth because of a hospital mix up. 'Frankie will go when this is finished,' said Bean, firmly.

Alison folded her arms. 'Both of you. Upstairs. Now.'

The base of Alison's bed was made of springs, not slats, so my hair got trapped in the coils as I slithered around in the dust. Bean slid out a suitcase and unzipped it. 'Is this *her* stuff? It's a bit ...' She pulled out a glittering bronze tunic, encrusted with beads. 'It even smells weird. Come out, Frankie, smell!' A clumsy snake, I reversed out from under the bed and inhaled obediently. It did smell weird – sour, tangy, slightly chilly. Was it rusting?

The door creaked open, and Alison appeared within the frame. 'Is that my Jasper Conran? I was wearing that when your father asked me to marry him.'

Bean wrinkled her nose. 'He *proposed* to you in that?' Alison went a little pink. 'It was very fashionable at the time. In fact, I've hung onto it because I'm certain that it's going to come back. We were on a boat—'

'Of course you were.' Bean's sarcasm was thrillingly adult.

Alison pretended not to notice. 'Well, you know. A booze cruise. A P&O ferry, really. He had volunteered to stock up for the golf club Christmas party. But we were on board, in the bar, and I had a Dubonnet.' Her pronunciation was exaggerated, theatrical. *Doobonairrrrr.* 'Moonlight fell, just as we left the harbour. That's when he told me he was head over heels in love with me.'

'Head over heels? Mum, seriously!' Somehow Bean rolled her eyes, her voice, her whole body.

'Your father was an old-fashioned romantic, girls. It's important that you know that. He was a good man.'

I shivered, dust prickling my nose. Alison said a lot of weird stuff about Dad, and I did my best to ignore it. He wasn't here, was he? I'd never know him. What was the point of this talk? But this made me feel raw, scraped at. Sad in a way I couldn't quite explain. 'And you loved him, too? He knew how you felt?' I asked.

117

The features on Alison's face blurred, almost shimmering, before hardening. She looked like the top smelled. 'Of course I did! And that's why this is so difficult—'

Bean interrupted. 'Mum, I think this is too lovely for Frankie to take to the photo shoot. There are so many memories attached to it. Imagine if it got lost, or if she damaged the beading? I think there's another big suitcase under the bed, let's see what's in there.' She took my hand, as though we were playing a game, and pulled me to the floor. Together, a pair of deep-sea divers questing for misplaced nostalgia, we dragged out the other suitcase. Together, Bean and Alison looked at old clothes, fought over them, and cried over them, late into the night.

I don't know if Alison still has the photographs. I remember her paying an extra £200 for giant, glossy prints. 'It's an investment,' she said.

It seemed like too much money for pictures of me in a very small Irish dancing costume; in a leotard and a scratchy skirt; in a black, sequined evening gown that had to be pinned with bulldog clips. On the way home, I fell asleep as she talked about the importance of showing my range. 'It's a shame we couldn't do more outfits, the camera really loved you!' she said, as the traffic slowed and drizzle turned the universe grey. *Yes, but the photographer hated you*, was my last, drowsy thought. Alison had been as noisy, as persistent, as pointless as a bluebottle, shouting instructions, making suggestions, shrieking, 'Doesn't she have *potential*? Don't you think she's a *natural*?'

I dreamed I was an octopus. No matter where I tried to put my hands, an extra set would spring up from a different part of my body. Someone screamed, 'Smile more! Smile harder! Look like you're enjoying yourself!' *I am smiling,* I tried to say, but water was filling the space, up to my neck, my nose, over my head, and I knew I was going to drown. 'Where is Bean?' I called out frantically. When I woke up, I was screaming for my sister, and my seatbelt was tangled. The traffic had started moving again, and Alison was turning on the radio. She looked at me tenderly, oblivious to my distress. 'Oh! You're awake! Didn't we have a lovely day?' she asked. It wasn't really a question.

Chapter Fourteen

Happy family

This time last Sunday, I was sitting exactly where I am now, feeling full of love and gravy. Now I'm just vibrating with anxiety. Three glasses of Rioja have done nothing to relax me, so I'm pinning all my hopes on number four.

I'm trying to summon the courage to tell Bean about the shoot. I was rehearsing my speech on the doorstep and was on the brink of blurting it out, but I was greeted by Jack, who wanted to sing a song about monkeys. Then I tried to bring it up when we were peeling potatoes, but Bean wanted to talk about meditation apps, and I couldn't very well say, 'Speaking of zen, here's something to shatter your sense of peace and obstruct the path to enlightenment.'

Bean is being odd, bright but hollow, saying some very un-Bean-like things. 'I've just got the *scrummiest* sourdough from the new bakery!' and 'Might redo the en suite next month. I've seen some *ravishing* tiles in the Fired Earth catalogue.' She seems to be channelling Alison. She looks manic, and she has a lot of makeup on – I'm watching her for secret signs of paleness, tiredness. I want to be delighted that she's trying to be positive, but there's something desperate about her. Frayed around the edges.

After my terse conversation with Paul, I assumed the Andersens wouldn't want me to come over, but Bean said she was keen to host. 'I might not be up to doing this for a little while,' she explained. 'And the boys don't know what's going on. They're just delighted that they get some days off school for a special Granny trip. If you're not there, they'll wonder why. You should come! There's no reason why we can't have our usual Sunday.'

Children do notice things, though. The boys are both remarkably intuitive, and I'd expected them to realise that something is up. Today, they seem like slightly more extreme versions of themselves. Jack is the caretaker, the cheerleader, performing and entertaining us all. Jon is sensitive and a little more withdrawn, pushing buttons to figure out what's wrong.

'I don't want to drown my potatoes in a lake of gravy,' says Jack, thoughtfully. 'Unless ... the gravy is a stream, or a river, and the potatoes are rocks and the peas are ... fish! Mummy, why is it called a gravy boat if the gravy is inside it? Wouldn't it make more sense for there to be little boats *in* the gravy?'

'He's got us there!' I say, cheerfully. 'Jon, what do you think?'

'I think,' he says, slowly, 'I think I want ... sausages!'

Bean winces. 'OK, darling, I can do it ... ' She's starting to get up from her chair.

Paul clamps a hand over her wrist. 'Babe, no, come on. We've talked about this. Jon, kiddo, eat your chicken. We're not having sausages today.'

121

'But I want ...' Jon's lips tremble, and his eyes start to fill up.

'Hey, Jon, I bet that if you eat your chicken, there will be a delicious pudding!' I beam at my nephew. He folds his arms and shakes his head.

Bean's face falls. 'I forgot to get the crumble out of the freezer,' she says. 'Fu ...'

'... dge?' says Paul, warily.

'I hate fudge!' says Jon, pushing his plate away. He starts to sob. He gets up from his chair and runs from the room. Bean's and Paul's eyes meet, and Jack responds to the situation immediately. 'Don't worry, he is being a silly billy. I'll go after him. Everything will be OK.' His expression is so world weary that I have to bite my lip to stop myself from giggling. Paul shakes his head.

'Another relaxing family meal.'

'Baby, don't.' Bean pats his hand again. 'They're just being kids. It is what it is.'

'I really wanted us all to have a happy family lunch, before tomorrow,' mutters Paul.

'Why do you keep saying "family"? It's a little creepy. It makes me think of Charles Manson.' As soon as I speak, I realise I shouldn't have said that out loud. On a good day, that would have made Paul laugh, but his face clouds.

'Of course "family" is a confusing concept for you, Frankie. You only understand the first part of the word, the "fame" part. To you, family is just a way to get yourself in the newspapers.'

I'm too angry to meet Paul's eyes, so I look down at the table, staring at the distorted reflection of the ceiling on the back of my spoon. 'Yeah, this was my plan all along,'

I say, sulkily. 'I wanted to use Bean's illness to further my art career. That's all I care about – being celebrated for my early crayon work.'

Bean shakes her head. 'Look, Paul, there's absolutely no point getting stressed about this. We've been through it. None of this is Frankie's fault. You know what our mother is like. We've raised loads of money for a good cause, by accident. Let's focus on having a nice day today.'

Paul is still looking at me balefully, but he gives me a faint smile. 'Sorry, Frankie, it's been a funny few days. I meant to say, a few of my mates keep sending me links and asking if you're single and as fit as your sister. I tell them it depends how they feel about the BFG.'

I pick up my spoon and examine it thoughtfully. I will not hit Paul over the head with it. I will not give his chair a big push. Bean stands up. 'Franks, will you help me with the washing up? Paul, I think the boys are probably in the den. Would you pop your head through and check on them? If you want to sit on the sofa and shut your eyes for a while, I won't judge.'

Paul grunts and gets up, and I follow Bean to the kitchen.

Before I can speak, Bean starts talking. 'I know, Frankie. We're all dealing with this differently, and this is what he does. He's scared, and that makes him uncomfortable, and that makes him an arsehole. And he's having an awful time at work. I'm desperate for him to change jobs, but on top of everything else ...'

I squeeze her shoulder. 'It's fine. Paul is Paul. It's not his fault that I'm taller than him.'

Right. Better out than in. I really do feel as though I'm going to be sick, although that might be the Rioja. 'Bean,'

I pause, and belch. 'I'm so sorry, that is not what I wanted to say. Bean, there is no good time or good way to tell you this, but I've fucked up. I have to be in the *Post*. Alison set it up, something to do with raising money for breast cancer charities. There's a photo shoot on Tuesday. But early in the morning, so I can come to the hospital in the afternoon.'

Bean says nothing. She picks up a dishcloth, squeezes it, and puts it down again.

I gulp at the air, trying to supress another surge of nausea. I pick up a mug from the draining board, fill it with water, and down it.

'If it's still OK for me to come in the afternoon, that is. I'm sorry, I failed to stand up to Alison, as always. You know what she's like. Maybe I can get out of the shoot. I'll give myself food poisoning, or break my leg ...'

Bean starts to speak. She sounds measured, composed, but she does not look at me. 'OK. I see. They don't want me to do it, do they? I'm not doing it.'

'No, even Alison seemed to understand that,' I say. 'But would you mind, much? I'm sure I can still find a way to get out of it.'

'I think you should do it.' She still sounds calm.

'Pardon?' Is this a trick?

'I remember some of these *Post* charity campaigns, and yeah, it's a horrible newspaper, but they do so much good. There was a dementia one a couple of years ago that had a huge impact. It funded part of a really significant study.' She puts an arm around my shoulder. 'Over the last few days I've heard from so many people. At first, I was furious, but I can see that this horrible thing connects us all. Everyone I know has a story, everyone has lost someone. I'm

124

so *fucking scared* but maybe this isn't all about me, right now. Or you. Or even bloody Alison.' She smiles, and now she looks really tired.

'How are you feeling?' I ask. 'What does "fucking scared" feel like?'

She shrugs. 'Right now, I'm knackered. And the mood swings are at teenage levels. I'm one dumb fight with Paul away from going to my room and playing Black Sabbath albums.'

'I didn't know you were a fan,' I say.

'I wasn't, Frankie, but these are strange times. I might be about to enter my black lipstick phase. That said, my consultant thinks I have every reason to be optimistic. There's even a good chance I won't need chemo, if everything goes to plan on Tuesday. She's a bit of a pioneer in the way she works with radiotherapy. It's supposed to be far less invasive.'

Making tight fists, I concentrate on not crying. *Optimistic. Invasive. Radiotherapy.* Bean has become fluent in the language of a country I hadn't even visited a week ago. And she sounds so brave.

'Then I'll be optimistic too,' I say, wrapping my arms around her. I can't cry. I won't cry. I bury my face in the top of Bean's head, hoping her hair absorbs the tears before they touch her scalp.

Chapter Fifteen

'It's for you'

It's 5.43. I have been awake for over an hour. At 4.57, I decided that I had to get back to sleep. At 5.08, I gave up, got up, and put a pair of teaspoons in my tiny freezer compartment. Now the teaspoons are out of the freezer and balanced on my eyelids.

Bean taught me this trick, before my first school disco. I was hoping that she might initiate me into the mysteries of body glitter, but she gave me a pair of cold spoons and told me to close my eyes. 'Models do it,' she explained. 'I read it in *Elle*.'

I did not ask any further questions.

When I was twelve I had no need of cold spoons, but now I require all the help I can get. And the weird little ritual makes me feel closer to my sister. I hope she's asleep. I hope she isn't thinking about any of the things I'm thinking about.

Bean is going to hospital. That's where they heal people. They will heal Bean. She's proactive. She knows herself. She looks after herself. She acted immediately. She's responsible.

Consider the alternative. In another reality, Bean's body

126

is a time bomb. She pats the lump, she thinks it's weird, she thinks it's hormonal, she thinks she's probably fine. Or she's too scared to investigate further. In that reality, we'd be going through this in a year from now, and the cancer might be much harder to treat.

And that's why I'm doing this shoot. For all the women, all the families who are scared and suffering now. I suspect we are legion.

This morning will be fine. It might even be fun.

Leticia has been very reassuring. We spoke on the phone yesterday, and she was not the woman I was expecting. 'Honestly, I can't tell you how grateful we are – I know this must be such a difficult time for you and your family. My mum had breast cancer a couple of years ago. She's in remission now, she's doing really well. But this means so much to me personally. Thank you,' she said, warmly. As Bean said, this awful thing connects us all. Maybe I am helping, in a tiny way.

I press the bowls of the spoons against my eyelids, creating dark, shimmering patterns, miniature firework displays. Then I let go of the spoons, pick up my phone, type a message:

HAPPY LUMPECTOMY DAY! XXXXX

I send it to Bean, followed by a suited Leonardo Di Caprio raising a champagne coupe, in front of a firework display. She replies immediately.

THANK YOU! Having a celebratory lumpy breakfast. Porridge, mashed potato, nachos and salsa. XXXXX

Then, NOT REALLY!

Then, (apart from nachos) XXX

SHALL I BRING SNACKS TO HOSP? I reply.

NOT LUMPY ONES OR THEY WILL OPERATE ON U2

Then, I don't think I can eat b4, might send you on a snack mission while I'm under.

Are you scared? I type, then delete. Then, I'm scared. I delete that too. I finally send, Alison is making me wear the wrap dress. LUMPS AHOY! XXX

Cannot wait to see pics! Good luck fitface. Don't forget to do blue steel XXX, replies Bean, before sending me a picture of Ben Stiller.

Somewhere at the bottom of the email chain from the *Post*, someone had grandly mentioned 'sending a car'. As though it might be summoned by remote control. I'd imagined all six feet of me being strapped to the top of Jack's Hot Wheels, wobbling down the streets and colliding with delivery drivers. Even though I knew this was unlikely, I politely declined. I'm prone to motion sickness on a good day, and today I'm feeling too raw, too jangly for strange synthetic air freshener and small talk. Or worse – radio phone-ins.

As I walk up Westbourne Terrace, past the row of glossy front doors, it starts to rain. The lenses of my glasses turn steamy and smeary. I'm being held in place by my own weather system, a soft grey fog. It's soothing. I should be nervous, but I don't feel it. Looking ahead, I can see a patch of shocking pink blossom blooming on a bare branch. That *can't* be real, not in February. I take my glasses off, wipe them on my sleeve and look again. Ah, a crisp packet. Prawn cocktail.

Following my phone, eyes on the blue dot, every turn seems to take me closer to Murderland. This can't be right. The postcode leads me towards a derelict industrial estate, and now my anxiety is ramping up. I'd assumed I'd be heading towards some shiny, happy magical photo factory, not this bleak grey expanse. Just because I can't see a chained-up Alsatian doesn't mean there isn't one somewhere on the premises. Perhaps Alison and I have been very naïve. It's a trick. It's a scam. It must be. Maybe the charity money is funding something nefarious on the dark web, and we're both going to be killed because we already know too much. It sounds far-fetched, but slightly less far-fetched than the idea of me launching a charity campaign for the *Post*.

I find Unit Nine: a black fire door, held open by a brick and adorned with a fluttering piece of paper that says SHOOT in black Sharpie. This does not look auspicious.

I could always phone Leticia to check I've got the address right. But then, what would she say? 'Don't worry, it's all legit, of course we're not going to murder you.' Then, as soon as I've descended the stairs, they will appear with chainsaws. Worryingly, the first thing I picture is Alison, standing over my disembodied corpse, weeping with remorse. 'Double tragedy for cancer mum.' Maybe she'd get the mortician to do some heavy contouring, while sobbing, 'I did keep telling her that she couldn't digest bread!'

The stairs creak and wheeze. Maybe they're just old and flimsy, but I assume they're protesting against the weight of my body. The women – the models, I suppose – who come down to the studio must be much slimmer than me. As I think of all the legitimate models who have ever walked down these steps, I consider the horror of having to stand beside one. What if they have brought in a couple of professional beauties to flank me, to emphasise my 'realness' and relatability?

That thought frightens me more than being murdered. Am I about to be exposed as a woman who Is Not Beautiful Enough and never will be? A woman who is Barely Presentable? I imagine the caption and wince. 'Introducing ... Frankie! She's the one with the cellulite.'

I wish I'd paid more attention to the email chain. I'm starting to worry that I've missed a crucial and humiliating detail. Was I supposed to let Leticia know about how tall I am, or what size I am? I don't trust Alison not to have lied on my behalf. This might end with me cringing awkwardly in a giant #BeKind4Cancer T-shirt, red in the face, giving a thumbs-up sign. The only good thing about this outcome is that it would make Bean laugh.

It's velvet dark at the bottom of the stairs, and it smells oddly bosky and botanical. Something is growing where it shouldn't be. I reach out for the wall, expecting to feel cool, soft moss – but rough brick scratches my wrist. I'm standing on the bottom step, my right foot hovering above the ground. Stick or twist? Stay or go? It's spooky here. Something just feels off, I know it.

A door swings open, and I scream.

'Hi, are you Frankie?'

The woman standing in front of me must be a full foot shorter than I am. Light is pouring out from behind her, hitting the top of her scalp. It takes me a moment to realise she has a perfectly trimmed, sixties Sassoon-style bob, and she hasn't had her hair cut into a tonsure.

'Yes?' Why am I answering her question with a question? Now is not the time for an existential crisis. This woman wouldn't understand, she's wearing a boiler suit. 'And you must be Leticia.' I'm about to go in for a hug, and she looks alarmed. It's fair enough; she's tiny. Already I feel clumsy and vulgar. A bully at the beach, kicking little kids' sandcastles.

'No, I'm Natasha. Leticia isn't here yet. Train trouble,' she shrugs. 'Although according to her Insta Stories, she was at the Maz Clarke event on the Southbank and had a late one, so ...' She rolls her eyes. 'Anyway, sorry, we should have warned you about the spooky building. I've never shot here before, and I nearly didn't make it down the stairs.' She holds the door open for me. 'Lovely place, though, very easy to light.'

I exhale, noisily. I no longer think anyone has lured me here to murder me.

The studio looks like a model town, a planned community. Everyone is moving with purpose. No one is slumped or shuffling. The room, or 'space', has been divided into three areas, the biggest being for the shoot itself. It's funny how piles of trailing cables in your house indicate chaos, but the piles of trailing cables here make it clear that serious work is being done. Under my coat, I start to sweat. It takes me a moment to realise that I can feel the lights on me. I see an old, freestanding oval mirror leaning against some exposed brickwork, and a sofa, not unlike Alison's. It would be nice to peel my coat off and put my feet up, but I suspect the sofa is some sort of prop.

I'm much more interested in the other parts of the room. In the far left, it appears that someone has set up a small branch of Waitrose. I stumble over to the magic table. I'm pretty sure my pupils are now shaped like pain au chocolates and popping out of my eyeballs. There are plates of cut fresh fruit – mango, melon, pineapple – and maybe fifty tiny triangles of sandwich. Is that ham, or salmon? Packs of Haribo, a fridge with a clear door. I can see a squadron of Diet Coke cans.

Is it OK to help myself? Flushing, I press a hand against my hot cheek. It's not the lights – I'm suddenly very self-conscious. Maybe this is all for someone else, the *real* shoot they're doing after this one. Any minute now, someone is going to come along and shoo me away.

Natasha is looking at her phone. No one is watching me. I call out, 'Um, is it OK if I have a Diet Coke?'

Natasha raises an eyebrow in my direction. 'Love, of course! It's for you!'

I'm not completely sure how I feel about that. This isn't something I thought I wanted. In fact, it's something I never allowed myself to want.

My biggest fear isn't being murdered on a murky stairwell. It's vanity. Being caught in the act of valuing myself, cherishing myself, thinking I might be worth something. Right now, I'm experiencing a thrilling moment of cognitive dissonance. I hadn't realised what my subconscious was really expecting. I thought someone would open the door, look me up and down and say, 'No thank you. Not you. Not today.' But I'm legitimate. Worthy enough to drink the Diet Coke. And yet, being able to roam around the buffet, unimpeded, makes me realise how I live in a strange state of self-consciousness. I'm used to being looked at, but I expect it to be followed with a taunt or a telling off.

I have always been the weird girl, the whispered-about girl. My father haunted me in the playground. Even though I barely remember him, I was constantly followed by his ghost. Everyone knew *about* me, and no one knew what to say *to* me. I was evidence that a child's worst fears could come true. The other children avoided me. Some of the teachers did too. The more I was ignored, the sadder and stranger I became. I was not spoken to, but I was stared at.

When everyone stares at you, you think there must be something wrong with you. You *know* there is. Even long after you've left school, and the stares keep coming, you can't bring yourself to believe that anyone is looking because they might like what they see. You know who you really are, and you can't hide it. It would be better if you thought people were picturing you naked. It's what's under your skin that must be bothering them.

I sip my drink and let the silver bubbles bounce on my tongue. Maybe I don't have to be that Frankie today. Perhaps I can shake off the sticky shame, that dull, numb, under-the-sea feeling, and become someone else. I'm not here to be laughed at. I'm here because the world believes I'm good and kind and inspiring. Instead of feeling bad about not being good *enough*, maybe I should try believing them. Just for a morning. It seems wrong, when this strange, scary afternoon is looming, but I'm jolted by an unexpected surge of hope, of optimism. I don't want to push it back down below the surface. After the last few days, I want to hold onto it and let it carry me away.

Chapter Sixteen

'Are you a photographer?'

Filled with light, warmth, and something close to joy, I'm on the brink of biting a salmon sandwich when I hear an unexpected sound, shattering and shrill.

'Hello, darling! Lovely to— oh, watch out for that fruit! Melon is surprisingly bloating.'

I'm so startled that I throw my sandwich up in the air behind me. I can't see where it has landed.

'Hello, Mum.'

Alison throws her arms wide, then squeezes me so tightly that I can detect a faint popping around my shoulder blades. She gives me a lip-gloss-sticky kiss that lands just below my chin. She smells of three times as much Elnett as usual. I worry that I'm going to break my nose on her hair.

'Frankie, you look absolutely lovely.' She catches my chin in her hands and tilts my face towards the light, frowning. 'You haven't been in makeup yet, have you? You've got a few blackheads on your chin. What happened to that nice Clarins exfoliator I got you for Christmas? You did bring contact lenses, didn't you?'

I wiggle away. 'They're in my pocket. I didn't realise you were coming.'

She beams. 'Surprise! Isn't it nice to see me? Leticia thought you might be nervous, so here I am.' She gestures to herself, as though she has just delighted a crowd by emerging from a cake. She is wearing a cerise skirt suit, with a petrol blue polo neck. Her earrings could broadcast FM radio.

'Anyway, we're not going to be nervous today, are we? Not now that I'm here. We're going to seize the day! We're not going to' – she forces a grin, and then reaches up to pinch the inside skin of my elbow. I know it's supposed to be affectionate, but she pinches hard. I can feel it through my thermals – '*eff* this up, are we? *Are we?*'

I don't know how to answer her. Instead, I call out into the room in the brightest voice I can muster. 'Where do you want me? Let me know when you're ready to get started!' I don't sound like myself, but I recognise the register. Alison's genes will out.

Natasha puts her phone in her pocket and comes over. 'I'll take you through to hair and makeup now. Leticia is on her way; apparently her train got cancelled so she's getting a cab.' I am ushered to the third corner, which has been partitioned off. It's the brightest, whitest space of all. I see a desk and three giant mirrors, all framed by swollen lightbulbs.

I'm assailed by a sense memory – a wash of comfort, and a pang of something sharp and sad. A long time ago, I owned the doll-sized pink version of this desk. When I was able to get hold of some batteries, I could switch the lights on.

It was my most prized possession, and I used to wonder

whether I could find a friendly scientist to zap the whole thing into life-sized splendour with a gamma ray. Bean was the scornful pin in my balloon. 'You don't want to be like bimbo Barbie, looking at herself all day long, loving herself, waiting for Action Man.'

I didn't cry and I certainly didn't tell her that it's Ken, and only Ken, that Barbie waits for. But I never switched the lights on again.

Today, at last, I get to be Barbie. No one would ever say that Barbie isn't beautiful. No one would ever expect her to be anything else.

'... so if you head into the cubicle you can put a robe on, then Jenny can get started. We'll bring through styling options when Leticia is here – she's in charge of the brief. It might be best to get undressed now, if that's OK. It saves us some time at the other end.'

Jenny – I assume – hands me a robe. 'Put that on in the cubicle, lovie. Just in the corner over there. It's *so* nice to meet you, Frankie. I'm really thrilled to be doing this today.' She is looking at me as though she has spent her whole life waiting to welcome me to Oz.

The joy surges again. Everyone here is so nice! Perhaps I am, too. Maybe the rest of my life has been a bad dream and I've woken up in photo-shoot land – a place where I'm pretty, and kind, and everyone is pleased to see me.

I am disabused of this delusion as soon as I enter the cubicle.

The light bounces off the four small walls of the tiny box. I feel more exposed than illuminated. Was the skin on my stomach always this mottled? My knees must have aged in the night. I bend down, trying to ease off my tights, and as my elbows fly up they knock the back of the cubicle, making it shake. As I unhook my bra my tits bounce out. They're not small, but today, in here, they seem enormous, vulgar. I feel as though I've turned up to a wake with a pair of striped beach balls.

The robe goes on. Again, I nearly knock the cubicle over. It looks soft, cosy and voluminous, but this is a lie perpetrated by the wizard sleeves. Fabric grazes my fingertips and renders me clumsy. I struggle to pull the robe across my chest, only just managing to tie it around my torso, even though my waist is relatively small. Alison has yanked enough tape measures around me over the years to reassure me of that. (Although it's 'an inch and a half bigger than mine, on my wedding day' – a fact that seems to bring her both sorrow and joy.)

I leave my knickers on, checking to make sure that they are still relatively new, white and plain. I'm genuinely concerned that they played a trick on me, that they're in cahoots with my oldest, grubbiest pants and have sneakily swapped places before I left the house. Or that they have cooked up a scheme with my menstrual cycle and brought my period on in the last hour.

I step out of the strange little hut and see that Jenny is waiting for me. She touches my sleeve and looks up hopefully. 'Ready to get started?' Maybe I have started a cult by accident. I'm in a white robe, being followed by people who seem creepily cheerful.

Jenny motions at me to sit in front of the Barbie mirror and fastens a black bib around my neck. 'You've got such lovely skin,' she coos. 'Really glowy. Do you use an LED mask?'

'I don't *think* so,' I reply, trying to remind myself of what an LED mask is. 'Are they the ones that make you look like you're in Daft Punk, and cost about a thousand pounds? No, I'd definitely remember that.' Perhaps this is a victory for Alison, and her Clinique and Clarins. She mustn't find out. I'll never hear the end of it.

'I'm going to put a tiny bit of primer on, if that's OK. You don't need much,' says Jenny, her hands cool and smooth on my flushed face. I want to say, 'Actually, loads, please! Pile it on! I need help!' But she keeps talking. Her voice is soft and soothing too. I'd guessed that she was around Alison's age, but she sounds young, the pitch of her sentences rising and falling. I picture a shoreline, clear warm water lapping at the sand.

Closing my eyes, I feel sleep starting to tug at me. I suppose I have been awake for hours. I catch the odd phrase. 'And when I heard about your sister, I was so moved ... adorable.'

I make a vague, grateful noise. I'm drifting away, hearing her words, but not understanding them immediately.

'My little sister ... her kidneys. Impossible to find a match. I was desperate to give her mine, but – just close your eyes for a minute, lovey. What fabulous lashes! Do you use a serum? – anyway, she's still with us, and dialysis is quite effective ... Just going to pop a tiny bit of highlighter here, it's a trade secret! Really opens up your brow bone.' Just as Alison did moments ago, Jenny holds my chin in her hands and forces my face up to the light. 'Very, very nice.'

It is all very nice, isn't it? I bask in the heat, the glow, coming from Jenny and the lightbulbs. 'Lovely, thank you ... hold on! You tried to give your sister your kidney? Oh my God! And she hasn't found a match? I'm so sorry.'

Jenny smiles, sadly. 'It's much more common than you think. I had no idea, before it happened to our family. Anyway, today is all about *you*. You're the real hero! Careful, sweetie, take your head out of your hands. In fact, don't touch your face before I use the setting spray.'

Sure. All about me. Because of something I wrote in crayon, when I was seven, with terrible spelling. I've tricked all these people, and I feel *horrible*. I wonder if I can give Jenny's sister my kidney.

'All done, Frankie. Gorgeous, absolutely gorgeous! It was a pleasure.' She squeezes my shoulder and drops her voice to a whisper. 'And I think you're so bloody brave.'

In the mirror, a slightly scared, slightly embarrassed woman stares back at us both.

I definitely don't look beautiful; however, I do seem sort of wholesome, I suppose. I wish Jenny hadn't soft pedalled the eyeliner. Or the bronzer. I don't look sexy at all – which is an horrific thing to think, under the circumstances. I look like me, just younger. I blink, smile and stick out my chin. 'Thank you very much!'

Natasha returns before I'm out of my seat. 'Oh, Frankie, you look beautiful, absolutely gorgeous. Fantastic job, Jenny! Lovely and natural, fresh and bright. Beautiful!' That must be an empty compliment, a word to throw around and make everybody feel good.

'Right, let's go get started, then!' Natasha starts walking quickly, and I'm tripping over my own feet as I get up and follow her. I change my pace into a lolloping trot to catch up. 'Leticia is finally here. Let's find a beautiful dress to go with that beautiful face.'

For a split second, I hope and pray that Jenny and

Natasha have discovered my beauty, and uncovered it. That after a lifetime of being good and patient, beauty finally arrived in the night. As Natasha leads me across the studio, I sneakily squint at reflective surfaces, but none of them reveal anything to justify all the compliments. I look like a human woman – albeit one who is maybe 30 per cent eyebrow. Nose is OK, mouth is OK, there seems to be a suggestion of a double chin. All of this fuss and effort to look average. This cannot be 'absolutely gorgeous'. I'm still the same, plain woman. I really shouldn't be here.

Leticia, on the other hand, is truly beautiful, quietly and with dignity. Strong brows, no visible makeup, wax-smooth skin with the slightest, softest pink on her cheeks. She's wearing those horrible stonewashed jeans that come up almost to her armpits, but they only serve to accentuate her utter loveliness. She looks like she's about to give me a tutorial on perfect organic overnight oats. She exudes calm. And beside her is Alison, vibrating with chaos.

'I'm just worried that the pink will *drain* Frankie,' she says, in her Talking To Idiots voice. 'Oh, hello, darling, you look very nice indeed. They did a lovely job on your pores. Although maybe a nice bright lip ... '

'Frankie! Can I give you a hug? It's so good to meet you.' Leticia is even more beautiful when her face is animated. Every word seems to be turning up an internal dimmer switch. 'This is a real honour for all of us, it's such an important campaign. We're lucky to be working with you.'

I don't know what to say, so I panic, and laugh. Everyone looks at me a little oddly and carries on. 'Great that your mum is here too, she's been really helpful,' says Leticia, and her right eyelid flickers, infinitesimally. She's on my side.

'We've got a gorgeous rack of dresses for you to choose from, some fabulous options here. We were thinking pink, because it's a colour traditionally associated with breast cancer, and it will focus everyone's minds on the cause. But your mum—'

'I think this is rather fetching!' cries Alison. 'So much fun!' She plucks a vast, bright, floaty sheet from the rack and thrusts it at me.

I hadn't realised the proffered garment was wearable. I assumed it was a collection of swatches, and that someone would hold different sections up to my face and make a mysterious declaration. 'Winter, with sallow undertones.' The dress Alison has shoved into my arms is an equilateral triangle with straps, made of layers of green, yellow, blue and red. It doesn't look like a dress. It looks like a diagram.

'It might be a little busy, for me,' I say, nervously. I have travelled back in time – I feel twelve again, about to have a futile argument with Alison in a department store changing room. 'This is lovely,' I say, longingly fingering a white cotton slip, plain but for the pink, yellow and blue buttons that run from the bodice to the hem. A sweetie dress. And maybe, a sexy dress. I wonder where it comes from? I'd wear this for my own photos, one strap sliding off my shoulder, a button undone here and there ...

Leticia and Alison exchange a look. Leticia was supposed to be on my team! Are they ganging up on me? 'It's a lovely dress,' Leticia says, diplomatically, 'but perhaps a bit, ah, booby, for today. What about this one?' She passes me a hanger and nods at Alison. 'I know we didn't want to go too pale, but let's give it a try. I've seen the page layouts, it's perfect for the campaign branding. It should show up a little bit brighter on the photographs.'

The dress is made of sugar pink, slippery satin. It has a high neck and a sash. I think it's supposed to be a maxi dress, but it will hit well above my ankle. It's not the sort of outfit I would ever have picked out for myself – mostly because it looks far too small.

'Lovely, I'll give it a try,' I say. 'But it might not fit.'

Tiny Leticia dismisses this with a wave of her hand. 'Oh, don't worry about that. It's what safety pins are for!'

I'm given a box of American tan tights (size medium – I'll be lucky if they come up to my knees) and a dinky pair of nude court shoes before I am shunted back to the cubicle.

Miraculously, the zip almost closes. It's concealed under the armpit so no one can see that it's slightly too small. The sleeves are tight, and my shoulders are raised, hoisted about half an inch above where they are supposed to sit. Constricted by the tights, I totter out. My feet registered a brief protest of pain as I forced them inside the court shoes, but now they're numb. I feel nothing. Maybe the numbness will creep up my legs, towards my torso, and inside my brain. I don't feel beautiful, but I won't mind if I'm not feeling anything at all.

Leticia and Alison are now both giving me the cult smile. 'Oh, Frances,' breathes Alison. 'I'm so, so proud of you.' And that cuts through the nothingness. It's a golden moment to hold, amid the grey. She hugs me and releases me abruptly when she starts to sniffle. 'Mustn't muss up your dress. Careful, don't cry. Keep smiling, for Bean.' Alison looks around the studio, as though she's expecting Bean to spring out from behind a plant pot or under a sofa cushion. 'It really is a shame that she's not here too.'

'Well, of course she can't come today,' I say. There's a

sting and a snap in my voice. I must neutralise it. I can't let on about later. 'She's got her team meeting,' I add, pointlessly.

A woman is waiting to approach the group, and I smile at her, recognising a kindred sartorial spirit. Grey T-shirt. Jeans that might have been black half a decade ago. There's a hole in her muddy Converse and a matching hole in her sock. She is also beautiful – and very familiar. 'Nice to see you!' I say, trying to figure out where I know her from.

Then I clap my hand over my mouth when I realise she's not an acquaintance I can't place but someone I must have seen on TV. She looks like the actress Taj Atwal. Maybe she *is*. Maybe she's doing a shoot, and we're standing in her way. She could pull off the mad triangle dress.

'You must be Frankie,' she says, taking my hand. 'I'm Hettie Bhaskar, and I'm doing the photos for' – she pauses. I think she's trying not to laugh – '"be kind for cancer". Or do I call it "hashtag be kind for cancer"?'

Leticia frowns. Is she going to tell Hettie off? 'Hettie, great to have you with us today. Hettie is an award-winning photographer, she's just got back from a big trip with Oxfam. We thought she'd be the perfect person to do this shoot.'

Hettie grins. 'I'm not allowed to tell you *who* I went with yet, because I signed an NDA. But I can tell you that she's a celebrated, venerated national treasure – an actual dame – and that I had the pleasure of watching her shit in a bin. Bad chicken, which is hilarious because she is famously usually vegetarian. But she's fine now. Her publicist *hates* me because I pretended to take a picture while it was happening. She thought it was hysterical. Right. Let's get set up.'

In the main body of the studio, there's a selection of blazing lights, coiled leads and what appears to be a large, silver umbrella. A giant roll of hot pink paper forms a wall and a floor. Everything seems slightly too bright, too vivid – as though it's lit by that sickly-sharp flash of sun you see before a storm. Perhaps this is how the *Post* people have chosen to manifest 'being kind'. I can't quite relax; I'm worried that if I do a gang of Munchkins might appear and batter me to death with lollipops.

At least Hettie seems sensible, scruffy, normal. 'Frankie, could you just stand in the middle of the pink?' she asks me. 'Lovely, yes, I'll get a read of the light. It's nice to be doing some portraiture, after weeks of crouching in a ditch, worried people were going to stand on my DSLR.' She stands behind her tripod, steps out, steps back and clicks. 'I was a bit worried about the pink on pink, but it's looking good.'

'So' – I know I'm about to ask a stupid question, but my curiosity has got the better of me – 'is that a DSLR that you're using at the moment? How does it compare with other cameras?'

'Can you take a step forward, slightly to the right? Great, now a step to the left for me? It's like I'm leading the calls for a hoedown,' she laughs. 'The DSLR is getting a bit old fashioned now, but I love using them for anything reportage-y – what you see through the lens is what you get. If you don't have much time to set up a shot, they are great. And I'm sentimental, I've had mine for years, and I've added all sorts of bits and pieces. But this is a mirrorless camera, which usually gives you more options when you edit.'

'Like filtering?' I ask.

'Oooh, yeah, good face, Frankie! Sort of "friendly

newsreader-y". Can you do that again?' I'm not sure. My face falls, and Hettie notices. 'Keep asking me questions. Ask me anything you like! Are you a photographer?'

'Me? Oh, no, no, no. I just mess about a bit on my phone sometimes.' I shrug. 'I like ProShot and Snapseed, and I've been having a look at Adobe Lightroom, but it's kind of pricey,' I say. 'Is it worth bothering with? Sorry, you probably use the proper, serious ones.'

'Perfect, yes, friendly newsreader is back! These are great! You've got such a good face to photograph, really animated. It's unusual, actually. Lots of younger women can only do "selfie face". You know, they don't *move*.' Hettie cackles. I do know. All too well.

She falls into a sort of drop squat while adjusting the height of the tripod. 'I'm doing some low-angle shots because they're supposed to make the subject look "sort of heroic".' She stretches her arms out and makes air quotes from either side of the camera. 'But then, I'm sure you know all about that.'

'About low-angle shots?' I ask. I did not know.

'About being sort of heroic! The *Post*'s hero of the hour, the nation's sweetheart.' She sounds sarcastic, but she's smiling, and I laugh. 'Lovely, lovely! Yeah, anyway, I think the apps are great. If you like ProShot, I reckon you'd get a lot out of Lightroom, it's really versatile. Can you look off into the distance for me. Like, like ... like you're sort of sad, but wistful. Trying not to think about things.'

How does she know?

I wobble on my feet, inhale, exhale and look up at the studio ceiling. 'Good, good,' says Hettie. 'Hey, I think I've got a free trial code for Lightroom. When we're done, I'll dig it out for you. You get three months; I'm allowed to share it with other pros.'

'Oh, but I'm really not—' I begin, and then I make a decision. 'Thank you, I'd love that,' I say. For the next few moments, joy can feel bigger than truth. Hettie thinks I'm a pro. She's speaking to me about her work, her art, as though I'm an equal. As though she respects me. Although, if she knew the truth about my photographs ... I don't want to think about it. Or about what it might really mean for me to be 'a pro'.

'Good, hold that face, I think we need some that are a bit sad, a bit serious ... and we've got it! We're all set.' Hettie steps out from behind her camera and walks towards me with her hand outstretched. 'That was a genuine pleasure, Frankie, thank you. As the kids say, you understood the assignment.'

As she shakes my hand, she lowers her voice. 'I *am* sorry about your sister. Between us, I've seen these campaigns and I know they can be quite a lot for everyone concerned. I hope it goes well. I hope you get what you want.'

She walks away from me, towards an open laptop where Natasha and Leticia are cooing. I squat down and try to pull at the heel of my shoe. It takes five tugs to wrench it off.

Hobbling over to the group, I realise I've lost all track of time. Where am I? Can I get across London in an hour?

'These are *lovely*, Frankie, we're really pleased,' says Leticia. 'Absolutely stunning.' It takes me a moment to work out why this sounds so strange and yet so familiar. It's the sort of comment I usually only see written, online. 'We thought we'd take you out for a celebratory lunch! Your mum too, of course! It would be good to discuss next steps, follow up features, that sort of thing.'

'I can't, I'm so sorry, I've got to ... get back to work.' Alison's face falls. 'Darling, surely Miriam would understand.'

'She's got an appointment this afternoon, I promised I'd hold the fort,' I lie, smoothly and easily. I wish Bean would just let me tell our mother. But then we all know where that might end. Alison, in her skirt suit, stage managing a photo shoot from hospital. ('Can't we get rid of the IV drips? They're a bit depressing, aren't they? Maybe some fairy lights instead!') 'But you should definitely go, Mum. You're in charge! You can be my manager, ha ha!' I regret the words instantly.

'Let me get that code for you, before you go,' says Hettie. Natasha and Leticia turn to me, awed, as though they are a pair of squirrels and I am St Francis of Assisi.

'Really, *really* good to meet you today,' says Natasha. 'Thank you. Thank you for everything you do. We are just so lucky to have you.'

'Absolutely,' adds Leticia. 'Kindness is *so* important right now. Listen, I just spoke to Polly and the label wants to gift you that dress. Keep it on. You deserve it, truly.' I have no idea who Polly is, but I'm glad I don't have to wrestle with the zip just yet.

As I gather my various layers and watch Alison glow with anticipation for her fancy business lunch, I start to wonder whether Leticia and Natasha might be right. Maybe I am a good person, after all. Maybe it's this easy.

Chapter Seventeen

Probably but not definitely

I promised Bean I'd be at the hospital by 1.45. It's 2.02 when the taxi pulls in. The driver was garrulous when I told him where I was going. Had I seen that thing in the paper? About 'that bird with the sister'? Really heart-warming. Nice to celebrate some old-fashioned family values – kindness, was that it? Five million, he reckoned they'd raised. Or point five million, he couldn't remember. Of course, charity these days is a racket, isn't it? A scam. Did I remember that scandal a few years back? Those poor kiddies. All that money, missing. Mind you, the money ought to be going to the kiddies, not the cats. His missus likes Cats Protection, but she did do a sponsored fun run for cancer a few years back, when her brother had something with his down-belows. Prostate, prostrate, he can never remember which one.

I smile, I nod, I alternate my *mmm*s and *oooh*s and *right*s. I sink down further into my seat. And when he misses the turning and we crawl around the block again, I swear in my head, pretending I am doing a sponsored silence.

Every few minutes, I'd thought about messaging to explain about the traffic. I'd texted, On my way!!! XXXXX at the start of the journey, but Bean once told me that she hates it when someone spends half an hour apologising for how late they are about to be. 'Just be late and take the hit. I probably won't even notice! I'm a busy woman, I don't have time to make you feel better about your lack of planning. I've got things to do. Packets of Kettle Chips to empty into small ornamental bowls.' Admittedly, this was specifically about parties, but I suspect the rule also applies today.

As the taxi crawls along, I start to panic about whether we are going to the right place, whether the mysterious combination of letters and numbers, units and blocks would get me to the correct bit of hospital. I picture myself running down endless corridors, flinging myself through doorways, a human gurney, screaming, 'WHERE IS MY SISTER?' It's a bit of an anticlimax to get to the carpark and be greeted by a grumpy man shrouded by a caramel-scented cloud that I could smell from inside the car. How long has he been out here, vaping? 'Paul!' I yell. *'Paul!'*

He smiles, sort of. I can see his teeth.

After a flurry of 'Great, thanks, fine, you too, lovely, lovely, thank you' and a small panic about payment (Why was my card declined? Oh, because I got my own PIN wrong), I fall out through the sliding door and attempt to hug my brother-in-law. He seems very small and very grey. It occurs to me that this pink, shiny dress is all wrong. I have come to this serious, sombre place in drag. Out of place, and out of time.

'Sorry I'm late,' I say. 'How is she? Where is she? How are you?'

'Can't be helped, I suppose,' he says, smiling tightly. 'You had your *thing*. Anyway, we got here ridiculously early, so she's already had her ultrasound. She's in the holding area.'

'The holding area? What's that? It sounds a bit *Border Force*. "No, officer, these live chickens are purely for domestic use, honest!"' It's a risk, and I wait for Paul to tell me off, but he laughs.

'I thought that,' he said. 'Bean went rude, obviously. She thinks it's about "holding your own". She said she could have a last go on her – and I quote – "jubblies".' I snort, and stop, abruptly.

'But it's not her *last*—'

Paul cuts me off. 'Frankie, I'm going to ask you to do what I'm doing. We can't make any predictions, good or bad. It doesn't help. It won't help her. We've just got to try, very hard, to take each bit as it comes.' He puts his vape in his pocket, and we walk through the doors.

I can hear someone laughing. How can *anyone* laugh at a time like this? But then, I was laughing too, a few moments ago. Nothing makes sense. I remind myself that this is a place of healing. This is where people come to get better.

We follow the sound of the laugh. Paul opens another door. We see a woman in blue scrubs, a stethoscope around her neck. She might be in her early forties, and she's absolutely cracking up. Standing, but bent double. And in a chair below her is Bean. She's in a white gown with blue spots, and barefoot. I stare at her feet.

It's so weird how you're sure you know every inch of a person, and yet you almost never consider their feet. Bean's are lovely, of course. Long toes, high arches, slim ankles. Her toenails match her fingernails, lilac, pale and glossy.

151

Her cheeks are flushed, and her eyes are sparkling, yet she seems paler than usual. Maybe it's the light. I hope it's the light.

'I'd never heard that before!' says the woman, wiping her eyes.

'It's Frankie's favourite joke,' says Bean. 'Well, one of them. Frankie, this is my consultant, Dr Zainab. I just told her about the difference between oral and anal sex.'

'Ah, yes. Oral sex makes your day, anal sex makes your whole week. And your hole weak,' I say. Paul looks quite shocked.

The woman laughs again, coughs, then straightens up and shakes my hand. 'Hello, Frankie! I keep telling your sister that just Zainab is fine.'

'No, no,' says Bean. 'Firstly, I think anyone who has been to medical school should remind us all of their hard work at every opportunity. Secondly, I want to remind myself that I am in a super-safe pair of hands.'

Dr Zainab smirks. 'Are you, though? How do you know I didn't just wander in off the street?' She plucks at her stethoscope. 'You put one of these on, they'll let you do *anything*. Frankie, do you want a go? We could swap clothes, and you could try your hand at a little brain surgery?' I squeak out a laugh but my face betrays me. 'Oh, sweetie, I'm kidding,' she says. 'I promise I'm an absolute expert. A breastspert. Ew, sorry, that's a horrible portmanteau.'

'But,' says Bean, solemnly, 'she has also promised to keep my breast pert. As much as possible.'

Dr Zainab nods. 'The great news is that it appears nothing has spread to the lymph nodes. We'll be able to confirm your sister's treatment plan after today. At the moment it looks like we're probably going to retain most of the breast—'

'Probably?' Bean's voice is raised, and wobbling. I reach to touch her, to squeeze her shoulder, but she shrugs me off. Then she continues, her voice now barely above a whisper, 'Dr Zainab, I thought you said ... well, probably isn't definitely, is it?'

Paul reaches for her other shoulder. 'Babe, we've had these conversations, we know there isn't any "definitely". One day at a time, like we said. And you couldn't be in a better place. The odds are good.'

'It's just that the goods are odd,' she says, and barks a laugh, before bursting into tears. 'I'm sorry, I'm sorry, Dr Zainab, I'm so sorry.'

I suspect this isn't the first time Dr Zainab has seen this. 'Listen, I hate to do this, but we must go in soon. But if you don't want to do it today, we don't have to do it today.' Paul and I look at each other with alarm. No, she *has* to do it today. If I have to do the surgery myself, it needs to happen today.

Bean shakes her head. A tear lands on my chin. 'No, today is good. I want to get it over with.'

She breathes out. 'I know this isn't logical, but I keep thinking, *It's not fair.* All I have ever done is try to keep myself safe. And keep my family safe. I don't take risks, ever. Because I don't do "probably", only "definitely". And what has been the fucking point of that? Sorry, I shouldn't swear here.'

Dr Zainab smiles wryly. 'It's fine, really. Everyone swears here, why wouldn't you? It's a place to be extra sweary, all things considered. Right, guys. You can come back and

153

collect her in about two hours. That allows us time for observation – and, crucially, admin. Masses of it. We love doing paperwork here. Love it.' She rolls her eyes.

'Is there anything useful we can do in the meantime?' I ask. 'Bean, do you need anything?'

Bean forces a smile. 'What I really want is every single trashy mag you can lay your hands on. *Take A Break. The National Enquirer.* It would really cheer me up to read about a woman whose husband cheated on her with a ghost.'

'On it!' I'm also going to hunt for green Jelly Babies.

Paul smacks his forehead, theatrically. 'Dinner! I was going to make you a fabulous dinner. I meant to see if that place on Northcote Road had any lobster. I could probably still find some lobster from somewhere.'

'Actually, I was hoping for Domino's. The cheeseburger one, with a stuffed crust,' says Bean. I know this voice. I've heard Jon use it when he claimed he'd heard about a law banning bedtime on the news.

'Are you sure that's OK? It's not very healthy, and I know that post recovery you're going to need fresh food, nutrients—'

Dr Zainab interrupts before Paul can go on. 'There's nothing wrong with pizza after a day like today,' she says, gently. 'By the way, I'm supposed to ask you not to smoke or vape outside the building, but there's a secret smoking area that some of the doctors use at the other end of the car park.'

She shakes my hand, then Paul's, and I bend over to hug Bean and kiss her on the cheek. I think about saying, 'You do not got this' to make her laugh, but it doesn't feel right. 'I love you,' I murmur. 'And you are the kindest human I know.'

154

'Wish on an eyelash for me,' she says, squeezing back.

Paul stares at me expectantly, and I know I need to let them have a moment together, alone. I turn away and walk through the doors, through the car park and over the main road. Then, stumbling up a side street, I sit beside the trunk of a tree on the freezing ground. I look up at the bare branches. The sky is opaque, pale grey. There is nothing to wish on. With my head in my hands, I cry, quietly.

Chapter Eighteen

Complete rest

'The paper shops and convenience stores have been good to us. Hot off the press, this week's *What A Shocker*: "Snakes on a plane – the airport surprise that slithered into my handbag!"' I unroll the magazine with a flourish.

'Also, *Time For Chat* has: "Caught Out During Special Delivery! Husband found postie in my box!" And best of all' – I drop the floppy, glossy magazine onto Bean's lap – 'In *Crazy Cuppa*: "My past-life sex life with Henry VIII!"'

She looks up at me and grins. 'I *knew* you'd understand the brief.' She seems grey, drained. I want to find Dr Zainab, or nudge Paul, and say, 'We *all* look like shit, right? Is it the lighting?' But I can't bring myself to draw attention to it. Bean is ill. She seems much more ill than she did a couple of hours ago. She's laughing but she looks exhausted by the effort of it.

How can I help? 'Shall I read you the Henry VIII one? I'll do a sexy, husky voice and everything.' Bean holds her hand up, and I try not to think about how hard this looks, how fragile she is. Her head seems much too big for her poor body. 'Frankie, I can't cope. I don't want to hear my little sister describing historical sex to me.'

Breathy, low, I begin. 'Henry slowly unrolled one leg of his weird Tudor man-tights and winked at me. "Baby, I need you to hold my ... doubloons ..."'

Bean honks. 'No, Frankie, I *mean* it. Don't make me laugh, it hurts. I don't think this dressing is secure enough. What is a doubloon, anyway? Isn't it pirate treasure? I thought it was a coin.'

'Frankie, you're thinking of doublet and hose,' says Paul. 'Can I have a quick chat with you for a second?' He nods at the doorway and then gives me a firm but gentle push.

As soon as we're outside, I start whispering, frantically. 'Have they told you anything? Because I know they said it all went fine, but she really does look pale; she doesn't look well at all.'

Paul sounds stern. 'Frankie, you need to go home.' For a moment, I assume he means *come* home, which is exactly what I've pictured. I'll be at Bean's side, a tea and biscuit machine, plumping pillows, making her laugh, finding her unwatched Netflix treasure.

'Go home?' I repeat, confused.

'Yeah. Bean is exhausted already, and you're tiring her out. I need to get back to Clapham and get her to bed – she needs a proper rest.'

'But I thought I'd be coming with you?' I say, too quickly. I sound shrill. 'To look after her?'

Paul's sigh is parental and familiar. I wonder whether he is about to tell me that *Stranger Things* is too scary, or that it's dangerous to put the slide in the paddling pool.

'Frankie, you can't look after Bean because she always

157

ends up looking after you. Everything ends up being about you, doesn't it? Dr Zainab has said she needs complete rest. No stress, *at all*. It's so important that she's as healthy as possible when she goes in for her radiotherapy. It doesn't matter about the supplements, the vitamins, all the rest of it – she can't get anxious, she can't get worked up, she can't have you bringing your usual chaos.'

It's suddenly strangely hot, in the hospital corridor. I feel slightly sick. I claw at the doorframe. 'But Paul, I can't not see her. That doesn't make any sense. God, I feel a bit ...' My vision starts to blur, and I slide down the wall.

'Fucksake,' he hisses. 'See? This is exactly what I mean. Typical Frankie drama. Now, you get back in there, you say a nice goodbye to my wife, and you leave us alone for a while. I will message you when I think she's up to seeing you. But if you love her half as much as I do, you'll do this for her. For the boys. For me.'

I think I'm blacking out, burning up. The air is too thick, my ears seem too thick. I'm trying to open my eyes but the dark swirls in front of me, a silver-edged pool about to suck me in. I gag, and swallow. Thank God I'm in a hospital.

Paul is pulling me to my feet; his fingers circle my wrists and they pinch. 'Don't go back in now. I don't want Bean seeing you like this. You are going to go to the toilet, where you will splash some cold water on your face and compose yourself.'

Dazed, I press my palms against the cool walls until I'm steady enough to open my eyes. Eventually, I'm able to find the loos.

In the toilets, I press down on the top of the tap, and it

dispenses a three-second dribble of water. I splash my face and press again.

Fuck him.
He hates me.
I hate him.

How come *he* gets to come home with Bean?

I splash my face again.

This isn't about me.

And again.

If eating a live toad every morning, every day, for the rest of my life would cure my sister, I'd do it. I'd shave my head for her. I'd join the foreign legion. I'd have sex with Rupert. But Paul isn't asking for a grand gesture. Bean needs rest.

And I need her to need me, but what I need doesn't matter right now.

I do need a hand towel, though. I try to pull one out of the dispenser and get a wasteful inch. I pluck one from the top and attempt to get the rest back in. Giving up, I pat my face. Layers of chalky orange come off, and I'm left with a death-mask pile. The Turin Shroud.

Bean has fallen asleep holding her copy of *Crazy Cuppa*. Paul holds a finger to his lips. He frowns as I press my mouth to the top of her head. She smells of English Pear and

Freesia, baby shampoo, plastic and plasticine and something I can't place – chemical, fetid. I make a heart shape with my fingers and blow her a kiss before walking away.

Chapter Nineteen

Obliteration

I didn't cry on the bus. I couldn't; nothing came out. The emotional storm clouds had been oppressive, and I needed a crash, a snap, a breaking after the rolling and gathering. But the liquid had become solid.

I thought something would hit me when I walked up my own road, when my key was in the door. It's like losing a sneeze, though. Now I'm sitting at the bottom of my bed, still in my coat, staring at the wall. Nearly numb, but not quite numb enough.

The familiar itch is tugging at the edges of my consciousness. The longing is a tendril of smoke, uncurling, making me softer, filling me up. I know what would make me feel OK, for a moment. But there must be better ways. Healthier ways.

I could call Paul and scream at him.

I could punch the wall. Or run towards it and knock myself unconscious. Maybe I could bring on a small, manageable coma. I'll come round, and Bean will be better.

I could go to the shop and buy a bottle of wine and race

myself. Will I finish it before I pass out? I could pick up some trashy mags, and maybe Bean will sense that we're together, reading the same silly stories.

I wish the ghost of Henry VIII would come along and fuck me. It would allow me to escape this for a few minutes.

It probably wouldn't be that satisfying. A little chilly, a little ticklish. And I wouldn't want foreplay. There might be poems – or worse, a lute.

But if I could summon a faceless spirit to tear my clothes off, slam the tension out of me, and leave, I might feel better. I might feel something. I don't want a person with a penis – and worse, their own wants and needs and feelings. I want to be fucked like a fairground ride. Or by a fairground ride. If only I could make it anonymous, keep it secret. No one would need to know.

As I pull my coat off, I remember the dress. Sweet, slippery, now slightly sweaty. I feel like an overgrown toddler. This is who I'm supposed to be: the nation's perfect little sister. Although I'm not perfect at all, am I? I'm so needy and annoying that I might make Bean even more ill. What kind of monster would think about fucking, now?

Monsters aren't meant to wear pretty pink dresses. I know what I am. Who I am.

I pull the dress over my head and it gets stuck. I'm alone. I can't move my arms. I can't reach the zip. Maybe I'll have to stay like this forever! Or *maybe* some faceless intruder will break in and bend me over . . .

I hear the sound of ripping, and then I'm free.

I can't fight myself, or my compulsions. I'm so desperate that I have become destructive.

I'm so anxious to get to The Drawer that I'm searching

162

and scrabbling before I've finished stepping out of my underwear. I almost fall and have to grab the handle for support. There's nothing here. Why is there nothing here for the woman – the *thing* – I need to be right now? What was I thinking? I want to look available for full sexual obliteration, but all I have is the sort of lingerie you'd wear if you were an Easter egg. Too many pastels, too many flowers. I don't understand what I want. I can't picture it. I'd *know* it, if only I could see it. I want to go to one of those truly terrifying Soho sex shops and buy something that is usually kept under lock and key. Something that would make the assistant turn pale and say, 'I'm not sure we're legally allowed to sell this.'

Panicking, I pick the pink dress up off the floor. I'm sure I have nail scissors, somewhere. *The brand wants to give you the dress, Frankie. Because you're special and magical and curing cancer.* They don't know the truth about me and my family. I'm toxic. A cause, not a cure. Hacking at a sleeve, I grunt, I feel a sense of release. I don't know what I'm doing but it feels good. I take off the other sleeve and slash at the skirt. Then, I cut a great big 'U' out of the front. This is either an act of genius or of madness. When I put the butchered dress on, I'll look so stupid that I'll be forced to finally have the big cry. *Then* I'll go and get wine.

I'll say this for my guerrilla tailoring: the dress is much more comfortable now. I close my eyes before I look in the mirror. There isn't a hope that this will have worked. I'm expecting to see what I saw under the fluorescent lights of the hospital toilets – a flushed, puffed, swollen, smeared, grubby woman.

But when I open my eyes, I am surprised. I have turned into Tinkerbell.

The reflected face is still a mess, albeit a fixable mess. The bitten lips look softer and pinker than usual. The eyes have settled, cooled by the winter air. Shining and feline, no longer red.

But the body has been reshaped, transformed by the altered line of the dress that encases it. It's all leg, all curve, pink satin on pink flesh, nipped in and falling out and torn and touchable.

The woman in the mirror is a gorgeous, haunted wreck. You could do anything to her. Everything has already happened to her.

I look so much better in this room, in this light, with a ripped dress and a ruined face. Hours ago, I was supposed to be 'beautiful'. I'm still far from it, but I feel so much closer. I don't understand.

It takes me a moment to find my phone, and as I'm hunting for it I remember Hettie and the conversation we had at the shoot. Should I download that app? I could really craft these pictures into something special. But I'm panicky, impatient, greedy to get going. I put some mascara on, and I resent the length of time that it takes. I search for shoes, and it's another boring, infuriating distraction. I can't name this craving, but it's unbearable. I'm swollen with it.

Standing on my tiptoes, looking over my shoulder, I turn towards the mirror, and it's no good. The fabric is too shiny, the back of the dress is too boring. I turn around, lean forward a little, my elbows bent back, my lashes lowered. That's a bit better. Now in the mirror I look luscious, overripe. I take a burst of pictures, moving backwards and forwards, smirking and pouting. But on my phone, they look flat. I look lifeless. Oh, for a proper studio! If only I could get my hands on Hettie's camera.

I turn the big light on and try again. But it's all wrong. In the mirror, the colours are strange, the dress is too pink and my skin is too red. Still, I take the pictures. I do not look like anyone's ultimate fantasy. I look like I have been hired to draw the raffle at a boat show.

I'll try the bed. Lying on my stomach, falling out of my dress, peering, post coitally, through my hair. The bedside lamp makes the photos softer, sexier. These are fine, I guess. Not great, but they'll do. But the itch stays unscratched; I'm still vibrating with longing and rage and something I simply cannot define.

Maybe I should take a shower, take a walk. It's too soon to post these. I'll wait until I've calmed down. I roll over and close my eyes. What does Miriam say? *Breathe in compassion for yourself. Breathe out compassion for everyone else.*

I breathe in, counting one, two, three, four, five, six ...

I've picked up my laptop before I start to exhale.

A smattering of flashing circles shows that I have nine new subscribers. It's a lot, for me. The itch, the edginess, starts to abate. I'm still tense, and scratchy, but my blood isn't prickling quite as badly.

As I upload the pictures, I notice the 'video chat' icon, winking away. I've seen it so many times, but I've never used it before. I've never felt that I needed it before.

I click.

Your fans have been notified that you are available for video chat. You will be paid by AutoBill, minus our administrative fees.

If I stay here, I am crossing a line. My finger hovers over the 'exit' button.

John_101 wants to chat

'Hello?' I hear a male voice. I can't guess an age, I can't detect an accent. His camera is off. I feel exposed – not because I'm falling out of my self-altered dress, but because of everything else that John_101 might see. My unmade bed. The open drawers. The plates and mugs and tatty tote bags.

'Hello,' I say, using my husky voice again. 'I'm F— Hi.'

'You haven't done this before, have you?' says the voice. It's almost robotic. I wonder whether it is automatically disguised, autotuned. 'I can see you haven't tidied up. Are you a bit of a slut? Have you been fucking in that bed?'

'Goodness me, no!' I say, blushing. Who is this rude man? And *why* is this kind of turning me on? Oh, who am I kidding with 'kind of'?

'I'm embarrassing you, Girl Going Alone. Perhaps I should put you over my knee and spank you,' says the voice. 'I bet you'd love it. I bet you don't have any knickers on.'

I am *curdling* with shame, and yet more aroused than I have ever been in my life. I breathe in . . . I don't know what I'm breathing in, but my exhale is finally slow, steady.

'I said, I bet you don't have any knickers on. Show me. Or I'll have to punish you for wasting my time.'

If there was a real man here, saying these things, what would I do? Would I want it? Would I run away? I don't know. But it's so easy to obey the voice.

Kneeling on the bed, I move my laptop away a little, so that just the lower half of my torso is in the frame. Slowly, I lift the fraying hem, letting myself enjoy the slide of satin against my bare skin. Lifting my hand higher, I start to stroke myself, the action hidden by the fabric.

'Would you like me to go higher?' I ask, politely.

A grunt, and a gasp. 'Please,' says the voice.

I could slam the laptop shut. I could disconnect from the internet. But I lift, half inch by half inch, all the way up the seam of my thighs. Only my hand is really visible, my fingers moving rapidly. I think I'm going to come. I need to come. I don't care what this man wants, or what happens next.

The voice speaks. 'I need you to pull your pussy apart and slide a finger inside yourself. I need to see how wet you are.'

I need you.

I do what I'm told, and my orgasm builds, and builds. I'm slippery, soaking, and surprised by the strangeness of myself on screen. It's funny to think that even though I must have spent hours looking at myself, I've never really *looked*. Is this hot? Is this how it's supposed to be?

Slowly, showily, I plunge my right index finger inside myself. I pull it out and hold it up to the lens, turning it to show this paying stranger how it shines in the light. And then I spread my legs even wider and rub it against my clit. 'Oh God, I'm going to— *Oh!*' My orgasm is an exorcism; something is pulling the sounds and sensations directly out of my gut.

'Good girl. Now I want you to—'

I have catapulted myself up into distant galaxies and fallen straight back down to Earth. The feelings flicker away and I'm bumped awake. What am I doing here?

The itch has gone. My breathing is steady again.

@girl_going_alone has terminated the chat.

Chapter Twenty

Secrets

When I was nine or ten, I overheard Alison claiming that she did not want to have her photograph taken. I was hovering in a doorway and almost walked in on my mother, the mayor, and a middle-aged man wielding a complicated-looking camera.

'Oh, no, I couldn't possibly! Please, I look an absolute state!' Alison held her hands up close to her face, framing it.

'Well, if you'd really rather not . . .' said the man with the camera, starting to turn away.

My mother all but grabbed him by his collar. 'No, no, it's fine, really, I am silly to make such a fuss. Please do!'

This resulted in a small picture being printed in one of the local papers. Alison obtained a print; she claimed that someone from the newspaper had been in touch and asked her if she would like one. (She also claimed that the only available size was eight inches by ten.) This photograph was framed, and it still sits in the centre of an occasional table in her maisonette. The lord mayor is in his ceremonial robes and chains. My mother is in a cream-coloured, fitted dress and a matching jacket. Very 'mother of the bride'. Less 'mother of the virgin child who has just given a rather wintry rendition of "Summertime"'.

Despite having firm evidence that my mother was wearing her usual Alison uniform – something from a mid-range department store with a dry-clean-only label – my memory lies to me. Whenever I think of that moment, the men, the pitch of her voice, I can't stop myself from seeing her dressed as a saloon girl from a western. Garters. Flounces. Tits spilling out of a corset like a pair of single-serve Christmas puddings. A fan, all the better to emphasise her girlish protests. *Me? My photograph? You mean, you think I'm pretty? Really and truly?*

It has taken me almost twenty years to come to terms with the fact that I am just like my mother.

Bean seemed to have been born knowing the secret. When anyone praises you for the way you look, deny, deny, deny. While Alison's denials were a burlesque of a protest, a fluting joke, Bean's were simply furious. She would fold her arms – or sometimes put her hands over her head, as if the compliment was an ill-timed summer rain shower. The harder she protested, the prettier she became. If a camera came close, she would not bat her eyes, nor pretend to hide behind an imaginary fan. If she had the option, she'd growl '*No*' and leave the room.

There are not many pictures of teenage Bean, and in nearly all of them, in spite of her great beauty, she has the air of a celebrity who has just been caught with a sex worker somewhere south of Santa Monica Boulevard. Panicked, and resentful.

Bean's beauty was unequivocal. Alison was – is – very

attractive. Sometimes, when Alison forgets herself and laughs, or lets her face relax, something strange and lovely shimmers to the surface. Her beauty was always buried, evanescent, elusive. And I was slow to catch on to the game.

School was full of pretty girls, and I was not one. My features were too heavy for my face. I was, for a long time, Big Fat Frankie. When we had our class photo taken, I mimicked Alison. 'Oh, no, I look a mess, I can't possibly have my picture taken today,' I said, hoping somebody would step into my trap and tell me that they needed me, and it wouldn't be the same without me.

No one did.

'You always look like that.' 'Good, because if you're in the picture you'll block out all the light. The photographer won't be able to see.' I can't remember who said it, but I will die with 'you'll block out all the light' ringing in my ears.

Still, even though I knew it was wicked and shameful and wrong, I wanted to have my picture taken. I wanted to feel pretty. And I lived in desperate hope that the camera would uncover a truth the mirror would not yield. Maybe I was beautiful, after all. Maybe I was scaring beauty away by wanting it so badly. Bean and I had complementary curses. I coveted her gift, and she hated it.

Perhaps surprisingly, my liberation came via a dating app.

The first time a man requested nudes, mid conversation, I assumed it was an odd joke. What could he possibly want with them?

I had vague memories of a stranger-danger sex education class. 'When someone asks you for a naked picture, you tell them NO!' said the teacher, while I thought, *I don't think anyone even wants a photograph of me with my clothes on.*

This is not something I will ever need to worry about. But it was just as Health and Social Care foretold.

Finally, I had permission to want to be in a photograph. I could even take the picture myself. I might be beautiful, at last. Or, if not beautiful, I could find validation, even salvation, through my own lens.

My early attempts were clumsy. I couldn't pose properly, and the lighting was too bright. But the responses were their own reward. The validation hit my bloodstream. I sent photos immediately, to anyone who asked for them.

The trouble was that most of these men wanted to return the favour.

The first penis made me throw up. It came without warning, unleashing a visceral, suffocating memory of my first, awful, time. I could smell the wine, sweat, stale vomit. Clammy hands, pinching and pulling at my body.

Something was very wrong with me. I was a hypocrite. How could I possibly think these men wanted to see me and then recoil when they showed me themselves? At first, I used fake enthusiasm to mask my real feelings, but I quickly learned that no man wants you to describe his penis as 'Very nice! Xxx'.

Then, I found a place where I could simply post my pictures to an admiring audience. I was down an internet rabbit hole, looking for more photography tips, and I was stunned to discover a place for girls like me. Girls who want their picture taken. Girls who want nothing more than for strangers to tell them that they are beautiful. I didn't know how ashamed I'd felt of my urges until some of that shame dissolved. I wasn't such a freak – there were enough of us to form a small industry.

I called myself @girl_going_alone because it made me feel brave. In real life, as I thought of it, I had disappointments, family dramas, money trouble – the same stream of unremarkable chaos as anyone else. The current was strong, and I let myself be carried by it. But to me, going alone meant making a choice. Swimming upstream, staying separate. Here, I ruled my own tiny kingdom. Here, I was undeniable. And no matter how explicit my pictures got, and how daring I became, the most perverse part of all was that I'd found a way to keep it a secret.

Chapter Twenty-One

Wednesday 22 February

In today's POST LIFE & TIMES . . .

Could your cat be making you stupider? We ask the experts

The deadly disease that might be lurking inside *your* shoe rack

7 women, 7 secrets – and one tub of hummus

Meet Frankie Howard – the courageous young activist inspiring us all to #BeKind4Cancer

Frankie says kindness is key

Sister spearheads emotional campaign to beat disease

When Frankie Howard, 29, found out that her

big sister Bean had been diagnosed with breast cancer, she wanted to pull out all the stops to show some support.

'Bean is my best friend,' says the courageous campaigner. 'We've always been so close, and I shared this list because I wanted the world to know how much I love her. I hoped to raise some money and awareness, but I had no idea that I was about to become a global phenomenon.'

The *Post* are proud to announce that we have selected the #BeKind4Cancer campaign as the charity for our annual Post Appeal. We encourage our readers to donate, fundraise and support, alongside Frankie.

'I hope everyone gets involved,' says Frankie. 'You can purchase artwork featuring the original list from the *Post* website, with all profits going to the appeal – but please do whatever you can. Even if it's just a bake sale. Kindness is more important now than ever.'

Want to look as sweet as Frankie? Top designer Angel Sundae is giving Post *readers* 10 per cent off her pink 'Adorable' dress. Just use the code KIND at the checkout.

Herald *Splashbar* – the sexiest scoops on the internet

Coming to your screens this summer – the show that promises to make *Love Island* look like 'a trip to church'

Nine nip slips that nearly ended presenters' careers

'SHOW SOME RESPECT!' fans scream at grieving billionaire pop widow as she is spotted in 'lingerie-style' outfit

TITS UP – internet charity sensation set to soar on sex-photo sharing platform

'Frankie in flagrante!'

BeKind4Cancer campaigner new star of controversial internet sex site

Campaigner Frankie Howard broke the internet when she asked us all to #BeKind4Cancer. But instead of raising awareness, she's looking to raise some other body parts instead, and giving her own profile a major boost.

She's joined one of the hottest and most controversial sex-photo-sharing platforms, and experts predict that she could be set to make over £10,000 a week.

The US-based porn star and sexologist Rita Ryder commented, 'When your profile is on the rise, the sky's the limit, and young women are making money hand over fist, as it were. And right now, subscribers to my new site, Ryding High, sponsored by 420 Edibles, will get a 10 per cent discount when signing up for three months. I wish Frankie every success with her own career in the sex industry.'

A spokesperson from Support For Sufferers told us, 'We're shocked by these images, which are in especially poor taste given Howard's link to breast cancer. It is saddening to see a young woman exploiting such a serious cause in order to further her own sordid ambitions.'

Frankie's on fire – click to see our scintillating selection of her most scandalous snaps

Chapter Twenty-Two

All over

'Frankie, what the fuck?'

Bean's voice jolts me awake, and I'm slow to detect the rage in her voice. 'Love! How are you? How are you feeling? How did you sleep?' I ask. 'Did you get your Domino's? I'm so happy to hear your—'

'When were you going to tell me that you were a porn star? I could have given you money, if you needed it that badly. Or helped you to find a proper job.' She says the last two words with total contempt.

'What are you talking about?' I sit up, trying to steady my breath. A mist of nausea thickens to a fog in the pit of my stomach.

Bean is speaking so quickly that it's a struggle to process her words. I wish I could switch her to half speed. 'What about Jack and Jon? How will they cope when everyone in the playground finds out about their Auntie Frankie? Because I know everyone is going to be whispering at the school gates. Was this really a career move for you? Are you really *that* selfish? It's like I don't know you at all.'

I've got to get control of this. 'Bean, slow down. I don't understand. What do you mean?' She *cannot* be talking about what I think she's talking about. Please, please let this be a bad dream. Let me have joined the wrong dots.

'It's all over the papers,' she says. As though I have spilled something revolting on her nice clean floor.

'The *Post*?' I say, dumbly. 'The campaign? Have they put it up already?'

'Your tits,' she says, darkly. 'Why? I get mine out in an MRI scanner, for doctors, so you become desperate to get yours out for any old weirdo? Is that it? Did you think, "Oh, my sister is having invasive, scary surgery on her breasts? That reminds me, mine are *fabulous*. I should show the world how good they look!" It's nice, actually. A bit of respite from one set of worries and anxieties. When I'm not contemplating my own death, I can think of those creepy men wanking over my little sister. Delightful!'

No one knows about my account. It *can't* be that. Maybe Alison gave Leticia the first photo, the bad-taste Valentine. Or it's something old from someone else's Facebook. I have some ancient headshots, where I'm in a vest top, and I suppose they could be cropped to look much more revealing than they are.

Why was Bean looking at the paper anyway? She is not supposed to be experiencing any stress at all. I had one job, one task, to keep my sister healthy and safe and alive, and all I had to do was *leave her in peace*. I have failed. I managed to keep my promise to Paul for slightly more than twelve hours.

'Bean, please. I don't know—'

She hangs up.

I search for my name online, seeking relief. It can't be the site. It just can't. It will be a mistake, and Bean will call back in five minutes, apologising for her mistake, her mood swings.

The *Post* campaign piece is the first result. I skim through it. This is fine, fine, fine. I didn't say any of those things, but it doesn't matter. I'm sure Alison came up with it over lunch. Whatever. The picture is fine too. A shiny girl in a shiny dress, smiling. She isn't beautiful. She isn't ugly. She doesn't look like me. I'm not connected to her. I feel like a hummingbird; I can't land on any part of this. I'm hovering, disconnected. Because there's a second search result that looks alarming.

The *Herald* piece.

As I click on it, I think, *Surely there's no way it can be that bad*, or *Maybe it's a mistake, a mix up*. Could there be a different Frankie Howard, getting naked, who looks enough like me to confuse Bean?

And everyone hates the *Herald*. It's grim, and salacious, and completely made up. No one actually reads it. Well, millions do, but no one will admit to it.

I fill the screen. Pouting. *Posing*. The words 'TITS UP' cast in illuminated Arial, 16-point type. It's me. Irrefutably, undeniably me. Filtered, edited and altered, but I recognise myself. I'm not the shiny girl in the *Post*. I'm a porn muppet. But it must be me because I'm wearing the pink dress in both pictures. Before and after. It's as though they have published my diary.

Last night, I must have crossed a line. I lost control. My urges became bigger than me, fierce and frightening. Is this my punishment?

I blink, repeatedly. Open-close. Me, not me. It can't be real. How did they even get these pictures? How dare they? I'll sue, for invasion of privacy.

Maybe the *Post* will sue me.

I feel ice cold. I imagine Leticia, Natasha, Jenny and Hettie reading this. They believed I was nice, and kind. Now they know exactly who I am. All of those people who were depending on me to help – I was meant to raise millions of pounds for people like Bean, people like us. I have ruined everything. I'm so ashamed.

I look at the horrible article again. The pink-dress picture isn't *so* bad. It's the context. The quotes. The spokesperson. Who the *fuck* is Rita Ryder? And how dare they say I'm exploiting the cause? Exploiting Bean! That isn't me. That can't be me.

Chapter Twenty-Three

Exposed

The horror keeps hitting me afresh, nanosecond by nano-second. I get out of bed, determined to go and buy some papers. Maybe it's a silly internet thing. Once I've figured out the full extent of the situation, I can try to do some damage limitation.

I've got one foot through my leggings when I think about Alison. My *mother*. My poor mother, reading those things about me. Cursed with one dying daughter and one porn-star daughter.

Maybe she won't hate this. She might surprise me! She's always telling me to 'put myself out there'. She's read plenty of Jackie Collins novels. We watched that Blondie documentary together, and she seemed surprisingly cool about Debbie Harry's pre-band Playboy Bunny career.

Or she will disown me.

Maybe if I call her before she sees it, I can prepare her for the worst. I pick up my phone. I feel sick, drop the phone and wonder if I'll be able to get to the bathroom in time. I leap over to the window. Scraping my fingertips on the screw, I force it loose and struggle with the stiff latch, swallowing down bile as my oesophagus seems to twist into a figure of eight. *That's ridiculous*, I think, watching my puke slide down the brickwork. *I don't know how the oesophagus works at all. I'm a dummy. A big, slutty, fucking dummy.*

The cold air is helping, and I pick up my phone again. I need to do this.

One and a half rings, and I hear the familiar trill. 'You're through to Alison Howard!'

'Mum! Mum! Oh, thank goodness, look, I don't know if you've seen the papers, but I have to tell you—'

'Please leave a message and I will endeavour to return your call as quickly as possible.'

'Mum, it's me. Please call. I really need to talk to you.' I rack my brains, trying to remember whether I have ever left a message for Alison before. She takes my calls in the bath. She's picked up, whispering loudly, 'Oh, hello, darling. I'm in the cinema.'

How can I control this? How did this happen?
Rupert.
This must be his fault. No one else knew.

I don't know what I'm going to say to him, but I need to speak to someone. I need to scream at someone. I'm searching, scrolling for his number. I've blocked him, and deleted all his messages, so I have to go through my call history using guesswork. And I'm going to do it now, while I'm motivated by white-hot fury.

'Frankie! How are you doing? Great to hear from you! I'm just going into the office. Can I call you back?' Rupert's drawl is warm and familiar and it's so novel to hear a friendly voice that I'm seconds away from saying, 'Of course, no worries!'

No. *Lots* of worries.

'You cunt! You utter fucking *shitweasel* of cuntery, you all-time arse! How dare you? How fucking dare you?' My heart is pumping, and I'm breathing through my mouth and sweating slightly. Did I just invent swearobics? *Frankie, focus.*

'Frankie? It's me, Rupert. Do you, ah, have the right number?' He sounds genuinely confused, but I don't buy it.

'You know what this is about,' I hiss. 'Why did you send my naked pictures to the *Herald*? How could you do this to me?' I need to be cool and collected. I'm about to say, 'Do the words *revenge porn* mean anything to you?' but instead, I burst into tears.

'What are you talking about? You sound really upset. Can I help?' He sounds so calm. How *fucking* dare he?

'Listen to me. You're the only one who knew about the pictures I was posting, and now they're all over the *Herald* – and a bunch of other newspapers, according to the internet. I told you to stop looking. I told you to go away.' Wincing, I can imagine the words *go away* being blown from my mouth and getting scraped along the gutter, inconsequential, pointless. Powerless.

'Frankie, give me a minute,' says Rupert. I hate him so much. Why isn't he screaming too? 'Ah, I've just googled. Right. Right. The thing is, I thought about what you said, and I did stop following you. I've been having quite a big think … anyway, Frankie … blimey. Your poor sister. I'm sorry, I didn't realise. I always liked Bean.'

184

'SHE HASN'T DIED!' I scream. How dare he use the past tense? How dare he say her name?

Rupert has the audacity to sound amused. 'Frankie, how anonymous did you think you could possibly be? I just stumbled across your account, and I wasn't looking. It never occurred to me that you might not want me to see it. It was there for anyone to find.'

I think I hate him even more now.

'Then who did this?' I cry. 'Someone did this to me! Someone exposed me!' As soon as I say those words, I realise how stupid I sound. 'Someone' is me. I'm the idiot who got herself here.

'If you're so upset, just take the account down! Stop shouting at *me*.' Rupert sounds exasperated, and I don't blame him.

'You're right. I'm sorry,' I say. I know this apology is costing me, but then I'm pretty much at the end of my moral overdraft limit. I hang up. I try to call my mother.

'You're through to Alison Howard!'

He's right. I could just take the account down.

Swallowing hard, I fight the urge to throw up again. Opening my laptop, I quail. It logs me back on to the site immediately, and I remember the chat. The strange voice.

The video icon is still winking. For half a second I feel a powerful tug. An electric shock jolts straight through my core and I want to do it all over again. I could cure this awful feeling with the thing that caused it. It's frightening. I feel like an addict.

With great difficulty, I try to push those feelings aside, and I start clicking at random. I don't know how to find what I need. Settings? Privacy and safety? There's no option to delete, to deactivate. It's a disaster movie: I've got ninety seconds to defuse the bomb and I can't even find the wire. Of course, this is the only part of the user experience that isn't frictionless. It's Hotel California – I can never leave. This is a different flavour of panic, oddly heavy, wet sand filling my chest. Why do I have all of these messages in screaming red?

The notifications make me wince. Hundreds and hundreds of them. Why won't anyone leave me alone? I can predict exactly what they will say. These are the people from the tabloids and news sites, and they will have come to hound me in my private, secret space. They will be telling me about how disgusting I am.

I could delete them all. Instead, I cannot resist, and I click. There is dread in the tips of my fingers.

New subscriber. New subscriber. New subscriber. I scan and skim, looking for angry messages, abuse, any threat that might fit my feelings, something to validate my fear and rage.

Maybe it's a joke or a trick, or someone at the *Herald* has come up with some other way to shame and humiliate me.

The last time I looked I had forty-seven subscribers, each paying £15 a month for photos. It's never been about the money, but the money has always been more useful than I want to admit. Now, I have 863 subscribers. When I refresh the total, it goes up to 867. I refresh again, 874. If they're each paying £15 a month, even if it's just for one month, that's . . . I wrestle with the maths, shocked, before my slow brain figures it out for me: *874 times ten, and then half of that again.*

I slam my laptop shut and breathe in, slowly.

I immediately open my laptop again and check the sum on the calculator. I must have got it wrong. Even if I'm out by a decimal place, that's still a cushion; that might almost get me out of my overdraft. But I was right first time.

I didn't think I cared about money, and by that I suppose I meant that I'd tried to come to terms with the idea that I'd never, ever have any.

Just moments ago, I thought I was cursed. I thought that Rupert had ruined my life, marked me with a label I would never be able to erase. That I had been trapped.

But this might mean freedom. I don't have to stay in a crappy, sublet bedsit, waiting for a little bit of luck to find me. Maybe this *is* the luck. I could buy a place to live. For a minute, I let myself imagine what it would be like to wake up in a clean, bright space, somewhere that belonged to me, out of the dark and damp.

Freedom, suddenly sponsored by my problem body, my too-big body. Finally, being visible in the *right* way. Useful, at last.

I'm tingling, giddy, hopeful. There are messages, too. I scan the compliments, expecting to land on something vulgar and cruel – there must be at least one bit of abuse – but the tone is strangely respectful. 'Can't wait for more pics!!!!' 'Frankie, you're beautiful!'

This time yesterday, I was longing to be seen through a lens and found beautiful. Jenny, Leticia and Natasha were happy to fill my ears with validation, but it never hit. I couldn't believe them. Yet, I might be able to believe in some of this.

My heartbeats are discrete again. I feel like a human with a pulse. The hummingbird buzz has slowed. I refresh my stats: 892 followers. Could this be a sign? Is this the universe telling me to embrace my secret self, go public? Could this be my calling, after all?

I shudder, thinking of Bean, thinking of what Alison would say. But Bean already knows the worst. And Alison has probably found it.

I hit refresh again. 904 followers. 904 fans, even. These might be the only people in the world who like me, who approve of me. The only ones who want to see me.

It would be crazy to delete this straight away.

I shut my laptop again.

I could stay here all day, clicking, refreshing, posting, googling. But I want to go to my day job, where it's safe. I need to see Miriam.

Chapter Twenty-Four

Past explosions

The older I get, the more confused I become about the way I'm supposed to feel about myself. It changes, arbitrarily. It depends entirely on who is looking, and who is judging. I'm mutable, cast and moulded by onlookers. When I reached my teens, I thought I'd start to have some control over the way I saw myself. I thought wrong.

'You really don't have to do this,' said Bean. She was lying across the bottom of my bed, left leg raised, right leg bent, her right foot flat to the wall. 'You've got to stand up to her and tell her that's it. You've had enough. Otherwise you'll be, I don't know, *forty*, standing around in draughty village halls in your knickers, singing "Over the Rainbow".'

'I will stop, soon,' I said. I wanted to trace the curves of Bean's body with my index finger. She looked like a sculpture, like something from the middle of a magazine – even in faded leggings and her old purple jumper. I sighed heavily and fished my leotard out of the crack between my buttocks.

'See, she needs to get you a costume that fits. This is far too small for you,' said Bean, shaking her head.

To be fair, Alison had made the same observation. I kept demurring, claiming I was perfectly comfy and didn't have the time or the inclination to go to the shops. My secret, the shameful joy that sustained me through the awkward, awful parts of my life was that I liked the way my body looked in the leotard. In the right light, if I pulled the right face, I looked like something from the middle of a magazine too. I felt like a firework. For so long, I'd been stubby, heavy, stuffed into my casing – and now, I was exploding. Now, I was dangerous.

'I think maybe this is the way it's supposed to look?' I ventured.

Bean shook her head. 'Franks, I've seen the way those creepy men look at you. The Rotary Club should change its name to Old Pervs Anonymous. "You're filling out nicely" – urgh! Doesn't it make you feel awful? That's why I quit. I got so self-conscious I couldn't bear it any more.'

'It's not so bad,' I said, pulling my stomach muscles taut. Even though my body had changed, I still couldn't quite get my fingertips to meet around my waist, no matter how hard I squeezed. I would never be Cinderella.

The other secret was that I really loved being on stage. And this information frightened me and embarrassed me. I couldn't begin to explain myself to Bean, because I didn't fully understand it.

Even then, I knew that 'being on stage' was a grandiose way to describe singing and dancing in front of a few rows of chairs in a small community centre. I also knew that I liked it for all the wrong reasons. It was supposed to be, as

Alison said, 'a chance to support good causes'. And 'a way to cheer up the old folk'. (Even I had a sneaking suspicion that Bean was right – the 'cheering up' had an unwholesome element that neither I nor Alison wished to dwell on.)

I loved being on stage because I felt safe there.

Everyone had to pay attention to me, but I could control it. No one could leap out from nowhere and shout or laugh. No one could demand anything from me, no one could accuse me of not giving my all or doing my best. I was lost and found, inhabiting the music that made up my imaginary world. I didn't perform to the audience, or even for them. But their presence protected me. It made the magic real.

Two hours later, at the Little Bidlington Rec centre, in my character shoes and home-made gingham skirt, cracking my imaginary whip as the Deadwood stage rolled over the plains, I gave it my all. I skipped, I sang, and in my heart I flew across the sky. This was my song, and it would keep me safe. I felt pure. I felt new.

I felt something hit my jaw.

Blinking, I touched my face. I must have imagined it, but my skin seemed tender, the bones jarred. I exhaled, shook it off, carried on, relishing the rhythm of the rhyme, the slide up 'Illinois' down to 'BOYS!'

Another hit, a pellet, at the top of my cheek just missing my left eye. I became aware of sniggering, of hissing. 'It's, it's.'

It's what?

I kept singing, even though my whole body was flashing a warning, flooding me with familiar sensations. That heaviness in my arms and legs had not been present a couple of minutes ago. There was the sense of being hemmed up, sewn in, an internal diminishing. If my fingertips were ever going to meet around my waist it would be now, with airless lungs and a shrunken heart.

'Tits! Tits! Tits!'

I looked up in time to see a third pellet tracing an arc in the air. Behind it, Sarah Hinchcliff, smiling evilly, sitting in the second row. Beside her, a shape I half recognised as Daniel Bowden, bent double, shoulders shaking.

It was only later that I realised Sophie then said, 'Get them off!' I heard 'Get off!' and ran. My tears were instant, my eyes were opaque. I fell into the tiny kitchen, I pressed the bar of the emergency exit door, and I kept running until I found Alison's car. Crying, shaking, I circled it, trying every single door until I realised it was locked and the only way to get the key was to go back inside. Collapsing on the grass, I howled. I wept into my sodden skirt, into hanks of my hair.

When I felt a hand on my bare shoulder, I screamed. 'Go away! Please leave me alone! PLEASE!'

'Frankie, darling, it's OK. It's me.'

Alison unpeeled me, separated my face from my skirt, and pulled me towards her.

'Going to get your blouse dirty,' I muttered, trying to wriggle away.

'Doesn't matter.' She held me tightly, her hands in my damp hair.

We stayed there, beside the car, until my breath slowed and the air felt cold on my arms.

'Do you think you're ready to go home now?' she asked, and I nodded.

As she twisted her key in the ignition, 'Move Over, Darling' began to play. She turned it off.

192

'Frankie, I don't know what happened in there, but ...'
She took one hand off the steering wheel, pressed it to her temple and sighed. 'You're very, very special. No, don't roll your eyes. I mean it. You are talented and you are beautiful. Unfortunately we live in a world where it's hard to be special. It's hard to stand out. It makes people uncomfortable. They don't know how to respond, how to pay attention, and so they ... do things like that.'

'Mum, those were people from school. They just think I'm an idiot.'

'People do the most awful things when they're jealous. And puberty, hormones, that doesn't help.'

'No, Mum, they're not jealous of me, I don't think that's it at all.' I thought about Bean's words, about the creepy men. The leotard rose up again, pinching and itching.

I thought about the free, flying feeling, the bliss of singing my own escape. I could never salute the Deadwood stage or lose a jolly hour on the trolley again. I'd be too fearful, waiting for the taunts, the attack.

I tried very hard not to start crying again when I said, 'Look, Mum, I don't think I want to do this any more. I think I'm too old, like Bean.'

Alison sighed and squeezed the steering wheel a little tighter. She stared out straight in front of her, contemplating the slow, snaking line of traffic.

'OK,' she said, at last. 'OK.'

Chapter Twenty-Five

An identity crisis

Alison is not a woman without fault, but she's never been an absent parent. She calls at lunchtime. She calls when you're trying to tap the front of your phone against a ticket barrier. She calls the second you step in the shower, the moment the microwave pings to tell you it's time to eat a baked potato. She has a spooky sixth sense for terrible timing. She's one of the most relentless, annoying and inconvenient people I have ever met.

But it's horrible when she doesn't call at all.

As I close my front door, I tell myself there is probably a perfectly logical explanation for her silence. After three yards, I call again, I leave another message, and realise I know what the perfectly logical explanation must be. She has not been mugged. She has not accidentally dropped her phone off the side of the Hungerford Bridge. She is not the victim of a technical error, in which the phone company have temporarily stopped connecting her number. She is not speaking to me because she is angry with me.

I walk eleven more yards. I take my phone out of my

pocket and hit redial. I need to hear her voice, even if it's shouting at me. She can scream, 'How dare you!' and 'That's not how I raised you!' and even 'I'm ashamed of you'. But I need her to say something.

I keep walking through the drizzle, flanked by a pair of pigeons who are going toe to toe over a packet of Frazzles. Redial, redial, redial. For a second, I think about trying Leticia. She's the last person I saw Alison with. Did Leticia murder her?

Just as I'm wondering whether it would be ridiculous to go to the police, the words 'Mommie Dearest' appear on the screen. The caption for a picture of Alison, chosen by Alison, taken at Aintree Races, in which it is impossible to ascertain the point at which her hair stops and her hat starts.

'Mum! How are you?' I say, breathlessly. 'I tried to call. I've been so worried!'

'Frances.' Shit.

'I don't know what to say. Well, I'm sorry. I'm deeply, deeply sorry. I never ever meant for any of this to happen.'

I hear a hissing, a fizzing. 'I'm so ashamed. Have you done a google of yourself lately?' I can picture Alison right now. I know the arches of her eyebrows will be pitched and pointed, a pair of perfect crayon roofs. I know her mouth will be pursed. Bean calls it her Cat's Bum Hepburn. And worst of all, I know that her fury and bluster is a front to hide her broken heart.

'Mum,' I say, stalling for time. 'I honestly don't know what to say. I'd do anything to fix it. This was supposed to be a secret. No one was ever meant to find out. I'm not proud of it.'

'Were you hacked?' says Alison, hysterical, but hopeful. 'I've read about this. Wicked men somehow break into your computer, they get down from the cloud – did someone take pictures when you weren't looking? We can sue!'

The pigeons have lost interest in the Frazzles. They are pecking and clawing each other instead. How do I tell my mother that I took these photographs? That this is who I am?

I have a brief brainwave. 'Maybe the *Post* can help,' I cry. 'Surely they can shut this down? It can't be good for their campaign.' A loophole! I jump up and down. I could dance in the street.

'Frankie, I've already spoken to Leticia and they're pulling the campaign, as of today. It's in today's paper, which is very embarrassing for them. She called me this morning. She says you're setting an appalling example to young women. She's talking about damage limitation. They may take legal action.'

Shit. They will sue me. They'll take my website money. Only I could randomly acquire thousands of pounds in one morning and lose it a couple of hours later.

'Mum ... ' I pause, because I daren't finish the sentence. *Will you ever forgive me? Do you still love me?* 'I don't know how to make this right. I don't care about the *Post*, I want to fix things with you.'

'Oh, darling,' she says, sounding softer. Then, the steel returns. 'You're not my little girl any more, are you? That picture you sent to your sister – I did think it was a bit raunchy, but then I thought, *Get with the times, Alison!* I thought it was your idea of a joke. I didn't know. It turns out I didn't know you, at all.'

'Mum, please don't say that.' I can't cry here, on the street.

'Well, I don't know what else I can say. I'm going to go now.' She hangs up.

I need to sit down. There's a branch of Oxfam up ahead, and as luck would have it, someone left a load of donations outside in the night. As soon as I spot the pile of black bin bags, my knees wobble, and I prepare to sink into them, letting the soft fabric receive me.

Cautiously, as I let the rubbish bags take my weight I breathe deeply and slowly. A sour, sewage smell assails my nostrils. These aren't charity shop donations.

This is just rubbish. From a bin.

Curling up, pushing my knees into my eye sockets, I think about weeping. Instead I let out a guttural, growling scream. It makes my diaphragm hurt. As I look up and start climbing off the bin bags, I notice an older man standing over me, peering down. He's wearing a hoodie under a shabby tweed blazer. 'Sorry, I was just having a moment,' I say, apologetically. 'I'll get out of your way, were you ...?' I trail off as I realise how offensive it sounds to suggest that he might have been purposefully seeking out my bin bags.

'You're that bird with the wabs, in the papers! I thought it was you!' he says. He offers me his hand. I go to shake it, but he pulls me up and draws me towards him, for closer inspection. 'You look different in real life, though,' he says.

He drops my hand abruptly. I fall down again.

Chapter Twenty-Six

Maz

**Nudes for you – Foxy Frankie stars in sexy
shoot DAYS after big sis cancer diagnosis**

**White women, fragility and privilege –
the lessons we must learn from so-called
'activists' like Frankie Howard**

**'Sex obsessed' Frankie flaunts
it for 'good causes'**

**Frankie Howard and the dark side of
self-appointed 'empowerment'**

As Miriam reads, I am compulsively slurping sugary tea
out of a Sports Direct mug. I'm sure this holds at least two
pints, and I've got through a pint and a half in six minutes.

'Frankie, I'm going to stop reading them out now. I don't
think this is doing you any good. I can feel your aura getting darker.'

'I'm sorry,' I tell my tea.

'Oh, love, it's a joke! You're in a bad way. Look, I think I've got some biscuits.' Miriam ducks under her desk and slides a packet of Choco Leibniz out of her handbag. 'If I were you, I'd skip town for a bit. Take the money and run. See the Mayan temples in Tulum! Watch the sun rise at Kanyakumari!'

'Firstly, I don't want to leave the country until Bean is better,' I reply, taking a biscuit. 'And secondly, it would probably make more sense for me to, I dunno, attempt to get on the property ladder in Croydon.'

Still, maybe Miriam has a point. Maybe I should go far, far away and hope everyone forgets me. Is there any point in hanging around trying to look after Bean when everything I do makes her feel worse?

'How was her surgery?' asks Miriam, tenderly, and I put my head in my hands.

'I'm really not sure. Fine, I think. She seemed so tired afterwards, but the internet thinks that's normal. But Paul has said that her recovery depends on her not being stressed, at all. Especially in the run up to her radiotherapy. And I've just landed her with a lifetime's worth of stress.'

My voice squeaks and breaks. Awkwardly, I look down at my hands and break my biscuit into two pieces. 'Miriam, Bean thinks I'm disgusting. Alison thinks I'm disgusting. I don't think they love me any more. Do you think I'm disgusting?'

'Oh, Flossie, love. Don't be so silly! Anyway, it's about how you feel, it doesn't matter what I think,' she says, shrugging.

'It does to me.' I'm desperate.

Miriam looks at me. 'Admittedly it took me a moment to get my head around it, but good for you! If I was a young woman now, that's exactly what I'd be doing. It makes a lot of sense to me. You're choosing, you're in control, and most importantly, you're making money. Look at Annie Sprinkle! You've got nothing to feel ashamed of. And *no one* can shame you unless you're ashamed first.'

I make a mental note to google Annie Sprinkle when I'm not at work. 'Yes, but I'm not sure I can call myself a feminist when I've been doing this in secret. If it was some proud, bold statement about body positivity I could style it out, but I'm not sure what it is. That's the trouble. I can't explain it to my family because I don't completely understand it myself.'

Miriam nods. 'We all have secrets, and yet we all *hate* the idea that the people we love have secrets we don't know about. Honestly, I believe they'll get over the pictures. So you've got nipples! So what? It's because you're the family baby, that's what's bothering them. They'll come round eventually.'

'I really hope so,' I say, glumly. 'I'm not holding my breath.'

Looking over at Miriam's screen, one of the search results catches my eye.

'Flossie, stop it, let's leave it for today,' she says, holding her hand in front of my eyes.

'No, Miriam, wait a minute. What's that top one?' I ask.

The first result is new. It's not from the *Post*, and it's not a hot take from a different tabloid. It's in the *Independent*.

Feminist firebrand Maz Clarke steps up to defend Frankie Howard following Boobgate

Leaning over Miriam, I click on the link.

> The feminist, activist and influencer Maz Clarke has waded into the Frankie Howard debate, sharing a post with 800k Instagram followers …

I click on another link. There I am. Or rather, there are my tits, again, falling out of the pink dress.

A different filter. Hearts over my nipples. And a caption:

> She has set herself on fire, and she's keeping us warm
>
> I #StandWithFrankie – @Maz_the_Clarke

More than 100,000 people have liked it in the last hour.

Biting my lip, I brace myself to wade through the comments for more 'whore' and 'slut' and 'attention seeker'.

I read:

> Frankie is brave
>
> Frankie is courageous

And then:

> Frankie is gorgeous

My palm becomes slick with sweat, and my phone slides straight out of it, hitting the floor. I join it, seconds later. I can't stop shaking.

'Maz,' I croak. 'Maz Clarke. She's standing with me.'

Chapter Twenty-Seven

*'A slut, a slag, a whore, a hussy,
a tart ... a philosopher'*

I can't believe Maz Clarke knows who I am. I don't know if I feel delighted or horrified, or both.

It's largely because of Maz that I know to call myself a feminist. Her words have reached me, and comforted me, during my darkest, loneliest moments. When I have doubted myself, when I've felt that I'm not sharp enough, or smart enough, or good enough to exist as a person in the world, it's Maz's voice in the dark that has nourished me, reassured me, lifted me up.

Bean and I discovered her blog around the same time, about five years ago. Even then, her voice was an established one, but her profile has since blown up – from respected commentator to media superstar. Still, when I share Maz's latest blog with Bean, I feel as though we're both in on a secret. She writes as one friend to another, and there's intimacy in her words. I suspect that's why everyone loves her so much.

It's because of Maz that I have been moved to learn about

period poverty, socialism, sexism, and the countless tiny, wonky, destructive threads of injustice that make up society at its weirdest and ugliest.

But while Maz has made me hate the system, she has forced me to fall in love with the English language. She doesn't simply point out the darkness, she paints with light. She wrote a post about the way young women dress for church in Koreatown, Los Angeles, and it was so beautiful I can still quote lines from memory. 'Sombre in the sunshine, girls in grey are gliding past my window, *literally* the living end. There is nothing more courageous or audacious than seeking salvation in Southern California. But then, hours later, I'll see them whispering over orange lip gloss in the discount drug stores, their laughter like a carol on a crisp December morning.' There's a page in her last book, four hundred words on the perfect cheese toastie, and it's *poetry*, not a mere essay.

The magic of Maz is that she makes you feel like you could belong. She refers to her 'mates', gives them nicknames and descriptors, and her gang becomes your gang. You know how everyone takes their tea and gets through their hangovers – and, through careful social media study, you also know exactly who each of her mates are. Artists, writers, telly presenters, all part of the cosy, spangled, Maz universe where everyone eats baked potatoes (just like us) and lusts over Capable Advert Dads (just like us) and writes books and wears couture and lives in the smarter parts of London (just like we dream of doing, one day, if only Maz, or someone like Maz, could leap out of the newspaper and take us under her wing).

A long time ago, on a school trip, I was sitting alone,

ignored, near the back of the coach, listening to some pop-
ular girls discussing Jodie, the girl I sat next to in English.
The popular girls were talking about a boy, and whether
Jodie had given him a handjob.

Generally speaking, Jodie was even more awkward than
I was. I suspected she hadn't given anyone a handjob, ever.
I held my breath, like a coward. I wanted to interrupt, but
I didn't want to admit that I had been listening in. The
popular girls, I assumed, felt that the details of lives were a
matter of public interest, but also that I was invading their
privacy by eavesdropping. I wasn't cool, interesting or special enough to hear their gossip, and I should temporarily
suspend my aural senses out of respect for their superior
social status. So, like a worm, I remained silent.

The next time I saw Jodie, the guilt got to me. Admittedly,
I had become curious too. Maybe she *had* done it. Maybe
she had a thrilling, secret life I was entirely unaware of.
Maybe everyone had secrets, apart from me. I told her what
I had heard.

Jodie listened, then exhaled heavily. I waited for her
to express distress, or to call me out on my betrayal. 'I
cannot believe,' she said, 'that those girls know who I am.
That's amazing!'

I get it now.

Miriam is blinking rapidly. 'Frankie, it keeps getting
more likes. Her followers love you, they're saying ... oh,
hold on, "brilliant blog". What blog?'

'What blog?' I echo, a fresh surge of adrenaline bolting
through my body.

She is flicking and scrolling frantically. 'Shall I read it out?'

I nod, dumbly.

Frankie Howard – she's got tits, and she's got balls

I should admit that I've always been slightly cynical about most mainstream charity campaigning. Days ago, when Frankie Howard demanded that I #BeKind4Cancer, I felt like retorting, 'OK, but what are we going to do about the diabetes you have just given me?' It was a message to rot your teeth, complete with a lisping list. If I was going to Be Kind, I'd have said it was trite. If I was going to Be Honest, I'd have said it was shite.

But now, Frankie's campaign has taken a surprise, outrageous twist. 'Kindness' clearly hasn't raised enough awareness, so she's getting her tits out. Is it simply a publicity stunt? Have we all been had? Or is this simply a sad sign that ultimately sex still sells? And why are we talking about this woman's body when she claims she wants us all to talk about cancer?

Even if Frankie isn't simply a self-satisfied narcissist, her behaviour is a little glib. 'Hot girls care too!' she seems to say, pouting like a Pound Shop Cheeky Girl. 'I'm sexy, I'm sultry, and I'm sad about your mastectomy.' It seems to trivialise the awful truth of the situation. I have lost friends to breast cancer. I have seen strong and brilliant women question their femininity – their personhood – and have their spirits drained by hospital neon. We all know cancer is a killer, but we don't talk enough about the way it destroys our dignity while disrupting our lives.

The disease is bad enough, but the ambulance chasers are worse. Cancer sufferers don't get to experience their pain and their panic in peace — they're forced to have it pointed out to them in primary colours. 'Busybodies' is an old-fashioned expression, but I can't think of anything more apt. These people are forced to keep their bodies busy in order to distract themselves from the silence, the emptiness of their own heads. Usually, the busybodies stick to bake sales — because we'll let women experience pleasure, as long as it's covered in sugar and can be crammed into the mouth. It's the best way to shut us up. Rumour has it that in the 1980s, the CIA was behind the crack cocaine epidemic, keeping society's most vulnerable people dependent and compliant. Decades later, we're up against a cupcake epidemic. The cancer feeds on the sugar we're force fed. Treat the cancer properly and the bake sales lose their raison d'être.

So at first, I was prepared to write off Frankie's stunt as another low-rent sugar hit, a desperate and pathetic attempt to grab our attention, wrestling it away from a more important cause.

She is the bake sale, offering herself up, climbing on the table and turning herself into a human buffet. Blonde, buxom and begging for the male gaze, a sight for sore eyes and a subject for a jaded commentariat. The nipples were simply cherries on the top.

But this seems far too straightforward. If Frankie is just another young, dumb, desperate girl, why are we all up in arms about her tits? Why are we shouting about her all over social media? Because fury feels good. It feels punk. And, once more for the people at the back, WHY ARE WE FOCUSING ON HER? WHY AREN'T WE SHOUTING ABOUT CANCER – THE CAUSE SHE PURPORTS TO STAND FOR?

Yet, amid all of the shouting, all of the noise, I'm starting to wonder whether Frankie is the most punk of all of us. She has set herself on fire and she's keeping us warm. She isn't simply posing, luscious and edible, offering 'coffee, tea, or me?' to all comers. She is cannibalising herself.

And it's feminist as fuck.

She's saying, 'This disease disembodies us, it breaks us down to our component parts. Society breaks women down to our component parts. Well, I'm doing it before you can. I'm getting in there first.'

We want women to be sexy, but never sexual. We want women to be available, but we're not allowed any autonomy over our availability. And we keep being told that the way we look matters – that, in fact, it is the only thing that matters.

Frankie has been called a slut, a slag, a whore, a hussy, a tart, a slattern, sex-vermin, rape bait, a desperate fame-hungry porn-star wannabe and a twenty-first-century Mary Magdalene. The world has fallen over itself to slut-shame her. I am going to slut-pride her. Who cares if she wants to capitalise on her body and make it our business? Who are we to look away, when we see one woman providing everything that we have asked her to offer? Yes,

208

of course it's crass and crude — even cancer isn't safe from sexy branding. But then, what is sex if it isn't about embracing your life force in the face of the inevitability of death? Maybe Frankie isn't a Girls Gone Wild-style cautionary tale. Maybe she's a philosopher.

As a feminist, I'd never judge another woman for anything that she chooses to do. However, it's impossible not to watch the public antics of one young woman and then worry about other, impressionable, young women. Luckily, my daughter knows her way around a role model — she's never been drawn into the tawdry temptations of reality TV. She chooses her icons; she is in charge of her own mind, and her own walls. Her bedroom is covered in pictures of Frida Kahlo, Georgia O'Keeffe, Deborah Meaden from *Dragons' Den*. But maybe Frankie should be up there too, everything out, for everyone to see.

Being a woman is nothing to be ashamed of. Wanting to objectify yourself, wanting the world to see your tits, shouldn't be anything to be ashamed of, either. And Frankie has got exactly what she wanted. We're all talking about her, and we're all talking about how to end a horrible disease. Not cancer — but our addiction to adulation and validation. Ultimately, why would anyone want to be the face of a cause, when they could be the tits?

Miriam's eyes are shining. 'Flossie, this is *brilliant*!'

'Is it?' I rest my palms on the scratchy carpet. It's slightly

209

damp to the touch, and I don't want to think about why or how that might be. 'She sounds a *tiny* bit mean, no?'

'No, this is her gift! She must acknowledge the fact that a lot of the press has been mean, sure, but she goes from low to high, here. Punk! A philosopher! A hot philosopher! You should message her.'

'You can't just DM Maz Clarke! It's like phoning Oprah. Or, you know, if thingy from the *Sunday Brunch* show moved to the top of the road and you knocked on the door for a chat on the way back from the shops.'

Miriam looks amused. 'Apparently someone from the telly *is* moving a few doors down from me. You know, some sort of chef. Twinkly eyed. Does a bit of business with a mandolin. I'm definitely going to be knocking on his door for a chat. Anyway, get your phone out. Do it now. Or I'll do it for you.'

I shake my head. 'I can't. I don't have a proper Instagram account.'

Miriam folds her arms. 'Yes, you do. I've seen you scrolling, and lurking. Yesterday you liked my post about rising signs.'

I hold my phone protectively. 'Wait a minute, let me think, I want to sound witty and cool.' I type, reading out loud for Miriam's approval. '*Maz, thank you so much for your support, I've followed your work for a long time, and it means a lot. Kiss kiss kiss. SEND.*'

'You didn't actually write the words "kiss kiss kiss", did you?' says Miriam, warily.

'Give me some credit.' Although I suspect that even the 'xxx' has diminished my credibility. Oh, well.

Wait, she's replied straight away.

'*OHMIGOD – spelled with an I, not a y – FRANKIE! HAI!!!!!*' I show Miriam.

'See? She's not worried about sounding witty and cool,' murmurs Miriam. 'She's farting exclamation marks.'

Maz is still typing. Her name appears again, in my inbox, winking and glittering.

Can you come for tea? Five-ish, tomorrow.

An address, a phone number, ten kisses and five thrilling words.

I have plans for you.

Chapter Twenty-Eight

We all come from warm water

'I have plans for you.'

It's not the first time in my life that I've heard those words. In Alison's mouth, they usually mean I should be very afraid. In Miriam's, they mean that the toner tray needs cleaning. But from Maz Clarke they sound biblical.

I have never needed Bean more badly. All I want to do is call and call and call her. At 4 a.m., frightened and exhausted, I thought about crawling out of bed and getting a taxi to Clapham. If only I could explain myself, I might be able to make things OK. But even if Paul hadn't banned me from seeing her or speaking to her, I don't know where I'd begin. I'm a virus, a vector. I could kill her. In fact, I am killing her, from a distance. I'm poisonous.

I have lost my protector, and my cheerleader. But I've also lost the person I support. Alison is overbearing and exasperating, but she needs – needed – me. Her attention has been relentless, fierce, hot and pure, giving me emotional sunstroke. But now everything seems so dark, so cold. It's not as though I haven't fucked up before, but I never, ever worried that my mother might stop loving me.

I'm starting to panic about the website as well. I now have over a thousand subscribers, which should be exciting, but the pressure is building. The idea of performing for all of these new people seems scary, not sexy. Going online no longer feels like an escape. The compliments are waning, and the requests are relentless. I stopped reading my messages when someone called RealBigGuy asked about my 'rates for anal'.

When I was quietly drifting along, with no real prospects, I secretly believed that eventually I'd get it together. Fate would force me to sort myself out and get a proper job one day. But who would hire me now? For the first time, I have money – but it might need to last me for the rest of my life.

As I make the journey to Maz's house, I think of everything I have ever run from, who I have lied to, why I hide. I have spun until I'm dizzy, attempting to trick myself into believing I was a real person. I've reached rock bottom. I have nothing to lose, and nothing to give. Maz called me Mary Magdalene. For her, feminism is a form of faith, and I hope she'll heal me. Or she might simply see me as I am, and turn me away.

Five stone steps lead to the dark green door of Maz's house. The door is framed by a pair of pillars, the white-grey of a cloud that has just registered the threat of rain.

I lift the dark brass knocker. I hold my breath. I let it fall.

The woman who answers the door is smaller than I expected, somehow less vivid. She does not look anything like her photos, but I know how that goes better than anyone. And if I were Maz, I'd want to keep my public and private faces as separate as possible, for the sake of my sanity. I can't imagine Elton John wears spectacles with fireworks on them when he's just pottering around the house.

She's wearing dark blue jeans and a pale grey jumper, but she has an arresting face. Her famous red hair looks silver – pewter, in fact, not even pale copper.

The more I look, the more I want to look. Her nose is long and narrow. Her teeth are straight, with a dramatic gap just off centre. I try not to stare at anyone – I know how it feels – but she's compelling. The only other word that might do her justice is sexy.

'Maz? Hello, I'm Frankie.' Please, I beg you, let me wash your feet. Let me touch the hem of your jumper for luck.

The woman rolls her eyes. 'I am not Maz. I am Laura, Maz's housekeeper. Follow me.'

'Sorry! I thought, um . . .' *Of course that's not Maz.* I trot behind Laura, glowing puce with embarrassment.

Obviously, Maz's house smells divine. The hall is womb dark, and I assume the flickering candles are filling the air with a scent that's creamy, fleshy, hothoused, with a low note of smoke and heat. It smells *sexy*. Expensive, but inviting. A space to taste and touch. I start to feel unknotted – as though the bones in my back were tied up tightly, and something has tugged at the bow.

The last time I had such a visceral reaction to a smell, an atmosphere, was in the hospital. Soap, sanitiser, Paul's vape. The bright lights bleaching everything grey. This is the sensory antidote.

To my left, shiny, dark wooden stairs twist all the way up into the dark. The hall ceiling seems too high to make architectural sense. How are the other floors supported?

214

As my eyes become accustomed to the lack of sunshine, I realise that it takes a lot of light to make a house this dark. Purple-pink glass shields line the walls, with bulbs that seem neither on nor off. In fact, the light makes my vision so dim that the last thing I notice is the most dramatic: a huge, golden, metal hoop, suspended from the too-high ceiling, studded with solid flowers and lightbulbs.

'That's beautiful,' I murmur, involuntarily. I'm rooted to the spot. There's something magical about the swooping and looping; it's so luscious, and feminine, but *solid*. Despite its delicacy, it appears robust enough to hold itself up.

Laura turns to face me. 'You should see it when it's on.' She appears to turn a dial on the wall, but she might have taken the roof off and changed the seasons. Suddenly light is all. I am following her into it, figuratively and literally. It's almost too bright; the details of the space are washed out, erased by the flash. Through the light, I can see the arch of a doorway. I squint at the neon above, also newly illuminated. Letters that must be a foot high spell out the descriptor **FEMINIST ICON**. And there, in the centre of the frame, unembarrassed by the trappings of her light and legend, is Maz.

'Oh, my love. I shall come to you.'

Before I have a chance to fully register Maz – the flaming hair, the leather, the smaller-than-Laura-yet-larger-than-life vibe of her – she's sliding off her stool and hugging me tightly.

She rocks me, backwards, forwards, side to side. Her head nestles against my clavicle, in the space just above my breasts. My nose and mouth seem to be full of her hair. I wait for her to drop me, to let me wiggle away and say,

'What a lovely house!' or 'So good to meet you!' but we are still swaying, and I allow the human contact to soothe me. 'Shake it, shake it, shake it,' Maz murmurs. 'Yeah, good girl, release, release.'

Fuck it. Maybe I need this hug. No one else wants to touch me. I try to relax.

In my arms, she feels a little like Alison, and my self-consciousness returns. I'm scared that I'm going to damage her. Awkwardly, I pat her on the back.

At a loss, I start counting. *One elephant, two elephants.* After seven elephants, I am released. As her arms fall from my body, I stagger, feeling slightly dizzy. Do I feel better? Am I beginning to heal? I wait for her to murmur some words of comfort, to say something profound.

'Goodness,' says the feminist icon, 'you're so … tall.'

'I know!' I gabble. 'It's a bit awkward, really. Everyone else in my family is really petite and feminine. Like you! My dad was tall' – *Frankie, stop talking* – 'but he died.'

Maz tilts her head to the right at a forty-five-degree angle. 'Frankie, I'm *so* sorry.'

'Oh, not to worry,' I say, breathlessly. *Not to worry?* 'I was very little when it happened. I don't remember him, really.' In that moment, I am aware of a sharp sensation in my chest, which I try to ignore. *I'm sorry, Dad,* I silently tell the sky. *That didn't come out right.*

'So, what's going on?' asks Maz. 'Laura, get us some— I don't know, Frankie, what do you want? Wine, water? Kombucha? Actually, do have a kombucha, they keep sending me crates of the stuff. Listen to me,' she says. Reaching up, she cradles my chin in both her hands, catching it like a bird. Is she going to feed me worms of wisdom, from her beak? 'Never, ever write a blog about the awesome female magic of yeast. Fucking yeast.'

She drops my head, and I commit her words to memory. No yeast.

'Right, Frankie Howard! I must say, you've taken an unusual path, but it's worked. Everyone is talking about you. I heard phone-ins on two separate radio stations this morning. I've even been asked to appear in a TV debate about you, but I think we can do better than that, can't we? What do you want to get out of this?' She looks at me expectantly, and I stammer.

'Um, well, I'm not sure. It's all been quite sudden. I guess . . . ' I'm panicking. I'm desperate to unburden myself, to seek absolution. But I have a sense that there is a right answer, and a wrong answer. ' . . . I really wish I could just start over. But I think all I can do is make the best of things.'

Laura places a pair of tall glasses between us. The one nearest me is filled with ice and a pale pink, fizzing liquid. The one nearest Maz looks like a gin and tonic. There's a slice of lime in it.

'Frankie, there is absolutely no point in me being anything but honest with you. Right now, you have been *called*. This is where lesser women fall. You've got to take action. You've got to be proactive. You cannot simply hope to "make the best of things".' Somehow, she takes my massive hands in her tiny ones. It's supposed to be a tender gesture, but her fingers scratch like claws. I feel like a bear being befriended by a chicken.

Maz lowers her voice. 'None of us simply stumble into the spotlight. You're a woman, and when people start to pay attention to you, you owe it to all women to come up with

217

something to say. It doesn't have to be the right thing, but you're honour bound to make some noise. Take up space.'

I nod. 'I know, Maz, honestly, and I know that's what you do. But – firstly, I have stumbled. I did *not* come up with #BeKind4Cancer.'

Maz snorts and shakes her head. 'Thank fuck for that! Although it has been strangely effective, as a slogan.'

'Yeah,' I drag out the syllable, trying to stop my voice from cracking, thinking about how this drama has hurt the one person it was supposed to help. 'Obviously, this all started with my sister. My mum wanted to do some fundraising, because she loves fuss, and drama. And then – everything else was supposed to be a secret. I never, ever meant to get my tits out. At least, no one was supposed to know about it.' I hang my head. 'I feel so exposed. So ashamed.' I wrap my arms around my chest tightly and start to cry. 'Maz, the last two days – in fact, the last two weeks of my life – have been unbearable. My family won't speak to me. I'd do anything for life to go back to normal. I just want Bean to get better!'

Rocking on my stool, I hug myself tighter. Poor little Frankie, poor big little Frankie. Big in body, small in spirit. I *have* stumbled into the spotlight, because it's the only way I move. I blunder about, crashing into things, making messes. I'm too clumsy to express tenderness. Look at how hard I have tried, and how horribly I have failed! And no one is ever, *ever* tender with me. I'm nobody's bird with a broken wing. I'm just a big girl with big tits who must take care of herself because no one else wants to. I won't be anything else to anyone, ever.

I'm howling with misery, screaming with rage, and

soaked with tears. Tears that smell, oddly, like tonic. Why is my hair wet? I open my eyes, and Maz is before me, her hands on her hips. Her empty glass is in front of her.

Did Maz Clarke just throw her drink at me?

'You ... why?' I say, pointing, blinking gin out of my eyes. 'Why did you do that?'

'Because you're out of control. Frankie, you need to calm down. Get a grip. I'm going to help you, but you need to listen to me. You must stop feeling sorry for yourself.'

She touches her fingertips to my temples and wipes some liquid away from my cheek. She has very long fingers, I notice. Like wires. Her fingernails gleam a deep electric pink.

'I know who you are – better than you do. You're not a victim. You're a survivor. You have been holding yourself back for so long, squeezing yourself into boxes. But no box is big enough to contain you. I am going to teach you how to breathe out. How to be. I'm going to teach you to stop wanting to be pretty, and average, and nice. I'm going to show you just how powerful you are.'

She looks at me, tilting her face so that it's an inch from mine. *Is she going to kiss me?* She has the strangest, loveliest, silver-green eyes. I feel as though I am watching the light shift on the forest floor. After a few seconds of staring into them, I look through the window again, mostly out of politeness. My gaze flicks back, and she's still staring. Is she going to hypnotise me? I thought Maz made her fortune from talks and seminars and merch and books, but maybe I'm wrong. Maybe she lures fans to her mansion, lulls them into a state of unconsciousness and then harvests their organs.

'You really do look different from your photos,' she

mutters. 'No matter. Listen, Frankie, I think you need a bath, don't you?'

Oh, no. I knew I was smelly and sweaty from the walk. I've blown it. Maz has realised that she's made a mistake. I don't have any power at all. 'I'll go,' I tell my trainers. 'Sorry.' Rejected, weary, aching, I let self-pity start to settle in my heels before thinking, *Wait a minute*. She's been touching me and hugging me non-stop. Feminist icon or not, it's quite rude to tell someone they need a bath.

Maz chuckles. 'Frankie, don't be ridiculous. I meant have a bath here. Upstairs.'

'Right,' I say, mystified. How can she accuse me of being the ridiculous one?

'Firstly, you are processing and releasing a trauma, and I think you're feeling vulnerable right now. The water will hold you, and nurture you. Secondly, I just threw a drink at you and you're all sticky.' She sounds entirely matter of fact about this. I suspect I am not the first person who has left this kitchen after taking a tumbler of gin to the face.

'A bath would be lovely,' I say. As though I am in the habit of going to celebrities' houses for an afternoon wash.

'We all come from warm water,' says Maz. 'You are ready for your rebirth. This is how I put broken girls back together. Follow me.'

She walks out of the kitchen, towards the stairs.

I pause, under the feminist icon sign, feeling anxious and unsure. Being asked to take a bath was strange enough, but *is she going to bathe me?*

Maybe this is an elaborate trap, and the bathroom will be filled with photographers from the *Herald*, lurking with cameras. I could hide away. I could go home.

But home is Bean, and Alison, and they don't want me any more. Maz does.

It doesn't matter what she wants me for.

I walk into the womb-dark hallway because broken girls don't get to make choices. If I do whatever Maz tells me, I might find that I can be fixed.

Chapter Twenty-Nine

Living in your skin

By the time I reach the foot of the staircase, I have lost sight of Maz. I'm expecting to find her waiting for me, loitering on a landing. I listen for the sound of her voice. Nothing. Not even the sound of passing cars, the hum of a radiator or the radio. Is this a test?

I creep up the first two stairs as quietly as I can, holding my breath, silently repeating her words. *You have been holding yourself back for so long.* Exhaling slowly, I stand up straight. There is room for me here. Each step can take my weight. I am not going to hit my head on the ceiling. It's terrifying and exhilarating to ascend the rest of the flight as though I'm a normal person. As though I don't care if the wood beneath my feet screeches and screams in protest. The stairs make no noise. I take off my glasses to see if my naked eyes can focus better in the darkness.

At the top of the stairs, I see a small puddle of golden light pooling on the floor in front of a door left ajar. I pull the handle and I'm in a very big, very purple room. This must be where Maz sleeps.

Putting my glasses back on, I try to take in as much as possible. I want to record as many details as I can, to tell Bean. Oh . . . I keep forgetting, and when I remember it feels as though someone has walked behind me and punched the base of my spine.

This is *hopeful* snooping. One day, Bean will be better, and we'll laugh about this, and I'll be able to share my weird adventure. Where is she, now? Is she napping, or watching Food Network under a blanket with her eyes closed? Are the boys back? Has she told Alison anything yet? When does her radiotherapy start? It seems so wrong, not knowing any of this. Bean tells me whenever she tries a different topping for her breakfast toast.

Sinking onto Maz's great big bed, I sigh. I need to get it together. I'm *here*. I'm not going to cry again.

To bring myself back to the present, I inspect the books on the bedside table. What is Maz reading? I recognise a few favourites. *Valley of the Dolls. Fear of Flying. Understanding Your White Privilege* does not look like it has been opened. However, *Loving Yourself and Your Success* is battered, a mess of bent-back pages and coffee stains.

'Frankie?' The light shifts, and as Maz appears in a different doorway, I can hear the sound of running water. Of course. She's been waiting in the en suite.

'Sorry, I was . . . looking at your books. I got distracted.' It's funny, if you were to tell someone that you had been going through their knicker drawer or looking at the contents of their medicine cabinet, they would be rightly horrified. Meanwhile, books are personal artefacts that people are usually glad to show off, but I believe they're much more intimate. I *had been* looking at her books, and her life.

Maz smiles. 'These are the books I take to bed with me. They're more important than the *people* I take to bed with me. But we're not here to discuss literature, are we? The water is waiting.'

She inclines her head towards the doorway, and I feel a stab of panic. Can't we stay here? Maybe I don't need a bath. I can be fixed with a few pages of *Loving Yourself and Your Success*.

Maz waits for me to get up, and then she walks so close behind me that she keeps catching the backs of my trainers. It's as if she knows I may bolt. What – or who – might be waiting for me behind the bathroom door? Laura, with a glass of kombucha? Leticia, with a lawsuit? Bean, to tell me that she's taking part in a reality show and this is all a prank that got out of hand?

Maz's bath appears to be in the middle of *Jurassic Park*.

The air is thick, fogged with steam. It takes me a moment to see the bath itself through the jungle of glossy, green ferns – if I was a couple of inches shorter, I'd be lost. As the air starts to clear, I notice the clutter. A pair of identical glass bottles of bath oil, both open. Listerine, with the lid off. The red hairs coiled around the sink.

'So?' Maz's voice floats over my shoulder, husky, expectant.

'It's very nice,' I say. 'Good plants!'

She puts her hands on my hips and pushes me to the left, making room to move past me. I feel self-conscious about taking up all of the space – even though there was definitely plenty of space for her. She shuts the lid of her toilet and sits down. 'I'm waiting,' she says, her arms folded. 'The bath is ready. I'm ready.'

'Right,' I say. 'I see.' I do not see. 'So I'll just go and change ...' I gesture to her bedroom behind me. Is she really going to sit here and watch while I take a bath?

'No, Frankie,' she says, silken and sure. 'We're both going to stay right here. Who are you hiding from?' She looks at me, and I look at my trainers again. When I look up, her eyes are still on my face. I don't think she has blinked.

'I'm not hiding!' I say, indignantly. 'But we've only just met, and I'm feeling a bit overwhelmed. This is a bit of a weird time for me. Can I take a minute? Or maybe we should do this another day?'

'The time is now,' says Maz, 'or it's never. Frankie, I can see why you're scared. The world has been weighing you and measuring you. It claims to find you wanting because *it wants you* – and it wants to stop women from stepping into their power.'

'What power?' I whisper. 'I don't think I have any to step into.'

She sighs, deeply. 'If you want to leave, you're free to go. But if you stay, here is my invitation. Step into my bath, and step into yourself. Unlike every single person who has been looking at your body, your photos, I am not going to judge. I am going to make room for you to enter your element. You will learn to live in your skin.'

I picture myself turning around, running down the stairs, through the hall, letting the front door slam shut behind me.

And then, in my mind's eye, I see my nightmare highlight reel, flickering away. I picture a portion of my body, captured by my laptop screen, following instructions from a stranger, and I squirm with delight, and shame. I picture my photos, the layers of me, distorted by me, and distorted again by

225

other, faceless editors. And I picture the other strange things I have done, my failed attempts to fill a void. All the wishes and rituals and escape routes that turned into dead ends.

It's just a body. Maybe this is a way to finally leave it behind.

'I will learn to live in my skin,' I say, making unbroken eye contact. I'm not sure whether I'm trying to sound defiant or compliant.

I pluck at the sleeves of my cardigan and peel them off. I throw it over my shoulder. I pull my polo neck over my head, and I do not care where it lands. I reach behind my back and try to unfasten my bra. Two attempts, three attempts, and Maz tries to intervene.

'Here,' she says. 'D'you want me to ...'

Her touch undoes me. A wave of rage rises up and crashes to the surface. 'No!' I shout, stepping back. 'I WILL DO IT MYSELF! I WILL LEARN TO LIVE IN MY SKIN!'

Maz is right. I've spent my whole life trying so hard to be nice, and good, and where has it got me? I wasn't even allowed one secret, one outlet. I have been punished for every single thing I have ever done.

Finally I unhook the bra, and I throw it over my head. There is a dull, splashing noise, which I ignore as I unbutton my fly.

'Frankie, slow down,' says Maz. I think I detect a laugh in her voice. 'This is supposed to be a ritual.' But I'm yanking at my jeans, trying to get my thumbs into the sides of my underwear while kicking off my trainers, digging at the tops of my socks with my toes. I am almost naked, almost free. But I'm top heavy, and as I reach to release my left ankle from its clothes prison, I fall into Maz's lap.

I should feel awkward and embarrassed. I have never done anything more ungainly in my life, which is quite a statement. But I'm angry. Fuck her. Fuck everyone. 'See?' I snarl, looking up at her. 'Nothing to hide. This is what you get. I'm just breasts and hair. Lumps of flesh.' I leap to my feet and shake like a dog. Everything wobbles.

'When I show my body, I reveal to conceal. My life isn't easy, Maz. It isn't fun. And I had one safe place, one special place where I was in control. Where I could decide how I showed myself and what I was worth. No one could accuse me of vanity. No one could accuse me of showing off, or attention seeking, *because they weren't supposed to know.* And now, through no fault of my own, it's been stolen. Now, I have nothing.'

Maz looks at me levelly. 'So you're upset because everyone knows who you are. Fine. Now, get in the bath.'

Chapter Thirty

'How are we supposed to feel?'

Maz has filled the bath to the very top. A normal person stepping in would cause a small flood – the water would come straight over the sides. And I'm not a normal person. If this were a physics equation, I reckon I'd count for two and a half normal people.

This is some sort of test, isn't it? She wants me to accept my body by measuring my shame – its volume being equal to the volume of water I'm going to displace when I get inside the tub. (If I was Archimedes making this discovery, I wouldn't have said 'Eureka!' I would have resolved to lay off the olives.)

Heavily, I get in. One step. Two steps. The water almost reaches my knees. It's scalding, but I won't gasp. I must pass this test. I thud to the bottom, aware of my flesh spreading and growing. My thighs smear the sides, my buttocks divide and conquer. I am bigger than water. The floor is soaked. My clothes are soaked. I don't think I can wear them home.

'Frankie,' says Maz, sternly. 'What are you doing?'

228

'You have made your point,' I say, sticking my chin out. 'So I'm big. So what?'

She sighs. 'You could have just let a bit of water out. That would have been the obvious thing to do. Look, you've gone very red. Take the plug out, put some cold in.' She picks a bottle up from the side of the sink and reaches over to hand it to me. 'Wash your face, first.'

I pump liquid into my left palm, and inhale. It smells of lemons, fresh tea, fresh starts. Money, or rather the *presence* of money. The opposite of worry. As I rub it over my cheeks and my forehead, I can feel the grubbiness melting away. My skin is softer than I realised. When I have finished, I fill my hands with cold water from the tap and splash it against my face. I feel better. I do it again.

'That's better,' says Maz. 'Now, tell me. How do you really feel about your breasts, and your body? Because I'm fascinated. I cannot reconcile Internet Frankie with the woman who just spilled bathwater all over my floor. I've looked at you from every conceivable angle, and I can't work it out.'

How does any woman feel about her breasts? How are we supposed to feel?

Our bodies carry secret weights. Muscle memories, feelings, not facts. A day at school, out on the field. The first warm day of the year. I had peeled off my vest in the changing room, and I savoured the sensation of my cotton T-shirt against my bare skin. It made me feel good, in a way that seemed new, then. I felt fresh, free. As though I was going on holiday.

It took me a long time to notice the way my nipples had stiffened in the breeze. The giggles. When Mrs Church shouted, 'Frankie, you're distracting the boys,' and everyone laughed at me, I had been daydreaming. I immediately thought I'd done something stupid, perhaps burst into song and danced around the rounders base without realising. 'Go and change.' Mrs Church looked at me and pointed at the building, as though I were a bad dog.

I remember putting my uniform back on, still confused. Sitting on the bench, the wooden slats sticky against my bare legs. The smell of stale sweat. I'd never noticed that smell before or realised how disgusting we all were. How disgusting I was. Am.

'Tits' was my nickname, for a long time. Even some of the teachers used it once or twice, by accident. When Will Homerton told everyone that he'd had sex with me, they believed him. He was the first to say it, but not the only one.

Maybe it's the heat or the lack of sleep on top of all the shock, shame and adrenaline, but my eyes flutter shut, and I let the back of my head meet the surface of the water.

'I don't know,' I admit. 'I think I'm waiting for someone to tell me how I'm allowed to feel. My head is swimming with other people's opinions, and I resent them, but I can't stop seeking them out. I've always wanted to be beautiful.' I feel embarrassed, so I amend this.

'To feel beautiful, anyway. Because that way, the good attention might balance out the bad attention. In real life, I don't even try to be pretty, so I can't fail. But online, I have a chance of passing the test.'

These are my biggest secrets. I have never said any of this out loud. I daren't open my eyes, and look at Maz, looking at me. Like a child, I shut them even more tightly, until I can see pink and silver patterns flickering, where my vision

230

should be. This is a confession for the sea bed. Curling my legs to one side, I bring the base of my neck to the bottom of the tub and start to silently count to ten. At five, I splutter to the surface, blinking.

Maz's face is impassive. How can I explain myself?

'My sister is beautiful. I'm not just saying that because that's what we must say about the women we love, as the greatest indication of our value. She is, objectively, perfect. She's also kind, and good, and clever, and funny, and everyone adores her. Beside her, I've always been this oaf, this clown.'

I look at Maz, waiting for her to interrupt me. When is she going to say, *But you're beautiful too?* Because even though I wouldn't believe her, I've just been telling her how badly I need to hear it.

Her face remains still. It's infuriating.

Her silence wrenches the words from me. 'Bean has always been better than me. She has always had more choices than me. She doesn't need to do anything, but people are happy to see her. I don't have that, so I need to fight for attention. And now she's ill, there's this disgusting, broken, ugly part of me that seems to keep fighting harder.' The words make me wince. I wish I could hold them under the surface of the water and drown them.

Why won't Maz say something?

I keep talking. 'Sometimes I think that if I could just love my body, or even like it slightly, I'd calm down. These awful urges would leave me in peace. I'm not beautiful enough to be a good person. But wanting to be beautiful also makes me a bad person.'

I wait for Maz to tell me that I am not a bad person.

Instead, she says, 'You know that none of this actually matters.'

There's a quiet anger in her voice. A steeliness – no, it's not a gravity, or an authority. It's a soft, creeping madness.

She gets up from the toilet seat and kneels beside the bath, in my giant pool of shame water.

'Poor Frankie,' she croons. 'Poor love. Nobody gets it, do they? Nobody knows who you really are. Not even you.'

Her hand is warm and dry on the back of my neck. 'Only' – her grip tightens, her breath quickens – 'you do. But you're scared to admit it. You're scared of what will happen if you show up, fully, and accept the consequences. The story you tell yourself is that you're a victim, a gentle giant, judged by everyone, understood by no one. But you also believe being a woman is a competition, and beauty is the ultimate prize. And you'll lash out at anyone who makes you feel as though you can't win.'

Maz is massaging my skin. Reflexively, I tense against her touch. I don't want this. I want to remain hunched and alone. But her fingers feel too good. She is rearranging my nerves and cells. It should make me feel scratchy and fractious, not peaceful. Yet, underneath her fingertips, my flesh is becoming molten.

'Frankie, people are always going to say things about you. I've said things about you. Everyone thinks you're beautiful, you're fat, you're too tall, you've got great breasts, you're a slut, you're a saint, whatever. Like I said, *it doesn't matter*. But you'll be cursed if you let yourself listen to the noise. You'll get stuck. And if you don't move soon, you'll suffocate. The stink of what has happened will linger. Everywhere you go, no matter what you try to do, you'll come reeking of "Wasn't that the girl who . . . ?" Everyone will talk *about* you. No one will talk *to* you. You'll get lonelier. You'll get even more lost in your own head. Because this is all about your head, isn't it? It doesn't really have anything to do with your body at all. This is about what Frankie thinks about Frankie.'

How *dare* she?

'Clearly you think I'm an awful, self-obsessed person too!' I say, sitting up, trying to wriggle away from her fingers. 'Fine. I shall get out of your bath and out of your life. Thanks for listening!' My sarcasm does not sound as clever or as cutting as I'd hoped.

'Frankie, *you're* not listening to *me*,' says Maz, exasperated. 'So you're a little self-obsessed. So what? So is everyone! You are *not*, ironically, the only one. You're hardly the only woman who doesn't know how she should feel about her body. Every one of us is struggling. I bet Bean struggles, huh? I bet she's not lying around thinking, "Oh, thank goodness I'm so beautiful and perfect, that will cure the cancer."'

In spite of myself, I laugh. Maz keeps talking. 'I've been trying to open up this discussion for a long time. At the moment, it's a space with complicated joining criteria. Body positivity has too many rules and no one feels that they're allowed to follow them. I get so many messages from women who are saying what you're saying. Every single one of them looks different, but they are all sick of being told to love their bodies. It's too big a leap for them. Some of them talk about wanting to lose weight and feeling terrible about it. They think the craving to control their body in any way makes them a bad feminist.'

233

I gasp. It's as though I've just worked out who the murderer is.

That's what I've been doing online. Trying to sate the craving to control my body. That's what I have been longing for. That's the urge I've been so ashamed of. It's about taking up space. My photos are just a way of constructing myself and containing myself. It's not so different from Alison and her Slim a Soups. Her craving to control her body is almost certainly leading to osteoporosis. And then, I am *electrified*. I am filled with fury, and it feels good. I stand up, dripping all over Maz.

'We keep being told what to think *about ourselves*,' I say. 'We're not allowed to decide *for ourselves*. "Love your body" is one more instruction, after *hundreds of years* of "Be thinner, be paler, be more tanned, have a flat chest, get a massive rack." We're confused, we're exhausted, we just want everyone to shut the fuck up and let us figure it out! I want to love my body. I want to feel sexy, and desirable, but how can I do that unless the desire is coming from me in the first place? How can we cut through this awful noise?'

Maz smiles serenely. She's looking at me as though, after countless, patient hours, I have finally grasped the rudiments of long division. 'At last. You get it.'

Chapter Thirty-One

Sitting tight

I am standing under the **FEMINIST ICON** sign, holding a
FEMINIST ICON tote bag, which contains my damp clothes.
'A gift!' Maz twinkled when she presented me with the bag.
I laughed, at first, thinking she was making a joke about
my soggy cardigan, and for less than a second, she looked
furious. I felt as though I'd caught a glimpse of something
unsettling, but maybe I imagined it. I'm wearing borrowed
leggings, which don't fully cover my crotch, and an XXL
FEMINIST ICON T-shirt.

'Do you want to take any kombucha with you?' asks
Maz. 'I can get Laura to grab a crate.' She's very generous
with her Maz merch, but what I really need from her is a
plan. Practical advice.

I shake my head. 'No kombucha, thank you, though. But
before I go, what happens next? Can I do anything about
the stories, the gossip? Should I take my profile down?'

'For now, we do nothing,' she says, solemnly. 'People
want to see how you'll react. They're waiting for it and
watching you. If you take it down, you look like you're

ashamed. Like you're apologising. Stand your ground, Frankie. Claim your space.'

Playing with the hem of my new T-shirt, I struggle to broach the other subject. 'So I should keep taking pictures?' It's strange, normally that would be my first response to stress, but ever since the *Herald* story – maybe ever since the video chat – I haven't felt the urge. When I think of posting now, it feels like just another task on a to-do list, not a constant craving.

Maz shakes her head. 'Stop fidgeting! Stand up straight. Plant your feet on the floor, hip width apart, speak slowly and clearly, and look at me. I just told you to claim your space!' *Who does she remind me of,* I think. *Bloody Alison, that's who.* Although it's oddly comforting to be bossed about again.

'As for posting more pictures, I wouldn't bother just now. Keep your powder dry. Again, people are watching. New stuff gives them something to talk about. Wait until we know exactly what we want to say.'

Although it makes me deeply uncomfortable, I look her in the eye and speak slowly and clearly. 'I'm worried about letting people down, I suppose. Everyone else is angry with me, and if I don't post anything new, the subscribers are going to be angry too. At the moment, they're the only people in the world who are on my side.'

She laughs. 'Fuck 'em. You've got to do this on your terms, and only your terms. Who *cares* what they think? It's just a lot of sad, desperate old men. If you want to take a break, take one. Stick two fingers up to the patriarchy. So what? You don't owe them anything.'

I want, so badly, to believe it. 'It's just the money ...' I've been walking around with the figures spinning at the edge of my vision, like a slot machine, thrilling and frightening. 'I think I'll really need the money, but I feel weird about taking it.'

Maz looks at me with a flicker of something like disdain. Maybe it's just confusion? 'Oh, who cares about money? It's boring,' she says, and I really want her to be right. What is it like to have so much money that you're *bored* by it?

'I'll sit tight,' I promise.

Chapter Thirty-Two

'It's hard for me'

I have been sitting tight for almost seventy-two hours. Walking, reading, downloading meditation apps. Lighting candles, saying prayers. Hoping for a message from Maz, from Alison, from Bean, from *anyone*. Even Paul.

Alison won't answer her phone. I didn't think she would be able to shut me out for more than a day. Surely by now she would have thawed enough to send her usual stream of skincare suggestions and warnings about wheat? I miss her desperately. Right now, there is nothing I wouldn't give for a passive aggressive 'reminder' about moisturising my neck.

I should be with Bean right now, in Clapham, full of Sunday lunch. I can't remember when I last went so long without speaking to her.

There were dark days at university, saving up calls, trying to sound bright, doing my best to hide the fear and sadness. Knowing that I had to protect her from my unhappiness, even if I couldn't protect myself. But that was different. I was in control, then. I could absorb all that pain in order to keep her safe. Now I am toxic, contagious. If I speak to Bean, I'll cause the sort of stress that could kill her.

Still, I can call Paul. I don't think he'll pick up, but speaking to someone who knows Bean might help, a little.

I'm stunned when I hear his voice after two rings. He actually sounds friendly when he says, 'Frankie!'

'Hello,' I say, briskly. 'Hope it's OK to call. Sorry to call. I just wanted to check in and say I'm thinking of Bean – and the boys, and, ha, you, of course! So anyway ...'

'Frankie?' he says again, sounding hesitant.

'Sorry, I'll go. I suppose I just thought I'd leave a message in case there was any news about Bean. How is she doing? Do you know what happens next?'

He clears his throat and I'm sure I can feel my heart shrivel. Is that a bad-news cough?

'She's sleeping a lot, but she's relatively cheerful, all things considered.' He chuckles. How dare he? 'Actually, that's a lie, I've never known her to be so grumpy. But I'm hoping that's a good sign, she's lively with it.'

Lively. I fix on that word. 'So, has she heard from the hospital? Was the lumpectomy ...' I don't know how that sentence is meant to end. 'Good?'

'Dr Zainab has told us that she's expecting the results on Wednesday,' says Paul. 'She's been great, actually. She's phoned Bean to see how she's doing, she was really reassuring. And she's recommended a local support group.'

I catch myself thinking, *Oh, so Dr Zainab is allowed to ring up my sister*, and feel ashamed.

Paul sounds cheery, but forced. 'Between us, Frankie, I'd mentioned looking at support groups before, and your sister

239

was having none of it. And suddenly she's all, "Oooh, Dr Zainab says they're great!" It's hard for me.'

'Is it?' I say, frostily. Then I remember that I can't afford to burn this bridge. I have too many questions. Does Bean mention me? Does she miss me? I take a deep breath. 'Will you phone me as soon as you've heard from Dr Zainab on Wednesday? Also, someone really needs to tell Alison. I'd do it, but she won't return my calls. And Bean asked me not to. But our mum needs to know.'

Paul sighs. 'Let's not get ahead of ourselves, shall we? I'll call you on Wednesday.'

'Thank you,' I say, softly. 'Actually, Paul, I just need to know that if anything happens *at all*, you'll call me.'

'Frankie, of course!' He sounds hurt. 'I promise, I won't let you miss anything. No news is good news – if you haven't heard from me, there's nothing to worry about.'

'You mean, nothing new to worry about,' I say, and he laughs. I wasn't joking.

'By the way, thank you,' he says, awkwardly. 'It's really good of you to give her a bit of space – it's helping. When I told you to back off, to be honest, I wasn't sure whether you'd actually do it.'

'Bye, Paul.'

It could have been worse. I say a little prayer of thanks to the universe. My sister is stable. And Paul says I'm helping. I can take any amount of pain if it makes Bean a little bit better.

Chapter Thirty-Three

Summoned

On Monday, morning, I start to feel anxious about my notoriety, and how it might affect the future of FinePrint. Well, obviously I don't give a shit about FinePrint, but I am worried about what might happen to Miriam. So I try to hand in my notice.

Miriam laughs at me. 'Flossie, if you go, I go. My goodness, the *glamour*, if the one remaining branch of FinePrint gets exposed in a thrilling sex scandal. To be honest, I think they'd love the publicity. Let's face it, neither of us are going to be here forever, but today's not our time. I don't feel it in my bones, just yet.'

So I'm still sitting tight. If I'm honest, I assumed Maz would spend the weekend scheming and planning on my behalf, and then I'd get a call, an early summons, demanding that I leap into action.

Monday comes and goes without a single message, and I tell myself, *Tomorrow.*

On Tuesday morning, I watch my phone and wait. Nothing from Maz – bad. Nothing from Paul – good.

By lunchtime, I'm starting to give up hope. To distract me, Miriam is workshopping the Alison Problem.

'I honestly think everything would be so much easier with your mother if she was prepared to try a light sage cleanse.'

Miriam is sitting on the edge of my desk, rubbing my back. It would be soothing if she wasn't also drinking mushroom tea that smells of spunk. In fairness, almost a week after the Oxfam incident, my coat still smells faintly of bins. For a brief period, the two fragrances circle each other courteously, bin smell giving spunk smell room to breathe and bloom. But then the two combine, passionately and voluptuously. I'm breathing through my mouth quite quickly, trying not to throw up.

'Flossie, what's wrong?' says Miriam, breathing directly into my face. 'Are you having a panic attack? Here, have a sip. It will help.'

I clamp my hand over my nose and shake my head. Angling my body away from her, I say, 'Sorry, it's that stuff. Bit potent for me. I think I must be at a sensitive point in my cycle.'

'Fair enough,' says Miriam. 'We don't fuck with Mother Moon. Seriously, though, sage would change everything. I've done plenty of stealth cleanses because the people who need it the most often don't want to be cleansed. I just break in, discreetly, with my smudging wand. We'd transform the space, and her life, and she'd be none the wiser!'

I can already picture Alison's place going up in flames as Miriam climbs out of the window, muttering, 'I was never here.'

Shaking my head, I reply, 'You tell me this all the time:

we have to open ourselves up, we can't force these things on anyone. Surely you don't condone spiritual sneakiness.'

'But I just thought—' I hold my hand up. 'Sorry,' says Miriam. 'Why don't you hold my lapis lazuli for a bit? That will stop you feeling pukey.' She burrows inside a bag and produces a small, smooth, blue stone. 'I must find a proper case for this. I keep almost eating it, it feels like a Tic Tac.'

I let Miriam place the stone in the centre of my palm, and I gingerly rub it with my thumb. 'I do feel a bit better,' I say, grudgingly. 'I was going to suggest taking you out for lunch today, if you fancy it. We could go to that nice Japanese place near Notting Hill?'

Miriam looks interested. 'You don't have to take me out, Floss. I'm happy with a sandwich. Although I do like their tempura ... '

'Go on, let me splash my ill-gotten gains,' I say, grinning. 'Lunch is on my tits!'

Miriam looks momentarily panicked. 'We won't have to eat sushi off a naked lady, will we? Are *you* the naked lady?'

'Generally speaking, yes. But I'm not getting my sashimi out today.' Miriam rolls her eyes at this, which is entirely fair.

There is some drama at 12.36, when a gaggle of American students come into the shop, led by a man in a duffel coat who asks us to recommend a 'good marmalade sandwich place'. We shrug.

'That's not *really* a thing ... '

' ... but you could try Patisserie Valerie ... '

'I mean, they'll have bread ... '

'And they do a marmalade jam tart ... '

The man with the duffel coat looks tearful. 'Thank you,

243

you've been really helpful. This is the fourth place we've asked, and everyone just laughs at us.' He leads his charges out of our shop. 'Good luck!' I call to their backs. Some version of this happens at least once a week, owing to our proximity to Paddington Station and the eponymous storybook bear.

Miriam sighs. 'Why doesn't some place do marmalade sandwiches? They'd clean up! I'd do it, if I had any business acumen, or any skills with a breadknife. In fact, that's not a bad option for when we inevitably go to the wall,' she says, thoughtfully. 'Anyway, lunch. Lead me to the nigiri!'

'I'll get my phone,' I say. I've buried it in a pile of old printer manuals to stop my obsessive checking. I'm about to shove it in my pocket when I notice it's winking, whistling and flashing festively. News! News for me! I have seven missed calls and a text.

Oh my God, it must be Paul. Something bad has happened. The results are a day early, perhaps they have found something so worrying that they rushed them through the lab and . . .

CALL ME MXXXXXX

I'm so relieved that it's not Paul that I don't remember who 'M' is until she picks up.

'Frankie, WHERE HAVE YOU BEEN? How soon can you get here?' It's hard to hear Maz over the music.

'Are you having a party?' Before one o'clock on a Tuesday afternoon?

'Hold on!' she cries. 'Just put it next to the champagne for now, it's fine. On the account, yeah?'

244

'Pardon? Maz, hello?'

'I need you to ...' the signal cuts out for a moment, and then she says, 'on Sunday!'

'You want me to come on Sunday?' I ask, confused.

'No!' Even though it's hard to hear what's happening, I can tell she's exasperated. 'The *News on Sunday*! I'll text the address. Just get in a cab for me? Quick as you can, darling!' She hangs up.

What is going on? I don't know if I feel thrilled or frightened, pushed or pulled. She can't just demand my presence when she feels like it, can she? Who ignores you for days on end after giving you a bath? But I told her I would trust her. And something about that final 'darling' lit a longing in me so palpable it's painful.

Miriam is now removing her arm from her coat. 'It sounds like we're not going to lunch, are we?'

'Did you hear that?' I say, frowning. '*I* could barely hear that.'

'You've been summoned,' she says, smiling. 'The universe is calling.'

'Mir, she can't just expect me to come on demand, like a takeaway,' I say. 'And I've just promised you lunch!'

She shrugs. 'So we'll go tomorrow. It's all good! And you'll have something to tell me. I don't know why, but I believe this Maz keeps turning up for a reason. If you don't go, I think you'll regret it. You'll come back with a story. This sounds like something you might not want to miss.'

I wrinkle my nose. 'I'm honestly not sure how I feel about this, or what the hell is going on.' I pause. 'I didn't tell you how weird it got with her the other day. But I've been waiting to hear from her. Wanting to hear from her.

Hoping something would happen. But I'm hesitating, and I don't know why.'

Miriam looks exasperated. 'Frankie, listen to me. Your problem isn't that you make bad decisions. It's that you don't make any decisions at all. I know you feel scared, and I know you feel guilty about doing anything exciting when Bean is sick. But you're stuck. You've been stuck for a long time. And I think Maz is going to push you. Go!'

She picks something up from my desk and hands it to me. 'Take the lapis lazuli. You don't want to puke in the cab.'

Chapter Thirty-Four

Dream girl

When I give the taxi driver the address that Maz has sent me, he asks me if it's 'the St John's Wood end'. 'Not sure, I think so!' I say, optimistically. Then I spend the fifteen-minute journey waiting for him to punish me for my geographical cluelessness by driving me down a quiet side street and murdering me. For some reason, I always leap to this conclusion. Even though I'm always doing stupid things with strangers and I haven't been murdered once.

I'm surprised when he says, 'Is this it, love?' and we're in front of a smart little mews cottage and not a haunted abattoir.

The walls are white, the door is white. A Perspex plaque screwed to the side of the building reads, **ANTHONY JACK PHOTOGRAPHY**. Inside, Anthony Jack, or someone, is playing 'Gimme Shelter' at a volume that makes the driver wince. 'Blimey, you'll have to get them to turn that down,' he says. 'Do you need a receipt?'

He drives off, and I stand in front of the doorway, psyching myself up to walk into the chaos. What's going on? I take one step forward and then another, and standing in the middle of the white floor, looking just like Mick Jagger, is Maz.

'Frankie, darling one! You made it!'

She seems sort of tiny and sort of enormous. A shock of teased hair, like Alison's, only Alison's looks like it might be protected by the National Trust, and Maz's looks like a tiny, magical witch might live in it. Her eyelids glitter – as though etched with miniature constellations, shimmering and sea coloured. She's wearing grey skinny jeans. I wear grey skinny jeans all the time, but I don't think it's possible for two garments to be less alike. Hers are seal sleek, precision engineered to go with her silver platforms. She looks delicate, powerful, gorgeous, furious, frail and wild. And I think she's a little drunk.

She walks towards me to hug me, stumbling slightly. 'Champagne! You must have champagne!'

'You look amazing, Maz!' I say, and mean it. 'Really dazzling. Are you having your picture taken?'

She laughs and picks up a glass. 'No, darling, you are!' She pours me an inch of champagne. 'Fuck, we're out. Oliver, is there any more of this? Can you get some?'

We both wait. Then Maz screams, 'OLIVER!' Instinctively, I take a step back. There seems to have been a shift in the last few seconds, as though she's passed a point of no return.

A man – a boy, really – struts out. He could be twenty-two, he could be twelve. 'MAZ!' he says, matching her rage. 'For FAHCK'S sake, I'm on the FAHCKING phone.' Then, resuming his conversation: 'I mean, why not orchids? Orchids are the new peonies! Orchids are so far out they're back in again, right? They have a terrible rep for being high maintenance but they take a *lot* of punishment.' Even over the music, I can hear the wink in his voice.

Maz shakes her head. 'Oliver is my nephew, and he's' – a florist? A trend forecaster? One hundred and forty-sixth in line to the throne? – 'an absolute nightmare. As is bloody Anthony, who isn't here yet. But come through, someone will find some drinks, and you need hair and makeup.'

'Lovely,' I say, politely. 'But what exactly am I doing? What's happening?'

'Hold on,' says Maz, tapping at her phone. She must have a brief for me, an email, some explanation that will clarify what happens next. But the Rolling Stones are replaced by a cacophony of rhythmic shrieks and thumps, music I don't recognise, and she puts her phone away again. 'That's better,' she says. 'I couldn't hear myself think. Now I explained this, didn't I?'

Did she? I must have missed a vital clue. 'When you called, my signal wasn't very good,' I say.

She rolls her eyes. 'Well, we're doing a shoot for the *News on Sunday*.' She waits for a response, and I don't manage to give her the right one. 'Which is *really exciting*, Frankie. Claiming space! Empowering women! Uncovering the ambivalence we have about our bodies! Slut pride!' She nudges me sharply in the ribs.

'Oh! I wasn't sure ...' I don't need to uncover my ambivalence; it's the only thing I am certain of.

'Well, Frankie, I'm sure for you,' she says, and laughs. 'Listen, one thing you've got to learn about me is that I'm not perfect. What woman is? I come up with these incredible schemes and plans, and other people think I'm quite impulsive, but I've got good instincts. It always works out for me.'

She leads me to a screened-off section of the studio that reminds me of the *Post* shoot. The bulbed mirror. The piles of bottles and tubes. And a rack. But there are no demure dresses, nothing pink and frilly that hits the calf. This is – well, I suppose the most broadly accurate thing you could call it is lingerie. Mostly black, although I'm troubled by what appears to be a swimsuit made from red fishnet material. 'Voila!' says Maz. Then, when I don't say anything, 'Ta-da! Where's Mollie gone? She should be around here, somewhere.'

A blonde head appears through a curtain in the corner. 'I've given up,' she says, glumly. 'They only had soy, and it won't foam properly.' She's wearing a boring dark blue dress with a huge white frilled collar. I imagine Bean sniggering, saying, 'Nice outfit; you forgot your buckled hat!' Mind you, I'd rather wear her frock than the fishnet swimsuit.

'Frankie is here, so let's get to it,' says Maz, seeming to sober up a little. 'Bloody Anthony is still AWOL. I need to interview her, so I'll sit and chat while you get to work.'

'Of course,' says Mollie, sounding slightly sulky about the prospect. She holds up the familiar black bib, and I sit down obediently. Now I know the drill.

Looking in the mirror, I watch Mollie frowning. 'Your features are quite heavy, and with your skin ...' She lets the ellipsis hang in the air, as if my skin is a distant relative of mine that died a little while ago. 'So we're going to go *dramatic*.' She picks up a brush, puts it down, and turns my chair away from the mirror to look at me. 'You're really nothing like you are in those photos, are you?' She spins me back towards the mirror. I'm forced to face myself. Mollie is right.

At first, we sit in near silence. Mollie seems to enter a flow state. Every so often she says, 'Sit *still*, please, Frankie!' and I become aware that I'm gripping the arms of my chair or grinding my teeth. Surely, at the end, she'll do a bit of strategic blending and wiping and I won't look quite so terrifying.

It takes me a moment to realise Maz is asking me a question and not simply talking to herself. 'So, your performed eroticism echoes the work of Cindy Sherman, yes? And the platforms currently available give women in particular a route to economic independence, as advocated by Virginia Woolf?'

'Er, I'm n—'

'Sorry, lovely, can you just shut your mouth and close your eyes for me,' says Mollie. It is not a question.

'And you consider your work a celebration – no, a clarion call – oooh, that's good! – to the body positivity movement. And you think it's never been more vital for women to celebrate their sexuality' – Maz tilts her head, and Mollie makes a low, sorrowful, cooing noise – 'as an act of defiance. You stick two fingers inside yourself and then up at the world. After all, sex is about the intensity of our life force!'

I have lost all control of the situation. Maz is interviewing herself.

'In fact, just like Anna in Lessing's seminal *The Golden Notebook*, your quest for pleasure, independence, for the orgasm . . .'

After I have felt the sharp side of Mollie's mascara brush against my eyeball, I try to reply to Maz. 'Can we just talk about Bean, for a moment? Virginia Woolf is great, obviously. But I'm here because of my sister. For my sister. It's what you said in the bath.' Mollie pauses, frowns, and then shakes her head as though she must have misheard.

I keep talking. 'I haven't been able to stop thinking about what you said, that beauty doesn't protect us. There must be lots of women who get told their bodies are beautiful and perfect, and they don't necessarily feel it, or believe it. Then they get sick.'

'That's really interesting,' says Mollie, but Maz speaks over her.

'Listen, Frankie, I know this is hard to hear, but basically at this point, if you're going to survive the media storm, you've got to pick a side. You can't do cancer *and* empowerment. Cancer doesn't want you any more, anyway.'

'What?' Maz's words have winded me. I'm stunned. I can't believe anyone could be quite so crass.

But as the shock starts to subside, I realise she's not wrong. So far, I've done plenty of damage by accident. How bad will things get if I start trying to be a cancer campaigner on purpose? More importantly, perhaps I don't have any right to talk about Bean, when Bean won't talk to me.

Maybe the best thing I can do is leave Bean out of it. If I turn up in the paper in my pants, blathering on about empowerment, the media might turn on me completely, but they'll forget all about her. She'll be left in peace, which is exactly what she wants. This is my one area of expertise. It's exactly what I am used to doing with Alison. I distract her, and she leaves Bean alone. If I can manage my mother, I can manage the national press.

I'm staring at my lap, so lost in thought that when Mollie

says, 'Look up for me, lovely,' I see a strange woman staring out at me from the mirror and I think, *Who the fuck is that?*

I can barely recognise my own face. It has become a palimpsest. My bones have been written over. I could be my own impersonator. My eyes are shrunken, heavy, beady currants in a sugar-glazed Chelsea bun. It's a struggle to see through my lashes. My nose has changed shape. It's always been a little ungainly, out of proportion – now it's nothing but a narrow line, a placeholder. Mollie has created a death mask with contouring powder. I look like a rat. My lips are paler than the skin on my face, huge and reflective. It's grotesque.

'It's ... different,' I manage.

Mollie smiles. 'Don't worry, I know it seems a bit dramatic, but it's all about how it looks on camera.' I fight the urge to say a sulky, stroppy *I know* and force a grin. I look like a Hogarth illustration.

'This is perfect, Mollie, exactly what I wanted,' says Maz. 'Sexy, strong, don't-give-a-fuck energy. And Anthony is going to take the most incredible pictures. If he ever gets here.'

Mollie flushes and peers into the mirror. 'I haven't seen Anthony for months, since we shot in Paris. I wonder if I've got time to sort my hair out. Are you excited, Frankie? Working with the legend himself!'

Maz looks at me expectantly. 'I've called in a lot of favours for you today. I expect you're still taking it all in.' She sips her champagne. I wonder when she refilled her glass.

'The legend himself!' I repeat, wondering whether I can sneak off for some speedy, secret googling. The name sounds sort of familiar. 'Yes, I'm so excited, and so grateful. Remind me, what's Anthony's surname, again?'

Maz catches Mollie's eye and they both burst out laughing. Maz is definitely drunk. 'Anthony *Jack*? You must remember, darling, the Jack the Lad calendars? That video with all the models – God, who was it for? Not Aerosmith but that kind of vibe. You know, it got banned from MTV.'

'The Helmut Newton of the nineties!' adds Mollie, helpfully.

Was Helmut Newton not the Helmut Newton of the nineties? 'Oh, of course, sorry! Anthony *Jack*,' I say. It's not technically a lie, I'm just repeating their words. I've just worked out where I've seen his name before: the sign on his own door.

'Such a coup,' says Maz. 'The *News on Sunday* loved the idea – so controversial! They've had so many worthy features lately, everything has become very earnest. They think a bit of sexy feminism might cheer everyone up. It's great for them.' She lowers her voice. 'Between us, it's great for Anthony too. He's not having the easiest time of it. I think people have been a little bit nervous about working with him because his early stuff was a *tad* scandalous.'

The alarm bells are ringing – in fact, my head is full of flashing lights and sirens and disembodied voices telling me to evacuate the building. But Maz places a cold glass of champagne in my hand – seemingly out of thin air. 'Frankie, darling, relax! You look so uptight, so stressed! Who died? For goodness' sake, this is supposed to be fun. A treat!'

There are so many things I want to say to her, but I take a sip of champagne and hold my tongue.

'You're going to love Anthony,' says Mollie, meaningfully.

254

'He knows exactly how to make you feel special. He's like human champagne, isn't he, Maz?'

'Yeah, vintage champagne, at this rate,' says Maz. 'Keeping us waiting at his own studio. If he didn't keep his key under the mat we'd still be out in the cold. He can be such a dick.'

'Hello, Maz! The dick is here,' says a voice. 'Sorry, sorry, I'm *so* sorry I'm so late, it's unforgivable. Frankie, thank you so much for trusting me to do this. It's a real privilege to meet you.'

He sounds golden. I hear linen, the clink of porcelain, good claret and boarding school, play up and play the game, and I-will-die-before-I-button-the-bottom-of-my-coat. But it's softened and roughened, artificially distressed; he has carefully applied the wire wool of clubs and cocaine and a friend of a friend who knows Banksy. The sort of man who makes Bean roll her eyes and shake her head in horror, while I nod and pretend to gag and say, 'urgh, I *know*' while secretly wanting. He sounds confident. Like a British man who has spent a lot of time in America.

Mollie squeaks with excitement and paints a pink line across her own cheek. I turn my head to look at the speaker.

His face matches his voice.

Surreptitiously, I scan for faults, flaws, anything to ground me and stop the electric current that is crackling and snapping from my lips to my ankles. His eyes are on the small side, I suppose. Perhaps his eyebrows are kind of goofy. No, they're solid and strong, all the better to frame his face and accentuate the movie-star jawline. He is ducking, slightly, to get through the doorway. The doorway I cleared by half an inch. (When you spend your whole, giant life calculating sizes and spaces and hoping to fit, you notice.)

He's taller than me. I'm done for.

He pushes his (promisingly large) hand through his (dark brown, glossy) hair, and it flops back into perfect place. I can hear Bean in my ear, sneering, 'Diet Coke break, is it?'

'Hello!' I say. I sound exactly like a seagull. I try to take a refreshing sip of champagne and discover my glass is empty. Anthony murmurs, 'May I?' and he's approaching me with a bottle he seems to have walked in with. Mollie's eyes meet mine in the mirror. I think she may faint.

'Hallo, little one,' he says to Maz, kissing both of her cheeks. 'You seem very grumpy. Will you ever forgive me? And, er, darling, *such* a pleasure to see you again!' he says to Mollie. 'It's been ages. Remind me, we were somewhere in Europe, yes?'

'I didn't think you'd remember me!' says Mollie, breathily.

Maz claps her hands. 'We need to get Frankie dressed, and then we'll get started. Have you got anything in mind?'

Anthony shrugs. 'Oh, you know what I like! We'll keep it classy. Listen, I meant to tell you, the boss wants to come by. He's a big fan of this one, apparently.' He gestures to me. I have no idea who the boss is, but I feel fluttery. Oh, *fie* sir! After almost two glasses of champagne, I'm starting to think, *Fuck it*.

When did I last relax? When did I last take leave of my life? I've been so worried, for so long. I've been so tired.

Miriam is right. I am stuck. I'm always feeling guilty, scared, ashamed. I've never had the chance to really be the woman in the newspapers, to inhabit her in any meaning-ful sense. I've never truly felt like the perfect little sister, or

'Foxy Frankie'. The former is a lost cause. But the latter sounds like fun. Freedom. Escape.

Maybe the makeup isn't so bad. This is a mask. It isn't me. All I want, right now, is a break from being me.

So when Maz hands me a pile of scratchy black lace, I think, *Fine*. And when I ask where I should go and change, and she says, 'Come on, you can just do it here, we've all seen it all before,' I think, *Fine*. And when Mollie teases my hair into a giant, candyfloss mass, as Maz mutters about stockings being a bit naff and 'sorting the cellulite out in post', I drain my glass and think, *This is great*. I've stopped feeling raw and punctured. In the mirror, I'm just a mass, a mess of eyes, lips, tits and hair. I'm everyone's dream girl – and I'm finally starting to feel as though I'm in the dream.

Wobbling a little in a pair of strappy black shoes, I feel delicate and giggly, not awkward and lumbering. Maybe this is the secret. No wonder I'm so miserable all the time, stomping around in my giant trainers. Everything is better when you're drunk and struggling to walk. The world loves an incapacitated woman!

But will Anthony?

I'm trying not to get my hopes up. It sounds as though he has shot actual supermodels, so I'm not expecting any compliments. He'll probably be brisk and business-like. But he really, *really* looks at me. He starts at my ankles, and scans, slowly, slowly, up my legs. His eyes linger on my breasts for a long time. When our eyes meet, I have to drop his gaze for a second. Even through my champagne haze, I'm embarrassed that he has caught me enjoying the attention.

I'm scared he can see that he is making me want him.

I'm imagining him sliding a firm, warm hand all the way up my thigh, touching me, in front of everyone. Or taking my bra off, and pulling my hair over my shoulders, so it just covers my nipples. I want him to tell me to arch my back, or spread my legs. Maybe he'd get slightly impatient and say, 'Not like that,' and force me into position, and then he'd tell me I was a good girl ...

'Frankie, you look incredible. That expression, right there – if you can do that again for me in two minutes when I've checked the light, that would be fantastic.' Anthony smiles. 'I think I'm going to really enjoy this.'

Was that sexy, or creepy? Sexy, surely. But maybe I should try to sober up a bit. I certainly don't want to *look* pissed in the pictures.

It might help if I ask an intelligent question and concentrate hard on the answer. 'There's so much natural light in here, does that change the way you shoot?' I'm genuinely curious – the whole space seems so bright and soft that it's as if the seasons have changed. For the first time this year, I have a sense that even if spring isn't quite here, winter will end eventually.

Anthony laughs. 'Oh, don't worry about that, it's really boring.'

'Honestly, I'm interested!' I say, and he takes a picture.

'Great stuff, hand on the hip, lovely silhouette. Can you do that sexy face again? Really, Frankie, I've been doing this for ages. I get so dull when I talk shop. I'd much rather talk about you. So, are you a natural blonde?'

I burst out laughing. 'Sure! And I assume you are too?'

'You got me!' he says. 'This is a wig. Now, have you ever been to Paris? Let me guess – some awful boy dragged you around the tourist spots and pawed at you ineptly. I'd love to take you to Paris.'

I stop breathing.

'Oh, yeah, nice, really nice.' He clicks. 'If that didn't make a bishop kick a hole in a stained-glass window it would have him committing an act of self-abuse in the christening font. Sorry, unforgivably vulgar of me,' he laughs. 'Actually, on the unforgivably vulgar front, I'll have to leave you for a minute. Derek is here.'

I look around for an extra person. I can see Oliver and Mollie, sitting in the corner and leaning towards each other intently. Oliver is saying, '. . . and you know she gave him chlamydia after the BAFTAs.' When he sees me looking, he claps his hand over his mouth. Maz is pacing, drinking, talking on the phone, either booking a flight or having an argument.

Maz's lack of involvement seems strange. I'd expected her to be right beside me – completely taking charge, calling the shots figuratively and literally. This is all her idea, after all. But maybe this is how it's supposed to work. I'm sure Anthony has been briefed, and he's going to make sure we get what she wants.

There is a new person here, an older man. He looks out of place, not as glossy as everyone else. He's small, and older, maybe in his seventies. He's wearing grey trousers, and a puffy, navy anorak that makes him seem fragile. The anorak looks expensive. The sort of thing you wear to go trekking in the Himalayas, not to keep the cold out in North London at the very end of February.

I smile politely – before remembering I'm nearly naked and surrounded by camera equipment. Anthony calls me

259

over. 'Frankie, come and meet the boss. This is Derek Sanderson, Mr *News on Sunday*. Well, Mr *News*, really.'

I've heard of Derek Sanderson, but in a vague, dull way. A share-price, takeover-bid, grey-men-in-grey-suits way. He sounds like a brand name. I'm not sure it ever occurred to me that he might be a proper person. Maz puts her phone in her pocket and scuttles over. I'm just a little too drunk to read her. Is this reverence, or fear? She is not the scuttling sort.

'Hello, I'm Frankie. Lovely to meet you!' I say, stooping slightly to shake his hand. It does not feel like the smooth, manicured, carefully scented hand of a wealthy, powerful man. It feels damp and smells of tuna sandwiches.

Derek Sanderson stares at my breasts for one, two, three full seconds, and then addresses Anthony. 'Can you do some on all fours? I like them on all fours.'

Did I hear that right? Surely this is when Maz steps in and says something, takes control?

'Is that for your personal collection?' says Maz, with a wink at me. 'You make yourself comfortable. I'll get you a drink.'

'Can I have another drink, Maz?' I say. There's a tremor in my voice. I look at the three faces in front of me. Sanderson, leering. Anthony, completely relaxed. And Maz – is she angry? Is she strained? I need a cue, a clue.

This feels wrong. What would happen if I ran away? Maz would be furious. Anthony would probably laugh at me. I'd slink back to FinePrint, and Miriam would be understanding, but disappointed. I'd keep living in the shadows, waiting for the stink of scandal to dissipate. Maybe I'd try to keep my website profile going, make some money and move on. But the thrill has gone. The longing has gone.

And if I stay, I get a profile in the *News on Sunday*. I stay in Maz's good graces. I have some control of who I am and what I stand for. It's my one chance to make some noise, to shake off the shame of 'Oh, wasn't that the girl who . . .' And I get to see what happens with Anthony.

All I have to do is endure the attentions of a letchy old man. He isn't going to touch me. It's no different from the website, really. He's just like a subscriber, commenting out loud. He may well *be* a subscriber. I'm being too sensitive; I just need to be a little braver. A venal inner voice whispers, *Derek Sanderson is a powerful man. Let him stare at your tits for an hour, and it just might change your fate.*

Still, Anthony seems to pick up on my hesitation. 'I'm just going to have a quick word with Frankie about the shots. Derek, do excuse us for a second.'

He rests a hand on my arm, and with his thumb he traces a small line on the inside of my elbow. 'Are you OK, darling? I know Derek can be a bit intimidating.'

I lower my voice. 'He's a tiny bit . . . you know. I'm probably being silly, but there was something strange about the way he looked at me.' I look down at my breasts, and Anthony looks at them too.

Then he laughs. 'Frankie, I've been looking at you that way since I came in, and you didn't seem to mind.' His hand is just above my hip. I have to concentrate very hard to stop myself from squirming against him. 'All I want to do is have fun and make sure you're comfortable. If you're not happy about *any* of it, just say the word, and we'll stop.'

His hand drops from my body. It's as though the sun has gone in.

'But,' he says, lazily, tracing another slow line, this time below my belly button, just above the black lace, 'I think you're incredible. I think you're really exciting. I'm enjoying working with you so much. And' – he takes the lace between his thumb and his forefinger and plucks it – 'I'd like to see you on all fours too.'

By the time Maz has produced another glass of champagne, I don't need it. My hair is a veil, falling into my face. I can barely see six inches in front of me. I can't see Sanderson. I'm only aware of Anthony's hands, bending me, beckoning me, never high enough or low enough for long enough, as he mutters 'perfect' or 'beautiful' or 'good girl'. When he says, 'I think we've got everything we need,' it takes me a minute to feel my way back to the room. It's as though I've crash landed.

I stagger to my feet and watch Anthony putting his equipment away. It's quiet, now. Everyone but Maz has left. She walks over to me. 'I was a bit worried at first, but you did really well today,' she says. 'Derek sends his apologies, he had to go, but he loved you. He's talking about a cover.'

'Great,' I say, weakly. 'I'm off, too,' says Maz. 'I've got to write this up. It's going in at the end of the week, apparently.'

'Oh! But we only started the interview, we didn't cover that much,' I say. 'I could come over tomorrow, maybe, and we could do it then?'

'No need,' says Maz. 'I've got loads, it's all good.'

How can Maz have 'loads'? All I remember is her talking at me about Cindy Sherman and Virginia Woolf while I was forbidden to speak or move. But then, this is *Maz*. One of my favourite writers. I've never read a piece she's written that I did not love. I have to trust her.

'Frankie?' says Anthony, walking up behind me and

262

putting an arm around my shoulder. 'Do you have any plans? You were asking about my camera. If you don't need to dash off, I could show you how it works?'

'I'll leave you to it,' says Maz. 'Frankie, I'll be in touch.' She walks towards the door and looks back at us, shaking her head, before disappearing into the twilight.

Chapter Thirty-Five

Basic instincts

As soon as the door has closed, Anthony says, 'Right. Drinks.'

'Surely there can't be any more champagne left?' I say. 'I think Maz finished it.'

He walks to the kitchen corner and opens a fridge, stacked with green bottles. 'I never run out. Always order more when you're down to your last six cases.' He pops the cork, opens a cupboard and produces two clean glasses.

'I'm honestly not sure I can manage any more,' I say. 'I think I'm getting a day-drinking hangover. The worst kind.'

'Then you need the hair of the dog, obviously,' he smiles, and lifts his glass to mine. 'To my new muse.' Anthony would be unbearably cheesy if he was even slightly less good looking.

'I should go and change,' I say. It's strange – I'd got used to being in a room filled with fully clothed people, while wearing just a bra and knickers. Now that everyone but Anthony has left, I suddenly feel especially self-conscious. I was longing to be alone with him. Now, I'm not sure what

I want. I'm desperate for him to touch me – and I'm also desperate to leave, go home, lock my bedroom door and think about him touching me.

'Wait.' Anthony gestures towards a heavy-looking camera, attached to a strap, resting on a table. He walks towards it and picks it up. 'This is my favourite one. I don't usually use it for work,' he explains. Is this still work? Am I?

'It's great for this light, now that the sun has gone in. You look really beautiful, right now. I could take some great shots. Head towards the window for me?'

The sky has darkened, but there's some illumination, still. A dusky, navy glow. And I look 'really beautiful', finally. After all these years of hoping, trying, waiting. Anthony can see me. I must be ready for this.

'Yeah, look out at the window, and then look at me ... lovely.' Anthony's voice is lower, a growl that comes straight from his gut. 'Do you want to come and have a look?' I pick up my glass and wobble over. Now that I'm beginning to sober up, my shoes are starting to pinch.

'So I've tried a thirty-five-millimetre prime lens, which I'd usually use for a landscape, but I thought I'd experiment a bit with that weird light.' He shows me the tiny screen. Is this what beautiful looks like, how he sees me? I can't quite reconcile the image with the image I carry in my head of how I'd like to look. The girl – she *is* a girl – looks fine. Attractive, in a generic way, but the picture doesn't make me feel anything. The person on screen doesn't seem to be feeling anything, either.

'I look very ... young. Dreamy. It feels quite abstract. I like it.' As I look at the tiny monitor, doing my best not to fog it up with my breath, Anthony turns his body to mine, briefly brushing a nipple with his arm. There's a perceptible jolt – I feel a shot of lust and longing. It's atmospheric. It's not coming from me, it's filling the room, and seeping inside me.

He smiles. 'Now, are you going to pose for me properly?' He waits for me to respond.

I daren't blink. I stand very, very still. Silence, it seems, is the right answer.

He runs a hand down my side until it is resting on my thigh. 'Or do I have to tell you what to do?'

I'm rooted to the spot. I do not trust myself to respond. My heart is beating, *thudding*, but between my legs. Dumbly, I open my mouth. *Yes please.*

I nod.

'OK, Frankie, back in the corner,' he says, casually. I feel like an animal. He is training me to recognise basic commands. I return to my spot, trying my hardest to walk slowly, sexily, not to fall over. 'No, don't try to move like a model, I want *you.*'

Anxiety snaps at my heels. I'm not good enough, pretty enough to be a model. I'm not even *like* a model. I push the thought away and turn around to face him.

'Good girl. Keep the heels on for me, for now, but take your knickers off.' It's his easy, offhand confidence that is making me crazy with want. The old urge, the old longing is back. In front of Anthony, I feel like my online self fully realised, come to life. Who is Frankie? Who *cares* about Frankie? I'm just a Girl, now.

Maz told me that I had to learn to live in my skin. Why would I want to try? It's too constricting, too complicated. I'd rather shed it entirely.

I hook my thumbs into my knickers and slide them off,

slowly. I'm aware of a repeated clicking, a flashing. Opening my eyes, I'm surprised to see that he's not using his special camera any more. He's just holding an iPhone. 'Nice, very nice, slow down a bit, yeah. Now I want you to touch yourself.'

Oh, *God*.

I'm glad he asked. I'm not sure I'm capable of anything else, right now.

As I reach down, I'm aware of an intense heat coming off my thighs, from ... *me*. With my thumb, I trace a line, where skin meets skin. I sigh, silently.

'Come on, Frankie, don't hold out on me. Touch yourself like I'm not here. Make yourself really wet. Otherwise I'll have to come over there and do it myself.' I have never wanted anything so badly, but I can't resist my own body. I writhe, I press the heel of my hand between my legs. I'm slippery, I'm soaking. It's as though I'm in a trance, drunk, wanton, pleasure seeking. I'm barely aware of Anthony's voice, hoarse and thickening, saying, 'That's good, don't stop, I love that. Mouth open, eyes closed ... fuck, that's nice, yeah.' My knees start to buckle, and I stumble, my thighs drenched, my ears ringing.

I've barely begun to catch my breath when Anthony says, 'Very good, Frankie. You're a real pro. Now, take the bra off for me. Keep the shoes on.'

What did he just say? Something about the word 'pro' has shaken me. My lust has started to ebb away. I'm being sensitive, ridiculous. I'm ruining this for myself. I should have another drink. But this has broken the surface of my fantasy. I'm rising above the dreamline, and I can't submerge myself again.

Anthony is impatient, gesturing at me with his phone in his hand. 'Frankie, I said bra off, now.' He's flushed, but focused, his features stilled. He drops the phone and walks towards me. Blinking, I'm aware of a strap being yanked. I raise my arms over my head, and in seconds I am naked, but for a pair of borrowed shoes. Anthony drops the bra onto the floor, and it crumples as it falls, as if haunted by something. With his right hand, he strokes me between my legs, for maybe half a second. *Do I want this? Of course I want this. I definitely want this.*

'Please,' I say, 'just a second. I need a ...' I can't find the words. A moment? A time out? A steadying breath?

He smiles and shakes his head. 'Not if you can't ask properly. Now,' – he picks the phone up, tilting it forward, and kneels before me – 'arch your back, please. Move your head, so your hair is falling, like ...' He gets up and his hands are in my hair, and then my hair is trailing against my breasts, brushing my nipples. 'Good, good.' He kneels again, his head almost between my legs. 'I need your legs wide apart. Wider, wider ...'

I realise I am powerless, now. Maybe I do want this, after all. Anthony's commands are strangely thrilling, obscene. Click, flash. 'Lean back, yeah, good girl.'

He is capturing all of me. I'm turned on, and terrified. The last time I felt this way, I was exposing myself to a stranger, on the video chat. My lust is an uroboros; I want to be wanted, his want makes mine greater, and nothing can sate or slake it. I don't know what this force is, but I would die for it, choking on my own tail. And I do not understand what makes me so desperate to give all of my power away.

He reaches for me, his fingers are inside me, his thumb

pressed against my most sensitive part, and I gasp. 'I could keep you here all night, Frankie, couldn't I? Holding back the thing you want the most.' I cry out, wanting to want what he's offering. I can do this. I can push myself away and bring back the girl from the photo.

'Shhh, that won't do. What if someone hears you? And what will they think of you? Bad girl.'

I gasp again.

'Oh, Frankie, I can't wait any longer.' Anthony stands up. 'Lie down for me.'

My vision is swimming, cloudy. I'm drunk on lust. The floor feels hard and cold against my bare back. Frankie floats away. I don't know who this is. I have finally left my body behind. I don't care what happens. I want Anthony's weight on me, crushing me. I want to feel everything and nothing, oblivion.

Maybe I just want him to rip me open, his fingers digging into my flesh, to feel him pulling me apart, to feel his hardness and my wetness, for him to be writhing and groaning and slamming into me, over and over and over, until my orgasm feels too big to bear, and my eyelids close. He's standing over me, and I'm swollen with want, turned liquid from navel to knee. It's like being underwater, until a noise, a shift in light, brings me back into the room. Click. Flash. Anthony has taken another picture.

'We'll have to send that one to Sanderson, won't we,' he says. 'He'll love that. Dirty slut. He's going to hear all about this. He's going to know all about you.'

Sanderson.

Slut.

And it's all over. I'm coming up far too fast, surging

through the warm water, breaking the surface while struggling for breath. My face is burning, but the air is icy.

Anthony, oblivious, starts to unzip his fly.

'Anthony,' I say, in a small voice, raising myself up on my elbows. 'I don't think I want to do this. We need to stop. Sorry. It's what you said, about Sanderson. Please don't talk about Sanderson.'

He isn't listening. He is still taking his trousers off. 'Yeah, Sanderson. You'd let him fuck you, wouldn't you, you filthy bitch? You'd let him do anything to you, wouldn't you? Just to get your picture in the papers.'

If I lie down and don't make a scene and pretend I haven't said stop, this is still fine.

If I follow my instincts and leap to my feet, this might become something else. I might be in more danger.

Anthony is bending over, looming closer. I stand up.

It's so cold in here, but I think I'm sweating. What do I tell him? It's not like leaving a restaurant after you've ordered dinner. *Terribly sorry but I've changed my mind about the sex, please let the kitchen know. I'll pay for the bread rolls.*

'I can't do this,' I hear myself telling him. 'I'm sorry. Really sorry. It doesn't feel right any more.' I take a step back.

'Oh, for fuck's sake,' he says. He sounds angry, impatient, frustrated. 'You little cunt, leading me on all afternoon. What the fuck is your problem?'

'Sanderson,' I say, apologetically. 'That whole thing got in my head. When you mentioned him just now, it took me out of the moment. It made me feel a bit' – I wrack my brains – 'cheap. I asked you to stop saying it, and you said it again.'

He looks confused. 'But that's exactly what you are, isn't it? That's the *point* of you. You're on that website, doing whatever, for money, for men. Bit late in the day to suddenly discover you have *morals*, Frankie.' He's speaking as though Noël Coward wrote his lines for him. The grunting, grasping man is gone, replaced by an old-fashioned aristocrat. Then, 'Is that why you won't put out? Because I'm not paying you for it?'

I don't think anyone has ever spoken to me with quite so much contempt.

Shame – old, familiar shame – turns me cloudy and opaque. I've been kicked, and shaken. Every separate part of me is muddled and tainted. I'm cheap. I'm a whore. Maybe I should lie back down on the floor.

But after the shaking, a distillation.

Who is this man to tell me who I am, and what I am worth?

The choices I make, how I live, and how I make my money are mine. All mine. I have to own them. I cannot allow myself to be ashamed of them. But I've seen something alarming in Anthony's eyes.

He wanted me because he made a mistake about me. Because he thought I was cheap. I think about the website, the men. Sanderson. The thoughts and feelings I haven't wanted to entertain. *I don't care what they think of me, as long as they want me. As long as they think I'm beautiful, or hot, or even simply pretty enough to hold their attention for a moment.*

I'm not sure I can still believe that. If there's a possibility that any of them think like Anthony, I can't afford to take their money any more.

As clarity comes, I can start to see Anthony as he is, too. It's dark now, but his outline seems sharper, starker. The glamour has gone. I don't need to impress him. He's just some man with a camera. He might have a dazzling reputation, a celebrity pedigree, but I don't think he's capable of seeing what – or who – is in front of him. What kind of professional photographer uses their iPhone, anyway?

I do, I think. And I wait for the moment when I automatically call myself delusional or ridiculous, but it doesn't come. Instead, my ego responds to my id with *interesting.* How odd. A brief flare of optimism, sparking in the dark.

'I'm really sorry, Anthony,' I say, and I mean it. I'm sorry for both of us. 'I thought this was everything I wanted. It was, and it wasn't. I made a mistake.'

'I'm really sorry that I almost slept with a whore. A cheap little whore. Although you're not so little, are you, Frankie? Don't worry, I'll Photoshop your thighs. I'm a nice guy, really.'

'Thank you,' I say. 'You just proved, beyond all doubt, that I've made the right decision. Not having sex with you might be the wisest thing I've ever done in my life.'

For a moment, I wish I could stride straight out into the night. Then I think, 'No. I'll take my time and make him really uncomfortable.' Slowly, I walk back to the hair and makeup area. As I tug my jeans back on, I look down at my thighs. Fuck Photoshop. I promise myself I'll never say a bad word about them again.

Fully dressed, I walk out and head towards the door. Anthony is standing in the kitchen, his back to the room, his arms folded.

I see a familiar black rectangle gleaming on the edge of

272

the counter. For a second, I think it's my phone. 'I'll never forget what happened here today,' I say. And then I pick up the rectangle and slip it into my pocket, maybe because I still think it's my phone. It's an easy mistake to make. 'Goodbye,' I say. Anthony does not turn around. I walk away and I keep walking.

In some cities, they say, you're never more than six feet away from a rat. Or fifty feet away from a branch of Pret A Manger. Or a hundred feet away from a building site.

I turn right, and right again before I find what I'm looking for.

A car passes. I watch a pair of women run down the other side of the road and listen to the percussive thud of their trainers as their ponytails bounce and swing.

When they turn the corner, I smile at the scaffolding, lift a protruding plank and throw Anthony's iPhone into the bottom of a skip. I really wish Bean could see me now. I walk away quietly, head down, coat buttoned against the final blast of February chill. In my heart, it's spring, and I'm whistling.

Chapter Thirty-Six

Fate, luck and circumstance

Living well is the best revenge but throwing someone's phone into a skip might come a close second. And walking away is a form of resistance. It is a choice. An expression of freedom.

Fifteen minutes after I have left Anthony's studio, I feel drunk on that freedom. High on the novelty of it. I am not usually the sort of person who says no, sets boundaries, or takes control. Maybe this marks a turning point. Maybe everything is going to be different from now on. This was not the first time that I have been alone with a man, unsure and afraid. But it wasn't like the last time. Today I left. I managed to save myself.

But the trouble with experiencing a single fleeting moment of power, or enjoying a tiny, solitary scrap of autonomy, is that it sometimes makes you realise you have absolutely no control over any other part of your life.

My mother still isn't speaking to me. She has been actively avoiding me ever since I was naked in a newspaper. How have I tried to make things right? By handing myself over to different bossy woman and agreeing to be naked in a different newspaper. All she had to do was bathe me, like a baby, and after that I did as I was told.

An 'iconic' photographer (his words, his website) called me a whore. I might have got rid of his phone but there's every chance that those photos have been automatically uploaded somewhere. Derek Sanderson might be looking at them right now. I can picture him, crouched over a screen fogged by his breath, nude but for his mountaineering anorak.

Before I can stop myself, I replay Anthony's awful, ringing words. 'That's exactly what you are.' He spoke with such confidence. He was so sure about me when I struggled to feel sure about him. He labelled me, even when I was still trying to override every one of my instincts and trick myself into believing that he was going to give me what I wanted, and what I deserved. How on Earth can he know when I don't know?

I start to feel heavy, and my spirits sink back down. The familiar ache comes. People don't change. I can't change. I realised what I am, who I am, a long time ago.

I have never believed I was allowed to call myself a victim. Victims have experienced evil, injustice. But I believe my bad luck was fated. Perhaps it began before I was born. I was always going to be crushed under the wheel. Perhaps it all happened at random. Sometimes I wonder whether it was already written.

I know that if I was different, it might have made me stronger. Instead, I let it destroy me.

I don't know if my expectations about university were

naïve, or optimistic, or both. After the hell of school, and spending the first eighteen years of my life stumbling through cramped, dark, stuffy hallways, I kept moving forward because I believed there must be a warm, bright room at the end of the corridor. A door would open, easily, and a crowd of people would throw their arms open. 'We've been waiting for you!' they would say. I'd join the laughter. I'd understand the jokes. My people must be out there, somewhere.

When I mentioned going to university, Bean and Alison were encouraging. I'd 'bloom'. It would be 'the making' of me. Both, in their different ways, seemed relieved. However, my teachers were not encouraging. I'd read too many books about dreaming spires, quads, Georgian red brick piles. Now I realise that I didn't actually want to go to university, I wanted to go to an Evelyn Waugh novel. Mrs Bates, who taught history, said something sneery to me about how further education 'isn't Hogwarts' – I thought she was being excessively cruel, but perhaps she had a point.

With the grades I was predicted, I found a place in a coastal town. It was shabby, dreamy, windy. Maybe my life would have been different if I had chosen a central, modern room in one of the larger halls of residence. Instead, I picked the storybook setting, high on a hill, falling down, wildly romantic and impossible to heat.

I had few neighbours in my collapsing turret. There was Judith, a PhD student with a Velma bob and matching glasses. I'd have put her in her early thirties, but I never got to find out. I knocked at her door hopefully, with my thumb and forefinger wrapped around the neck of a bottle of supermarket merlot.

It took her maybe two minutes to come out. I still remember the terror, and the hope. Was I disturbing a minotaur? Would I be laughed at, scorned, rejected? Or was I on the brink of friendship? Was this the bright room I'd been walking towards?

'Hello, I'm Frankie! I've brought some wine. Are you going to the thing tonight? Maybe we can walk up together!' I was breathless, panicking, not expecting Judith to be a real adult. When she shook her head, I was crushed – but a little bit relieved.

'Sorry, I've got plans.' She shut the door. Oh.

I had promised Bean that I would try, very hard, to make friends of my own. Bean was very confident about these hypothetical friends; she seemed to set a lot of store by them. She'd promised me that the people here would be 'more mature' and 'friendly'. Neither of us had come up with a contingency plan for when doors were shut in my face.

The 'thing' was a drinks reception, a chance for new students to meet the faculty and each other. After being rejected by Judith, I would like to have stayed in my room. However, the only thing more daunting than walking into a room full of people by myself was the prospect of calling Bean and telling her that I had failed my only real challenge and spent my first night at university alone.

Still, I had my wine, and I had a new dress.

I believed in dresses, then, and I read the sort of books that encouraged me to maintain the myth. The sort of clothes I loved had been all wrong in the southern suburbs. At school, when out of uniform, you were expected to wear shrunken tees and low slung, embellished jeans, or tracksuits. You try being six foot tall and fourteen and a

D cup, wearing a Tammy Girl crop top. Alison would sigh over those clothes. We'd go on fruitless shopping trips, her begging me to try jeans that would get stuck on my shins, gathering piles of pink, glittery, little-girl clothes for the little girl I was failing to be. It would end in a row, and her buying me giant things from the men's section, shapeless things emblazoned with Nike and Adidas logos.

I left all of those sports jumpers at home, even though they would have offered some useful protection against the sharp wind, and swore I would dress exactly how I wanted, which was an approximation of what I imagined Elfine in *Cold Comfort Farm* wearing immediately after her introduction to sparkling London society.

The dress was from a junk shop, not a charity shop. A dark and dusty repository of various house clearances. The kind woman, behind the counter had said, 'It could be a Frank Usher,' and I nodded, not understanding what she meant but feeling as though I should be flattered that she thought I might know. I googled, later, and thought her theory didn't hold up. It was much more likely to be something cheap from a chain store with the label cut out, but that didn't matter much.

It was a fabulous, synthetic pink. Tailfin pink. Diner-waitress-lipstick pink. The colour of old America. Loose, with a low, scooped front and a lower back, polyester that felt like silk, looped chiffon ribbon trimming the hem. If I'd been six inches shorter, and significantly narrower, it would have looked like a slightly matronly nightie. But then, it felt like a proper party dress. The first thing I had really chosen for myself. It made me want to smile. It made me want to move.

It didn't absolutely go with my trainers, and so I made my first mistake and put on my hateful, cheap, satin peep-toe shoes, the result of another fight with Alison, who was upset when I told her I had no intention of ever trying to wear heels. I knew I'd lost the fight when she retorted, 'But the supermodels do it!'

The angle of the heel and the length and width of my foot forced my middle toes outwards. Moving made me think of Hans Christian Andersen's Little Mermaid, knifed by every step she took on land. Still, I put on my coat, opened my wine and started walking, hoping that numbness would come sooner or later.

I could have owned that moment. I could have changed everything for myself if I'd had the courage to be a lioness, a leopard, the six-foot-something woman in the bright pink dress. When I walked into the hall, people stopped talking and stared. Not all of them, but enough. I had their full attention, and it did not make me feel warm, or safe. It stung like an ice burn.

I felt sober, and cold. Too scared to take my coat off. I scanned the space, searching for a corner to hide in. Every one was occupied.

I feel quite fatalistic about many things. 'What's for you won't go by you,' as every other person's great-grandmother apparently used to say. I believed it – what I really believed was that nothing was for me. 'What's for you won't go by you' means 'You'll get exactly what you deserve', and I could not conceive of a reality where I deserved anything, even though I'd spent so long hoping, trying and waiting for a start. For something.

That night, I was tremulous with hope, yet quite resigned

to fate. We are all capable of believing entirely contradictory things at once, and the greatest cognitive dissonance we carry is about ourselves. I longed for it to be the first night of the rest of my life, but I believed this was unlikely. A few people might stare at the height, the exposed legs, the general effect. No one would approach me. I'd make a half-hearted effort, a quarter-hearted effort, and go home desolate and alone, and the next day I could call Bean and say, 'See? See?'

If nothing had happened, I'd believe that to be written in the stars too. Three sparkling ellipses, a celestial 'So what?' But it was the first night of the rest of my life and it still feels like all my fault. If I'd tried a little harder with Judith, perhaps we would have found common ground eventually. If I'd tried a little harder at school, just enough to convince the teachers that I wasn't a bimbo, or a shambling, dreamy idiot, they might have been more encouraging when I made my applications. I wouldn't have landed in that place, on that day.

Here is the contradiction that sits within my soul. I believe it was coming for me. I believe it was all I deserved. But I also know he didn't really *want* me. He wasn't moved by me. He was waiting for the first girl who seemed alone.

He was standing beside a trestle table, filling plastic cups with red wine. He seemed much older than me. He said hello, and I responded with deference. I assumed he must be a lecturer and, like a teacher, he was looking out for the wallflower. A good guy.

We sat on a pair of chairs, by the wall, and he talked about himself. He was in his final year, his dissertation was something to do with Communism, he was an active member of the film society. I remember letting the words wash over me. Thinking about how kind he was, as he kept bringing me more and more wine. I felt suddenly sleepy and then even more suddenly sick.

For a long time I thought I'd dreamed the rest. I feel flashes of it. The awful, visceral weight of him on me, him trying to get into my mouth, into my body, and thinking, 'But I've just been sick! But my dress is covered in sick!'

I remember the next morning clearly. First, I was awoken by the smell. Then adrenaline, shame, panic.

Ever since, I've read and heard the words of countless women who have been in a similar situation, and they have all mentioned the feeling of shame. Yet their shame seems carved from grace and granite – heavy, spiritual. The sort that ends in beatification. Mine was tar and treacle. I had become stinky, sticky, dirty. If I had been different, if I had been better, I'd have been in control. I would have enjoyed it. But I'd failed a test, one I would never be allowed to take again.

I looked at this man, pallid, slightly greasy, a spot forming on his chin, and felt overwhelmed by an urge to shake him awake and apologise. I was sorry for not being better at sex. I was sorry for not having a better body, for not being sufficiently scented and sophisticated.

My lovely dress was ruined. It was half unzipped, slipping off my shoulders, my plain, white cotton knickers (Why hadn't I learned lingerie, before my rape?) balled around my left ankle. I was glad, at least, that I wasn't naked – not just because it would have been so horribly exposing, but because I don't think I would have had the emotional or physical strength to pull that damp, crumpled dress back over my head. I was gathering myself together as silently

281

as I could, and my assailant opened one eye. 'Take it easy, yeah?' he said, before turning over and pushing his head under a nest of pillows.

Sometimes people vomit in the night, and they choke on it and they die, I thought, as the wind whipped my cold, sticky dress against my legs. I must be lucky. Then, *No. There is no luck here, for me. I wish I had died. Why didn't I die?*

When I got home and opened the door, Judith was coming out of the kitchen. She looked me up and down. 'I see.' Then, 'My work requires a lot of peace and quiet. This isn't really the right place for a fresher. If you're going to make a lot of noise and fuss, Frankie, maybe you could move to one of the bigger halls.'

I showered, I fell asleep, I showered again, I rang Bean. Her voice was bright with hope. Was I having fun? Meeting people? I needed a prize for her, a present, so I volunteered all I could muster. 'I met a guy. Don't think I'll see him again.'

Bean was delighted. 'Nice work, Franks! Don't meet a guy on your first night. Play the field!' She sounded wistful. I remembered she had met Paul in her halls.

At my first seminar, there was some whispering and giggling. One girl muttered, 'Get out your damp cloth, here comes the Puker!' And I had a nickname.

Strangely, it helped me to reconfigure my awful, heavy shame, to shrink it down to a size that made it easier to carry around with me. The sex was not the headline. No one cared about the fact that some fresher had gone home with a guy she'd just met. I wasn't a slut. No one knew I'd arrived as an awkward, anxious virgin.

Still, life was hard. I hated talking to people and I hated being by myself. I'm sure some people thought me rude or standoffish. Once, caught out by surprise tears, I saw a girl I knew walking towards me, and I jumped into a hedge, scratching my face on the brambles.

I was crying because I didn't know there was a name for what had happened, a label – or rather, I knew there was, but I didn't think I was worthy of it. I didn't think I counted. I was crying because I hated myself. For making such a stupid mistake, and for my failure to put it behind me. Most of all, I was crying because I was grieving all my old hope. The weeks and months I had spent surviving school in a dream of university, thinking my life was just about to start.

A better girl would have been able to bury all her shame and sadness in academic work. I was not better, and I seized up. Some mornings I felt dense and furred, thick and slow. Too heavy to sit up properly, sludge in my veins. The only thoughts I could consciously formulate were *I'm so tired* and *I want to die*. I wept for Alison, and for Bean, and for their tragedies, a dead dad and a suicidal sister. Bean, I knew, had been sad sometimes. But Bean had also done everything she could to protect me from her pain. I wept for myself because I couldn't kill myself and I felt ashamed of that too. At least I had people who loved me, and wanted me around, even if I didn't want to be around. How dare I feel this way?

Most days, the sun seemed to fall straight out of the sky after rising, and there was no light at all. I'd read and write all morning, and then sleep long into the afternoon. I'd wake up and hope night had fallen. Occasionally, if I ventured outside after waking, I was surprised to find visibility, and other people, normal people, going around, doing things. They seemed to be managing to buy milk and catch buses without falling to their knees, bawling for their families. I felt so far away from Alison and Bean, even though Bean was a grown-up now, with a life of her own. I tried to hustle my way out of my feelings. *You're silly. You're too sensitive.* True. *It will pass.* A lie.

There were other days when I would leap up with purpose, determined to fix myself, change myself, start anew. I'd see the sun rise through the mist, and watch the walls became silken, molten pale gold. Then something happened in the afternoon. If the sun shone, which was rare, my little world turned Uranium yellow. It took me weeks to realise that this colour triggered a crushing, shapeless, nameless sense of dread. I'd want to weep, and search for something to be frightened of – because the idea that my fear was not attached to anything was the most alarming thing of all.

The fear would arrive often and without warning. I could be walking by the sea and my heart would start to beat slightly faster, my cheeks would become warm, the gorgeous crash of the waves would become roaring static and I'd break into a breathless run, to my own silent soundtrack of 'No exit no exit no exit'.

I diagnosed myself with flu and missed two seminars. When I skipped the third one, I was called into a meeting and then sent to see a counsellor. The counsellor suggested I might like to do something nice for myself. *Like killing myself*, I thought, and then bit my lip. At the beginning, she'd made it clear that if I told her I was thinking about it, people would be 'notified'. Again, I thought of the pain it might cause Alison and Bean, and I stayed silent. I fantasised about being in freak accidents. I stopped looking when I crossed the road.

There were more meetings, and I didn't know how to advocate for myself, or how to explain myself. I came across as sullen, stuck up, uncommunicative. I don't remember those meetings well. I know that at one point, my supervisor said, 'Frances, we are trying to help you, but you might be a lost cause.' At one point, the notion that I was 'on drugs' was floated.

I failed all my first-year exams. When Alison came to pick me up at the end of the year I braced myself for furious invective, a tale of opportunities wasted and money spent. Instead, I stood hunched over in a grey coat I don't remember buying, and she put her arms around me, bone on bone. The tears were falling down my face even before I could smell her Diorella. She wasn't perfect, but she was my home. 'Frankie, you're so thin,' she murmured. Only now do I realise this wasn't praise, but concern.

Alison knew how to be kind when it counted. She didn't ask me any questions, not even, 'How are you?' She would bring me breakfast in the mornings, and she cut the crusts off my toast. I was deeply touched, and a little confused. 'Mum, I'm nineteen, I can manage crusts!' I said, after a few weeks, laughing.

'You laughed!' she said, and then pressed her forearm against her eyes. 'Thank goodness! I was worried I would never hear that sound again.'

Bean would come to visit at the weekends. She brought Paul sometimes, and I felt shy of him, embarrassed about not being a worthy sister to the love of his life. Bean was shiny, impressive, competent, and she deserved a sibling who matched. I played down my pain. 'I had to drop out, I'm just a bit thick,' I explained, but this would make Bean angry. Once we almost had a physical fight about it. 'Frankie, never, ever say that about yourself! It isn't true!' She shook me, and then dropped me, abruptly. 'I'm so sorry, I don't know what came over me.'

Neither Bean nor Alison ever asked me to talk about what happened, or why I had to leave, and I was grateful. I think they knew I couldn't explain myself. I sometimes wonder whether they guessed.

I did a little temping, and Alison would find scraps and snippets of work, tiny jobs for would-bes and wannabes. She'd buy *The Stage* at the newsagents and make a big fuss of telling the person behind the counter that it was 'for my daughter. She's very talented!'

She'd tell me, 'You need to get back out there.' It was so nice to be believed in. Even though I was never, ever out there in the first place.

I also tried to get a 'proper' job, but without a degree it seemed pointless. Interviews were even worse than auditions, where occasionally I'd get down to the final three and nearly be a 'woman who just loves Oxyfresh ultra whitening toothpaste' – I was far less convincing as a 'woman who longs to become a junior marketing executive'. Months drifted into years, and Alison became hardened by faded hope. 'You've got to get a thicker skin, Frankie, to be in this game,' she'd say, after she, not I, had wept over my failure to secure a walk-on part in an obscure Dutch drama.

A thicker skin. If I had a thicker skin, I could be all kinds of things. A graduate. A success. A real person in the world.

Everything would be for me, and nothing would go by me. I would be worth looking at, worth seeing. If only the right person paid attention to my hidden potential, I would be able to bloom. I could make my family proud of me at last.

But I didn't have potential. I had been exposed, and the whole world could see exactly what I was. A dropout, a drifter, a puker with too many feelings. I wasn't broken – I had been faulty from the start.

Chapter Thirty-Seven

News

When the pounding beat of my heart shocks me awake on Wednesday morning, it instructs me to worry. Do I have to sit an exam? Attend a job interview? The paranoia buzzes and builds, and I wonder whether I need to check for blood or bruises. This isn't anxiety, this is *fear*, thick and dark. It's as if I came home, went straight out again and got blackout drunk. But my coat is on its hook on the back of the door. I remember drinking a glass of water and putting my T-shirt on before going to sleep. What's going on?

Bean. Today is results day.

Paul will call – he *promised*. But what if the results don't come in for a while? Or the news is bad, and he doesn't know how to tell me? If the news *is* bad, it might be all my fault. I have caused Bean so much stress and worry, not just over the last month. A lifetime's worth.

I edge and stumble my way through the next few hours, waves of adrenaline occasionally sharpening the dull edge of despair. I don't know how I managed to walk to work.

Miriam looks at my face and says, 'It's today, isn't it?

I'm not going to say anything at all unless you want me to. In which case I will chat absolute, endless, distracting bollocks. You know I'm capable of it. I'm not even going to ask you what happened with Maz yesterday. Unless you want to tell me.'

If I hug her, I'll cry, so I give her a thumbs up.

When Paul calls at 11.03, Miriam leaps to her feet and knocks her glass of kefir into her handbag. She vaults over a chair and reaches for the radio, and there's a sharp, sudden blast of Rick Astley, followed by a secondary blast of yelping.

'Shit! *Shit!* Flossie, I'm so sorry, I didn't mean to, the volume is stuck. Sorry, sorry!'

And then everything goes quiet, too quiet, and I can hear Paul crying.

I say his name. 'I'm so, so sorry, I missed what you just said, it was a bit loud in here.'

'Oh, Frankie, I can't . . . ' and he's sobbing still.

Miriam is looking at me, and I realise she's trying to breathe with me, for me.

'Paul, we will get through this.' If I can make myself sound brave, if I can *do* brave, I can *be* brave. 'Can you tell me exactly what Dr Zainab said?'

'Non-invasive.' I latch onto the last three syllables and feel a flash of panic before Paul says, 'Frankie, it's *good* news. There's healthy tissue. It doesn't seem to have spread.'

I burst into tears, too. 'Are you *sure*?' I wail.

'She'll need to have a course of radiotherapy, starting in about four weeks. Oh, I've been so scared for her. For us. And I didn't want to say anything – she'd convinced herself that this would happen, and that everything would be OK.

289

She'd designed her own treatment plan in her head, and I'd convinced myself of the opposite as a form of insurance. I'd decided this was a death sentence.' He starts sobbing again.

'It's OK, please don't cry,' I say, even though I can feel fresh tears hitting my own cheeks. 'I'd really, really love to see her,' I say. Then, thinking quickly, 'What about Alison? Has she spoken to her? Have you?'

'It might not be possible, right now.' Paul suddenly sounds business-like, as though he's dealing with a double-glazing salesman. What happened to the tender, weeping man I was speaking to seconds ago?

'What do you mean?' I say. 'The news is good. Our mum needs to know. She deserves to know. And I promised to give Bean this time and let her recover, and I kept that promise.'

'Frankie, I know this is hard to hear but she doesn't want to see you just yet,' Paul says, still sounding like Mr Reasonable. Fuck him. I hate him so much.

'How can you possibly know that?' I say, attempting to channel Mrs Reasonable and coming out Mrs Squeaky. 'It's not up to you to decide!'

'It's not up to me, no,' says Paul. 'It's up to Bean, and as soon as we heard the news, it was the first thing I asked her.'

'I don't understand,' I say.

'Frankie, the stuff in the papers . . . she's taken it pretty hard,' Paul says, gently. 'I think she just needs time.'

I could cope when I could blame Paul for this. The idea that it's Bean's choice is unbearable.

'Fine.' I kick at the wastepaper bin and hurt my foot. 'She doesn't want to see me because I'm a big slutty slut. Well, tell her she's a judgemental . . . tell her that I've definitely seen at least one picture of *her* when she was a sexy zombie nurse at a fresher's Halloween ball, and how is it different—'

He cuts me off. 'Frankie, it isn't that. You're her baby sister. And this is a lot for her to get her head around. She's struggling because this happened the moment she wasn't there to look after you.'

I bend down and rub at my toe. It doesn't help. Miriam has sat down again and turned her handbag inside out, and she's systematically going through its contents with a wet wipe.

Paul keeps speaking. 'She needs to tell Alison but she's furious with her, too. Bean blames her for all of this. We're going to see some friends in Brighton this weekend – we could all do with a break. Can you just give her a bit more time and space? She'll be ready when she's ready. Maybe you can talk to your mum and tell her!' He says this as though he's awarding me a small prize. 'That's a nice thing you can do for Bean.'

'Well, technically Bean made me promise not to. And Alison still isn't—'

'Good, good! Nice one! Thanks, Frankie, speak soon!' Paul hangs up.

I'd *love* to tell Alison, but I'm still waiting for her to break her silence and return one of my thirty-eight voicemails. Short of turning up on her doorstep and shouting through her letterbox, I don't know what to do.

Miriam puts down her wet wipe. 'So, is that what it sounds like? Good news?'

'Yeah,' I say, trying to smile. 'Good news.'

Chapter Thirty-Eight

The feelings will still be there

The next few days are strange. Half the time, I feel ener-
vated, emotionally jetlagged – and then I'm thrown by
strange surges of angry energy, an itch that starts deep
within the skin. I call Alison every morning, only to be
told that her inbox is not accepting messages. On Thursday
night I go on a pointless pilgrimage to Southfields. I find her
house in darkness, then I get stuck on a rail replacement bus
and spend a long forty-five minutes in a depot in Streatham.

By the end of the week, I catch myself snapping at Miriam
when she suggests that Bean might benefit from a course of
activated charcoal. Then, I immediately spend forty pounds
on a tub of charcoal pills. I can't stop shopping for Bean.
Every time I google 'radiotherapy side effects', it triggers an
internet trolley dash. She's going to be very tired, so I spend
more than a month's rent on a stunning pair of electric-pink
silk pyjamas.

Then I panic, because all breast cancer branding seems to
be pink, and she might never want to see the colour again,
so I add a crisp cotton blue-and-white-striped set to the

pile. I buy medicated moisturisers, organic throat lozenges, dusts to put in your tea that claim to boost your mood. I'm looking at luxury sun loungers – by the time she has finished treatment, it might be warm enough to read in the garden! – when Miriam intervenes.

'Flossie, this big Bean binge – well, firstly, I think she probably already has some garden furniture, yes?'

I look at my screen and shrug. 'I'm sure she could always use more. And apparently, this reclining chair is built with NASA technology.'

'This is not what Paul meant when he told you to give your sister some space.' She puts a hand on my shoulder. 'You have a lot of feelings right now. You're not shopping them away, you're refusing to feel them. When you've spent all your money, the feelings will still be there.'

Miriam can be very irritating. 'But I don't want to feel this way!' I cry. 'It's horrible. I can't control anything. Yes, of course, it's wonderful about Bean, but the best case scenario is still a shitty scenario. She's still got to have this treatment. She's still not speaking to me.' I hang my head, feeling tears start to come. 'Neither is Alison. Neither is Maz.'

The truth is that Maz is the one person I have made no effort to contact. I don't know how I feel about her, any more, and I don't know how to tell her what happened with Anthony. He's her friend. He must have told her his side of the story already. She hasn't called me to ask me about it, or to see if I'm OK. I suspect she wouldn't be on my side. Sometimes I'm not sure if *I'm* on my side.

Every day that goes by without a message from her feels like a reprieve. Perhaps the Anthony business made her decide not to bother with the piece. Or Sanderson is sulking because he didn't get his grubby pictures, and he decided to cancel the whole thing. Maz barely interviewed me, after all. The barrage of articles about me is grinding to a halt; everyone has lost interest, and they are finally leaving me alone. It's a relief.

Still, I miss the Maz who used to live in my imagination. I trusted her. I'm not sure about the real one.

'I don't understand why you don't just call Maz, like a normal person,' says Miriam. 'Or go to her house. You know where she lives.'

I knit my fingers together and twist them around and around. 'It's not that simple.'

'Why not?' says Miriam.

'I don't know,' I say, after a pause. 'Everything has got away from me.'

Miriam sighs. 'There's so much stuff going on in your life right now that you can't control. But you can control this. I thought this was going to be empowering for you, Frankie. A celebration of body positivity! The moment when you really show up!' She sounds so disappointed.

I haven't been able to explain the shoot to Miriam – I change the subject whenever she brings it up. But the word 'empowering' is painful to hear. Before I can stop myself, I picture Anthony's face. The things he called me. Slow-acting acid, eating away at me from the inside out.

I don't think I want to show up any more.

Chapter Thirty-Nine

The worst that could happen

When I walk to the newsagent on Sunday morning, the sun has just started rising. It's shockingly, thrillingly, cold and bright. The air feels sharp against my cheeks, almost painful.

I'm 99.9 per cent certain that I won't be in the paper. Maz would definitely have called, or texted, or said *something* before now, if I was. I'll just buy the *News on Sunday* as a precaution, a superstition. When I have checked it thoroughly, I can finally move on with my life. Maybe I'll go on a long walk to a café and have a wholesome breakfast as a reward . . . or, I think, scanning the shelves, I could buy that family-sized bag of chocolate buttons. Families are wholesome.

Then, I see it. The *News on Sunday* headline is so stark and startling that I jump. I am briefly airborne.

SANDERSON DEAD

72-year-old mogul dies in hospital following suspected heart attack

Oh my God.

It's in the *Post*, too.

ENQUIRIES EXPECTED TO FOLLOW SANDERSON'S DEATH

Historical allegations to haunt controversial media magnate

The *Herald*, classily, has gone with:

ME TOO! I WANT SANDERSON DOSH

Accusers hope to get their hands on mogul millions

I pick up the *News* and the *Post* and stare at the two photos. The *News* shows him in a smart black suit, stepping out of a private jet, his face set, blank and expressionless. The *Post* has picked a picture that might be ten or fifteen years old. He looks a little younger in it – and he has his arm around a blonde woman in a strapless dress who might be in her early twenties. She stares at the camera. He stares at her breasts.

I wish I felt vindicated. I wish I could simply think, 'Good. Fuck him!' But I'm frightened, and sick, and guilty and scared. I'm not sure why.

Each paper is heavy. I arrange them under my forearm to carry them both to the till, sorting out the bags filled with thick supplements and pamphlets. The *News on Sunday* flops open to reveal the magazine, and there I am.

The cover is bright pink, and I'm in my skimpy black

296

underwear, leaning forward, eyes half shut, falling out of my bra. Stamped over me, the caption reads:

SEXY FEMINIST?

Then,

> Meet Frankie Howard. She thinks her breasts can empower you. Maz Clarke speaks to the controversial 'campaigner babe'.

I slam it shut.

Then I start laughing, hysterically. Because this is the worst thing that could have happened. I kept making all those deals with the universe, promising I'd do *anything* if Bean got better. Bean is getting better, and Sanderson is dead, and I'm still here. Showing up, in my bra. I could kill Maz. I want to weep. Then another wave of giggles engulfs me. This is truly in the worst possible taste. It isn't sinking in, at all. It's ridiculous. *I'm* ridiculous.

I'm so overcome, and tired, and mad, that as I try to put the papers back together, I think I can see my mother on the front of the *Post*.

I'm tempted to ask the cashier, 'Am I losing my mind, or can you see that lady on the masthead? With the hair that looks not unlike the sail on the *Cutty Sark*?'

> This week, our #BeKind4Cancer columnist shows us how we can boost our mental wellbeing.

It *is* her. What the hell is going on?

Staggering to a bench, I sit down with my newspapers, staring at her face again. Alison looks at home on the cover – much more so than I do. This is utterly improbable and *completely* plausible. This is Alison helping, in the most Alison way she knows. It hurts that she hasn't told me – but it stings when I wonder *why* she hasn't told me. I've been so self-obsessed, convinced she has been ignoring me and punishing me. But she's been busy, thinking about Bean. Not about me, at all.

Of course, she's got it wrong. But so have I. We've ended up in bad places, with good intentions. Like mother, like daughter. Here's me, in my bra. There's Alison, claiming that the best way to '#BeKind4Cancer' is to try 'a lovely indoor picnic'. Most of the page is taken up by a picture of Alison clutching a tiered cake stand piled high with jam tarts and custard creams.

'Careful, they'll bloat you,' I mutter.

It's been so long since I've heard her voice. I wish she was here. I'd do absolutely anything to have her here beside me, criticising my clothes and then telling me off for frowning. I want my mum so badly. I miss her so much that I want to press my face against the page.

Then, bracing myself for the worst, I pick up the *News on Sunday*.

I try and fail to see myself in the woman on the pages. Big hair, expensive underwear, attractive enough – striking, maybe?

No, that's the last word I'd use. She really could be anybody. Her bare body is neither sexy nor unsexy. It's about as exciting as a deodorant advert. The face, too, is generic. It doesn't yield any special mysteries. These are Anthony's pictures. Not pictures of me.

I try to project a hint of sadness, madness, anything, into the expression, but it's as blank as Derek Sanderson's face on the front page. When I take my own picture, at least I look like *someone*. Like I have a story.

Not for the first time, I think that perhaps Anthony Jack isn't such a good photographer, after all.

I start to read the piece.

Blonde ambition

Maz Clarke gets up close and personal with DIY porn star Frankie Howard

'If I have a message, I guess it's this: there's nothing wrong with being sexy.' Frankie Howard shakes her golden curls as the celebrated photographer Anthony Jack snaps away. 'I believe in empowerment, for all of us. I believe in sexy feminism. I am an artist. This is my art. And I want to be an example of what's possible.'

Frankie is one of a growing number of women who are taking their careers and reputations into their own hands by becoming self-styled, DIY 'porn stars'. Howard is far from a traditional pin-up, but she's paving a path that allows women of all shapes and sizes to pursue 'erotic empowerment'. She says, 'It's a struggle to find space for women to express their sexuality, so I'm fighting back.'

A growing number of 'sex-positive' social media networks are allowing people like Frankie to connect with a fan base, and even profit from it. Globally, experts predict that the industry will be worth half a billion dollars in the next five years. Frankie has plenty of detractors, online and off, but she doesn't care what people say. 'I want to love my body! I want to feel sexy, and desirable, but how can I do that unless the desire is coming from me in the first place? This is how I'm learning to live in my skin.'

Over the last decade, the exploitation of women has dominated the headlines, following growing concerns and protests about abuse, harassment and the prevalence of 'rape culture'. Many feel that Howard's work is totally insensitive – but for others, it represents a timely vibe shift. If she says, 'Let's celebrate our bodies', we think it's time to join the party.

I believed Maz was better than this.

I thought we had talked about complications and contradictions. I thought she understood why it's so hard to love our bodies while living in the world. I hoped we'd create something that helped other women to feel seen. This is just tits and bullshit. It's not an article – it's a long, crass caption.

There's nothing wrong with being sexy. There is everything wrong with being a literal dumb blonde. I need to speak up.

Maz has made me a puppet. The girl in the pictures might not mind, but I do. I need to go and see her. Now, before I lose my nerve.

Chapter Forty

A lesson

'It is very early, Frankie,' says Laura, her arms folded. 'Have you called first? She didn't mention you coming. She's still sleeping.'

'That's OK, I don't mind waiting!' I smile. I suspect that getting an audience with Maz will require ignoring all social cues. Then I see a plume of red hair over Laura's shoulder, hear a familiar 'Darling'. Then, 'You do it! You put her on a plane! I don't see why I should pick her up from *fucking Gstaad*.'

'Oh, look at that, she's up!' I start to force my way through, expecting resistance – Laura is about a quarter of my size, but I'm certain she's stronger than me. However, she steps aside and I sprint past.

'Hallo, Maz! Great to see you!' I tap her on the shoulder, and she turns around and scowls at me. For a moment, I feel awful. Maz looks exhausted, eyes framed by smudge and sparkle. Has she been to bed? Is that a silky nightie, or a party dress? 'Ah, you're on the phone! I'll wait in the kitchen,' I say.

Pulling up a stool, I see the Sunday papers, open and spread all over the table.

She follows me. 'My fucking ex,' she explains. 'I said I'd call him back tomorrow, it's late there. Not a fun conversation to have on a Sunday morning. My daughter lives with him, in America.'

'That must be tough,' I say, softly. 'Do you get to see her often?'

'It's a lot of admin,' she snorts. 'And it's disruptive. I've got my own life to lead, I'm not going to drop everything to organise her Easter vacation.'

Right.

'So,' I say, holding up the magazine. 'It's in. It would have been nice if you'd told me, no? Or asked me for any input whatsoever. Because, Maz, what you've done here doesn't feel very "empowering".' Before I can stop myself, I'm making air quotes with my fingers. 'In fact, I'd describe it as "reductive". But hey, what do I know? I'm just a "sexy feminist".'

'Oh, I don't choose the headline, the subs do. And you never know if any piece is going to run or not until the paper actually comes out,' she says, airily. 'It's a good piece, I thought. Strong. Fun. Clear messaging.'

I can't believe I'm thinking this but I wish Paul were here, with his stupid 'reasonable' voice. 'What messaging?' I spit. 'I trusted you. I believed you were the one person who got it, who might be able to make a difference. We had a real opportunity here. This wasn't for me. This was for the millions of women who feel like me, which is what we talked about. It's hard to love your body – and harder when it's sold to us as feminist obligation *and* a slogan on a shower gel advert. It's hard to celebrate your sexuality, and harder when you're ashamed of what gets you off because it technically makes you a tool of the patriarchy. We had a chance to speak to people, and you fucked it up. I thought you were a good writer.'

She raises her eyebrows. 'You told me you wanted to love your body. You told me you wanted to feel sexy and desirable. You told me you wanted to learn to live in your skin. Is that not what this is? Have I not been teaching you?' She exhales sharply. 'It's Anthony, isn't it? He said you were all over him, at the shoot, and he had to let you down gently. Don't be embarrassed. Apparently, it happens a lot.' She tilts her head and looks almost sympathetic.

I stand up. 'It was the other way round.' I shove the *Post* at her. 'Well, sort of. By the way, I don't know if you've noticed every single headline here, but his friend and yours, Derek Sanderson, just died. It's hilarious, isn't it, for me to discover that you both invited a known predator to gawp at me during our sexy feminist empowerment shoot.'

Maz flushes slightly. 'You don't invite Derek; he decides – decided – to come.'

'Oh, I bet he did,' I say. The flash of fury is igniting.

Maz, oblivious, gestures at the papers. 'This is really unfortunate timing, Frankie, I'm afraid. Because if there's a great big wave of #MeToo stuff, your piece in the *News* isn't going to land well. There might be a bit of a backlash. Although I haven't seen anything about you online yet, it's all just Sanderson, Sanderson, Sanderson.'

Please stop saying his name.

'So, here's what we're going to do. You sit tight, and trust me, and I'll be in touch when I've figured out the next stage

303

of the plan. Actually,' she says, thoughtfully, 'I don't want to burn any bridges with the *News*, but everyone else is denouncing Sanderson. Maybe you could join in? I mean, he was a bit touchy-feely with you; we all saw it.' She nods emphatically, concerned.

She saw it. She did nothing. She offered the man a drink. Even Anthony Jack did more to help than she did. But now, it could be part of a cause. Now my connection with the dead abuser could be convenient for Maz.

She is unbelievable.

'Maz, I think we're done here,' I say.

It's taken me a long time to work it out. The only empowerment Maz cares about is her own.

Finally, I am ready to stop giving all my power away.

Chapter Forty-One

To do, and not to 'be'

As I walk home, I think about the article Maz wrote. Just as I did when the *Herald* piece came out, I imagine every single person I know reading it, and I wonder about how they might be judging me. Then I think about imaginary 'me' – the version of Frankie Howard that Maz described.

That Frankie might be a little much, a little unsubtle, but she's *confident*. She does not believe there is anything wrong with making money from her body or making her body work for her. She seems to like herself. There's no trace of vulnerability or anxiety there. What would it feel like to be *that* Frankie?

I think of some of the things I've been called by strangers, by Anthony, by Maz. By Bean, and Alison. I've never answered back. I have never stood up and shouted, 'That's not who I am. *This* is.'

But who am I?

An insecure, horny, lonely, confused woman who dared to dance into the tractor beam of the male gaze. A bad sister. A disappointing daughter. A ghost tenant, a dull neighbour, the employee of a business with dubious legal status. A subletter who does not pay her own council tax or have a GP.

If my flat fell down right now, the people in charge would never know I had been there in the first place. Never mind FinePrint – on paper, *I* don't exist. Do I even have adult dental records?

Anthony called me many things, but he also said I was beautiful. I don't know why I have been so quick to discount that as a potential identity when it's been my biggest ambition for so long. It's not even the first time it's happened; I see it in 'fan' comments and messages. Still, no one has ever been able to make me believe it for more than a moment. Maybe that's because it's the only thing I do know about myself: I am not beautiful.

'I am not beautiful,' I say, quietly.

A short, sharp pang of grief rips through my body. I wait for further feelings. Despair shall set in. This is my tragedy. My bones shall shatter. A woman who is not beautiful cannot be useful to anyone.

But I'm still here. Still breathing. Still a person. Poor – unless I count the strange swell of website income. Obscure – apart from my media infamy. Plain – maybe. Definitely not little. What about my heart and soul?

Bean is beautiful, and I am never going to be like Bean. I'm never going to graduate to her level, never going to become what she represents. *I'm never going to be good enough. I'm never going to become as loved as she is,* I think.

Is that true?

Or have I just been looking in all the wrong places?

Love looks like family. It looks like Miriam, the only person in the world who has never judged me and who speaks a love language of crystals and strange-smelling teas. It looks like Mrs Antrobus, worrying about my wellbeing and inviting me into her home.

There has been barely any romantic love in my life, but that's a choice I've made. I have never wanted a man to get close to me. I have dated rarely and chosen badly – Rupert – because I decided, ahead of time, that I was damned and doomed. I have not loved myself enough to be loved in that way.

Instead, I waited for strangers to validate me. I wanted their attention to fill me up. I thought they could stop me from feeling worthless. It never occurred to me that instead, I could declare myself priceless.

I told myself I was celebrating my body, claiming it, and taking control of my image. I was doing creative work. It was proof of my confidence. But seeing Maz's words makes me realise I'm not confident – that's the quality I believed beauty would bestow on me. If I truly believed in what I was doing, I wouldn't have wanted to keep it a secret.

The *Herald* quoted that woman, Rita someone, who spoke openly about her own work. In fact, she sounded downright proud.

Out of curiosity, I google 'Rita pornstar'. The results fill pages. This is someone who wants to be searched for and seen.

The internet is not a reliable indicator of anyone's interior life, but as far as I can tell Rita seems robust. She has a logo, merchandise – I can buy a T-shirt that says 'Ryde

Me' for $29.99. The first pictures of her are not naked and exploitative but images of her meeting thousands of fans at something called PornCon '22. (Cum On Down!!!!!)

There isn't anything shameful about Rita's world. But I don't think it's where I belong. While there is nothing wrong with making a living from the way you choose to use your body, if that's your job you need to treat it like one: With some perspective. With some distance. And I'm beginning to realise that beauty is a useless qualification. The true entry requirement is rock-solid self-esteem.

I never really wanted to be paid in money. I craved compliments. Fifteen pounds a month is neither here nor there; I just wanted to earn fifteen minutes of a stranger's undivided attention and approval, to seem worthy of something. I have been trying to fill a bottomless bucket with enough validation to build a life on. To be someone else's fantasy, a picture-perfect girl. I thought attention was the solution.

And that's why #BeKind4Cancer is such a stupid slogan. Because 'be kind' is an empty instruction. How do you measure or qualify kindness? You can wander the world wishing people well and thinking sweet thoughts, but if you really want to show up and help, you have to *do*. I've done nothing. Everyone was falling over themselves to praise me for the list – and then to call me names, and curse me, and judge me, and be frankly *unkind* when it made them feel better.

I've been desperate for attention. Begging for it. Demanding it. But I haven't been *paying* attention. Staring at my reflection, literally and figuratively, has shrunk my world. Maybe that's why my life feels so small and sad sometimes. The silver of the mirror turns everything grey. If I look up and look out, I might start to lose my *self* and find my *purpose*. I'm too big to keep living small.

I want to show up. I want to help.

Chapter Forty-Two

Something that's yours

As I approach the front of my building I notice a familiar flash of hair. The bouffant helmet beehive, matchless and immovable. And underneath it, a face that looks all wrong – crumpled, craven.

Have I manifested Alison?

She's always on my mind, and I was going to track her down today, no matter what it took. I blinked, and she travelled from my mind's eye straight to the pavement. I'm even more shocked than I was when I saw her on the front of the *Post*. This makes no sense. But nothing does.

'Mum!' I say. 'Thank God! I know you probably want to shout at me – in fact, I want you to shout at me—' I say, but she holds her hand up and speaks over me.

'Frankie, thank goodness you're here. I've been so worried, wondering where you might have got to.' She sounds as though she's been crying.

I want to run to her. Why isn't she hugging me? 'Why didn't you phone? You could have tried Mrs Antrobus – actually, I think she's away ...'

She looks exhausted, frightened. 'You're right.' I don't think Alison has ever said these words together before. 'I wasn't thinking straight. You're here now. Can I come in for a cup of tea?' She sounds timid and uncertain.

'Of course, of course!' She looks at me, and I look at her. She opens her mouth, and shuts it. I gather her into my arms and push us both through the door. Slowly and awkwardly, we guide each other up the stairwell.

It's strange to see Alison in my bedsit. Usually I come to her; I don't think she has visited since I first moved in. Her gloss, her grooming, throws the shabbiness of the surroundings into sharp relief. However, today the space overpowers her. She becomes stale and grey, greasy and dusty. She sits on the corner of my unmade bed, and I wait for her to comment or simply wrinkle her nose. I am wrinkling my nose. I can smell my unwashed ghosts.

The room is gloomy, and it is taking my eyes longer than usual to become accustomed to the lack of light and the general sense of squalor. How long have I lived here, now? It was only ever supposed to be six months, a year at most. I meant to build up an emergency fund, sort my life out, buy myself some time and some freedom. Instead, I simply got used to it.

If I am so afraid of everyone dying, why am I living like this? I'm barely living at all.

You'd feel sad for the girl who lived here. I do. And I feel sad for her mother. Alison is slumped, round and lashless, like a mole. A heartbroken mole. I'm not sure I have ever seen her without mascara before.

Alison opens her mouth and shuts it again. I breathe in and brace for criticism, waiting for my home to get a verbal kicking. It deserves it. I deserve it. But she simply says, 'Frankie, I can't do this any more, it's too much.'

Sitting beside her on the edge of the bed, I take her hands. 'What happened?'

'Well, I've been writing this column.' She gestures vaguely.

'I just saw in today's paper,' I say. 'I wish you'd told me before.' I'm longing to ask how it happened, and why it happened, and what possessed her to jump on the *Post*'s stupid bandwagon. But I can't do it yet. Everything between us feels too delicate, too fragile. 'Congratulations,' I say instead, squeezing her hand.

She gives me a watery smile and takes her hand away. 'No, I'm officially a liar. It's all gone wrong, Frankie. Everyone hates me. Your sister won't return my calls.'

I'm confused. 'But it's not like the list, at least you don't mention Bean. It's just about biscuits.'

Alison sighs. 'She's furious about the whole thing. Leticia was keen to keep the campaign going and said this was a way to make sure everyone at the *Post* had what they needed. They were going to sue you, Frankie. I tried to explain to Bean that I was doing it for you. I don't think she believed me.'

She lowers her voice. 'To be honest, I thought it would be fun, too. A nice distraction from everything. And I *did* think I might have something to say about grief, mother-hood, losing a partner. I've lived through a lot.'

'Right,' I say. 'So, picnics . . .'

'Leticia rewrites it all. She takes my copy and turns it into drivel, about how lovely things are just lovely. Positive vibes all round! Isn't it nice how you can get so many different kinds of hummus now?' She looks angry. 'I'm a widow, I'm estranged from both my daughters, I'm desperately worried

312

about them both, and I've come to regret starting this chain of events in the first place. I've got things to say – but no, it's just my name, and my photo, and then an advert for *fucking hummus*.'

I gasp, and Alison gasps, and we both start to laugh.

'Sorry,' she says.

'Don't be! I don't think I've heard you use that word before,' I say, still slightly stunned.

'Do you need me to explain what it means?' says Alison, with a smirk, and then we're both laughing again. When she gets her breath back, she says, 'I saw your photos in the *News*, and your interview, and I wanted to say that I'm proud of you. It's taken me some time to come to terms with everything that has happened, but I'm your mother and I want to support you in all your choices.'

I shake my head. 'Mum, that piece didn't get it quite right, either. I didn't say most of those things.'

'But you sounded so confident, darling. Up the women!' Alison makes her delicate hand into a fist and punches the air. 'Anyway, I wouldn't have seen it at all, but Leticia phoned earlier. She wants me to write about it. Well, *she* wants to write about it, really. After this horrid Sanderson business, she wants to have me saying awful things about you, and the bad example I think you're setting, as a sort of one-off opinion piece. I've said no, but she keeps offering me more money.'

'Oh,' I say, numb. 'I suppose, if that's your job now—'

She interrupts. 'Frankie, for goodness' sake, of *course* I'm not going to do that to you. What must you think of me?' She lowers her head. 'After you were in all the papers before, I never stopped to think what it might be like for you. How scary it must have been, how lonely you must

313

have felt. It's only now that I've been – what is it, gnomed? Elfed? People have said horrible things about me, anyway, about how insipid I am, about my *hair* ...'

She holds me tight. 'It made me think of what happened to you at school, too. I haven't always done right by you, have I? I haven't always understood. I've pushed you into things I thought were best. And I know that because I lost sight of what matters, I pushed Bean away. I've been calling and calling. Occasionally she'll text to say, "I'm fine, I'll call you back." She never does.' Usually, Alison would relay this information in a state of fury and indignation. Now, she simply sounds quietly resigned. Quietly heartbroken.

It's time to tell her. 'Mum, there's really good news about Bean. I've spoken to Paul. It looks like her cancer hasn't spread, it's non-invasive, and she's due to start radiotherapy in a few weeks.'

Alison sighs. 'Oh, thank goodness. I've been praying for it, wishing for it. You know, I've started going to a support group, a little local thing. Mostly for families. A few of the women have been through it themselves. I thought they'd tell me how to help – but mostly, we've talked about how our "helping" is about fear, and panic, and control. I'm starting to realise how I did that, with your dad. My grief got stuck. I stayed in denial, for a long time. I'm doing it to Bean, too.'

'That makes a lot of sense. And I'm glad you found the support group. Going to something like that takes a lot of courage,' I say, and I really mean it.

'I've been feeling so guilty, for so long.' Alison looks away. '*Months* ago, Bean told me she had a feeling that

314

something wasn't quite right, health-wise. I told her she was much too young, and that obsessing about it would probably make it worse. I thought I was reassuring her, but maybe I just didn't want to hear it. Then I turned it into a project because I wanted to pretend it was something that happened to other people. Not us. Not again.'

She looks so sad. Gently, I say, 'Everything should have been about Bean, all along. She isn't speaking to me, either. If I'd paid more attention to what she needed – in fact, if I'd paid enough attention to what was happening around me – we wouldn't be apart. I miss her so, so much.'

Alison reaches for her black leather handbag and starts to unzip a pocket in the lining. 'It's funny, I don't know what made me think of this. But I look at it every single day. You should have your own copy. Have you seen it?'

She hands me something, soft, creased, worn, folded in two. 'Please be careful, it's very precious. I should have framed it. It was in a frame, once.'

At the centre of a photograph, there's a white bed. At the centre of the bed, there's a woman. Young, wild haired, with huge, luminous eyes. It makes me think of Renaissance pictures of saints being visited by spirits. The woman is holding a tiny, red, cross baby. A small girl is standing beside them both. Her eyes are huge and luminous too. And she is gazing at the baby with reverence – no, *awe*. Beams of love are shining out of her face, as well as from her Care Bears T-shirt.

'You were about six hours old when that was taken. And Bean has never stopped looking at you that way. So I never worry about you two, really. I know you'll always love each other. I know you'll always come good.'

315

Gently, taking care of the precious picture, I stroke Bean's tiny face. I wonder if I can wish on her, summon her. 'Who took the picture?'

Alison smiles, sadly and sweetly. 'Who do you think? Your dad.'

I frown. 'I wish I could remember him better.' I try as hard as I can to picture him holding me. Even though I know it's not a real memory, I want to believe I can recall the softness of a blanket, his solid arms.

'He made a great big fuss of you and Bean. And me, sometimes. He wasn't usually given to making a fuss about anything, but we were the exceptions. I think he loved being a dad. In fact, I know he did. He used to say that when you were born, he finally felt right.'

'What made you fall in love with him?' I blurt out the question, and I wish I had bitten my tongue. I'm anxious about the answer. If Alison makes something up, I'll know that it's not true. What if she says something about it being different then, that love wasn't so important to her? That would be even worse.

Alison looks lost, for a moment. When she starts speaking, she sounds far away. 'I was going to say that it took me a long time to fall in love with him, but that isn't quite right. I suppose it took me a long time to realise I had fallen in love. I'd had a few boyfriends, but no one who felt special. Your grandparents, my mum and dad, never seemed that happy. I thought love meant you were constantly kissing, or at each other's throats. I wanted romance, glamour, escape.' She smiles to herself. 'I had a *terrible* thing for boys who liked nice cars. All awful.'

'But dad wasn't awful?' I prompt her.

'Not at all. He was quite senior in the firm where I was a PA. It was a time when going to bed with your boss was not encouraged exactly, but normal. A blind eye was turned. And he wasn't my boss, and I didn't think he wanted to go to bed with me. He was just funny and kind and decent, and I liked spending time with him more than I wanted to admit.'

Why haven't I heard this before? Maybe I didn't ask. 'You still haven't answered my question. When did you know?'

She smiles, and she's miles away. Years away. 'I got another job. More money, more opportunities, all very exciting stuff, and I was *devastated*, Frankie. I cried. That was when I knew I didn't want to be away from him, and I didn't know what to do. I didn't want to declare myself to him – what if I'd made a mistake? What if I was just a silly girl with a crush? So I asked his advice about the job, and he told me to take it. Then he told me he'd miss me very much, and he cried, and I cried, and then we knew.'

Her eyes are shining, and I ache for both of us. A nice man. My dad was simply a sweet, decent person who had treated my mother with love and respect. Alison chose well. Maybe that's my legacy. Not just the height, and the awkwardness. If I'd known Dad, would I have made better choices? I can never know. More importantly, I can't keep limping around, tragic and unlucky in love, with a dead dad.

'Paul is not unlike your father,' says Alison, and I grimace. 'No, not in a creepy way, just – he's kind. He's consistent. He treats Bean well.'

'Why did you stay single? Why haven't you had any boyfriends?' I say, out loud. I don't mean to, but curiosity trumps good sense.

Alison smirks. 'Ah, there was the odd chap here and there but no one I really liked. Well, there was Terry,' she says, correcting herself. 'So embarrassing to have your heart broken by a man named Terry. I was a young widow, and I don't think I realised quite how vulnerable I was. Terry promised me the moon, he told me he couldn't believe how fast he was falling for me, all that stuff. Then he wanted a business loan, tried to get me to remortgage the house. I didn't want to – not when you girls were little – and I never heard from him again.'

'I'm so sorry, Mum, that's awful.' There must be so many details of my mother's life that I don't know.

She shrugs. 'It's more common than you'd think. Some of the stories I've heard – well. That's why I was so keen for you and Bean to do something with your looks, your talent. I wanted you to have something that was yours. I didn't want you to wait for a man to come and look after you. And I wanted you to know you were special, without some man having to tell you.'

I look at my mother's face. Alison knows her lines, as always. She's convinced by what she is saying. But her words aren't landing with me.

Usually, I would make my protest silent. I'd think it, shelve it, and bitch to Bean. I'd be too cowardly to tell Alison what I truly thought and felt – and then resentful, angry with her for not listening to what I hadn't said.

'There were men around, though, weren't there?' I say. 'At all the concerts and pageants and fundraisers. Everywhere we went, there would be middle-aged men who'd support any charitable cause if it meant they got to gawk at teen-age girls in leotards. I know it was a different time.' I sigh, heavily. 'Actually, no. Don't tell me it was a different time and use that as a defence. I don't want to hear an excuse. I want you to know that it was strange, and scary. I hated them for looking, and I wanted them to look. I hated myself for craving the attention. I hated you for doing that to both of us.'

Heat rises to my cheeks. Holding my breath, I wait for Alison to jump to her feet, scream, storm out.

She sits still and does not look away. 'I'm really sorry. I hope you'll forgive me, one day. My darling girl, please forgive yourself too. Please don't hate yourself. You haven't done anything wrong.'

Chapter Forty-Three

Creative

Here we are. Two women, sitting side by side in a shabby bedsit, mired in grief, surrounded by ghosts. A pair of attention seekers.

The woman in front of me is infuriating, self-absorbed and difficult to love. But she has the best intentions. I look at her, and see myself, and see her again, our flaws reflected and magnified in a magic mirror bounce. If I can start to forgive one of us, I can forgive both of us. It will be difficult, but worth the work.

'So what ...' We speak at the same time, but Alison finishes. 'What are you going to do now, Frankie? If you want to make a go of this sexy stuff, I'll support you. It might even be fun! Lots of girls – young women, I guess – are doing that sort of thing. I'll get with the times!'

This is Alison at her best. Even when it's entirely misguided, her passion and enthusiasm is endearing. She'd take to the industry with alacrity. She'd become my manager. She'd sell 'Fuck-Me Frankie' T-shirts for thirty quid a pop.

'I'm not sure, Mum,' I say. 'Honestly, I thought I was

enjoying that tiny bit of attention, but it felt more like a secret art project. I liked making photos, having control of something. Playing with the camera settings. It felt ...' and I hesitate, because I know exactly how it felt but there is something daunting and audacious about naming it. 'Creative,' I manage, eventually.

'Of course it did! You're *very* creative,' she says, patting my hand.

I roll my eyes. 'Obviously you have to say that, you're my mother.'

'Frankie, darling, seriously. You've always been very visual, very expressive. Ever since you were little. Even in those charity shows, you had a way of moving, making things your own. Like a tiny director!'

I laugh. 'Maybe I got that from Bean. She always seemed to know what she was doing.'

But Alison shakes her head. 'No, you're different in that way. Bean is methodical, almost mathematical. That's another form of creativity, of course. But it was fascinating for me, watching you growing up together, and noticing the tiny differences. It's an amazing lesson to learn, as a parent. There isn't one right way to be. It took me a long time to realise that, with you two. When you were little I compared you to Bean, and I shouldn't have done.'

Somewhere deep inside my chest, I feel a small but definite shift. Something clenched, and buried, is opening up.

'So, what does a creative person do?' I say, thinking, *I hope it doesn't involve character shoes.*

Of course, Alison has some thoughts. 'In your interview in the *News*, you were talking about wanting to feel empowered, wanting to feel desirable— no, Frankie, don't make that face. It's OK to want those things. We talked about that in the group, we talked about you!' Alison's tiny hands are clasping my meaty forearms. I don't know if it's an expression of love or a response to the fact that I look like I want to jump out of the window.

'Your lovely, kind, wise, supportive cancer people talked about me? About my ... photos?' I say. I can't look my mother in the eye.

'Yes, Frankie. They were the ones who helped me to get my head around it. We talked about sexuality and confidence. People from all walks of life want to feel desired, and desirable. No matter who they are, or what they've been through. Not a single person in that room judged you. Some said that they would want to do what you did, if they felt brave enough.'

I think for a minute. 'Maz wasn't wrong. I would love to empower people, as much as I hate that word. But – is there a way I could show people? I don't think me getting naked is going to inspire anyone else to get naked, but maybe if I could help people take their pictures. Or just take the pictures myself!'

I wait for Alison to tell me I'm being ridiculous, that this isn't a thing. But she smiles. 'Do you remember that nice Hettie woman, the photographer at the *Post* shoot? We had a great chat. I've still got her card. She told me that she loved your enthusiasm, and she's always looking to support women trying to get into the industry. I said I'd tell you to get in touch with her to chat about photography.'

'Mum, your group.' I'm thinking fast now. 'Where do they meet? I wonder if we could do a sort of exhibition? Probably not – no one's going to let me take their photo,

I've not even got a proper camera – but maybe it could be a fundraising thing? Or would that be crass?' The words are tumbling out, my brain is too fast for my mouth. 'But I'd *love* to try to take great photos of women, different women. Maybe I could ask Hettie for some advice? I suppose she might not want to talk to me, if she's been reading the papers.' I sigh.

Alison ignores me for a few minutes, while she taps at her phone. Then she looks up. 'It's on. Tuesday night. At our next meeting. You can have the community centre, and I've got you three models so far. You ask Miriam. Oh, what about your nice lady next door?'

'Isn't this supposed to be for people with breast cancer? We can't just ask everyone! Mrs Antrobus won't want to do this anyway,' I say, slightly sulkily. Typical Alison, taking over, being bossy, issuing instructions before she's made a proper plan.

Still, I've missed this. And my mother occasionally does know best. Usually, I'm pushing against her all-powerful pull. But if we were working on the same project, and heading in the same direction, I might fly.

Alison raises her eyebrows. 'We *can* just ask everyone, Frankie. And I think we should.' She waves her phone in my face. 'Some of these women are keen, but they're a bit worried that it's going to be "cancer themed". I say we make it woman themed. Everyone is welcome.'

And can I see it. A photography essay. Everything I wanted Maz's piece to say, told in pictures, by as many different women as possible. Women who don't feel beautiful, who *want* to feel beautiful, who feel excluded because they are not enough and they dream of too much.

If I can get Miriam to print out the pictures – and she will – we'll have a proper exhibition.

'Can you give me Hettie's card?' I ask. 'She might be able to give me some advice, or tell me where to get some basic equipment. What are you going to do about your column?'

'It's supposed to run in tomorrow's paper, so if I file it late enough there might not be time for Leticia to change it. I've had an idea, I'll see if I can pull it off. Leave it with me,' she says, echoing Maz unknowingly. And while I never truly trusted Maz, I trust my mother.

Chapter Forty-Four

The ask and the answer

I'm still not convinced that Mrs Antrobus is right for the shoot. I want to take pictures of women who want to feel better in their bodies, and I get the impression that my next-door neighbour already feels great.

She might say no. She might not be in. She might have read about me in the papers and slam the door in my face.

But I have to see her at some point. And I suspect she's a photographer's dream. I really would love to take her picture, if she'll let me. So I'm standing on her mat in a second-hand slip dress with a full face of makeup and a bottle of champagne in my hand.

The door opens just before I let go of the knocker. A flaxen-haired apparition in diaphanous blue chiffon presents me with a five-pound note. 'Tell me you remembered the prawn crackers this time,' she says, grumpily, before doing a double take. 'Frankie! You're a delivery girl? *This* is the job you dress up for?'

'Not exactly.' I hold the bottle aloft. 'I don't know if you have plans, obviously you have plans, you're getting food delivered. But I'd love to hang out. If you don't mind. If you want to see me.'

'Why wouldn't I want to see you, dollface?' She takes the champagne from me with surprising force.

She walks towards her kitchen. 'Let me get some glasses. This is already chilled, isn't it? Clever girl.'

Her flat has the same layout as mine. I've been here before, and I remember a general impression of rose pink and gleaming white, monochrome photographs, tasselled lamps and vintage splendour. But now I feel as though I'm finally seeing it properly. I notice each deliberate detail. The glossy kitchen tiles, the fan-shaped wall lights. It's as beautiful as Maz's house – but it feels more like a home. Everything that surrounded Maz was made to impress, as though it was waiting to be judged. Here, I get a sense that while my hostess has deliberately created a feast for the senses, she's ultimately cooking for one.

I hear a muffed thump, a thud, and Mrs Antrobus says, 'Now *that* must be the guy.'

'Your boyfriend?'

Her look is sharp. 'No, the *noodle* guy. No "guy" guys are coming, OK? You fix the drinks.' She makes for the door, and I pour champagne into the pair of coupe glasses on the kitchen counter. Then I pick mine up and roam around the room, inspecting the walls. There's a photograph of my hostess, I'd guess it's fifty years old. She's as blonde as she is now and signing something for a stunned teenage girl.

'Chow mein OK? I've got some little pot stickers too. Goodness, that was taken a long time ago.' She points at the photograph. 'Nineteen seventy something, I think.'

'I was being nosy, I didn't mean to pry,' I say, gesturing at the wall. 'These are fabulous. *You're* fabulous!'

'They're on my wall to be looked at. There's nothing wrong with being nosy. My favourite people are curious people.' Mrs Antrobus sits down and pats the space beside her. 'So, what's going on with you? You live inches away from me, and I know next to nothing about your life!'

I take a deep breath. 'Ah, I assumed you might have been reading all about it . . . in the tabloids.'

She opens her mouth wide. 'No! Oh my *God*! What did you do?' She claps her tiny hands together, and I notice her nails are shimmering amethyst.

'I can tell you, or I can show you,' I say, gesturing to my phone. 'And when you know what happened, you might want me to leave your home. Or move away.'

I guide her through the Google highlights. She laughs. She raises her eyebrows. She says, 'Wow', then, 'No way', then, 'Fuck me!' Finally, 'Frankie, let me give you some advice.'

Oh, no. Is it *Don't let the door hit your ass on the way out*? She sounds full of fury.

'*Tell* this story. It's yours. It can be sad, it can be funny, it can be sexy, but it belongs to you. You know who it doesn't belong to?' She flicks and scrolls, to indicate various comments and digital catcalls. 'These *clowns*. This is a riot – dine out on it.' She laughs, and her eyes are sparkling. 'Thank fuck! I was worried you were wasting your youth. You were having an adventure.'

'An adventure,' I repeat. 'I hadn't thought of it that way,' I say slowly. As I speak those words, I'm aware that they're melting some of my lingering shards of shame, making me feel a little lighter and brighter.

Mrs Antrobus keeps speaking. I'm sorry about your sister, though. How is she?'

'It's looking good. The surgery went well. I think she's going to be OK.' And I promised the universe I would do *anything* to make Bean OK. I must be brave. I must be bold.

I don't understand it – taking sexy selfies and posting them online was easy, but asking my neighbour to pose for me is terrifying.

'Mrs— Estelle,' I begin, clumsily. 'I came here to ask you a favour. I'm putting on an exhibition. I'm going to take some pictures, and I'm looking for models.'

'And you want me to open my address book?' she grins. 'I'll ask any woman who's still alive!'

'It's your picture I want to take,' I say. 'If you're up for it.'

'Oh, no one knows who I am any more. That ship has sailed.' She sounds sanguine; there isn't a trace of bitterness in her voice.

'You used to act?' Proof that I need to start paying more attention. I live next door to an actual movie star, and I have only just noticed.

She chuckles. 'Oh, honey, did I! I was *really fucking good*, too. Still, you know, mine is the tale as old as time. Same story as nine out of ten girls. Gorgeous, talented, ruined by an asshole. You ever hear of Connor Dean?'

I scratch my chin. 'Hang on – yes! *Dancer on the Ledge*? *The Great Electric*?'

'You got it. What a toad! He promised me the part of Moira in *Dancer* if I slept with him.'

'And you wouldn't do it,' I say, sagely. 'You wouldn't compromise your artistic integrity.'

328

She narrows her eyes. 'Jesus Christ, Frankie, of course I slept with him. I wanted the job! This is why I worry about you – girls today are such prudes. But if you're sure you want me, of course you can take my picture.'

Chapter Forty-Five

'For this, you'll need Lightroom'

'Hello, Hettie Bhaskar photography.'

'Oh, hello! Um, may I speak to Hettie?'

'You are.'

'Right, great. I'm sure you don't remember me. My name is Frankie Howard, we met at a shoot for the *Post*—'

'Oh, Frankie, hello! Great to hear from you. How's Lightroom working out? Did you get it in the end?'

'Not yet; I will, though. Listen, I'm so sorry to bother you, but I'm doing this project, I guess it's a shoot, tomorrow night. I'm taking pictures of different women, friends of my mum, my boss, my neighbour, she might bring a mate. It's supposed to be sort of sexy, and "empowering" – urgh. Anyway, it's just in a little community centre, and I was wondering whether you had any tips, I suppose. Is there anywhere you'd recommend I go to hire some lights, or maybe a backdrop? I only need basic stuff.'

Silence.

'Sorry, it was silly, wasn't it? I shouldn't have called.'

'It sounds like a great idea. I've got some bits you can borrow. Did you say tomorrow night? Is it in London?'

'That's really kind, but I'm sure your stuff is really sophisticated. What if I broke it, or—'

'It will be fine. Why don't I come along and help? I had a *News on Sunday* shoot lined up for tomorrow, but it's been cancelled, so I'm at a loose end.'

'Yeah? Yeah! Oh my God, are you sure?'

'Cool, of course. Text me the address. Have you still got that discount code? I'll text it to you. For this, you'll need Lightroom.'

Chapter Forty-Six

News on Tuesday 7 March

Trending on Dailypost.com

WHY I'M PROUD OF MY 'PORN STAR' DAUGHTER

Posted by Alison Howard

In her final column, our former #BeKind4Cancer campaigner says goodbye – while making a controversial claim for 'sexy feminism'.

Modern life isn't always easy.

Every day, social media presents me with reasons to be cheerful, reasons to be grateful. Symbols of kindness. Butterflies, puppies, sunsets. A big sale on appliquéd cushions.

But at the same time, social media can be quite unkind. Especially if you're a young woman, like my daughter, Frankie. When I was her age, the world was quick to shame any woman who wanted to explore her sexuality on her own terms. We called them 'attention seekers'.

I thought my daughters would grow up with more freedom, but things have become worse. It's a struggle for all of us. And we can't afford to ignore it any more. In the last week, I've been amazed to discover just how many women feel ignored.

Women of all ages, backgrounds and experiences are still longing to feel beautiful and desirable. They're still working out how to accept themselves. They fantasise about ways to feel better, and they worry that it's too late to make a change.

Is that you?

On Tuesday 7 March at 6 p.m., at Beaumont Road Community Centre in Southfields, London, Frankie will be taking photographs for her first ever exhibition, Look at Me. She would like to invite you to model. We're generously hosted by the Southfields Breast Cancer Support Group, but all women are welcome. This is for everyone. Older women, younger women; cis and trans women; women of all backgrounds, shapes and sizes.

We've all been made to feel bad about the way we look, and bad for caring about the way we look. Frankie's photographs will make you look good and feel good.

If you can't make it this time, don't worry. This will be the first of many such exhibitions. Thanks for reading, and remember: Being kind won't cure cancer. But it's the only way to live.

Chapter Forty-Seven

Queens

'Apparently, it's one of the most read pieces on the site! Leticia is furious, but her boss overruled her. After the Sanderson business, all the feminist stuff is doing well for the papers.'

Alison is holding court. Miriam, and two of the ladies of the Southfield Breast Cancer Survivors Group – Georgette, and her daughter Clementine – are hanging on her every word.

'I suppose it's clickbait, isn't it?' says Miriam. 'Eyeballs are eyeballs.'

'I don't want to brag, but I think my choice of title helped,' says Alison, a little smugly. 'As I've always said, sex sells! I've certainly learned a trick or two, as a national news journalist. I think I've certainly got a flair for it. Maybe I should offer my services to the *Mail* ...'

My mother is in her element. I wish I could say the same. I've only just met Georgette and Clementine, and I'm already terrified of letting them down. They have given up their evening for this. What if the pictures are awful?

What if Hettie doesn't come? I can't quite believe she would volunteer to give up her evening, too.

'Are you OK? Is anyone cold? Shall I put the heating on? Cup of tea?' I'm pacing and pawing at the blinds. 'I'm so sorry Hettie isn't here yet.' I knew I should have bought a giant lighting rig. Or hired a studio. Or not had this terrible idea in the first place.

'Frankie, sweetheart, calm down. You're vibrating all over the place. Come to Earth,' says Georgette, warmly. 'We have everything we need. I have jumpers, I have a robe, I have my wigs. It's going to be OK.'

'It's only five to,' says Clementine. 'It's still early.'

She looks at us all, furtively, and then pulls something pink and lacy from her bag. 'Frankie, will this be OK? I haven't been able to wear a *nice* bra for a while. I used to have some amazing bras. I still do, but they're all wired and they hurt. And I look weird in them. Anyway, I found this – it's the first bra I will have worn in ages that doesn't look as though it's supposed to attach a suitcase to a luggage rack.'

'It's really beautiful,' I say, reverentially. 'I think you'll look amazing in it.'

'I have matching knickers too, but ...' She looks shy. 'I'm not sure I have the guts for, you know, the full thing.'

'That's OK, see how you feel. You could try bra and jeans, a sort of old-school Calvin Klein vibe. If you want to do more, we'll do more – and we don't have to do everything today. This is about making it fun for you, making you feel good.'

She smiles. 'Thank you. You have turned my nerves into total excitement. You're like a horse whisperer – a tit whisperer. Can we get started?'

335

I shrug. 'It will just be me and my phone; we don't have any lights yet. Are you sure you don't want to wait?'

'Nah,' says Clementine. 'Let's do it, before I change my mind.'

She pulls off her jumper, and instinctively I turn around. 'It's OK,' she says. 'You can look.'

Objectively, Clementine is stunning. Huge, dark eyes, a perfect V-line jaw, cheekbones that make me think I didn't really understand what cheekbones were before I met her. But if I shake off labels like *beautiful*, *gorgeous*, *pretty* and *sexy*, her face and her body become much more interesting.

The scar is diagonal and precise, running from the middle of her left armpit to where a nipple might be. It shines – no, it bisects the space, so that the light falls and gleams on either side of it. The scar is like the lead in a stained-glass window.

'I want to get a tattoo there,' she tells me. 'It would really annoy my mum. In fact, I might get an old-school "MUM" one.'

'But Georgette has tattoos!' I say. 'I can see something on her wrist.'

'Yeah, it says, "Clementine". My mother is a logic-defying, ocean-going, full-fat nightmare,' she says, wryly. 'But I love her to the end of everything.'

Same, I think.

For now, I stand Clementine in front of a pale blue noticeboard, after strategically unpinning a few signs claiming that anyone who leaves teabags in the sink AGAIN will have to go before a judge. The evening light coming through the window reminds me of being in Anthony's studio. I shudder, and then I realise that a week has passed and there's a little more brightness in the sky. It is a great light.

'What do you want me to do? How should I stand?' calls Clementine.

'On one leg!' shouts Georgette. Clementine shouts, 'Oh, Mum, for FUCK'S SAKE,' and she looks so fierce, and gorgeous, and pissed off, that I shoot a burst of photos.

'Frankie, what are you doing? I wasn't ready!' she cries.

I show her my phone. 'Look at your face here. You look like an Elizabethan queen. You could be on stage, doing Shakespeare. You look amazing.'

A slow smile lights up Clementine's face. 'I do, don't I?' she says, quietly.

We take a few more before Clementine decides she's done as much as she's comfortable with. As she puts her jumper back on, I hear someone entering the room, muted voices and footsteps getting louder. Thank goodness – Hettie has finally arrived.

But then Miriam says, 'Oh my *God*, Flossie, did you know about this?' and Alison is saying, 'Goodness, gracious, did you read my little column?' and I hear two familiar voices. One belongs to Mrs Antrobus. The other is one I've heard on screen, berating coachmen, wisecracking with Stephen Fry, and once – memorably and not entirely convincingly – emerging from a papier mâché alien.

Clementine's mouth falls open. 'I didn't know that an actual queen was going to show up.'

Chapter Forty-Eight

Going to work

Hettie is following close behind, her arms full of bags and leads, and greets the movie star like an old friend. 'I didn't know you'd be here! It's so good to see you!' She drops a handful of cables and goes in for a hug. As if it's totally normal to just touch this woman.

The movie star hugs her hard and addresses the room. 'Funny story,' she says, in her velvet voice, loud enough to be heard down the road. 'Last time this woman took my photograph, I was shitting in a bin!'

'It's a small world,' says Mrs Antrobus, dryly. 'Frankie, come and say hello. We'll do introductions. Not that this one needs any introduction!'

Trying to stay calm, I address our visiting dignitary. 'I'm so glad you're here. Thank you so much for coming!' *Your Majesty*, I almost say. Should I curtsy?

'Fabulous idea, I was so pleased when Estelle called me. And what timing! We're about to start doing the *Shipwreck* promotion, so I'm in town for once. And don't get me wrong, I adore Jonathan Ross, delightful fellow. But one

338

runs out of things to say. All I've got is the story of when Jennifer and I had to go into Chris's trailer and catch a giant spider. Being naked in an exhibition is a much better thing to talk about.'

Mrs Antrobus shrugs. 'I'm sure you don't have to be fully nude. Frankie, talk us through your artistic vision.'

'Oh, but I want to! I wouldn't get my kit off for Kubrick – bloody agent advised against it, actually. But I'll do it for you. For this!' She beams. 'Even though I'm still not entirely sure what *this* is. Now, Henrietta, we must catch up. Last time I saw you, I was going to show you my Hamlet ...'

Our nation's unofficial queen starts an animated discussion with Hettie, and I hug Mrs Antrobus again. 'Blimey. Thank you! How do you know her?'

She shrugs. 'Oh, you know, around. We were both in California in the seventies. She did some godawful walk-ons in cop shows. Her American accent was quite something. "Hayulp! Off-i-sur! Thayt offal mayn stole mah purse!" She changed her name, then came home to London and changed it back.'

'I had no idea!'

'Oh, we all thought about it,' she grins. 'After a week of duff auditions, we'd be working out whether our tips would cover a plane ticket, practising our best "A handbag?" Anyway, she's a doll.'

I look over at her, and Hettie is waving at me. 'Frankie, come on! This is your project. I've brought my DSLR.' She gestures up at the noticeboard. 'This is a lovely spot. Nice framing. We'll see how these come out, and if they're not working I'll stick some lights up. I think we're going fully nude with these.'

'You don't have to if you don't want to,' I say, to the movie star. I think I'd feel more comfortable taking fully nude photos of Alison. But she's already removed her coat, her shirt and her shoes. 'It was my idea,' she says, indignant. Navy twill trousers hit her ankles, and she stretches her arms wide.

'Make me look like Vitruvian Man!' she bellows.

Hettie hands me her camera and I almost drop it. 'Are you sure?' I say, meaning, *I'm not sure.*

She's completely calm. 'Just point and shoot, it's all digital, we can do loads. If you can take a photo with your phone, this is easy.'

I remember our last shoot. 'Oh, I should make her look heroic. Low angles!' Crouching, I look at the famous head, blocked in blue. 'Can you take your feet in a little, and make your arms even wider? Lovely, a strong warrior pose.' There's a shaft of light coming through the window. If I can get her to move, this might be great, but I feel slightly awkward. 'Ah, maybe lean back just a little, shift your weight into your left hip. Yes!'

'Nice one,' murmurs Hettie. 'You got the pubes.'

I take a few more shots. At least half are, frankly, awful – lifeless and lightless, and I don't fully understand why – but some are OK. Good, even. I hand Hettie the camera, and she flicks through the images. 'Yeah. You've got some really strong ones here.'

'I want to see!' My subject grabs the camera, giggling. 'Not bad at all, might use some of these for press shots.'

More women are arriving. I count almost thirty – the youngest are in their mid-twenties, but quite a few have a good decade on Alison.

I can hear her corralling everyone, organising them into groups and lines, and feel a giant surge of love. 'It's so good of you to come. We're going to take as many photos as we can tonight, but we'll definitely do it again another time, so if we don't get to you, you must leave your name ... ' She claps her hands. 'Right, Frankie, Hettie, are you ready for the next one?'

I've got work to do.

Chapter Forty-Nine

Reunion

My fingertips are numb, my thighs are aching and my stomach is roaring. I should have stopped for a snack hours ago. I've been squatting, crouching and planking, trying to find everyone's best angles. Admittedly, my technique is hit and miss. I've had tearful, tender gratitude. I've also had a very grand woman looking at her picture with horror, crying, 'Fucking hell, you've made me look like a scrotum on legs.'

Hettie has been relentlessly kind and encouraging, talking me through the techniques with the utmost patience. She only got upset once, when I said, 'Sorry, that's a bit shit,' and she said, 'OF COURSE it is. That's how you improve. You start by being a bit shit.' Then she apologised and I apologised, and we were fine.

Apart from one embarrassing moment when I forgot to take the lens cap off, I'm learning to love the weight and feel of a proper camera. It's frustrating using one, though. Sometimes I want to throw the bastard thing to the floor (I suspect that's why they have the big straps that go around your neck). I'm having micro mood swings – elated when it goes right, 5 per cent of the time, and tense and tearful for the 95 per cent of the time when I'm fucking it up. But it's addictive. Even though I'm audibly howling with frustration, I want to keep trying.

After a slightly warm pint of tap water in the grubby galley kitchen, I decide I need some fresh air.

It would make sense to go for a walk, move around, do something about my scrunched-up vertebrae, but I don't even have the energy to go for a crawl. Instead, I lean against the wall and hold my head up to the sky. My face is tensed against the cold – but I notice that the air feels a little softer, a little milder. One day soon, winter will be completely over.

Yawning, I stretch up, waving my arms, wiggling my fingers. Pressing my shoulder blades into the brick work behind me, I groan with pleasure. There is so much of me. And I've got so used to squashing it down, knocking it back. I'm Diet Girl – now with 25 per cent less Frankie. When I am alone, I can draw myself to my full height and breathe freely.

'Are you doing the Inflatable Man dance? Are you out here to make me aware of great deals on used cars?'

That voice. Bean's voice. My heart's metronome. The girl guiding me through the dark.

And a small woman is bearing down on me, in a thick, navy wool coat, a red hat, a tartan scarf. 'Oh my God! What are you doing here?' I hug her, I squeeze her. I try to work out whether she feels even thinner, smaller, through the fabric. 'I missed you. I missed you so, so much.'

'I missed you too,' she says, gruffly, and nestles into me.

'How was Brighton?' I ask politely. I don't quite know

343

what to say. 'Forgive me,' and 'Why wouldn't you speak to me?' and 'I love you' and 'How could you?' and 'I'm sorry' are on the tip of my tongue, but I'm so scared of shattering this moment. One wrong word and she'll go home.

'Lovely, thanks,' she says. 'We had a very nice time.'

'Is there any more news about treatment? When does it start? How does it work?' I ask, as though I haven't been memorising every WebMD page about radiotherapy.

She drops her arms and stands, stiffly. 'End of the month. It's good, really, it means it's the beginning of the end. Or the end of the beginning. I'm lucky that I don't need chemo first – Dr Zainab said I should be pleased about that. But I've got to go in five days a week, for six weeks. It's going to be intense.'

There are so many things I want to ask her. Is she scared? Do the boys know? Has she been sleeping? But the words won't come. There is still a tension between us, separating us.

It is a relief when she says, 'I'm still really angry with you.'

'I'm sorry. I brought you all that shame and stress and I made you even more ill. I couldn't even help you with Alison. You must hate me ...' I have so much to apologise for.

She cuts me off. 'No! I'm angry because you kept this massive, massive secret! I thought I knew everything about you. I don't know why you didn't tell me! I hated – hate – the idea of not knowing about any parts of your life!' Her chest is rising and falling, rapidly, and I start to panic. 'Don't get stressed! You're not supposed to ...' I place a hand on her shoulder, and she shakes me off.

'I feel like it was my job to have worked this out, and I didn't know. I never guessed!' she shouts. Her face is flushed, too bright against the darkening sky. 'I never gave you a chance to tell me. So I hate me, too.' She hangs her head.

I'm stunned. 'Bean, no. I fucked up, completely. Hate me, but don't hate you,' I say, hurriedly, echoing the words Alison said to me. I really am just like my mother – and my sister. I realise Bean and I both want exactly the same things – to know everything about each other, while protecting each other from the worst of ourselves. We can't have it both ways. 'How did you hear about this, anyway? How did you find me?'

'I talked to Alison,' she says. 'I should have talked to her a long time ago. I've been deliberately pushing her away. You know I hate needing anyone, but I need my family. You're both my family, just as much as Paul, and Jack and Jon.'

My fingertips are numb, so I rub them together, trying to create some defence against the cold. Our connection seems so fragile, so vulnerable, that I'm scared of saying anything that might break it. But if I don't speak up now, I never will. 'Bean, we do need each other. All of us. And we both know, better than anyone, how needy Alison is. How hard she makes things for us.'

I stop, to take a steadying breath, trying to iron out the tremor in my voice. I want to give Bean room to interrupt me, but she's listening intently.

'Obviously it was – is – my job to save you from that, at the moment. But I can't do it alone. You know that. And more to the point, you can't push her away completely, because she's difficult. You can't just say, "Well, I'm an Andersen, the Howard stuff is not my problem," and put up the barricades.'

Bean pouts. 'Paul is *very* protective, and ...' she sighs,

shakes her head, starts again. 'You're right. I know you're right.'

'Paul did call, to let me know what was happening,' I say, gently. 'I'm grateful for that. And so grateful that the news is good. I guess.'

'Honestly, I'm not grateful at all,' says Bean, with feeling. 'I feel like I'm supposed to be patient, and good, and kind, when every other day I want to just go around kicking things. I'm too tired to kick, but I am angry.' She whispers the word, as though it's a confession. The heat drains from her voice.

I open my mouth, wanting to tell her it's OK, that she's allowed to feel whatever she needs to feel, but she holds a hand up to quiet me.

'I don't know why I'm so angry. I'm not supposed to be. I'm trying not to tell people that I'm ill, because they all talk to me with a tilted head and a soft voice. It's as though they expect woodland creatures to emerge from my hair. Birds landing on my shoulders.' Bean rolls her eyes.

'You could get a falcon,' I say, gravely.

'What?' Bean laughs, and I know we're going to be OK.

'Become a falcon woman. Get one of those massive gloves. I think falcons are quite violent. You could really fuck people up with a falcon.'

'Listen to my apology or I will set a falcon on *you*. I'm really trying. I know I've been taking things out on you, like I used to do when we were little. I could be nice and sweet and good 90 per cent of the time, and the other part had to go somewhere, and the only safe place was on you and Alison.'

'I'm sorry,' I say. 'We didn't listen, we didn't give you

346

room, we didn't give you anything you needed. We will make this right, I promise.'

'Frankie, I'm not quite sure how to say this.' Bean frowns for a minute, a crease forming under the brim of her hat. 'It's not easy, having you as a little sister. I worry about you. I've been waiting for you to show some initiative, some sense of direction, and then, when you do . . .' She throws her hands up.

'It's usually the wrong direction,' I say, sadly, feeling the weight of the old shame gathering in my shoulders. Bean has set the best of all possible examples, and I haven't just failed to live up to the standard she's set. I've failed in every way.

Then, in the corner of my eye, I notice more lights going on in the building, and I think I hear someone calling my name. Tonight, right now, I'm creating something. I'm part of something positive.

The woman in front of me has never asked me to copy her. She's never told me that she's the person I must try and be. She's never asked me to be anything but myself. I take her hands in mine. 'I've spent my whole life wishing I was more like you, and looking up to you, and *studying* you for clues, and I don't know how to be you. I don't think I can. So maybe it's just . . . a different direction?'

'Exactly,' says Bean. 'I thought the problem was that you are my little shadow.'

'Not so little,' I say, jokingly.

'Well, I guess real shadows aren't, are they? They're taller than that which casts them. But I've been waiting for you to step out and do your own thing, and it happened, and it wasn't what I was expecting.' She looks at me and says, simply, 'I was kind of jealous.'

'I don't understand.' I shake my head.

'I'd never felt that way about you before. I didn't know I could. But I felt so grey, and frightened. And the surgery, fucking hell. I'm supposed to be *pleased*. Glad this thing is treatable and manageable. Remembering the people who have it worse than I do. But I feel like I've lost my essence, some fundamental spark. Like I will never feel good about my body again, not that I've ever felt great about it.'

'But Bean, you're *beautiful*,' I say, shocked. 'Seriously. You must know that you on a bad day is better than most people on their best days.'

She shakes her head. 'Shut up. Thank you, I love you, but that's not the point, is it? You might see me one way. I might see me a different way. There isn't a definitive viewpoint here. But I didn't realise how miserable I felt until I saw those photos of you. You looked so young, and hot, and vital, and *different*. What a secret to keep about yourself! And I thought, I couldn't do that if I wanted to. I missed the window.'

'Why do you think I did it?' I ask. 'It was a way to feel good about something I felt bad about. You're right, I don't look like that. But I can make myself look like that.' My breath rises, like smoke, in the cool air. 'I'm not beautiful, and I'm starting to realise that I'm not going to wake up one morning and have turned beautiful in the night.' With those words I feel a short shot of sadness, but the Earth does not crater and the sky does not fall in. I can hear the rumble of traffic in the distance, and feel the solid, scratchy wall behind me. I'm still here. I keep speaking. 'So I'm trying to find a way to be useful. And I'm not bad at taking photos.'

'Actually, Frankie, I came here to ask you something.' She looks nervous.

'You can ask me anything.'

'Will you take my picture?'

Chapter Fifty

The light

This has never happened before. As I lead Bean inside and over towards Hettie, I realise that I'm the one in charge. It's my job to protect her. More than that – I want her to shine. I want everyone here to know I'm so proud of her.

Bean whispers, 'This isn't a tragic cancer shoot, is it? That's not the theme? Alison was a bit vague. I got the impression that she had just invited everyone she had ever met and hoped for the best.'

I look around at the room, still filling up with women. 'That's exactly what she did. There is no theme. This is classic Alison: she just went ahead and did it, without stopping to think about what "it" was going to be. But for once, I think it might have worked out.'

Wanting to reassure her, I add, 'But we've roped in a proper grown-up. Come and meet Hettie, she's a real photographer. She's making sure I don't fuck this up. Hettie, this is my sister, Bean.'

Hettie pushes a palm through her hair. 'Ignore Frankie, she's doing good work. Great to meet you, Bean!'

Hettie looks at my sister. She looks at me. She looks at Bean again. Dainty, delicate, bewitching Bean, and her great big little sister. I think I can predict exactly what she's going to say. I've heard it so many times. 'Oooh, it's Little and Large!' Or 'Ant and Dec!' Or 'How much do you both weigh?'

Eventually, Hettie speaks. 'You're so similar! It's as though the same artist drew you. The proportions of your face, the depth and planes and things. It's uncanny.' She tilts her head. 'Oh, I could do a picture of both of you!'

Hettie's words are a benediction, a release. All I have ever wanted is to look like Bean's sister, to *feel* like Bean's sister – to feel the way I imagine she feels, all the time. Something in my soul shifts, and pops. We're sisters, but we can stand separately and together. I don't need the validation from the camera lens, right now. But I think my sister does, today.

I look at Bean for a moment and shake my head. 'No, just Bean. And I'd really like to take it.'

I wait for Hettie to register the significance of my gesture, but she's already focusing on her next task. 'Cool, cool. Shout if you need me.' Hettie goes back to her laptop, and I take my sister's hand. She's shaking a little.

'Are you feeling OK? Do you want some water?' I ask.

Bean hugs her own body, appearing to burrow into herself. 'I'm fine, I'm just nervous, I guess. Frankie, what if I just look stupid? What if I show Paul the pictures and he says something like "very brave"? I hate being brave. I need an hour off being brave. I want to look sexy. Just for a minute.'

'You will! You do! You are!' I say. Then, I look at Bean closely, carefully. She doesn't have her usual glow. Her face

351

is thinner than I remember. She's always seemed much more delicate than me, fine-boned. But now, she looks fragile.

How can I make her feel comfortable? What can I say, to bring out her Beanness?

'The most important thing is that this feels good for you, and fun. If you get too tired, we'll stop. We can do this any time. But I promise I can make you look like the sexiest woman in the world – with your coat on, if you like.'

She tugs at her sleeve. 'Yeah, but where's the fun in that?' Her eyes shine, and she smiles. Now she's glimmering, glowing – not at her highest wattage, but there's some sparkle there.

'I can find you somewhere a bit more private, where you can go and change?' Guiltily, I realise I'm frightened of what I might be about to see. But I can't show my fear. It's my turn to take care of Bean.

She shrugs. 'I'm not feeling especially private at the moment. I'll pretend I'm in a room full of medical professionals.'

'Take your time,' I say. 'Let me know if I can do anything to make you more comfortable.'

'I'm fine. Just promise you won't tell me to relax. Allow me to feel as stressed, anxious and uptight as I need to be.' Elegantly, she peels off the roll neck, pulling it up over her torso and off her head in one fluid movement. Should I look away, or keep looking? I don't want Bean to feel anything less than loved.

'Nice bra,' I say, and it is – sheer, pale, blossom-tinted tulle, embroidered with small, stylised bluebells. Moss green straps.

Bean smiles shyly. 'I bought it especially.'

Then she reaches both hands behind her back and unclips it.

'Can I see?' I walk towards her, not knowing what I'm asking for, or what I'm doing. Waiting for her to tell me no, that I'm being intrusive. But she beckons me towards her.

Bean's left breast is an almost perfect, slightly sunken sphere. Her skin is the palest pink, the colour of old newspaper, her nipple a tawny orange red, a distended Jelly Tot. I remember when Jack was born, and what a shock it was to see Bean's breasts *all the time*, and then how quickly I got used to it. Jack's soft little head, resting in place.

Her right breast seems to have been folded into itself. Her line is smaller than Clementine's, a little off-centre, haloed with faint yellow bruising. It's a shock, for maybe half a second.

I realise that I don't really understand what I'm looking at. I cannot see what a doctor can see. But I do know that this doesn't have to define her, or us. And that I have a chance to show Bean to herself. Less than a square inch of her body has been breaking her heart and writing the script of all her nightmares. I can't make her better, but I can offer a form of healing.

'You're absolutely beautiful,' I tell her. 'All of you.'

I pick up the camera. My arms are aching, but I pull it towards my body and focus my attention on the woman in front of me and her story. To me, she's a sister, a daughter, a mother and a wife. To the world, she's Clapham, big kitchens, expensive perfume, school runs and pension plans. She's vulnerable. She's fragile. She's a patient. She struggles and suffers with big things, and small things.

But Bean wants to look at these photos and forget

353

everything. She needs me to capture the part of herself that she's never able to show. She's trying to find a way back into herself. She's a woman who is so, so loved. A woman who deserves good luck, and happy secrets. Her life has been shaped by grief, by tragedy – yet she's the funniest person I will ever know.

'Can you take a step towards me? Right into the light, if that's OK. Gorgeous! Lovely! Perfect!' I adjust the lens, and crouch. 'Yes! You're so good at this, Bean. Look down for a second, and then back up at me? Wonderful!'

'Oh my God, Frankie!'

'What? Are you OK?' I put the camera down, trying to be concerned, not annoyed. We're sisters again.

'I'm really impressed,' she says. 'You know what you're doing. You're a proper photographer. A professional.'

Privately, secretly, I take a mental picture of the expression on her face. I will keep this forever and look at it whenever I need to remember it.

I take photos where she looks flirtatious, and photos where she looks defiant. I take photos of her turning around and smiling over her shoulder. And at the same time, we both forget ourselves and say, simultaneously, 'This is really fucking weird,' and she bursts out laughing.

She doesn't need to be in the light – she is the light. I get my shot. Sexy, happy, carefree, beautiful Bean.

Chapter Fifty-One

Exhibitionist

In a cramped, narrow corner of the Beaumont Road Community Centre, my shadow self stretches up and along the floor. My breasts have become a single hump. My legs and arms are thick tubes. I'm an amorphous mass. I stand on my right leg and lift my left behind me. Then, I step forwards and backwards, toe-heel-toe. *Would I waltz into the underworld with you? If I could stand on your giant shadow feet, would you take me where it's dark and soft and silent?*

Alison is annoyed. 'Frankie, stop that! You're making me nervous!'

'Sorry. But why are you nervous?' I say. 'You're not in the exhibition.'

'It's not that,' she hisses. 'I invited the mayor! He said he'd come!'

'Of London?' I say, beginning to panic. Alison's column has caused a stir but I didn't realise she'd had that kind of impact.

'Don't be ridiculous, Frankie, the Mayor of Merton! He's

responsible for all four parishes!' I'm not sure that Alison is making any sense, but at least I know why she's wearing a hat indoors – if you can call it a hat. It's a stiff, bottle green flying saucer, glued to an Alice band.

I'm about to ask her if she considered whether my models will mind the mayor gawping at their tits, but I think better of it. After all, none of this would have happened without her, and I've spent the last couple of days taking photographs of different women with one thing in common: They want this. They want to be seen. They want a moment to take up space, and celebrate themselves, and feel sexy, in a world that keeps telling them they will never be sexy enough. It's about the way they see themselves. No one gives a shit about the mayor.

Hettie joins us. 'Frankie, we're full up. Everyone's got prosecco, so I reckon it's speech time. Shall I introduce you?'

I palm the crumpled piece of paper in my pocket. A couple of days ago, when I was high on pride and fatigue, the speech seemed like a brilliant idea. Now I'm not so sure.

'Shall we give it another fifteen minutes?' I say, desperately. 'Or perhaps half an hour?'

Alison gives me a little shove, and then smiles sweetly at Hettie. 'Please do, darling. That would be lovely.'

I watch Hettie take a few steps forward. She picks up a full glass and taps it daintily, before resorting to an 'Oi!'

There's polite laughter, then silence.

'Hello, everyone. Thanks so much for coming to Look at Me – the very first exhibition by a brand-new talent, Frankie Howard. My first exhibition took about eighteen months to put together – Frankie has done this in a week!' She pauses for applause. 'We're all hugely grateful to the Beaumont

Road Community Centre for having us, and giving us this space, at such short notice. We have many thank-yous, so I'm going to hand over to Frankie because I suspect her list is going to be a lot more thorough than mine.'

There is more applause, and a small hand shoves the small of my back again. I look at the crowd, and my vision swims, before my eyes alight on Bean. She's mouthing 'You do not got this'. Then she blows me a kiss.

I look at the ceiling, I look at my feet, and think *the sooner I start this, the sooner I can stop.* 'Thank you so much for coming,' I squeak, before forcing my voice down into its normal register. 'Firstly, we wouldn't be here without Hettie Bhaskar, who has been beyond generous with her equipment, her advice, her time and her kindness. I have learned so much from her over the last few days, which have been some of the most exciting days of my life.'

That wasn't so bad. I feel for my paper and look up. There must be at least 100 people here, maybe more. Where have they all come from? Is Mrs Antrobus wearing mesh? Her dress looks like a magical silver fishing net. She gives me a little wave.

'With all my heart, thank you to Clementine, Georgette, Estelle, Darcy, Lauren, Angeli, Grace, Beth, Olivia, Madge, Dorothy, Hannah, Ana, Lucy, Caro, Char, Nicola, Julia, Marnie, Amber, Liz, Jayne, Corrie, Corinne, Rachel, Becky, Susie, Sophie, Lisa, Jo, Jude, Marian, Nina, Gayle, Rosh, Leiyah, Jade, Cesca, Amy, Rosie, Issy, Nat, Emma, Claire, Sheryl, Bryony, Diana, Megan, Ruby, Fatima and Ashley. These are the gorgeous, courageous women who you see all around you. These women gave up their time to take part in this exhibition. It's bloody brave to respond to a call-out from an amateur photographer – especially one who's asking you for nudes!'

'Thanks for leaving my pubes in!' The crisp, clear voice carries. It's coming from a familiar face beside Mrs Antrobus. The laughter isn't polite, this time – it's a proper chuckle.

I wait for the sound to subside. The next part is important. 'Most of all, I want to thank my family. Bean, my sister; Alison, my mother; Miriam, my – my Miriam. Technically my boss, truly my guardian angel. She's the one who helped me to get these pictures printed.' Miriam steps to the front of the crowd and takes a small, brief bow.

I take a deep breath. 'Bean has told me it's OK to talk about this. She's recently had a lumpectomy, to remove a small tumour in her breast, and she's about to undergo radiotherapy. I know some of you have been affected by cancer. You've been through it, or you have been there for the people you love during their treatment.'

The crowd seems to become quieter and even more attentive. I keep speaking. 'Bean has always been my idol. She's funny, she's clever, and she's beautiful. I've always assumed she has known that about herself. I was shocked to realise that she doesn't always feel good about the way she looks because she always looks so good to me. I know that sounds trivial, under the circumstances. Bean knows her treatment is going to save her life. But the treatment is also diminishing her confidence, her sense of identity, her life force. I was grateful that she let me take her picture, and I hope I've shown her as I see her. Not "beautiful, considering the circumstances". Just beautiful.'

I pause. I need to take several more deep breaths before

I'm able to start speaking again. 'I've grown up with so many issues about the way I look. I'm a big girl, a tall girl, and I've always felt wrong in my body and dreamed of feeling desirable. Some of you might have seen some of my public attempts to rectify this.' I wait for laughter, expecting jeering. I hear applause, and whooping. 'In trying to boost my body confidence and become reconciled to my sexual self, I've taken a few interesting turns, and got lost. I do not recommend outsourcing your self-esteem to the men of the internet. But I hope to keep exploring this idea of image and identity. I'd love to work with any women who feel like me. Women who want to feel desirable. Women who don't feel seen, and who crave a little attention. I'm new to photography, but I can promise you my undivided attention.'

The room fills with the joyful noise of women applauding, sobbing, and drumming their feet on the floor as though it's the last school assembly before the summer holidays. It's a force, a magical thing, women coming together to be even greater than the sum of their parts.

I wait for the sound to subside. Then I wait a little longer. 'Sorry, this is the last bit, this is a very long speech. Finally, I want to say another thank you to Alison, my mother. Because she raised Bean and me, and she loves us. I'm inspired by her energy, her optimism and her self-belief. She's a force of nature. I didn't think I could do any of this, but she believed I could. Everything here has been made possible by amazing women, and she is one of the most amazing. Thank you.'

Impulsively, I walk towards Alison, and take her hand, wanting her to stand with me. As my palm touches hers, I feel my other arm being pulled in a different direction.

Bean is holding my other hand. Together, we form a circle. Three women, protecting each other, lifting each other up. Making each other powerful. Making each other feel beautiful.

Epilogue

'I'm watching a swallow trace a path across the sky, its wings tipped in gold. The sun is sinking, slowly. And – oh, there's a pigeon. Is it going for the swallow? No, it's got a – hold on, is that a Caramac wrapper? I thought they stopped making those.' I look at Bean for confirmation, and she wiggles under her blanket.

'Dunno, Franks. I thought you said you'd be my eyes.' She's wearing an eye mask that I had made for her especially. Electric blue satin with gold embroidery. #BeKind4Cancer. I thought that it was in such bad taste it would make her laugh, and I was right.

'Can I get you anything?' I ask. 'How are you feeling?'

'Same as I was ten minutes ago! You could go and wrestle that pigeon for me – I want a Caramac.' She yawns.

'Just let me know if you want to go to sleep, or if you want the telly on,' I say.

'No, it's nice to have you here, chatting nonsense. Soothing. I hadn't realised how weird I'd feel about going back into hospital. And I'll do it all again tomorrow. I'm going to feel worse before I get better, apparently. But I'm glad I've got the first one out the way.'

361

'It feels a bit like one of the days after Christmas,' I say. 'Being here with you, under blankets, raiding your fridge for picky bits and buffet food.'

'The boys running amok,' murmurs Bean. 'Taking full advantage of being surrounded by various relatives, demanding sugar and plastic tat.'

'I should have got a huge tub of chocolates,' I say. 'It just doesn't feel like Christmas unless Alison is aggressively shaking her head at a tub of Quality Street.'

Bean laughs. 'Hopefully, this isn't like Christmas and it won't be happening once a year. But there are no guarantees – cancer comes back. I must learn to live like this. I find that frightening. But sometimes I think, well, the worst is happening, and I'm still here. We've all got to learn to live with "it", and "it" is something different for all of us.'

'Yeah,' I say, sighing. 'I often think about the "what ifs". Wouldn't it be lovely if we could cure you by worrying? You'd live to be a million! But then, I'm having a lovely time with you, right now. I suppose you're technically healthier than you were twenty-four hours ago.'

'I'll be getting better every day,' says Bean, drily. 'Anyway, have you heard anything yet? Any news?'

'The course? It's a bit early. Hettie reckons I'll know by the end of the week.'

Hettie found a good part-time photography course with spaces in the summer term, and she's written me a glowing reference. Thank goodness she did, because the one Miriam gave me was of no help. I'll treasure it forever, but I don't know what the admissions tutors would have made of 'Frances is a child of light'. Mrs Antrobus wanted her to add, 'with an ass that won't quit'.

362

(They're currently in Morocco together, having a fairly 'mellow' time, according to their postcards. I described them to Bean as the ultimate odd couple, but Bean thinks this makes perfect sense. Alison is threatening to go out and join them for a holiday. We don't know whether to put her off or make an offer for the movie rights.)

'I might not get on it,' I say, carefully. 'Mustn't get my hopes up.'

Bean shakes her head, and her eye mask slips down. 'Well, I think they'd be mad not to take you. And if they don't, someone else will. You'll get there.'

I still feel shy about admitting just how excited, passionate and *nerdy* I'm feeling. 'I can't believe I might get to go back and study,' I say. 'I won't be a dropout, any more. Just think about how much more there is to know! All of the terms and techniques I haven't even heard of yet. And every so often, I find out that I knew more than I realised.'

'I like Hettie,' says Bean. 'She seems solid. I approve of her, although I don't think she's as well connected as Miriam. I'm all for your career change, but I'm a bit sad that your new boss is never going to offer me magic mushrooms.'

'Never say never.' I shrug. 'And I still talk to Miriam all the time. If you want any hallucinogenics, they're yours.'

'I'm alright for the moment, but I'd love it if you could ask her to recommend a good place for acupuncture. Are you doing any more shoots with Hettie?'

'She needs an assistant for one next week, up in Manchester. But she said she'd understand if I didn't want to leave London for the next few weeks.'

Bean sits up. 'You should go.' She smirks. 'It might be

good to have some stuff in your portfolio where the models have their clothes *on*. Although it sounds as though the Beaumont Road ladies are keeping you busy.'

Ever since the exhibition, I've had a weekly date in Southfields at the community centre, with my new camera. I've met so many women. Women who tell me that they have felt desperate, vulnerable, inadequate, broken. They want to find a place for themselves in the world, and while they worry that it makes them bad feminists, they want to feel beautiful and desirable. That's what I'm good at.

Every single one of these women has their own beauty, and every single one of them carries some pain and trauma. We have all been made to feel inadequate, and ashamed – not just of our looks and our bodies themselves, but of *wanting* to be pretty, wanting to be sexy. It's a privilege to do this work and hear these stories. The more time I spend behind the camera, the happier I feel. It's an act of connection, and communion.

Maz taught me that. She didn't listen, she didn't respond and she didn't pay attention to anyone else. But because she tried to exploit me, she forced me to seek agency. Because she claimed she was giving me the answer, I ask more questions. I'm determined to give the women I work with time, space and respect, because I know how it feels when those things are taken from you. I'm grateful to Maz because she forced me to work out what my values are. Still, I never want to see her again. (The last I heard she was in the throes of a mysterious public spat between period poverty activists and menopause activists. Bean and I went through the Twitter thread together for over an hour, and we couldn't work out which side she was on.)

Connection, I'm learning, is what makes us powerful and what makes us vulnerable. We need it. It's what love does. What family does. Their love makes life worth living, although that's not always the same as making us feel safe.

I think that's why I have always wanted to be beautiful. I thought it would make me safe. I believed that if I could only become beautiful, I would be forever protected from grief, shame and pain. If I was a beautiful woman, no one would want to hurt me.

There is no protection from grief, shame or pain, for anyone. That's all we have in common with each other. We can hide from pain, or we can choose to live through it.

For a while, I sought solace online because that was the one place where I felt hidden. The screen seemed like a strong, secure barrier between me and the men whose gaze I sought. It was my drug of choice. It felt good because it made me numb, for a moment.

I don't need to be numb now.

I refuse to feel ashamed of my old pictures. In taking those photos, I started to teach myself my craft. And I made a tiny sacred space for myself. I discovered my power. I brought myself back to life, from the brink of the darkest place I've known. It's something I did for as long as I had to. Now, I've deleted my account. The time felt right. I'm not @girl_going_alone any more. I'm not alone; I never was. I don't need to keep a secret.

Bean makes a snuffing, snoring sound. Very gently, I lift her blanket up to her chin and kiss her softly on the cheek, brushing off a loose eyelash. I place it in the palm of my hand and make the most obvious wish. Then I add a postscript.

I make a wish for women like me. For everyone who has felt ashamed of their bodies, and ashamed of that shame. For everyone who has ever felt like the weird one. The ugly one. The worst one. For everyone who fears this means they are less loved. For everyone who has found themselves in dark and desperate places while searching for self-worth. For everyone who has ever felt beauty is binary, a mandatory test with a 100 per cent pass mark, and every day is a failure. I wish for us to forgive ourselves.

May we let go. May we stop hoping and waiting to be worthy of placement on someone else's pedestal. May we pay less attention to fixing our own perceived flaws, and more attention to life itself. Let us stop waiting for someone to tell us we are good enough to start living.

May we all find the courage to live in our skin, and in the light.

Acknowledgements

Firstly, the most enormous thanks to my editor Darcy Nicholson, and her colleagues Sophie and Ruth. You have transformed this book and I can never thank you enough. I am so very proud of what we made together. Thank you for all of your hard work – and for making me work so hard. I'm so glad I did. Also, enormous thanks to Jon Appleton (I will never forget your great catch on that reference to phoning the Queen!) and Maya Berger for their great care and editorial insight.

A special thanks to Thalia Proctor, and much love to her family. It was a great honour to work with her, and I miss her.

I would also like to thank the amazing Stephie Melrose, Natasha Gill and Brionee Fenlon for all of the amazing work they do. I'm so lucky to work with such a brilliant team – if you're reading this, it's because of them! Special thanks to Bekki Guyatt, for another *iconic* cover. I feel like I've won the author lottery, cover wise, it's the greatest privilege to have your beautiful artwork accompanying my words.

Enormous thanks to 'Agent' Diana Beaumont who always works far beyond her paygrade – as a cheerleader, author whisperer and spiritual advisor. Love and thanks to the rest of the magnificent Marjacq team – Leah Middleton, Imogen Pelham, Sandra Sawicka, Catherine Pellegrino and Philip Patterson. Special thanks to Guy Herbert for your wise counsel, support and tweets!

Huge thanks to everyone at the Tape Agency – Laura Coe, Natalie Young, MK, Camilla and Becky – it's a treat to be powered by your enthusiasm and support. Thanks to JP (and Ida B!) and the Pound Project – because writing *Burn Before Reading* made *Limelight* so much better.

Enormous thanks to the independent booksellers who support me as a writer and a reader – especially Fran at The Margate Bookshop, Gayle at the LRB Bookshop, Gem at The Deal Bookshop, Chrissy at Bookbar, Simon at The Big Green Bookshop, Jo at Red Lion Books, Clare at Harbour Books, the team at Bookish in Crickhowell and the team at Fox Lane Books. And huge thanks to everyone who has listened to You're Booked, and Daisy Is ... I'm so grateful for your support and the loan of your ears.

A giant thank you to all of the writers, readers and creators whose generosity, kindness and good cheer make my life, bookshelves and literary festivals better and brighter. Lauren Bravo, Jude Leavy, Marian Keyes, Jo West, Kat Brown, Nina Stibbe, Dolly Alderton, Ayisha Malik, Cathy Rentzenbrink, Lucy Easthope, Emma Gannon, Charlotte Mendelson, Sophia Money-Coutts, Jilly Cooper, Fern Brady, Laura Jane Williams, Sarra Manning, Louise O'Neill, AJ Pearce, Rosa Rankin Gee, Lindsey Kelk, Lucy Vine, Caroline Corcoran, Lucy Foley, Holly Bourne, Sarah Knight, Claire Cohen, Holly Williams, Rowan Pelling, Annabel Rivkin, Emilie McMeekan, Cesca Major, Rosie

Walsh, Kate Riordan, Amy Rowland, Isabelle Broom, Jade Beer, Bryony Gordon, Nell Frizzell, Julia Raeside, Marina O'Loughlin, Flora Gill, Adele Parks, Giovanna Fletcher, Sophie Morris, Lisa Jayne Harris, Evie Lynch, Isy Suttie, Amber Butchart, Rebecca Humphries, Katherine Heiny, Sheryl Garrat, Ayesha Hazarika, Ashley Audrain, Nicola Daley – you've all been very kind to me, I think of you often and I feel very grateful. And if you're reading this and you feel missed off the list (for I have definitely missed someone) get in touch. I owe you a big lunch.

Huge thanks to my family, for your love and support (and your continued not minding/ignoring the sex scenes. Sorry about those.) Thanks to the South London Lovers, the Jillies, Hogsnet, the Radiant Boilers, the Sober Social crew and the Skinnydip team, especially Charlee – because you all kept me sane and cheerful and without you there would honestly be no book.

Thank you, Dale. I am only able to write about darkness because you fill my life with light. You are my all-time favourite writer, reader and human. I love you.